Living with Abi

Other Book

Too Much Gold to Flush

If you have not read *Too Much Gold to Flush*, you need to. In it, Pat Grissom shares the story of her three-month marriage ending in betrayal. She fills *Too Much Gold to Flush* with quotes on every page along with an honest self-evaluation of who she was when she married that creep. By doing so, she found the courage and the strength to shift from victim to living a vital life. Plus, she gives half of the proceeds to women's shelters.

Call It Quits

Abi Martin is 29 years old, has been married to Vince since she graduated from high school, and more than anything wants to go to college. It is 1973 and they live in Quits, a little town in the Texas Panhandle that has to be the belt-buckle of the Bible-belt. When Vince's rage lands Abi in the hospital, she overhears her father-in-law asking Vince about Abi going to school. Vince reluctantly agrees. At college, Abi gets into a situation that requires her to make impossible decisions. Travel back to 1973 and accompany Abi through a year of shifting how she sees herself and others.

Living with Abi

PAT GRISSOM

Permission requests should be directed to:
Patricia Ann Grissom
c/o Dedicated to Empowering Women, LLC.
P.O. Box 2235
Friendswood, Texas 77549
www.patgrissom.com

Dedicated to Empowering Women, LLC. (DEW)

Copy editing: Deborah K. Frontiera of Jade Enterprises

Cover & Layout Design – Yvonne Vermillion

First Edition

Paperback edition ISBN 978-0-9853813-4-9
eBook edition ISBN 978-0-9853813-5-6

Library of Congress Control Number: 2018908919

Printed in the United States

To Mother,
as unique and special as her name,
Myrethia.

Chapter One

A thick fog lingered in Abi's head. The high ceiling and pale green walls didn't look right. Where were her paintings, her books? Oh yes, she had checked into the hospital yesterday, immediately after she spoke with Dr. Cook about her test results. He wouldn't let her go home, birthday or not. This morning before dawn, a nurse apologized for waking her, not that Abi had slept, so somebody else could shortly put her back to sleep.

Movements at her side made Abi gaze at the three people she loved most in the world. They stood next to each other, nervously grinning at her.

"*Kia Ora. Tena koutou tamariki ma,*" Moa asked, giving her a Maori greeting and inquiring after her condition, which was not good, but how bad she did not know.

Abi flopped a deadweight hand toward Moa, her nine-year-old son, Takahe, her best friend, a tall, dark-skinned Maori, and Colin, the sailor who had brought her and Moa to New Zealand from the States. Takahe, rubbed her nose against Abi's in a traditional New Zealand greeting.

Abi chuckled, which awakened the newly sutured muscles of her abdomen. Takahe had welcomed her to Birdsong Inn, a bed and breakfast in New Zealand, with that same gesture when Abi still carried Morgan in her arms, before Takahe dubbed him Moa, before she took them in and treated them like family.

Through parched lips, Abi whispered, "Have you talked to the doctor yet?"

Takahe moved her face from side to side, shaking her dark, wavy hair, now prominently streaked with gray. "The nurse said he would be around soon." She poured a glass of water and held it to Abi's mouth.

It helped, although the dryness in her mouth felt permanent.

"We brought your sketch pad like you asked and a surprise." Gripping her fingers, Moa pointed to a chair where a cake sat. Something Abi couldn't read from her perspective had been written in the icing. She attempted to raise her head, but shooting pain stopped her.

"You picked a hell of a way to celebrate your fortieth birthday," Colin said.

Abi held his calloused hand. "That was yesterday. You missed the party." Since bringing her to New Zealand, Colin had drifted in and out of their lives, pursuing his love of the sea, but always returning to Birdsong Inn for short visits.

"Afraid you're the one who wasn't there." His broad, tanned face broke into a mischievous grin. "So we had to celebrate without you."

"I wouldn't have it any other way." She kissed his scarred knuckles.

The door opened, and Dr. Cook walked in, his small, white face more grim than yesterday when he spoke of possible ways to put this cancerous growth in check. Takahe and Colin introduced themselves and Moa.

Dr. Cook, American by birth, shook hands with everyone, ending with Moa, who was small for his age. He bent over so his head was level with the boy's. "What grade are you in?"

"I'm not, sir. Mum teaches me at home," Moa answered formally, just as Abi had instructed him to respond.

Her heart swelled with pride. He was everything to her, absolutely everything.

"And why is that?" Dr. Cook asked.

"There aren't very many children in our village. 'Sides, we can't find a teacher to come to Jacob's Springs," Moa said, slipping back into his standard speech.

The doctor chuckled affably. Takahe and Colin followed suit while Moa looked pleased with himself.

Abi stroked Moa's mop of curly, golden brown hair. By the thickness of the folder under Dr. Cook's arm and his seriousness masked by forced pleasantries, Abi suspected the worst. "Colin, would you mind taking Moa for a walk while Takahe and I talk to Dr. Cook?"

"Not a problem." Colin wrapped an arm around Moa's shoulders and guided him out the door.

Moa poked his head back in, his green eyes glimmering. "We'll make it our mission to get milk to go with the cake."

"Good idea." Abi blew him a kiss.

He caught it, high and outside, exactly where she had thrown it. Clutching it to his heart, he disappeared.

"He's a fine young man," Dr. Cook stated, his somber tone asking what would become of him when the awful thing that had invaded her body had run its course.

"Give it to me straight." Abi braced herself.

Her request seemed to catch her doctor off guard. "I wish you had come earlier, when you first started feeling the pain." He had expressed this sentiment several times last week during their initial meeting.

"So you didn't get it all, huh?" she asked, avoiding the dreaded term for the demon that slowly consumed her.

"You have to remember it's the eighties. Advances in treating cancer are being made every day. A colleague of mine in Houston, Texas, is showing amazing results in arresting ovarian cancer. Since you're from Texas, perhaps you'd like to go there and . . ."

"No," Abi snapped, unable to stop herself. Dr. Cook had no idea what had forced her to flee Texas, but that didn't stop Abi from remaining terrified at the prospect of ever going back.

Dr. Cook's brow wrinkled, and his mouth gathered in a pout. She had offended him by rejecting his lifeline or maybe he had wanted to rid himself of her advanced condition. "But I don't have *just* ovarian cancer, do I?" she observed.

"No, you don't. Chemotherapy is still an option. While I can't make promises for a full recovery, we can slow it down."

"You mean prolong my death."

"Give you more time – with your son and your friends." He glanced at Takahe's grave face. "You'll need to get your affairs in order, determine a guardian for your son, make sure your will is up to date, all of that. Maybe spend some time with your mother. You said you hadn't seen her in a while."

"How long do I have?" Abi asked, drained by the prospect of putting a timeline on her remaining days.

"A year at the most – with treatments," he replied.

"And without?" she prodded.

He glanced at his closed folder as if he might see the answer on the cover. "It's hard to say. Six months, perhaps more. There's no way of knowing."

Loud footsteps slapped on the tile floor down the hallway, Moa's sneakers.

Before he had time to charge back inside, Abi pasted on a smile and touched Dr. Cook's sleeve. "Thanks, you've done all you could. I prefer to proceed without intervention." Her words sounded so rational, like she knew what she would do with Moa, like she had a goddamn plan.

"You don't have to decide now. Think about it," Dr. Cook urged.

"I have," Abi assured him. She had also thought about the fact that Moa's father, who didn't know Moa existed, was married and already had a son. Worse than that, as far as she knew, he still lived in Texas, a big state, but obviously not big enough for Abi to get away from Vince, the monster Abi had been married to. When Moa was only a few weeks old, Abi had made the mistake of calling her mother and telling her she lived in Austin. Before Abi could get off the phone, her son started crying. Mama must have put two and two together and came up with a grandchild, which she sent Vince to find.

When Abi started feeling abdominal pain three months ago, she tried to ignore it. That didn't work, so she willed it to go away. After that, she prayed and bargained with God. Now she must face it – and what to do with her nine-year-old son.

* * *

Garrett blinked and tried to focus on the red digital numbers of the clock that sat at the far side of his office desk. His damp forehead rested on the blotter. He felt wet all over. While he had been unconscious, he must have sweated. He dragged his arm that felt like it had weights tied to it toward his face, feeling for the negatives of Abi that he had been examining when he passed out. The narrow strips of plastic, his only concrete proof that she had existed, were still there. Thank God he had thought to lock his door before he pulled them out and lined them up on his desk, an insane, yet compulsive habit he had acquired in recent days. Delthea, his wife, would not understand if she walked in and saw them lying there.

How long had passed since he blacked out? He couldn't remember what time it had been when he couldn't hold up his head any longer, and he had felt himself collapsing onto his desk, much like a child falling asleep in his highchair. When he began feeling drowsy, he wondered if it had something to do with the constant discomfort in his gut that had gradually intensified over the last three months.

When he regained consciousness, he still felt bad, although his abdominal area felt semi-numb like the sensation that remains for hours after getting a tooth filled. It was nice to lack sensation in the area that usually pained him, but while he was unconscious, he had emptied his bladder and his bowels, so he needed to get cleaned up – if he could muster the strength to do so. Luckily, Judy, his secretary, and Delthea, his co-therapist and wife, were leaving him alone. Delthea probably told Judy not to disturb him since he had been listless yesterday when he arrived back in Houston after a month long book tour. By now his wife had left the office to prepare for his birthday party.

She wanted to surprise him, and he had played along, never mentioning the messages he heard on their home answering machine when he called from hotel rooms and checked it. He had not given Bud Anderson his home phone since he dared not let Delthea know he had hired a private eye to find Abi. Bud was touted as an individual who pulled information out of thin air, things like phone numbers. Supposedly, he could find anyone, even a mistress who had disappeared ten years ago.

*   *   *

Delthea Richards glanced at her watch. Then she tossed a roll of black crepe paper to her sister who stood on top of a stepladder. "Can you move a little faster? We've still got balloons to blow up and posters to hang. Garrett will be home in less than an hour, and the guests will be here any minute."

"Don't get your panties in a wad, Deli," Elaine drawled while she fiddled with a roll of tape. She had an infuriating habit of moving at a snail's pace, yet somehow working circles around Delthea. She always had.

Frustrated from a day full of setbacks and delays, Delthea threw her arms in the air and marched into the kitchen. Even though the caterer had spelled Garrett with one 't' on the cake and brought the wrong brand of champagne, he *had* arrived. She couldn't say as much for the piano player who had promised to come an hour early and warm up on the newly-tuned baby grand. Neither Delthea nor Garrett were musical, so this seemed like the perfect opportunity to actually utilize an extravagance bought simply to fill that corner of the living room.

While Elaine puffed on balloons, Delthea emptied the refrigerator of serving platters piled with a variety of cheeses, boiled shrimp, and vegetables and fruit cut into decorative pieces and assembled into recognizable shapes like birds and fish. She laid out her china, silverware, and linen napkins – none of that paper stuff for this special occasion.

When people responded to the invitation, they said how eager they were to see Garrett since he had been away so much promoting his book. Delthea hoped his schedule had finally slowed down some. At the beginning of their relationship, Garrett delayed marriage until they both finished their doctoral degree in psychology. When they finally married, Delthea was ready to start a family, but on their wedding night, Garrett convinced her to help him manifest his dream of a successful counseling practice before they had a child. As soon as their business had taken off, her dear, sweet husband plunged into writing a book. Now it was her turn. More than anything Delthea wanted a baby.

Garrett looked and sounded so tired last night. He fell asleep wearing his traveling clothes. Jet lag, she supposed. Who wouldn't be tired after thirty cities in as many days? He didn't have another book tour on his calendar. At last, they could finally enjoy being together. She had turned down several speaking engagements in lieu of spending time with her absentee husband, preferably in bed.

After finding the perfect spot for a bouquet of long-stemmed red roses, Delthea glanced out the window of their fifth floor condominium and noted the profusion of pink azaleas.

March in Houston. Spring came earlier, and it got hotter here faster than any place she had ever lived. Still it was a lucrative city, and if you didn't go see your shrink once a week, you had "not arrived." Delthea hoped those with disposable income continued to think that way. She had sacrificed her most fertile years to help Garrett start a practice and then to keep it all going while he followed yet another of his dreams. Now he could see their patients while she took time off.

Oliver Matthew's car pulled into the drive. He had been compulsively punctual since the day she and Garrett both showed up to start interning at his psychology clinic nearly ten years ago. From the very beginning, Delthea fell in love with Garrett's green eyes, his short, muscular frame, his caring demeanor, his confidence, wit, humor, everything – except his marital status. Neither ethical nor prudent nor wise, Delthea had hopelessly fallen in love with a married man.

Although Garrett openly admitted that he remained with his wife out of obligation, having brought her and their child from Vietnam, he was indeed taken and a father to boot. On top of that, Garrett was recuperating from a failed affair. His mistress, Abi, had disappeared about the same time Delthea met Garrett. A year later, Garrett seemed to be coping with losing Abi when his wife and child tragically died in a car accident. Delthea's willingness to listen and comfort Garrett through both ordeals eventually brought them together.

The phone rang and Delthea answered it. She told Milton, the doorman, to admit Oliver and anyone who mentioned they were here for Garrett's birthday party. She asked Milton to give her a warning call when Garrett arrived. As she hung up the phone, she shouted to Elaine, "The first guest is on his way up. Let's change our clothes."

She prayed Elaine didn't plan to put on that purple dress she had worn to Garrett's first book signing. What little there was of it fit too snugly in what Elaine would consider all the right places. Elaine was well endowed; Delthea couldn't argue that, but she was also thirty pounds overweight.

Soon the apartment teemed with friends and colleagues. Delthea, now wearing a long, black evening gown, circulated among them, smiling, offering more wine, and periodically checking her watch. Noting the phone remained disturbingly quiet, she picked it up to make sure it had a dial tone.

Oliver cornered Delthea and asked if she still planned to cover for him in October. At first she drew a blank. Then she remembered their telephone conversation about his inadvertently booking two speaking engagements for the same night, one in Austin with the Cattlemen Convention and the other in Houston with a group of dermatologists. Once she assured him that she wouldn't think of letting him down, he asked her which she preferred. She opted for Houston since, hopefully, Garrett would be home. Besides, she doubted anything she said to a herd of cowboys would mean anything to them.

An hour after she expected Garrett, Delthea sought out their secretary and pulled Judy aside. "Was Garrett at the office when you left?"

"Yes, he said something when I said I was going, but I couldn't understand him through the door." She winked at Delthea. "I nearly said I'd see him when he got here – of course, I didn't."

Good thing Garrett had been out of the office most of the last month. Judy used no discretion about saying things on the telephone loud enough for anyone to hear or leaving notes on her desk about so and so RSVPing.

Across the room, Elaine chatted with a group of prospects for husband number three, their enraptured faces all spellbound by her skimpy, purple dress and candid stories of life as a nurse in the ER. Invariably she repeated that hideous story about the three-hundred-pound woman who was dropped off wearing nothing but a gee-string. Delthea hated to see Elaine embarrass herself with junior high humor, not to mention how her behavior reflected on Delthea. When Elaine paused for air, Delthea grabbed her elbow and guided her to the kitchen.

"Hey, Deli, what's the big idea? I was just getting warmed up?" Elaine protested too loudly.

Delthea pulled her sister toward the pantry, out of sight and earshot of the crowd. "I need you to drive to my office and see if Garrett is still there."

"You go. I'm having a good time." She shrugged off Delthea's hand. "Anyway, I've drunk too much. I can't drive."

"I thought you were doing a night shift later." Elaine had agreed to help with the party but made it clear she must leave by nine to go by and check on her sons before she went to work. "What about Kent and David?" Delthea reminded her.

"Who's that?" Elaine laughed and tipped her empty glass to her lips. "Call Garrett and tell him to get his butt home."

Delthea grabbed the wall phone and punched in the office number, certainly not because Elaine had told her to. It was simply the most logical thing to do. The phone rang until the machine answered. Yes, she had an emergency, but the number the recording said to dial wasn't going to help her find Garrett. She slammed the receiver back onto the cradle.

"I'm driving over there," she announced to Elaine who looked none too steady. "Make some coffee and sober up."

"Maybe he had an accident," Elaine offered grimly, probably reflecting on what she saw wheeled into the ER every night.

Delthea grabbed her purse from the pantry. "Call the office again in a few minutes. Garrett might have gone to the john. If anyone asks, tell them I've run out for ice."

"Right," Elaine affirmed with little enthusiasm. "And if I reach Garrett, should I tell him there's a house full of people here waiting to celebrate his fortieth birthday?"

"No, just – just tell him to get his butt home." Delthea rushed out the door, ignoring the questioning gazes that followed her, the woman who had planned a party for three months but had failed to make sure the guest of honor would show up.

*   *   *

The phone rang – again. Garrett knew he should answer it. Delthea was probably beside herself with worry. What would he tell her? As much as Garrett hated the idea of disappointing Delthea, he could not muster the courage to face a crowd of people, especially after what had happened today. Garrett had thought he could show up, smile, and go through the motions, but not after the episode just after noon that left him even more drained and drooling while sitting in his own shit.

Down the hall, a door opened and immediately slammed shut. "I know you're here," Delthea yelled. "I saw your car outside."

A fresh crop of sweat erupted over Garrett's entire body. Panicky, he swept the photo negatives that lay in neat rows on his desk into his lap. He thought since the phone had rung recently that he had more time – to hide them, to think of an excuse for not going home.

Delthea tried the door, and then apparently using the key at the top of the door-frame, opened it and hurried inside, wearing the dress he had given her for Christmas. Her beautifully thin body leaned against the door facing while she bent over and gasped for air. "Why didn't you answer the phone?"

His mind whirled. It did that so often nowadays. Today was worse than usual. Along with the fatigue, he felt drugged and disoriented after he regained consciousness. He might not have survived except for the numbing sensation that lingered. "I felt bad," he mumbled, unable to look her in the eye.

She charged his desk and reached across it, placing her fingers on his forehead. "Do you have a fever?"

"I don't think so." He grabbed for her hand and noticed a photo negative stuck to his sweaty wrist.

Her questioning eyes registered the long strip of brown plastic. Then she closely scrutinized his face. "What's that?"

"Just something I happened onto in an old file . . . ." months ago after he searched for several days.

Delthea pealed the incriminating evidence from his skin and held it up to the light. Her expression turned hard. "This is Abi. I thought you got rid of this a long time ago."

"I meant to. I guess that one got caught on something." Delthea would never understand the compelling force that had driven him to find the only keepsakes he owned of that brief but once in a lifetime affair. A mysterious power drove him to have two sets of photos printed from the negatives, one for himself and one for Detective Bud. He couldn't quit thinking of Abi, not that he dreamed of returning to what they once shared. That was gone. He needed to find Abi, though, to know she was all right, to somehow assure himself of . . . of what? He had no idea. How could he explain this obsession to his wife, a woman he loved without question, if he couldn't explain it to himself.

"You really don't look well." With an air of disgust, Delthea tossed the negative into the trash.

"Really, I'm feeling better." He brushed the incriminating evidence to the floor and rose, thankful for the strength that had failed him all day. If she saw the rest of the negatives, Delthea would realize he had tried to hide them, and, like any spouse, assume the worst.

"Are you sure? You're so white." Delthea caressed his cheek with her tender fingertips.

Garrett grasped her slender hand and kissed her smooth knuckles. "As long as I've got you, I'll be just fine."

While he concentrated on walking around the desk, he said a quick prayer that she would not notice the disaster that had accompanied his loss of consciousness. On the way down the hall, he planned to excuse himself and duck inside the restroom. He could hide his underwear and say he splashed water on his front. All afternoon, he had sat in his own shit and prayed for a glimmer of understanding about what had taken hold of him.

Delthea sniffed and wrinkled her nose. She gawked at his fly. "Your pants are wet . . . and you smell as though . . . . Oh, Garrett, you are sick. What has happened? We've got to get you cleaned up." She wrapped her arm around his waist, as always right by his side when he needed her most.

*   *   *

Shifting in the bed next to his mother while trying to get comfortable before they read, Moa accidentally jabbed his elbow in Mum's tummy. She caught her breath and grabbed his arm with her free hand, the one that wasn't wrapped around his shoulders. She breathed long and hard and her eyes watered. He hated this place. It stank, and it sure hadn't helped Mum feel any better.

"Sorry." It made his chest tight and achy to see her like that. "Did I hurt you?"

"I'm okay." She turned the page on the book they had read every night for as long as Moa could remember. "Did you practice the piano after I left the inn?"

"Not exactly," he admitted, looking at his hands. He curled his fingers, so she couldn't see he needed to clip his nails – again. "Colin got home right after you left, so we went for a shoot and before we knew it . . ." He looked to see if she was buying his excuse. "Well, you know how it is."

She took one of those huge breaths that meant she was trying to be patient. "I do, but you still need to practice. I wish I had learned to play as a child. When you get good at it, you'll enjoy the piano as much as you like to hunt."

Her mentioning shooting a gun made Moa think of his sixth birthday. "The day you started teaching me to shoot, you said I might need to protect myself someday. What did you mean?"

"I don't know." She chewed her bottom lip, the way she did when she had more she could say if she just would. "Takahe and Colin will be back soon. Then you're bound for home. It'll take you a couple of hours to get there." She cleared her throat and began reading, *"Calmness of mind is one of the beautiful jewels of wisdom."*

While Mum said the words they both knew from memory since they had repeated them so many times, Moa thought about the book they came from, *As a Man Thinketh*. Every page was covered with underlining and notes written along the edges. On the front inside cover, the name, Garrett Morgan Clay, was handwritten. When Moa had gotten old enough to figure out that Morgan Clay, his first and middle names, came from that person, he asked Mum who Garrett Clay was. She stalled and then said he was a friend, but she wouldn't say anything else. That happened a couple of years ago, and ever since then, Moa had wondered if Garrett wasn't his dad, the man who died when he was just a baby, the man Mum constantly painted pictures of, the man neither Colin nor Takahe knew anything about.

Mum's words trailed off, and her eyelids shut for just a second then she stirred with a start. "Huh. I'm drifting off to sleep. It's that damned sleeping pill." She tried to sit up, but stopped when her face started looking pained again.

"You never did eat any of your cake," Moa said, wanting to make her feel better.

"That's an excellent idea. Would you do the honors and cut me a piece?" She lifted her arm, so he could get down.

Moa carried the cake to her bed and sat it on the sheets, so Mum could see what he had written with white icing.

"Abigale Barker, March 6, 1983, 40 Years Old," she read aloud. "You made this yesterday, thinking I was coming home."

He nodded.

She chewed her bottom lip. "Moa, I never told you before, but your dad and I were born on the same day. In fact, we were born at the same time of day."

"To the minute?" he asked, thrilled she was finally telling him something about his father.

She laughed softly. "I think we were both born in the afternoon. Yesterday was my birthday, but in Texas it's our yesterday right now. So this is his birthday."

"Except he's dead, right?" Moa asked, making sure she wasn't changing the story she had always told him.

"Right," she answered, but she sounded like Moa did when he lied. Her eyes started doing that fluttering business again.

Moa got the plates, forks, and knife that the nurse had brought and cut Mum a huge piece of cake. He needed to keep her awake and talking now that he had her going. Sticking a fork between her limp fingers, he asked, "What else do you remember about my dad?"

Mum studied the cake and then she looked at him. "Moa, you need to understand that things are going to change a lot in the next year or so."

"What did the doctor find?" According to Colin, Dr. Cook had done something he called exploration surgery, so surely he had found something to help his mum.

A tear rolled down her cheek.

Seeing his mum cry made Moa want to cry, too.

"Dr. Cook decided that I am very sick." She looked at him with that no nonsense way she had.

"Are you going to die?" he asked, hating himself for saying the words out loud, for jinxing her with the idea of it.

Mum let the fork fall from her fingers and grabbed Moa's hand. She swallowed slowly while grimacing. "Not tomorrow or even the day after, but long before either of us is ready, I will die."

Moa couldn't stand it. He shoved the cake aside and reached for her like he had as a little boy when he got hurt. She wrapped her arms around him and squeezed so hard it forced the air out of his lungs. At the same time, she made the sharp cry that a rabbit or weasel makes when it's shot and hurt but not badly enough to die. He hated that sound. It meant his aim had not been quite true. It meant he had caused something to suffer rather than killing it outright.

What kind of crazy thinking was that? He loved his mum. He didn't want her to die. Who would take care of him? Where would he live? Takahe was too old, and Colin was always gone. He'd be an orphan, like a fawn left on its own in the forest.

Chapter Two

O nce more Delthea ignored the telephone while she continued scribbling notes about her last patient, Mrs. Wood. Since she did all the work in this two-counselor practice, she didn't have time to take every call her incompetent secretary rang through.

A minute later, Judy bolted through the door. "Please pick up line three. That creep, Bud Anderson, is calling – again."

"Look, my job is to see patients. Your job is to deal with people like Bud. Now get rid of him." Earlier Delthea made the mistake of answering an unauthorized phone call Judy rang through and ended up wasting thirty minutes talking to a damn salesman.

Judy folded her arms across her thin frame and cocked her head to the side in that stubborn little girl pose of hers.

"Tell him I'm with a patient." Gripping the pen so hard her fingers cramped, Delthea returned to her paperwork.

"I have – five times this morning and ten times yesterday." When Delthea didn't reply, Judy added, "He said he's a private detective, and he has valuable information concerning Garrett, details you'll want."

"Right, he and every other leech in this world." Delthea peered through the veil of her blonde hair at the picture Garrett had used for his book jacket. She admired his once engaging smile. Did this jerk have a clue who had taken her healthy husband and left an invalid in his place, or was he like the other swindlers who called, willing to say anything in order to get his foot in the door? "Tell Bud I'll be with him shortly."

Judy left, shutting the door behind her.

After finishing Mrs. Wood's chart, Delthea punched line three. "This is Dr. Richards. May I help you?"

"It's about time," barked a man with a New York accent. "I been trying to get through to Dr. Clay for three months. Your secretary finally told me he's not even coming into the office."

That did it. When Delthea found the time to train someone new, Judy would be history. She had been told numerous times to take messages without offering explanations concerning Garrett's whereabouts. "I have no idea what you want."

"Your husband hired me to find somebody," Bud stated.

A likely story. "Well, he no longer needs your services."

"That's fine," Bud said confidently. "I didn't find her anyway, but what I did find, I think you'll pay to keep the rest of the world from knowing about."

"What are you talking about?" Garrett looked at Abi's pictures when he thought Delthea was unaware, but surely he hadn't hired someone to find her, not after all this time.

"It's against my principles to divulge a confidence, especially to a spouse, but since you're the one with the check book, I'll make an exception. Back in January, Garrett hired me to find Abi Barker-Martin."

Delthea tried to swallow, but her mouth had gone completely dry. "Go on," she whispered.

"I've checked every source, and like I said, she didn't surface, but I did find an address in Austin where she lived, and I found out she had a baby seven months after she left the Panhandle, or rather that little town where she lived – Quits."

"So what?" Delthea asked, a fresh wave of panic rising in her chest. "Abi was married – to someone other than Garrett." Stretching the telephone cord, Delthea walked to the window. The first year Delthea knew Garrett, he talked about Abi constantly, but he never once mentioned a pregnancy.

"The certificate names Garrett Morgan Clay as the father."

Delthea sucked in a long breath and held it. She gazed through the huge expanse of glass at Houston's 610 Loop where cars sat motionless in bumper-to-bumper traffic. She identified with every one of those frustrated motorists. A force outside their control held them captive with no end in sight. "Do you have a copy of the birth certificate?" Delthea asked, somehow managing to sound reasonably calm, at least, to her own ears.

"You better believe it. And if I don't get a check today, I'm taking it straight over to my friends at the Post. They'll pay mega-bucks for this and the details." Bud cleared his throat. "Your husband's quite the celebrity with that book he wrote. People love to read about dirt on successful people."

Too exhausted to stand, Delthea crossed the room and dropped into her chair. She hated this leech and all the media hyenas who called daily wanting to know about Garrett. Not only were they ganging up on her, but now she had to deal with this preposterous story about Garrett fathering Abi's child. Plus, he had started looking for Abi back when he was promoting his damn book.

"They could do a follow-up story on what's become of Dr. Clay," Bud droned. "People also love stories about headliners who have dropped out of sight."

When Judy buzzed twice, signaling Delthea that a patient was waiting, she forced herself to speak. "I'll pay your bill, but everything you've found and your silence concerning this matter are mine. No one, including Garrett, is to know about this."

"Fine," Bud agreed. "Write me a check for two grand."

Delthea opened her mouth to protest, but decided any amount was worth getting rid of this sleaze-bag. "Make sure it's in a sealed envelope before you give it to my secretary. I'll have your money waiting. After this, leave my husband and me alone."

"Don't worry. It's cash in advance before I deal with either one of you again." He slammed the phone in her ear.

After dropping the check sealed in an envelope addressed to Bud on Judy's desk, Delthea smiled at Mrs. Hightower, her next patient. "Sorry to keep you waiting."

Mrs. Hightower followed Delthea down the hall. When they passed Garrett's office, she whined, "When will Dr. Clay return?"

"Not too much longer. He's finishing his new book." Delthea had said this so often, it almost sounded believable.

* * *

Evening's darkness settled over the condo, but Garrett lacked the energy to struggle to his feet and turn on the light. He flipped through Abi's pictures once more, getting one last look at them before Delthea arrived. Every day he swore to himself that this was the last time, but every day he found himself doing it all over again. His need to see her and to find her grew as the days ground past.

As crazy as it seemed, his addiction for Abi in no way diminished his love for Delthea and her never-ending strength. For the last ten years, she had been there for him, when he struggled to cope with Abi's disappearance, when Trang and his beloved son, Loc, died in the car accident. Through it all, she offered compassion and support. What would he have done without her?

Someone banged on the front door. "Garrett, let me in," Delthea called. "My hands are full." She nearly always said that, but tonight she sounded more frustrated than usual.

Garrett couldn't blame her, but he also couldn't find the energy to do more than stick Abi's pictures inside his journal.

Following more banging, Delthea flung the door open. Loaded down with two bags of groceries, she used her shoulder to turn on the wall light switch. Then she staggered into the living room and dropped both damp, dilapidated paper bags onto the coffee table. She tossed a handful of mail and her purse next to the pile of canned peas, crackers, sweating ice cream, and frozen dinners.

Garrett glanced down at his lap where he noted the corners of Abi's pictures peeking out from beneath the front cover of his journal. He should have hidden them better, but Delthea hadn't given him much time. She had become efficient at letting herself in, even with her arms full.

"Didn't you hear me screaming?" Rage seethed in every word.

Garrett didn't reply for fear of her comeback. As good as Delthea had been to him, lately her patience had grown thin.

"Garrett, answer me!" Her voice broke.

He wanted more than anything to say exactly what she wanted to hear, to be the man she had married, to be normal again.

Delthea walked to the sofa and sank into its billowy, velvet cushions. After watching Garrett for several minutes, she asked, "Do you know Bud Anderson?"

Shit. Garrett knew this might happen. He should have called Bud and given him his home phone number. Only Garrett didn't have Bud's business card. It was in the briefcase he had left in the office – along with Abi's negatives scattered on the floor. The cleaning crew had surely thrown those out, or possibly stuck them in the desk drawer. Thank God, the extra set of prints he ordered when he had pictures blown up for Bud was in the bottom of his sweater drawer. Why was he grateful for that? His insatiable need to stare at them all day only fueled the deterioration of his mind along with his body.

"Answer me," she demanded, her voice raising an octave.

"What was the question?" He really didn't remember, but he also knew he didn't want to.

"Bud Anderson," she repeated loudly as if he was a ninety-year-old. "Do you know him?"

Garrett nodded slightly.

"I talked to him today." Delthea examined his face like she would one of their patients. "He said you hired him to find Abi. Did you ask this creep to find your lost mistress?"

Delthea had been more than understanding, but accepting his obsessive need to find Abi went beyond even her capabilities.

"Bud said she's nowhere to be found, and he's taking himself off the case," Delthea announced with finality. "What I want to know is why you hired him? Why are you looking for her now?"

Garrett returned his gaze to the corners of Abi's pictures. He couldn't see them, but he knew every detail, her serene face looking back at him, the flow of her auburn hair, and the curve of her smile. Every line was etched in his mind and on his soul.

"Look at me," Delthea said like a mother getting ready to discipline her two-year-old.

He wanted to assure her that his need to find Abi in no way negated his love for her. The more he tried, though, the harder it seemed to communicate anything at all, much less such an illogical and sensitive point.

Delthea crossed the carpeted expanse between them and dropped down beside his chair. Her troubled blue eyes searched his. "Every day you get farther and farther away from me."

Garrett glanced down, praying the infernal corners had magically disappeared, praying she would not see them.

During a chilling silence, Garrett felt Delthea follow his gaze. Her hand shot to his lap and deftly extracted the photos. She shuffled through them, now bent and frayed with his handling. The crease between her brows grew deeper.

A wave of relief washed over Garrett. She finally knew. He could quit hiding them. Maybe now Delthea would talk to him about Abi as she had when they first met.

Delthea jumped to her feet. "I can't believe you're doing this to me." She held out the evidence of his crime.

"I d-d-d-idn't mean to," he protested.

"I've put up with a lot, but this is the limit." Delthea sneered at the pictures with revulsion. "Your detective is paid off, and we are through with this insanity." She gripped the pictures with both hands and ripped them down the middle.

Garrett's already weak breath caught in his throat. He didn't just *want* the pictures. He *had* to have them. They were his only tangible proof that Abi existed. His hands trembled as he reached out to Delthea. Her image wavered as his eyes filled with tears. She took a step backwards and ripped the pictures again. Oh, God, it felt like she was obliterating him.

"Don't throw this garbage in my face again!" The veins in Delthea's long, graceful neck stood out. "I want her out of my house." Her arms shook with exertion as she attempted to shred the thick wad in her hands once more. "I will not share my husband and my life with some fantasy woman you've built up in your mind." With a final effort, the paper tore and then the jagged squares of paper sprayed from her hands like confetti.

Delthea extracted her purse from the mess on the coffee table and announced, "I've got to get out of here. I'm going to Elaine's." She marched to the door, jerked it open, and slammed it shut behind her.

Garrett gazed at Abi's mutilated, scattered images. Her hold on him remained. In fact, it felt stronger than ever. With his heart as torn as the pictures, Garrett inched his way out of his chair and onto the floor. He had to put her back together. He had to. For some strange, unfathomable reason, what remained of his existence depended on it.

Lying on his stomach and propped on his forearms, Garrett futilely manipulated the unworkable jigsaw puzzle for what felt like hours. Then he collapsed on the carpet, the torn picture pieces beneath his cheek. He closed his eyes and wished he could be anywhere, except where he was at that moment.

He took a few deep breaths and then peacefully fell into a deep sleep. Almost immediately the familiar setting of the park where he had taken the very pictures he was trying to piece together began to form around him. He felt the West Texas wind on his face and watched the limbs of the elm trees wave in the breeze. Although he knew this was not real, he was amazed at how realistic it seemed. Then he marveled at something even better; he felt well and healthy. For the first time in many months, he felt like a normal human being. There was no sign of Abi, but that did not matter. What he held onto, what he could not let go of was the fact that he actually felt good, almost youthful.

Afraid it might not last, but willing to enjoy it while it did, Garrett tested his legs to see if they would run. They did, by God. He sped around a tree, up a shallow knoll, and then back again. All of this, and he barely even felt winded. When he looked down at his legs, he saw the oddest thing – ragged jeans and boots like he had worn in college. Of course, this was a dream about that time. It made sense he would be dressed that way and have the same degree of health and energy. Garrett didn't care how he looked as long as he felt this way. He would give anything if he could remain feeling well.

* * *

Intent on getting the green of Garrett's eyes exactly right, Abi held her palette in a pool of noonday sunlight that had puddled on her bed. She decided the paint needed just a smidgen of cobalt. Colin had been so sweet to modify an easel to work like a bed table. When a fresh wave of pain washed over Abi, she stuck her paintbrush in a jar of turpentine and lay back on her pillow. The unrelenting ache of the cancer kept Abi from painting more than a few minutes at a time. If Abi rang the bell, Takahe would bring her another pill, but that meant lapsing into a drugged state for the rest of the day.

In the living area, just down the hall, Moa plunked away on the piano, offering a crude rendition of "Bridge Over Troubled Waters," her favorite song from the 70's. Garrett had been her bridge over troubled waters. He gave her the strength to escape an abusive marriage. He gave her a son, the joy of her life. He could not give her himself, though. He already had a wife and a son.

Recently, Abi lived in the massive four-poster bed and used the potty chair Takahe had placed nearby rather than cross the hall with someone's help to the toilet. Takahe and Colin, when he was home, constantly waited on Abi, bringing her meals, fresh flowers, and popping in to smooth her covers or fluff her pillows.

And Moa. He came to her almost hourly during the day. They read for a few minutes, or drew a picture, or talked. His visits were so regular and so short that Abi knew Takahe must regulate them, trying desperately to stretch out what little time Abi had left.

Right after Abi came home from the hospital, she spent the mornings in her studio, a separate building behind the inn. When she and Moa moved to New Zealand, Colin had built it for her, reclaiming a dilapidated garden shed and building onto it to make one large room with four walls of windows. Abi loved it. Initially, her canvases filled with scenes of the exquisite New Zealand countryside. Its lushness and color contrasted with the barren, flat land of the Texas panhandle where she grew up.

Having satisfied her desire to paint what she saw around her, Abi returned to her greatest love, Moa. And always, in spite of her will not to, Abi painted pictures of Garrett, the man she would always love. Since her illness began, she could not stop herself from returning to his image time and time again. It beamed back from the canvas before her, his long loopy hair, his beard, his clear, green eyes, Moa's eyes.

During their brief relationship, he had taught her that she chose her life and everything that happened. From that, she had garnered the courage to leave Vince, but life by herself with a tiny infant had been lonely. In a weak moment, she had called home and her mother had heard the baby cry. A few days later, Abi heard Mr. Truman, her landlord, arguing with Vince outside her apartment. She didn't have to see Vince's angry face to believe him when he said he would do anything to get his son.

That night one of her customers at the restaurant asked her why she was crying. She told him, and the next morning the customer, Colin, arrived at her apartment with a plan to take her to New Zealand aboard the freighter on which he worked. Although terrified of leaving the country, she was more scared of Vince. So here she sat, a Kiwi for the better part of a decade.

Over the years, Garrett's message of self-empowerment and choosing her own fate had served Abi well. Recently though, she had begun to question its merit. She could not accept the idea that she had chosen the cancer that ate away at her body. Why would a mother willingly die and leave her little boy? Abi couldn't believe she had. It didn't make sense. Nothing made sense any more.

Abi studied her painting. Garrett looked the same as he had ten years ago. He had not aged. She had, especially of late with her hair graying and her body withering to nothing.

Following a light knock, Takahe stuck her head in the door. "Are you up to a bowl of pumpkin soup?"

That was Abi's favorite, but the idea of food made her nauseous. "Sorry, I don't think I could keep it down."

Takahe stepped inside the room. "Would you like another pill?"

Abi closed her eyes. "I want to escape. I want to go somewhere else and be someone else for just a little while, but I don't want to wake up in a fog and feeling grouchy."

"Perhaps you would like to try self-hypnosis." Takahe sat on the side of the bed. "It may not take the pain away entirely, but it may make it more manageable."

They had discussed this concept before, and Abi had dismissed it as the witchcraft that Takahe used on the locals. Now, she was ready to try anything, absolutely anything that would give her an iota of relief. "Okay, let's do it."

"Are you in a comfortable position?"

Abi nodded. Comfort was a foreign term to her now. She had forgotten how that felt.

"Take a few deep cleansing breaths." Takahe breathed with her. "Continue to breathe slowly and deeply. You are relaxing, starting at your feet. Each one of your toes is limp, limp." Her voice sounded as soothing as the words she uttered. Takahe verbally traveled up Abi's body until she had talked her through releasing the tension in every limb and joint. Then she said, "Turn your face to the sun, and the shadows fall behind you. Imagine you are in the most pleasant setting possible."

Nothing came to mind – except Garrett. It was an image that often followed her into the oblivion induced by the pills. With Takahe's voice in the background, a heavy cloak of sleep drifted over Abi, and she gave in to it.

Immediately she found herself in a park she had not seen in many years, a small grassy area on a back street in Oaces, Texas. It was the park where she and Garrett had once met. She recognized the elm trees, the children's playground. Garrett had shown up with a 35mm camera and shot a half-dozen pictures of her in spite of her protests. She glanced at the street behind her and noted a black Volkswagen Beetle like the one she had driven. Abi looked around.

Across the way, she spotted the knoll where a man stood. He had long curly hair, a beard, a leather hat with a floppy brim, tattered jeans just like Garrett used to wear. She walked toward him, and he looked up. It was Garrett. The green eyes and ready smile were unmistakable. He immediately waved and motioned for her to join him.

Abi waved back, knowing he wasn't real, but unable to stop herself. Then she realized an incredible thing; she did not feel bad. In fact, she felt great. She felt like she did when she knew Garrett, when she was alive and not getting ready to die.

Again, he motioned for her to come closer. She wanted to. Oh, how she yearned to, but she couldn't get close to him again, not even in a dream. She had to protect Moa. If Garrett found out about his son, he would bring Moa back to Texas after she died. It was the only decent thing to do. Then somehow Vince would find Moa and out of pure meanness he would take Moa away.

When Garrett motioned again, Abi waved and shook her head. She knew her fears were unfounded, that this was just a silly dream, that none of this was real, but it allowed her to escape the pain for a few minutes, and for right now, that was all she wanted. Seeing Garrett, even though he was simply her imagination, was an added bonus.

*   *   *

While she ate supper with Elaine and her two boys, Kent and David, Delthea worried about Garrett. She had not left him at night since his illness became apparent. Could he feed himself? Would he leave the apartment to look for her?

Halfway through his second piece of pizza, with most of it still in his mouth, Kent, the fifteen-year-old asked, "Where's Uncle Garrett?"

"He's at home writing." Delthea responded out of habit.

Kent grunted.

Elaine gave Delthea a questioning look but said nothing.

"How's school going, David?" Delthea asked the twelve-year-old, steering the conversation away from Garrett.

"I hate it," he replied flatly.

"What don't you like about it?" she asked, immediately in therapist mode.

"My teacher hates me," he retorted.

"So how come every teacher you ever had hated you? You ever think it could be you?" Kent asked pointedly.

"Shut up!" David snapped and returned to his pizza.

Elaine seemed oblivious to their exchange.

"Have you tried talking to your teacher?" Delthea suggested.

David pounded his fists on the table. "I said she hates me!" He ran to the living room and switched on the TV.

Elaine kept eating. Kent finished one piece of pizza and grabbed another before joining his brother.

"I'm worried about David," Delthea whispered to Elaine. "This isn't a passing phase. He said the same thing about his teacher last year. Don't you hear his anger?"

She gave Delthea a condescending roll of her eyes. "You worry too much, Miss Therapist."

Delthea returned to her beer and a permanent headache.

"Boys, it's time for bed," Elaine announced. As soon as their bedroom door shut, she leveled Delthea with a stern look. "What's going on, Deli? You look like crap."

"Thanks. I needed to hear that." Delthea ran her fingers through her hair and away from her face. "It's been a bad day."

"One of your regulars decide to switch from therapy to yoga?" Elaine asked with a sneer.

"No, it's Garrett," Delthea admitted. She had not told anyone about his condition, not even Judy.

"Is he having an affair?" Elaine asked casually.

Delthea choked on her beer. "What makes you say that?"

Elaine rocked her head from side to side as if planning her attack. "It's a no-brainer. Most of the gunshot victims in the ER got caught dipping their wick where they shouldn't have. Plus, you don't know where the hell he is. You told me when you first got here he was with his editor. Then you told Kent he was home writing." She took another bite. "Third, he had just had an affair when you first met him. Men don't change."

Delthea swigged her beer and decided to face this thing head on. "You're right. He's still crazy about her."

Elaine thudded her beer on the table. "Who's 'her'? Abi?"

"Yes, Abi. Today I spoke with a detective who claims Garrett hired him to find Abi," Delthea admitted.

"Damn," Elaine commented between bites, obviously delighted. "I thought you two were inseparable. What's going on?"

"Tonight I confronted him about the detective and the photos of her that he secretly drools over while he sits at home alone all day, every day." She swigged her beer.

"How long has this been going on?" Elaine asked.

"Since his birthday party six months ago," Delthea admitted.

"You mean the one he didn't attend," Elaine added with a smirk.

Nodding her head, Delthea said, "At first I thought he was just tired from promoting his book, but it's more than that. I've taken him to five different doctors." Delthea drank deeply from her bottle of beer. "They all say the same thing; there's nothing physically wrong with him."

"What do they recommend?"

"Three of them said he should get a psychiatric evaluation."

"It does sort of sound like he's losing it," Elaine said. "I mean hiring a detective to find somebody he hasn't seen in ten years and then fixating on pictures of her is not normal."

"I know. It's bizarre. But I'm no better off. Tonight, I confronted him about the stupid pictures, and then tore them up like that would do any good. On top of that, I've covered up Garrett's invalid state by doing his work and mine and telling everyone he's at home writing."

"Wow, is he really that bad?" Elaine asked with genuine concern.

"He sits in his chair all day, reads this little book, *As a Man Thinketh*, and writes in the journal where he keeps her pictures. I've looked at them after he's gone to sleep." Delthea's voice broke.

Elaine lit a cigarette.

"I can't lose him, not to her, not after all this time," Delthea whined, hating herself for being so weak, for admitting all this to Elaine of all people.

"Get help. I know a lady who used to work for a home health care agency. She'd be great." Elaine blew out a cloud of smoke.

"I can't. I've taken care of him myself, so no one in Houston would know about his condition."

"That's your problem. You're always there for someone else. You never take care of yourself." While Elaine dumped leftover pizza into a plastic bag, she continued, "You took care of Daddy until he drank himself to death. Now you call Mother every Saturday morning. Don't think she misses a chance to throw that in my face every chance she gets."

Her truthful assessment of the situation ground salt into old wounds. Delthea bowed her head and waited.

Elaine flung the pizza into the refrigerator and turned to her sister. "For once, ignore the rest of the fucking world."

Delthea finished her beer. "I'm really glad I came here."

"Why? So I could holler at you?"

"No, I needed someone to force me to be honest with myself." She smiled at Elaine. "I can always count on you for that."

"Telling people off is my best and worst quality." Elaine got a beer out of the refrigerator and held it up to Delthea.

She shook her head. "I need to check on Garrett."

All the way home, Delthea thought about her purchase from Bud and Elaine's suggestion that she take care of herself. The two ideas throbbed in her head like a song that wouldn't quit repeating itself. She could go to that address in Austin that Bud had included with the birth certificate, but what good would that do? If he couldn't find Abi, what made her think she could?

And what would she do if she actually did unearth this demon from the past? Threaten her with . . . with what? Abi had committed no crime. In fact, she held the high trump card. She had given birth to Garrett's son, something Delthea had always wanted to do. Would Abi care that he was too sick to be a father to her child, to their child?

Chapter Three

*A*s he slowly turned the page, Moa glanced at his mum to see if she was still awake. Most of the time she was so *knackered* that she drifted off while he read. It used to bother him, but in the last few weeks, he had begun to realize that if she slept, she probably was not hurting so bad. Her eyes were closed, and her breathing was slow and steady. In a few minutes, Takahe would come in and make him leave, saying Mum needed to rest.

He watched Mum breathe in and out, in and out. He wanted to stop time and keep Mum with him forever. Mum had spoken with him about the fact that she was dying; only she never had spelled out what would become of him. Moa had worried about this since that night in the hospital when she told him she would die before either one of them was ready.

It didn't seem fair that he didn't have a father. Colin had tried to hang around, especially in the last couple of months, but Moa could tell he was getting itchy to get back to the sea. As Mum said, he had salt water in his veins.

Mum's face had grown so thin, and the circles under her eyes were darker every day. As gently as he could, Moa touched the corners of Mum's mouth where she used to always have a smile. He couldn't help himself, his fingers had to hold her cheek and feel her velvety soft skin. Someday she wouldn't be here, and he wouldn't be able to touch her. That thought made tears fill his eyes.

Mum's hand covered his, holding it on her face. "You're my sweet angel," she whispered.

"What do you think death will be like?" It was a question that would not leave him.

She opened her eyes and looked at him. "Peaceful, I think. No pain." Mum collected one of his tears on her fingertip and brought it to her dry, cracked lips.

He smiled and said, "Nectar of the Gods," before she could.

Mum grinned. "Truthfully, I'm scared about dying since I don't know what it will be like." She took a deep breath. "The main thing is I hate leaving you."

He nodded. "I think it's a bad idea." It helped right now to sort of joke about the whole thing, but Moa didn't think it would make him feel any better when he had to face the real thing.

"Me, too. I think it's a terrible idea." She wrapped her arms around Moa and held him to her chest. "Sometimes I get downright mad at God or whoever thought up this whole business."

Moa was past being mad at God. By the way things were going, God didn't have a snowball's chance in hell of getting back on Moa's good side unless He did some big time miracles. Thinking about what Takahe had said about not squeezing too tight, Moa reached around his mum and hugged her. He could feel her ribs and backbone. She felt so small and fragile. If God was planning a miracle, He'd better get busy. He was running out of time.

* * *

When Delthea arrived home from work, Garrett lay in bed where she left him that morning. She coaxed him to the bathroom. As she eased him onto the commode, her fingers settled into the grooves between his ribs. His middle age gut had disappeared along with all of his other fat. Soon he would be too weak to stand.

"Elaine thinks I'm crazy for staying in this situation." Not that she had any choice in the matter. Delthea watched his face for the slightest hint of the man she had married.

Garrett's stoic, feeble expression revealed nothing.

She moved him to a steamy bath where he slouched forward like a very old man. After soaping and rinsing him, she helped him out of the tub, and gently patted dry his skeleton-like frame. "I fantasize about getting on a plane without even knowing where it will go," she said, mostly to herself.

Garrett swallowed and fumbled for her hand. Their eyes connected for the first time in what seemed like weeks. "Don't leave me," he whispered.

Delthea held his thin, naked body, relieved that she had finally reached him, but ashamed she had been so cruel in doing it. "Garrett, I love you. I could never desert you."

After settling Garrett in his chair, Delthea heated two microwave dinners. She fed him hamburger steak and mashed potatoes until he clamped his mouth shut.

"You need to eat more than that," she prodded.

When he stubbornly refused to continue, she sat on the floor where she had been kneeling and ate her enchiladas, too tired and hungry to force the issue. The phone rang, and Delthea scurried across the floor toward it on hands and knees.

She answered, and Milton said, "Your sister and her friend are on their way up."

"What friend? Who-?"

The doorbell rang. Delthea slammed the phone back into the cradle and crawled to her feet on the way to the door. She opened it, and saw Elaine in scrubs next to a woman who looked to be in her sixties wearing a white uniform style dress.

"I brought someone to help with Garrett," Elaine announced. "This is Berta Powers." She gestured to the short, stout woman.

"I don't need help," Delthea said through gritted teeth while glaring at her sister.

"Yes, you do, and Berta's perfect. She's retired and wants to pick up some unreported income – if you know what I mean." Elaine breezed past Delthea to Garrett's side.

Delthea followed with Berta trailing them. While Elaine assessed Garrett from a distance, he stared at his lap, deep furrows radiating from the corners of his eyes.

"Elaine came to see you." Delthea squatted by his chair.

He refused to acknowledge them.

"Hey, you've lost some weight," Elaine said too cheerfully.

Nodding stiffly while still looking down, Garrett's eyes widened. He acted more like someone with a brain injury rather than her brilliant husband.

Elaine knelt on the other side of his chair. "I brought a friend to meet you. This is Berta." Elaine pointed to the detached looking woman. "She's a visiting nurse."

His head swung slowly from side to side.

Berta's steely gaze darted around the room, stopping at the ice cream stain on the carpet under the coffee table and six months' worth of dust on everything in the place.

Delthea grabbed Garrett's hand. "He's tired." Urging him from the chair, she added, "Elaine, find something to drink."

Garrett walked stiffly and slowly to bed where he fell into it, grabbing Delthea's arm.

She pried his fingers loose. "Try to sleep."

His terrified eyes followed her out of the room.

In the kitchen, Delthea found Elaine surveying the empty pantry. Berta sat at the table with her ankles crossed and her arms folded over her barrel-like torso.

"I've got a bottle of red wine," Delthea offered.

"Why not?" Elaine retrieved three glasses. "We found the remains of Abi's pictures." She gestured toward the trashcan.

That's all Delthea needed, Elaine telling Berta everything she couldn't already see. Delthea opened the wine. "So, you've stayed with people before?" she asked Berta.

"I worked for an agency the last ten years before I retired a year ago," Berta reported. "Usually took care of terminal cases." Their eyes met. "Not that I'm assuming that's your husband's situation."

"What have you done since you retired?" Delthea poured the wine, trying not to think about Berta's last comment.

"Visited the relatives, but after a while you both get tired of that," Berta said dryly.

Delthea thought of Bud Anderson and the way he capitalized on their misfortune. Would Berta Powers do the same? "Garrett is well known in the media. They would have a field day if details of his condition leaked out." She leveled her gaze at Berta. "How do I know I can trust you?"

"You don't," Berta replied. "But you can." After an awkward silence, she cleared her throat. "Elaine said the doctors haven't given your husband's ailment a name."

"No, they haven't. We've been to five specialists, and none of them can explain his pain or fatigue." As much as Delthea felt trapped by her sister's boldness in bringing a stranger into her house, she also needed to prove she had done everything humanly possible for Garrett. "What do you charge?" she asked, eager to get through this ordeal.

"Twenty dollars an hour – cash."

That seemed high, but not outrageous for professional help. "What are your credentials?"

"Would I drag somebody here that wasn't qualified?" Elaine interjected indignantly.

"No, she needs to know." Berta summarized her impressive training and from her purse pulled a folded piece of paper that listed references and phone numbers in neat handwriting.

"When could you start?" Delthea asked meekly.

"Tomorrow. I prefer Monday through Friday, instead of skipping, 'cause it ends up being twice as much work when I come sporadically. Weekends or overnight is two-hundred a day."

"I understand," Delthea said. "Do you think the physical aspect of handling him might be too much?"

"Naw, I been lifting these babies my whole career. You got to know how to do it." She studied her untouched wine.

Berta's confidence impressed Delthea. In fact, she envied it. "Let's start tomorrow and see how it goes."

Elaine drank more wine and recounted getting drunk at Garrett's birthday party, along with the humiliating details of Delthea throwing a party which the guest of honor did not attend. While Elaine jabbered, Delthea questioned the wisdom of what she had done. Still, she desperately needed the help.

On the way to the door, Berta turned to Delthea. "I don't know how you'd find out, but you might, so I guess I'd better tell you up front. I'm an alcoholic. Haven't drank for seven years, but you never quit being one. If you want to back out now, I understand."

Torn between anger at Elaine and disappointment that an unexpected blessing had evaporated, Delthea gawked at Berta.

"Hell, you don't care, do you?" Elaine grabbed Berta's arm. "Delthea counsels people like you. She'd be the first to understand, and the last to pass judgement before she got to know you." She winked at Delthea and led Berta out the door.

Too tired to fight that battle, Delthea let them go. She re-heated Garrett's food and tried to feed him. He refused, so Delthea walked to the door and turned out the overhead light.

"Del-Delthea," Garrett whispered.

"What is it?"

"Berta. Too much money."

It surprised her how much he had heard. "No, I need help. You need help. We can't do this by ourselves." As she left the room, his muffled sobs made her heart ache.

*   *   *

Long before sunrise, Garrett lay awake, half-dreading Berta's arrival and half anticipating it. He hated for anyone to see him in his miserable condition. Still, she was someone, and he had been starving for human contact. Last night when they were talking about her salary, he got that same panicky feeling about money that had plagued him since he had been unable to work. He felt terrible about Delthea carrying the entire burden, and he worried the money would run out. The doorbell rang.

"Thanks for arriving on time," Delthea said as she opened the door. "The phone numbers for here and my office are under a magnet on the refrigerator. Our home line is unlisted. I'd prefer you only give it to people who really need to know. See you around six-thirty."

It had been a typical Delthea speech, professional yet polite enough to override her tendency to cover up insecurity with bitchiness.

The front door shut, and Berta walked into his bedroom. "Rise and shine." She sounded as confident as he felt unsure.

Shortly, Berta had him up, dressed in a navy blue jogging suit, and seated at the kitchen table. She fussed over his tea until Garrett said it had gotten strong enough. Then she cooked oatmeal but did not find any milk or butter as he requested, so she improvised with cinnamon and powdered coffee creamer. While sitting in the other chair and crocheting, she told him about the grandbaby due in January who would one day use the afghan under construction and the three others in Dallas, Washington State, and Florida.

"Sounds like your family is spread out," Garrett observed as he concentrated on feeding himself, a chore he had not done in a while. It amazed him that he could.

"What about you? Got any kids?" Berta asked, continuing to crochet. People asked that sort of thing all the time, not knowing how a simple question could hurt so deeply.

"I had one son." Garrett studied the oatmeal stuck to the side of the bowl and thought of his affair with Abi. Loc had been the only reason he didn't drop everything to find her when she left. "He and his mother died in a car accident."

She inhaled sharply. "I'm sorry. How long ago was that?"

Garrett closed his eyes. No one had asked him to think in so long that it felt odd and scary and a little confusing. "Eight, nearly nine years. He was eight at the time. He would be seventeen now, a senior in high school. Wow."

After breakfast, Berta insisted that Garrett brush his teeth. As he focused on the stranger in the mirror, toothpaste dripped from his mouth and into his gray-streaked beard. He had not worn facial hair since his college days, specifically since his brief affair with Abi. That seemed so long ago and yet the most significant five months of his life. Dear God, he loved Delthea. Why couldn't he let Abi go?

Next, Garrett sat in his armchair, his primary spot lately. Berta pulled a newspaper from her bag and asked him to catch her up on everything while she dusted. He read aloud about the Cabbage Patch doll craze and the hysteria associated with getting one. If Loc were alive what would he want for Christmas? Terrified of going through the pain of losing another child, Garrett had put off starting a family with Delthea twice. Once, by insisting they wait to get married until they finished their doctoral degrees and later when he devoted himself to his book. He loved Delthea and wanted to make her happy, but he couldn't face fatherhood again.

At Berta's prodding, he scanned an article about the USSR shooting and destroying a South Korean airplane back the first of September. He hated senseless killing and war. Only one good thing had ever come of it – his stint in Vietnam, which resulted in him fathering Loc, his dear sweet dead boy.

Delthea called at noon. By then Berta had heated a can of soup and showed him how to freshen crackers in the microwave. She briefed Delthea on their morning, adhering to the facts until she gave Garrett a conspirator's wink and finished with, "We're just discussing going out for a jog."

While they ate lunch, Garrett eyed the trashcan. Sure she had seen him peering that direction, Garrett said, "Could you help me get Abi's pictures out? I heard Elaine say something about them yesterday, so I know you know about them."

Berta chomped another cracker. "That would make me an accessory to a crime, don't you think?"

"Yes," Garrett answered.

Laughing and shaking her head, she said, "So what are we gonna do with them once we pull them out of there?"

"Glue them together," Garrett said. "There are paper and glue in the drawers of my desk." He motioned toward the study.

"And what will we do with it when Miss Hothead gets ahold of them again?" she countered.

Noting the bag Berta had left by the front door, Garrett answered calmly, "We'll keep them in your tote."

"Smart boy." Berta collected their dirty dishes, put them in the sink, and began rummaging through the trash.

While they matched torn edges and colors, Garrett related details of the relationship, how Abi and he had known each other for only a few months, her abusive marriage, and how stupid he felt when he finally realized her dangerous situation. He bragged about how Abi had grown emotionally in such a short period of time. As the six different pictures took shape, Garrett pointed out the features that held him captive.

"She's very pretty," Berta remarked, lining up the blue and white stripes of her sweater.

"You already think I'm crazy, so I can tell you something else, and it won't make any difference, will it?" Strangely, he felt totally comfortable with Berta. She was the ally he had needed all along.

"Probably not."

"I saw Abi in a dream. It was the night Delthea tore up her pictures. I have been searching for her all this time, and then she showed up in that dream, looking as real as you do to me right now. Sorry, I just needed to tell somebody."

"I'm glad you felt like you could." Berta patted his hand.

"Abi was a woman I had an affair with when I was married before." It was too late to take back what he had said, so Garrett wadded in deeper. "You must think that's terrible, but I can't get her off my mind. Several times while the affair was going on, I sensed there was something wrong, and sure enough it was. I'm getting the same vibes, but it's also affecting me physically. I don't want to renew the affair. I'd just like to know she's okay. And I'd like to return to normal."

After a thoughtful moment, Berta said, "I reckon everybody wonders about people we've loved."

They finished reconstructing the pictures and glued them to a paper backing. He marveled at how well they had gone back together. A few pieces were missing, but they were not in crucial locations. Berta gathered up the trash from all over the condo and took it down to the dumpster to avoid raising Delthea's suspicions. When Delthea walked in the door, Berta stood at the stove stirring two pots, one with spaghetti and the other contained sauce out of a jar. Garrett sat in his chair reading a book, feeling only slightly guilty for their ruse.

Berta picked up her bag while Delthea opened her purse.

Delthea handed Berta a stack of bills. "It's amazing what you've done in just one day. What did you find to cook?"

Berta stuck the money in her billfold. "Very little, but we made do. If you leave some cash, I'll do some shopping, or there's a service I've used that delivers. I can give you their number."

"I'd prefer you do it. Use Garrett's car. It needs to be driven anyway. In the morning, I'll show you where the keys are." She pulled two hundreds from her purse and handed them to Berta. "Tell me when you run out. Oh, and I will need you for an overnight stay in a couple of weeks. I have a speaking engagement in Austin."

While she tucked the money away, Berta said, "Sure."

"Great. I'll let you know about dates and times after I make my reservations."

A little boy's fear of being deserted played along the edges of Garrett's mind. Delthea had mentioned getting on a plane without regard for where it went. Was Austin merely a ploy to walk out the door forever?

*   *   *

Moa continued to read, and Abi drank in the melodic flow of his words. They sounded as glorious as the sweetest bird's song. Bird, the nickname Garrett had called her, starting with their first meeting. Moa, a huge New Zealand land bird that had been hunted into extinction, the name Takahe had derived out of Morgan. Takahe, a bird that had been thought extinct until recent years, a woman who had been their adopted mother and grandmother. And Birdsong Inn, their haven when she needed it most, the place where she would eventually die. Birds, birds, everywhere birds, but no wings to help her escape.

While Moa's sweet voice tinkled in her ears, Abi drifted in and out of sleep. She wanted to hold onto every precious moment with Moa, but her mind was not cooperating. Details of the park where she had seen Garrett kept coming in and out of focus in her mind. Finally, she succumbed to her desire to see him again and let herself shift totally into that place. Once she was fully there, her constant pain immediately disappeared, and again she had the same sensation of being in a real place, not the foggy, ambiguous feeling she got with her other dreams.

Both relieved and disappointed, Abi noted that she was alone in the park. She walked, relishing the ease with which her legs moved. It was heavenly escaping her agony as well as reclaiming her physical strength. Finding the spot next to a huge elm where they had sat on Garrett's bedspread, Abi lowered herself to the grass and the hard ground below it. Though Abi hated admitting it, even to herself, she wanted desperately to see Garrett. It did not feel right to be here without him. She ran her fingers along the rough bark of the tree and turned her face toward the warmth of the sun that peeked through the swaying limbs.

"Bird, I hoped you would come back," said a voice she had not heard in many years.

Abi spun around to see the youthful Garrett standing beside her. "Do you come here often?" It was a stupid question, but also the most coherent thing she could think to say.

"Only that other time when I waved at you." His mesmerizing green eyes searched her face. "I take it you don't frequent this place."

"No, I don't. I didn't really intend to come today. I just showed up."

"Me, too." He smiled, looking so much like Moa. "God, it's good to see you. I can't tell you how often I've wished for this very moment."

"This must be your doings. You'd better explain yourself." Abi patted the grass beside her. She would let him talk all he wanted to, but she had no intentions of telling him about Moa or her illness.

He lowered himself into a cross-legged sitting position. "I just can't get over this. You're here. Now, you have to tell me. Where did you go? Where have you been all this time?"

"All this time? Let's get a couple of things straight. What year is it?" she asked, struggling with her own amazement.

"It's September 21, 1983, but you haven't aged a day since 1973. In fact, you're wearing the same sweater that you wore the day I took your picture here."

Abi looked down at her clothes. "How do you remember?"

"I look at those pictures daily."

She examined his bearded face and long hair. "And you're identical to the way you were then."

He glanced down at his shirt and pants. "You're right, I am dressed like I did then." He felt his face with both hands. "And I am currently wearing a beard, but I'm sure what you're seeing doesn't look at all like I actually look now."

"Well, it is a dream, isn't it? We can appear however we want, can't we?" The comment about him looking at her picture sank in. "Doesn't Trang mind you looking at pictures of me?"

The shadow of pain crossed his face. "She and Loc died in a car accident nine years ago." He looked down at his interlaced fingers and then back up at her. "I'm remarried." He smiled as if he'd told himself a joke. "And, yes, Delthea does mind me looking at your pictures. In fact, she tore them up because she got so mad about it."

Abi grimaced. "I can't say that I blame her. It's not exactly what a happily married man does." It shouldn't be, but this was music to Abi's ears. She had never really given up wanting Garrett.

"You're right, but I actually do love Delthea. It's just that I've had this overwhelming need for the last nine months to know where you are and how you're doing." He studied her closely as though trying to verify the answers. "I detect a bit of an accent, English maybe, but not quite."

"Well, as you can see, I'm perfectly fine," Abi said, ignoring his last comment. She held out her arm and flexed it like a muscle man showing off. "See?" The irony of her words struck her. Even in a dream, she couldn't tell him what she desperately needed to tell him in real life.

"I see that." He gently squeezed her arm muscle.

Electricity seemed to flow from his fingers straight to her heart. It beat like it had when she first met him, like it did when he kissed her, when he made love to her, when she left his apartment for the last time, knowing she would never see him again. Yet, here he was touching her.

His fingertips lightly stroked her cheek. "You okay?"

She swallowed and tried to speak, but words would not come. Abruptly, she felt herself yanked back into her bed like someone had pulled her through a tiny hole at lightning speed.

"Mum, are you all right?" Moa asked in a panic, his hands on her arms and then her face.

"I'm fine. I'm fine," she assured him, aware that she had upset Moa but she was also overcome with a need to somehow manage the pain that came back to her like a punch to her gut. Her insides wrenched like someone had grabbed them and twisted. She reached for the bottle of pain pills on the bed stand, knocking off a glass of water in the process.

Takahe rushed into the room, shouting at Moa, "I told you to tell me before your mum started feeling bad again."

"Please, don't fuss at him." She reached for Moa, but he had jumped off the bed and was standing halfway to the door, looking scared and hurt. Abi held out her arms to him.

He shook his head and looked at her like he was not sure what she had become, like he was too scared to go near her. That hurt – worse than the cancer ever had. She had to spare him the pain of seeing her die. As much as she needed and wanted him, she would not force him to carry that image with him for the rest of his life.

Chapter Four

Scraggly elm trees blocked Austin's noonday sun as Delthea's rental car crept along. She scrutinized one tiny house after another for the address Bud had left with the birth certificate, one-thousand-thirty-and-a-half. It did not exist. She had found the whole numbers, but not the half. Finally, Delthea parked on the street since an old Plymouth occupied the single car drive of the house numbered with the correct digit, minus the half. Nearly out of the car, she grabbed Morgan Clay Barker's birth certificate as proof that she was whom she said.

Unsure what she would say to the occupants, Delthea walked up the cracked and undulating sidewalk. A crumbling brick planter box surrounded the front porch. Not finding a doorbell, she knocked on the screen door, the only thing that separated her from the shadowed room where a game show blared from a hidden television.

A round, Hispanic woman walked across the linoleum floor toward her. She wiped her hands on a small towel. "Help you?"

"Yes, I'm looking for Abi Barker. Do you know her?"

Shuffling sounds preceded the appearance of a tall, elderly man. "Who is it?" he asked, drawing closer.

"She looks for someone named Abi Barker," she shouted in his ear.

"There was a guy by here some time back wanting to find her," he said thoughtfully.

Shrugging her shoulders, the woman sauntered away.

"Does she still live here?" Delthea asked.

"Run off not too long after she come." He shifted his towering frame and appeared close to toppling over.

"Do you know where she went or why she left?"

"Nope," he answered stubbornly.

Delthea guessed that he knew quite a bit, but he wasn't going to tell a stranger without knowing what she wanted. It would take time to convince him, time she didn't have. She needed to get back to the hotel and look over Oliver's notes. She had barely glanced over them on the plane earlier that morning. "My name is Delthea Richards. I am married to Garrett Clay. He is Morgan Barker's father. Abi was in an abusive relationship with someone else when Garrett fathered this child. She never told Garrett about the baby, but we recently learned of his existence." She held up the birth certificate.

His thick eyebrows knitted, and he peered through the screen door at the paper in question. "Let's see. Your name is Richards. Your husband's name is Clay. And that baby . . ."

"It's very complicated, but I assure you my intentions are pure. My husband wants to find his son." Or he would if he knew about Morgan, so it wasn't a complete lie.

The old man's face, patterned with tiny squares of light from the wire mesh between them, softened. "Why isn't he here?"

"Garrett's very ill. In fact, we're afraid he might die before he gets to see Morgan." As much as Delthea had avoided the idea of Garrett dying, it occurred to her often.

"You don't say. What's he got?" The old man opened the door and motioned Delthea inside.

"Heart trouble." It was the easiest explanation and truthfully the most accurate conclusion Delthea could make. His heart belonged to Abi, and Delthea intended to get it back.

The old man turned and shuffled toward the television. He turned it off. "I haven't seen Abi in going on ten years now. She disappeared right after her husband showed up."

"Did she go with him?" Delthea hated the idea of anyone going back into an abusive marriage, but it would certainly solve her problems concerning Abi and her son.

"I don't think so. He came back looking for her again. Plus, she left a note asking me to keep her stuff and to not let him have it."

"Do you still have her things?" Delthea asked, sure he had gotten rid of it by now, but also clear she needed to make sure.

"Yep, I got it. Thought she'd come back for it by now."

"Could I see?" The question had popped out of her mouth. Delthea dreaded looking at or touching Abi's things, but she couldn't leave anything here that might implicate Garrett.

"Only if you'll take it with you." The old man shuffled to the kitchen where he rummaged through a drawer full of hardware, including nuts, bolts, and hand tools. At last, he produced a key and turned his turtle like progress toward the backdoor.

Delthea followed him outside. While he unlocked a storage shed, the man introduced himself as Mr. Truman, like the president, and explained that Abi had lived in his garage apartment that faced the alley. It was now rented by a group of noisy college boys. Once inside the metal structure, Mr. Truman pointed to several boxes labeled clothes, art supplies, and personal. The last title concerned Delthea.

"I'd like to pay you for storing these things all this time." Delthea pulled out her wallet and handed Mr. Truman one of the one-hundred-dollar bills earmarked for Berta.

Mr. Truman took the money and chuckled. "I guess ten dollars a year ain't too much for storing somebody's stuff."

"Do you think I should pay you more?" Delthea pulled out another one-hundred-dollar bill.

"Naw, I never expected to get anything for it. Maria can help you load it in your car. She comes twice a week since my wife died, and she's strong as a mule."

Delthea accepted the offer. After speaking to The Cattlemen of America, she would spend every minute if necessary until her plane left in the morning sorting through this stuff. It wasn't going back to Houston with her.

While Maria and Delthea filled her trunk, Delthea asked the old man why he had not given Abi's things to Bud Anderson. No doubt he was 'the guy' Mr. Truman had mentioned earlier.

"Him?" Mr. Truman snorted. "He reminded me of her ex, who is the reason Abi left. Just about broke Ellie's heart."

"Garrett told me he was very violent with Abi," Delthea said, struggling with the last box.

"Yeah, he was a big guy. Acted pretty hot under the collar. Me and Ellie expected Abi to come back. She was crazy about those two, chiefly little Morgan. We never had none of our own."

After apologizing that she could not visit longer, Delthea traded his phone number for a promise that she would keep Mr. Truman abreast of her progress. No telling what questions would come up after exploring Abi's castoffs.

On the way back to the hotel, Delthea took in a long, deep breath. She had trouble getting enough air. Being this close to a woman who held Garrett spellbound had a suffocating effect. Although she hated to admit it, Abi controlled Delthea as well. Otherwise, she would confront Berta about what she and Garrett had done with Abi's torn pictures. From the way Garrett and Berta had immediately bonded and Garrett's never saying another word about the pictures let Delthea know the pictures had been instrumental in bringing them together. While Abi had acted like glue for Garrett and Berta, she continued to separate Delthea and Garrett. Damn Abi Barker. Damn her to hell.

*   *   *

After lunch, instead of sitting in his chair, Garrett crept down the hallway to his bedroom. Delthea had gotten up early to leave for her trip to Austin. Something about her being out of town bothered him. He told himself it was simply the fact that they had not spent the night apart in six months, but there was more to it than that.

His agitation started when she mentioned the trip to Berta a week ago. Something told him then that she had a reason for going to Austin that did not have to do with filling in for Oliver. Later, the way she diverted her eyes and used a slightly higher tone of voice when she talked about going made him even more suspicious. Over and over again, she assured him that she would only be gone one night, which further convinced him that she had a secret mission.

As Garrett lowered himself onto the bed, Berta appeared in the doorway. "You taking a horizontal nap today?" she asked.

"I woke up early this morning." He usually nodded in his chair after lunch, but today he wanted to sleep soundly, maybe even dream about a certain park.

Berta shut the door. Garrett slipped off his house shoes and stretched out on top of the bedspread. Within a few minutes, the vacuum cleaner began humming in the background. Closing his eyes, Garrett thought of the last time he had dreamed of Abi and how she suddenly disappeared. He tried to recall exactly what he had said or done prior to that. This was only a dream, but, hey, it gave him a reprieve from the pain, the only relief he had discovered since all of this began.

Even before the reality of his bedroom fully disappeared, Garrett began shifting to that back street in Oaces, Texas, to a park where he hoped to find an auburn-haired girl whose radiant smile said she was also glad to see him. Once fully there, he walked to the tree where they had previously met, but he did not see her. Finally, he saw a woman with long, brown hair sitting in a swing at the far end of the park. He walked that direction.

As he approached her, Abi looked up at him and smiled. "I wondered if you would be here today." He noted the faint accent that he had detected on their earlier visit. It had a melodic quality that wasn't exactly English.

He wanted to touch her again, but he recalled that was something he had done prior to her disappearing, so he sat in the swing next to hers. "Have you been here when I wasn't?"

"No, I haven't," she answered. "It seems like every time I dream of you, you magically appear."

"Same here. Since this is only a dream, I guess, we can do it however we want." He reflected on their previous encounter. "But you abruptly left last time. Was there a problem?"

"Since this is a dream, I guess I can be perfectly honest."

"Go right ahead." Garrett stroked his hand through the air as though offering her the floor.

Bird, that painfully shy woman he had known ten years ago, looked up at him. "You touched me . . . and I simply couldn't hang around." She studied her hands while one thumbnail picked at the other. "It was like electricity running through me."

Garrett had felt the same sensation. Of course, he had. He was the one making up this dream. He was the one who had searched for Abi. It made sense he would finally find her in a dream, something he could control. Then why had he allowed her to disappear?

"You mentioned that you married again after your wife and son died. Tell me about her – Delthea, is it?" Bird wore that open, gullible expression that had captured his heart long ago.

"Yes, she's a psychologist, too. We met when we were both doing our internship." Garrett thought about how attentive and helpful Delthea had been almost from the very beginning of their association. "She and I have a private practice, but she's run it by herself for the last couple of years."

"Why?" Abi asked, having lost interest in her fingernails.

"For a while I was finishing up my book." He was only fooling himself by talking about his success rather than his illness, but it felt good, so why not continue? "Then I was busy promoting it."

"What's the name of it? What's it about?" she asked like an excited child on Christmas Eve.

"It's entitled, *I Am*," he said, glad she had interrupted before he got to the part about being sick and staying home while Delthea went to work. "It deals with the idea that people's thoughts create their reality. Whatever you think is what you are or what you become."

"Like in *As a Man Thinketh*. I used to buy into that, back when you introduced me to that idea, but now I'm not so sure." Her eyes had grown dark and skeptical.

Garrett nodded, realizing his need to come to terms with what was happening had likely prompted him to manufacture this dream scene. "I know what you mean. I've been sick – to the point that I can't even go to work. A lady comes and helps me dress in the morning, fixes my lunch, and does practically everything for me. I'm a goddamn invalid."

"What kind of illness do you have?" Bird asked.

"I've been to five doctors and none of them can diagnose it. Each one puts me through a battery of tests and then tells me they haven't a clue, so they give me a prescription for pain pills."

"I'm sorry to hear that . . . really sorry. What about your wife? How is she coping?" She sounded genuinely concerned.

"Like I said earlier, Delthea has been holding the fort by herself. This morning, she left for Austin to speak to a group. Usually, she puts in fifty hours a week seeing clients." It felt strange telling Abi about Delthea. When he and Abi met, he had purposely not told her about Trang and Loc. Even though it was only his imagination, he was determined to be honest this time.

"Austin is where I lived when I left Oaces," Bird admitted, grinning mischievously. "Are you still in Houston?"

"Yes, I am." Bud would have found her in Austin, but this was only a dream. He decided to play along and enjoy the escape. "What made you leave Austin?"

Again, she was preoccupied with her thumbnails. "I made the mistake of telling Mama where I was, and she told Vince."

"You were afraid he would make you go back to Quits?" Garrett offered.

"That's exactly right. If he hadn't dragged me back to that little town screaming and kicking, he would have killed me." The more candidly she spoke, the more clearly he heard the melodic quality that had invaded her speech.

"What changed? When you left Quits, he didn't try to stop you, did he?" Garrett asked.

Bird glanced around the park, a wild animal looking for a hiding place. She jumped out of the swing. "I've got to go."

"No, please don't." He reached out and grabbed her hand. "We don't have to talk about that. We can go on . . ." Before he finished what he had started to say, she disappeared, and he immediately woke up, his body wracked with pain and exhausted. Welcome back to reality.

*   *   *

Movement within the bedroom awoke Abi. She gasped for breath and forced her eyes open. It was only a dream, only a dream. No matter how many times she told herself, it still felt more real than the bed she lay on or Takahe walking toward her.

"Sorry to disturb you." Takahe set the tray on the nightstand.

"I'm glad you're here." Abi's teeth clattered together. "I woke up in a cold sweat. Can you help me change?" Agitation at talking to Garrett had caused her to sweat while the cool room chilled her and magnified the pain.

"Hold your hands up." Takahe slipped Abi's cotton gown over her head. Then she pulled another one from the drawer.

Relishing the soft, dry material against her skin, Abi said, "It's incredible how good something as simple as fresh clothes can feel while the rest of me is feeling terrible."

"Your illness must have heightened your sensitivity." Takahe unfolded the lap table and placed it over Abi's legs. She set the breakfast tray on it.

Ravenous, Abi spooned pumpkin soup into her mouth. "You know the other day when you helped me do some self-hypnotism?"

"You slept deeply after that. Did it help?" Never idle, Takahe sat in the chair next to Abi's bed and pulled from her pocket one of Moa's socks, a spool of thread, and a needle.

"Yes, very much." Abi confided. "I imagined a park where Garrett and I once met."

"You're always painting pictures of him; I guess that's logical that you would think of something to do with him when you are trying to relax." She examined the hole in the sock.

"I suppose that's right. It seemed so real, like he was really there. The first time I dreamed about him, we didn't talk. He motioned for me to come over to him, but I didn't go."

"What stopped you?" Takahe held the needle up and poked the thread through the eye.

"It sounds stupid, but I'm terrified that he'll find out about Moa and take him back to the States after I'm gone. I've dreamed about him two other times, and I talked with him both of those times. Neither time did he seem threatening."

"Remember, it's only a dream – simply what you create in your mind." Takahe took a stitch.

"In my dream, we were both young, the same age we were when we knew each other. And I felt healthy. The pain was completely gone. The disturbing part is that he told me he is sick like me."

"You should try going back to talk to Garrett again." Takahe took another stitch. "It has helped you escape the pain and God is talking to you in this way."

"I can't imagine what God is saying. Maybe He's trying to tell me not to contact Garrett? Or maybe He's trying to point out that things are not the way they appear to be." Again she sipped from a spoonful of pumpkin soup, the one thing she could sometimes eat without vomiting. "The oddest part about all this is these dreams don't feel imaginary. They feel like I'm really there."

"I'm sure there is a message even if it is not yet apparent," Takahe said.

"He told me he was sick, too sick to take care of a child, and that his mysterious disease has been going on for a while – just like mine. That must be my fear, that he wouldn't want Moa, that I would be opening Moa and me up to a lot of heartache if we did contact him." Abi reached out and held Takahe's hand. She needed someone to help her decide whether or not to contact Garrett.

The wise Maori woman placed her other hand on top of Abi's, sandwiching it between her own. "Whether you tell him now or wait for him to decide on his own, Moa will want to know his father. Everybody does. He will have more reason than most."

"I told him his father was dead."

"I know, but he will want to visit the grave someday."

Abi had thought about that fact, but she had not let herself dwell upon it. Mostly she did not want to address how mad Moa might be if she kept Garrett's existence a secret until he eventually discovered him on his own. Takahe was right. Moa would eventually look for some tangible evidence of Garrett with or without her help.

All of this unknowing was compounded by the fact that Moa was scheduled to leave for boarding school next week. As much as Abi treasured their time together, she would not allow him to see her in the final stages of this horrible disease. She was an awful sight now, and she would only get worse.

*   *   *

The American Cattlemen of America politely clapped in response to Delthea's less than stirring speech on how to increase their sales. She knew nothing about marketing cattle, certainly less than Oliver whose speech had fallen on blank faces. Oh well, she had fulfilled her obligation to her former supervisor, and she had a mountain of stuff to sift through in her hotel room, not that she relished the thought. Still, the idea of discovering more about Abi and her whereabouts had been the reason she negotiated with Oliver to do the Austin speaking engagement instead of the one in Houston.

The crowded ballroom emptied slowly. As Delthea made her way to the exit, men, most of them balding and weathered by years of dealing with the elements, smiled and nodded. She returned their silent greeting.

Someone at Delthea's side leaned toward her and said softly, "You don't know jackshit about cattle, do you?"

She turned to look at the tall, dark-haired man whom she estimated to be around her age. He had sat in the front row, his youth contrasting with the older gentlemen surrounding him. "Not a thing. I delivered this speech to help out a friend."

As they inched forward, his thick Texas accent charmed Delthea into telling him how she liked Austin, where she lived, what she did for a living, but nothing about the fact that she was married. A neglected part of her desperately needed to talk to someone who saw her as an individual, someone not linked to a man whose problems constantly weighted her down.

When they finally reached the hallway, her companion of the last five minutes said, "How about dinner?"

"You mean tonight?" She stuck her left hand in her pocket and slipped off her grandmother's wedding ring, the ring Garrett had placed on her finger more than five years ago right before they both promised to love one another exclusively.

"Sure if you don't have plans." He smiled, revealing teeth that looked particularly white against his dark tan.

"I-I don't even know your name," Delthea sputtered.

"Rhett Butler." He beamed, apparently ready for the predictable reaction.

"So your mother was enamored with the movie, huh?"

"Yep, she had a thing about *Gone with the Wind*. She used to say she married my dad to use his name." He stuck out his hand.

She shook it, and pulled her left hand out of her pocket, minus the ring. He never had to know about Garrett. After all, Rhett had asked her to dinner, not to sleep with him.

Delthea reminded herself of her innocence as she and Rhett dined at a seafood restaurant. They discussed his family and hers, the fact that Elaine was a nurse, and that he was getting his nursing license, the first man in his part of the world to do such a thing. She was merely enjoying a break from reality – while avoiding the woman who occupied her hotel room and her husband's mind and heart. Then why did she feel so guilty?

*   *   *

Saturday Night Live ended as Garrett sat in his chair. Berta slept on the couch, her crocheting sprawled across her chest. When she asked him two hours ago if he wasn't ready to call it a night, he stalled, sure Delthea would phone to check on him. She had not. In fact, the phone had not rung all day. He hated to admit it, but dreaming about Abi had added to his agitation. Again, she had left abruptly when he touched her. He couldn't tell Delthea about Abi, although in the past Delthea had been his stabilizing force.

Garrett picked up the phone and pushed the on button again. For the third time since Berta fell asleep, the dial tone hummed in his ear. He punched in the number for the hotel that Delthea had written on a piece of paper and given to him as she walked out the door. Garrett asked the desk clerk to ring Delthea's room. No one answered. He declined to leave a message.

Where was she? She could have gotten mugged or hurt. Or maybe she met someone. That idea scared Garrett the most. It had occurred to him frequently in the last six months. She might have gone to Austin with someone or to meet a lover. A year ago, he would never have thought such a thing. Now she had every reason to look for companionship elsewhere. They had not conversed meaningfully, much less made love since this wretched condition began. Garrett thudded his head against the back of the chair. Dear God, he was tired of it all. Why couldn't he go ahead and die and break out of this insane prison.

* * *

In the elevator Rhett nibbled Delthea's ear lobe and throat. She let him, aroused and flattered by his attention. Tomorrow she would fly back to Houston, and he would get in his big red pickup truck and drive to Opedyke or Hurlwood, whatever he called his hometown. After eating, they had gone to the clubs on Sixth Street where they danced and drank and laughed. After three frozen margaritas, she couldn't read her watch, and she did not care – about anything.

Outside her room, Rhett unlocked the door and flung it open. "Your bed awaits us."

"Not on a first date." Once again, laughter bubbled out of her throat. "Thanks for a fun time."

"Are you sure? I could make it worth your while." He flashed her that little boy grin he had been using all night.

"I'm sure you could, but my carriage turned into a pumpkin several hours ago," Delthea answered with surprising resolve. She was tempted, though. It had been too long since she felt a strong man press against her and moan with desire.

Rhett wrapped his arms around her waist and pulled her closer. Their lips met. He tasted of bourbon and a spicy after-shave. She pulled away, fully conscious of crossing the line between flirtation and intimacy. His dark, piercing eyes searched her face longingly.

Delthea stepped back and drew in a long steadying breath. "I better go in before I do something I regret."

That made him grin. "I'm not far if you change your mind. Five-twenty-three. And I've got a fresh bottle of Jack." He sauntered down the hall, unlocked his door, waved, and disappeared, three doors away.

The irony of befriending someone staying in a room so close by struck Delthea. What were the odds? She stepped inside, closed the door, and leaned on it. Then she saw the pile of boxes at the foot of the bed. She had to sort through their contents before asking housekeeping to throw them out. Otherwise, she would always wonder when something hidden within this trash would come back to haunt her. Creeps like Bud Anderson showed up daily. No doubt someone would go through all this, if for no other reason than to see if they could use the clothes or books.

After slipping off her shoes, Delthea sat on the bed and opened the flaps of the top box, the one marked personal, the one she dreaded the most. She pulled out a sketchbook and began thumbing through it. Drawings of Garrett filled every page. Although his beard and hair had recently grown out to semi-match the drawn images, the man who stared back at her looked decidedly different. It wasn't just his age. He was happy, happier than Delthea had ever seen him. No wonder he longed to find Abi.

The next sketchbook featured pictures of Garrett holding a baby. Delthea could imagine Abi drawing Garrett while they were together, but realizing she had done these after they parted sent a chill up her spine. His image was obviously etched in Abi's mind. She was and probably is as crazy about him as he was and is about her. Every detailed drawing struck Delthea like a physical blow.

Unable to look further, she threw the sketchbooks back in the box. The next spiral she picked up said 'Journal' on the outside cover. Dreading what she might find there, Delthea took a breath and opened it to the first page.

My Dearest Garrett,
May 18, 1973

As I lay awake and hold your dog tag to my heart, I picture your face – the way you smile, your gorgeous green eyes, the tiny lines that radiate from the corners of them like rays from the sun. I must remember every detail for our child. He will know you in his heart even though he may never feel your gentle touch in person.

It's only been a few days since we lay in each other's arms, but I miss you. Christ, how I miss you. I already doubt the wisdom of leaving Oaces, but I couldn't do anything else and not destroy your family. Forgive me.

Someday we'll be together again. Someday.

I love you, Abi (Bird)

Delthea thumbed through the rest of the book, her heartbeat picking up speed with every passage she read. Abi loved Garrett as much as was humanly possible. She had loved him enough to sacrifice their relationship in order to preserve his family. A wave of panic coursed through Delthea when she looked at the box and saw at least five more spirals that probably contained more of the same. She could not read them. She couldn't even stay in the same room with them.

Throwing the spiral on the bed, she ran from the room. What had possessed her to find Abi's landlord, to burden herself with these relics of the past? She looked at her open door and realized she could not return. There was no way, absolutely no way. Rhett's offer echoed in her thoughts. Perhaps with a couple of drinks from his 'fresh bottle of Jack' she could face packing up that shit.

Chapter Five

*T*he roar of the plane engine magnified the pounding in Delthea's head. Thank God she sat on an aisle seat, easier to jump up and run to the restroom. A smiling stewardess stopped and handed Delthea the Bloody Mary she had ordered. Delthea's hand shook, spilling a drop of tomato juice on her skirt, the one she found at dawn on Rhett's hotel room floor next to the empty whiskey bottle and the rest of her clothes. Oh, God, why had she taken off her ring? Delthea dug in her pocket. She found nothing.

She had been a complete idiot to come to Austin. How could she ever undo what happened last night? One drink led to the next, the intimate dance . . . . Thank God Rhett still slept when she left. By the time she found someone to help her tape up the boxes and load them into the rental car, she nearly missed her plane. Dealing with Rhett as well would have been too much.

How could Delthea face Garrett? He would take one look at her and know. His ability to accurately read her was one of the qualities she loved about him – before she had secrets like his son, Abi's things, and most especially her unfaithfulness. Why, oh why, had she pursued that stupid birth certificate? She should have torn it into tiny pieces and thrown it away.

Delthea downed her drink and pushed the call button. She needed another one, a double.

* * *

Using the lap table, Takahe and Abi played the only card game they knew. A guest at the inn had taught it to them years ago. Abi never thought she'd spend hour upon hour in bed.

"Gin," Takahe announced, turning her discard face down.

Abi laid her cards on the table, too tired to count the points.

"Do you need a pain pill?" Takahe asked, concern etched in the wrinkles that framed her face.

"Later." Abi didn't know which was worse, the pain or the drugged feeling that lingered after taking the pills. "Mostly I'm tired. I haven't slept much." Every time she drifted off, she wondered if she would see Garrett again. Part of her dreaded the idea, a larger part of her looked forward to their next encounter.

Takahe gathered the cards. "I have been thinking about your ability to move through time and space with your thoughts. From what you describe, it's more than just dreaming. Perhaps your spirit is preparing itself for a time when your body will no longer house it."

"After I'm dead, you mean." The inevitable event was a topic Abi thought about constantly, but avoided discussing.

"Yes." Takahe shuffled the cards. "What do you think will happen after you die?"

"I'll go to heaven if I've gotten enough points, and to hell if I don't," Abi said caustically, repeating the concept pounded into her head as a child. She refused to buy it, then and now.

"What do you want to believe?" Takahe's dark eyes reached into the part of Abi that could not be destroyed by rampant, mutated cells, that part in question. Her soul.

"I'd like to work a deal with God and get to hang around and watch over Moa. That's what I really want." Tears sprang to her eyes. She could not think of leaving him without crying.

"You can. God is showing you the way."

Abi wondered what Takahe was saying. The old woman seemed to have a connection to the spirit world, and Abi trusted her friend to know more about all that than she did.

Takahe set the lap table on the floor, quietly walked out of the door, and pulled it shut, whispering, "Go to sleep."

At Takahe's suggestion, Abi shut her eyes. After a few minutes of shifting to find a more comfortable position, Abi's mind began drifting out of consciousness. Her dream world immediately took her to the park where she saw Garrett sitting on the merry-go-round next to the swings. "Hello," she called. "You're already here."

"I've been waiting for you." His brow was bunched with either concentration or worry as he looked down at a tablet in his hands. "Do you remember the drawings you did of me?"

"Of course. Now I paint pictures of you. Let me see what you're drawing."

He flipped the tablet over and held up a picture that was a perfect likeness of Morgan at his present age. The young boy was laughing. Even his hair was the same mop of curly ringlets. The image took Abi's breath away. She took the pad from Garrett and examined it closely.

"Morgan," she whispered, the name spilling off her lips involuntarily. "I can't believe it."

"Who's Morgan?" Garrett quizzed, with the eagerness of a dog with a bone. "That's the name of your roommate – the one you told me about when you called in December after you left."

"Wow, this is crazy." Abi raked her fingers through her hair. "It's uncanny." She looked up at him. "This is a dream, so I guess I can tell you, huh?"

"Tell me what?" Garrett demanded.

"That's your son. That's Morgan."

"What?" Garrett grabbed the drawing pad back. "My son?"

"He was born December 8th, 1973. He's the reason I left Oaces. He's the reason I left Austin. I can't believe you drew that."

Garrett gawked at her, open-mouthed. "I didn't draw that. You did. It was lying on the ground when I arrived. It has your signature in the bottom right hand corner."

Abi yanked the tablet back from him and saw 'Abi', the way she signed all of her work, hidden in the folds of Morgan's shirt. It was a drawing she had done over a month ago, using a photo Colin had taken. How had it gotten here? All at once, it dawned on her that the dream, like Takahe, was encouraging her to tell Garrett, sort of giving her a practice venue.

She studied his face, hidden behind a beard and in the shadow of his ever-present leather wide-brimmed hat. "I wasn't going to tell you. I never wanted you to know about Morgan."

"Is that my punishment for not admitting I was married when I knew you in Oaces?" he asked, his brows bunched.

"No, I was afraid you'd bring him back to the States and somehow Vince would find out and take him away from you because I was married to Vince when I got pregnant."

Total bewilderment clouded Garrett's face. "I don't get it. Where are you? Why would I have him instead of you?"

Unable to keep her hands off of him, Abi reached out and stroked his cheek with her thumb. When a current of electricity coursed through her, she closed her eyes and took it in. "I can't explain. I can't explain," she muttered, while she felt herself being sucked back to her bed at Birdsong Inn and once more away from Garrett.

*   *   *

Imagining Abi held the pen in Garrett's hand, he moved it across the page to form the jawline of the picture he had seen in his dream. Another line all but drew itself, forming the bridge of his nose. Seeing the young boy's face in his mind, his hand traced the lines of the portrait, the face of his son. His pen effortlessly followed the image that had etched itself in his mind. Giddy with excitement, his hand moved faster, rapidly sketching an exact replica of the sketch he had seen in the park, a boy laughing, his son. But that couldn't be. It was only a dream.

Garrett ran his fingers over the drawing, bewildered and scared and wondering what had possessed him.

Delthea walked into the living room from the kitchen. "Elaine and the boys are bringing a pizza over tonight. Would you like someth – . . ." She gazed at the drawing in Garrett's lap. "When did you start drawing?" Her voice shook while she stared at his open journal.

"I don't. It just came out on its own." Garrett couldn't tell her about finding the drawing at the park. He hadn't told her about talking to Abi in his dreams, and he sure couldn't open a can of worms like telling her Abi had told him he had a son. God, what a preposterous idea. Was this some kind of unresolved loss of Loc? But the drawing didn't look like Loc. He looked like Garrett, like a son that Abi could have given him.

"On its own," Delthea repeated indignantly. "When did she give you that?"

She didn't have to say Abi's name. "She didn't. I drew it."

"You just said you don't draw, so where did you get it?" she demanded.

"Sorry. I misspoke. I did draw it." Ever since Delthea had returned from Austin, she had been acting strangely, at first like she had a hangover, which Garrett couldn't blame her for having a few drinks. More than that, she had hardly touched him – and her ring was gone. He had noticed her bare finger within minutes after she walked in the door. The night before when he had called her hotel room again at two, four and six o'clock, she had not been there.

Delthea walked away, shaking her head and muttering something under her breath.

Almost without effort, Garrett drew one page after another of the same boy in various poses. The idea that Abi had given birth to his son was simply too bizarre to entertain, but like always, the dream had seemed more real than his current reality of being sick. The sketches reminded him of Abi. She had drawn portraits of him and these were similar to what he remembered of her style. Delthea had thrown out Abi's drawings not long after they moved in together. It had been the source of their first major disagreement. But who was this boy? And why did Garrett suddenly have the ability to draw?

Although Garrett could not stop his hand from performing his newfound talent, he tried to keep Delthea from seeing them when she passed through the room.

Elaine and the boys arrived with two huge pizzas. Garrett couldn't remember the last time he saw his nephews. They had grown from rowdy, happy children to sullen ones in adult size bodies.

Kent handed Delthea his pizza box and approached Garrett. "How you doing, Unc?" He stuck out his hand.

Garrett took it, wondering how Elaine had bribed him into this visit. "You've grown up. What grade are you in?"

"Eighth," he answered

David knelt by Garrett's chair and peered into his face. "What's wrong, Uncle Garrett? You look like an old man."

"David!" Elaine scolded from across the room.

"It's okay." Garrett appreciated his candor, the very thing a twelve-year-old might say.

"Hey, this is cool," Kent commented, picking up Garrett's journal. He flipped through the drawings. "Who's this dude?"

"I don't know. He sort of appeared on his own." Garrett took the book from him, and seeing Delthea's face, wished he had closed it when they arrived.

"Can you draw me?" David asked, his eyes suddenly alive.

"I'm not sure." Garrett flipped to a fresh page. When he started to sketch, the pen practically worked by itself. He glanced back and forth from the paper to his posing nephew, amazed by the likeness that was forming there.

Everyone but Delthea admired Garrett's drawing. She refused to comment, her mouth set into a hard, straight line.

"Do me," Kent demanded. He struck a pose and Garrett began drawing. Again, the pen seemed to know exactly where to mark in order to capture an incredible likeness. He found his own actions as fascinating as Elaine and the boys seemed to.

"Let's eat," Delthea called, her voice strained.

They gathered around the dining room table since the kitchen wasn't big enough. David and Kent jockeyed for seats next to Garrett. He had become the cool guy to sit beside. That pleased him. Having people around again felt good.

*   *   *

After eating while the boys and Garrett were settling in front of the television, Delthea pulled Elaine aside. "Let's take a walk."

"Sure. The boys are entertaining Garrett, and I need a smoke." Elaine grabbed her ratty vinyl purse.

In the elevator, Elaine pulled out a cigarette and a lighter from the depths of the huge bag. "How was Austin?"

"Terrible," Delthea answered, sorting out what to share.

"I figured that from the look on your face and the shitty way you've been treating Garrett."

"What do you mean by that?" Delthea despised Elaine's ability to see through her.

The elevator doors opened before Elaine could answer. They walked across the lobby striped with vacuum cleaner lines and outside to a sidewalk flanked by manicured flowerbeds.

"You can't hide your feelings. Remember that time you came over after you figured out Garrett was obsessing over Abi?"

"Yes, the day I found out he has a son by her," Delthea recalled. Her problems had not changed, merely magnified.

"You're acting bitchy again, just like you did then. What happened in Austin?" Elaine lit a cigarette as they walked.

"I went to the address the investigator gave me along with Morgan's birth certificate, where Abi used to live. Her landlord had three boxes of Abi's old stuff." The impact of recalling Abi's journal stopped Delthea.

"Did you figure out where she went?"

"I think she's here in Houston," Delthea said. "While I was gone this weekend I suspect she and Garrett were together. In fact, I'd venture to guess they've seen each other quite a bit over the last few months." She gave a weary laugh. "Maybe that's why I'm treating him so 'shitty,' as you say."

"Did Berta tell you about Abi visiting?" Elaine asked.

"She didn't have to. Those sketches he's doing are exactly like the ones I found in her sketchbooks. Abi must have taught him." It all sounded too preposterous to be credible. Delthea wouldn't believe this bizarre tale, except she had seen it.

"How long has he been sketching?" Elaine asked.

"This is the first time I've seen it," Delthea admitted.

"That's kind of farfetched that she'd sneak in, and in one weekend's time teach him something like that," Elaine said.

"Let me show you what I found." Delthea marched into the lobby, approached the front desk, and requested her car key.

In the garage, she opened her trunk and revealed the boxes she had brought home with her. After ripping the tape off of the one marked personal, she pulled out a sketchbook and handed it to Elaine.

"Holy shit," Elaine commented as she flipped the pages. "These *are* the same style. No wonder you're so creeped out."

Delthea didn't dare tell Elaine about Rhett. Although he had everything to do with the guilt that weighed on her, he had nothing to do with Abi. Delthea hoped to erase him from her memory with time.

"Have you told Garrett about this?" Elaine began pilfering through the rest of the box.

"No, and I don't intend to. I need to dispose of this stuff without it ending up in the wrong hands." When Elaine picked up the journal that had sent Delthea running out into the hotel hallway, Delthea reached for it. "I'd rather you not look at the rest of that crap."

"Why? Is there something juicy in here?" Elaine flipped open the thick, tattered book.

Delthea jerked it out of her hands, tossed it back inside the box, and slammed the trunk lid. "I don't intend for you or anyone else to see that."

"Gee, Deli, you take all the fun out of finding all this cool stuff."

"Right. That's me, Miss Party-Pooper." Delthea walked toward the lobby. She was exhausted. It had been an awful night, followed by a long day.

Elaine caught up with her. "I talked to Mother this morning. Since you were gone, she called me. She wants to know if you're coming for Thanksgiving. I told her I didn't think you were since you and I had planned to get together."

"Thanks for covering for me." Someday Delthea would have to tell her mother and Garrett's parents about his condition. She had kept it a secret for so long that it was easier to continue doing so.

"Why don't you and Garrett come over? The boys would enjoy it. Hell, we've never had company for a holiday."

They got in the elevator.

"I'd like to, but while Garrett seems stronger emotionally, he keeps getting weaker every day. He's doing better tonight with the boys than he has in weeks." That along with his drawing ability had Delthea mystified. She didn't know what to make of the latest twist in his unpredictable condition.

When they walked into the apartment, Elaine announced to the boys, "Time to go. You've got school tomorrow."

They grumbled while gathering up the drawings Garrett had done of them.

"Quit your bitchin.' Garrett and Delthea are coming over for Thanksgiving. You can talk him out of another Picasso then." Elaine shooed them out the door, giving Garrett and Delthea each quick hugs. "See you in a few weeks." She waved and shut the door behind her.

Delthea collapsed on the couch.

"Are we really going there for Thanksgiving?" Garrett asked sounding no older than David. His pen moved as he looked at her and back at the paper.

"Don't do that," Delthea shrieked, exasperated by his newest obsession.

He stopped. "Sorry, I didn't realize it would upset you."

"Has Abi been here?" she asked, her voice steady and level, considering the rage that churned within her.

"No, I haven't seen her," he mumbled, his head bent.

"You're lying," she accused.

"I haven't seen Abi," he repeated, more adamantly, but still not looking at her.

"We'll see what Berta says about that." Delthea picked up the phone, wondering if he realized she had no idea where to find Berta's number at that moment. "Of course, she may lie too. She never has fessed up to her part in getting Abi's pictures out of the trash." Delthea hated herself for saying such tacky things; she hated the wrath that brewed inside her. Why were they playing this silly game?

"Where were you last night?" Garrett asked, a master at disarming her at the peak of an argument.

"Asleep in my bed," she spat back.

"You didn't answer when I called."

"I met a friend and we went out to eat and to the theater." A partial truth might make her sound more credible. She hung up the phone, her hand shaking. Then she lined up the pillows on the couch, anything to put a little order in her life.

"Until past six this morning?" he persisted in that way he had of latching onto something and not letting it go.

"They must have been ringing the wrong room." Her words sounded hollow, and she realized it.

Garrett and Delthea glared at one another.

"Where's your ring?" His voice quivered with emotion.

Delthea looked at her hand and wished with all her heart that she could make it magically reappear, that she could push a reset button for this weekend. "I lost it in Austin."

He nodded, his expression clearly saying that he knew she had taken it off for one reason, to do exactly what she did.

"It's not what you think. I love you," she pleaded.

"I love you, too." He picked up the goddamned pen and started drawing again.

Tired, confused, and full of guilt, Delthea marched to the extra bedroom and slammed the door. She fell on the bed and lay in a daze for an hour or more. When she got up to check on Garrett, he was asleep in his chair. Drawings of the baby in Abi's sketchbook grown into a young man littered the floor around him.

Delthea swallowed two sleeping pills with a glass of wine. She needed to rest. Someone had to get up in the morning and run their practice. Someone had to hold their crumbling lives together.

*   *   *

While Mum ate a late lunch, Moa sat next to her and read out of his history text. When he finally got to the end of the page, after stumbling over nearly every sentence, she put her hand over his, keeping him from going on.

"We need to talk," she said, which meant she would tell him something he did not want to hear.

"What is it?" He was almost sure it had something to do with her illness, probably more specifically about dying.

She put her spoon down. "I'm concerned about my inability to really help you with your studies. You're getting behind."

"It's not your fault. It's mine. I haven't been reading on my own like you asked me to." He knew sneaking off to hunt would catch up with him; he just didn't know how quickly.

"You shouldn't have to. Part of home study is that we do it together like we've always done in the past." She lay back on the pillows. "I've contacted the nearest boarding school, St. Anthony's over at Harrington. We have an appointment to check you in there tomorrow."

"That's not fair. You can't do that!" He hadn't meant to shout.

Tears spilled down her cheeks. "I'm sorry, Moa, but I cannot subject you to more of this than you have already endured. That's what is not fair."

"I don't understand." Now he was doing it too, crying like a baby. "I love you. I don't want to leave. I want to be here as long as you're here."

She reached out and took his hand with her cold, bony fingers. "That's just it; there's not a whole lot of me left."

"That's not true. You're here with me right now."

"I'm not," she muttered. "If I'm awake, I'm in pain, and if I'm asleep, I'm having crazy dreams." She wrapped her stick-like arms around his torso and pulled him to her, chest to chest. "Let's play that imaginary game we used to play when you were little," she whispered in his ear.

He wriggled down, settling his head on her chest. "You mean where we make up a story?"

"There once was a little boy who lived in New Zealand," she began. "He was really a Texan."

"You always start that way." It felt good to go back to something they did before Mum got sick.

She ran her fingers through his hair. "I know, but I've got a new idea."

"What is it?" he asked, not sure he wanted to try something new, not after her saying he was going to a boarding school.

"Instead of the boy's father dying, let's say the boy's father is not the man who the mother was married to. So when the woman realizes she is pregnant and that the real father is already married and has a child, she runs away." She stroked his back. "Have I lost you yet?"

Moa's arms and back felt prickly. "No, but why wouldn't the woman stay with her husband, so the boy would have a father?" Moa asked, as usual worried about the boy in the story.

"Her husband had a bad temper. Sometimes he got mad for no reason and hit her. She lived with his abuse for years, and she couldn't imagine him doing that to my – her baby."

"This isn't a made up story any more, is it? My dad's alive." Moa felt all funny inside.

Mum looked at him with sad eyes for a long time. Then she said, "That's right, Garrett Clay is your father."

"The name in the book – Garrett Morgan Clay." Moa jumped off the bed and retrieved *As a Man Thinketh* from the shelf. He opened the front cover and pointed to it. "See."

"That's right," Abi said. "I have no idea where he is or what has happened to him. When you were born, he lived in Houston."

Moa returned to her chest and wrapped his thin arms around her waist. "We should call him and see if he is still there."

"I don't think we should." Mum reached inside her gown and fished out a chain that hung around her neck. "I want to show you something."

Again, Moa sat up, fascinated by the silver disk that dangled before him.

"This is one of your father's dog tags. He was in the army during the Vietnam War." She slipped the chain and dog tag back inside her gown.

"Let's call Dad, so I can talk to him." Moa felt good again for the first time in days.

"We can't. Your father doesn't know about you. When you were conceived, he had a son and a wife. I couldn't ask him to give them up, so I left without telling him I was pregnant. This dog tag, that floppy leather hat, and the vest with fringe are all I have of his."

Moa bolted for the closet and emerged seconds later, wearing the vest and hat she had never allowed him to wear outside this room, in spite of his constant pleas. The fringe sown into a seam across the chest hung down to his knees. The hat covered his eyes, so he peeked out beneath it. They swallowed him, although not like they once had.

"Your father was wearing those the day I met him. We accidentally collided in the bookstore at the University of the Panhandle where I was attending college." Her eyes began watering again, and she held out her arms.

Moa crawled back on the bed. "What's the matter, Mum?"

"You remind me so much of Garrett. You always have." Her voice broke, and more tears ran down her cheeks.

He snuggled next to her again. Mum combed her fingers through his hair. After a few minutes, he cried even though he was trying his best not to.

She cried with him and kissed his head. "What if we call your grandmother? She knows about you. I phoned her when you were just a tiny baby. I didn't really tell her about you, but I think she heard you cry and realized you exist."

Head down and clinging to her, he said, "Maybe she'll take me when . . . ." He couldn't say the rest of it.

"No!" Mum said, nearly shouting, although she was weak.

He sat up, not knowing what to say. Surely she knew that in time he needed some place to live besides a boarding school. Takahe would always let him stay at the inn, but she was getting old, and Colin was gone most of the time.

"Your grandmother lives close to my ex-husband. If he found out about you, he would try to take you."

"We could still call her, though. I bet she would be so glad to hear from you that she'd promise not to tell anyone," Moa said, wiping the tears from his eyes.

"Perhaps we could ask her to come here," Mum said. "In the States, they set aside a day to give thanks. That's only a few weeks away."

"Right, Thanksgiving. We read about that. We could cook a turkey and all kinds of pie and cakes. Just like in the book." Celebrating would make everybody feel better.

"If we do call her, we have to make her promise not to tell Vince – the man I was married to – and she has to understand you can't ever go there. Okay?"

"He wouldn't want me if I'm not his son," Moa said, trying to assure his mother.

"Yes, he would. He may be married again, but he couldn't father children, and he wanted kids worse than I did. You can't ever go back there. Grandmother can come here, but that's all. Promise?" Mum argued stronger than she ever had about anything.

He was so stunned by her tone that he stared at her unable to speak.

She held his shoulders and shook him. "You have to promise, Moa. Tell me you'll never go back to the States."

"I promise," he answered and a chill moved over him as the word 'back' wiggled around in his mind. If he had been there, it was possible to go back – even though he had told Mum he would not. Before she changed her mind, he hurried to the kitchen and got the cordless phone. She switched it on and began punching in numbers that she must have memorized.

Chapter Six

"**W**e have several new students starting in February after the summer holiday," the headmaster said to Takahe and Mum. "Since Morgan is starting now, he will already be at home here by then."

Mr. Perkins wore a blue blazer and a red tie, the same uniform every boy at the school wore, only the headmaster looked old enough to be a grandfather. He had already told them a sappy story about the boys of St. Anthony being his family since he had never married.

Moa didn't care what some bald fart with a big belly said about 'these boys' being his sons. That would not stop Moa from being alone – no matter where he lived or how many boys 'of a similar situation' lived here. None of their mums were close to death; none of their mothers were dumping them in this creepy place, not knowing if they would ever see them again. None of them had never known their father.

Even though Mum was standing next to him, he felt as alone as anybody could and still be alive. How much worse would it be when Mum actually died, and he could not look forward to going home to see her? As it was, he only had three weeks to make it through before Grandmother arrived, and he returned to Birdsong Inn for her visit. This was just a 'trial run' – for when Mum was dead, and he had to be here all the time, except holidays. That dark, hollow feeling that started back in March when Mum was in the hospital was getting stronger.

At least, this school didn't have reminders of his mum everywhere he looked. Still, he would miss seeing her pictures, lying on her bed, and smelling her special smell, a strange combination of turpentine and soap and, lately, sickness.

Takahe nudged Moa and gave him one of her stern looks. "Mr. Perkins is speaking to you."

Moa didn't have a clue what the old man had said, but rather than admit it, he stared at the hair growing out of the mole on Mr. Perkin's cheek.

"Do you play sports?" the headmaster asked.

"No, sir. We ain't got any —"

"We don't have any," Mum said, barely able to stand, but not too sick to correct him.

Ignoring her, Moa repeated louder than before, "We ain't got any kids in Jacob's Springs. Well, one, but his mum won't . . . ." Moa didn't figure he wanted to know about their only neighbor, Tommy, who wasn't allowed to climb trees, much less join Moa and Colin on a hunting trip.

Mum had taught Moa to shoot. Her aim was better than Colin or Moa's. After she came home from the hospital, she went hunting with them, but they hadn't been out long before she started looking spooky white. Colin said he wanted to carry her, but she wouldn't let him.

Takahe laid her hand on Moa's shoulder. "I'm sorry, Mr. Perkins. Moa has not been himself lately. Hopefully, a change of scenery will do him good."

Moa's face burned with shame. He had embarrassed her by drifting off into his own world, and she was dishing it back at him. Not really mad at Takahe, but hating everything and everybody, Moa leapt to his feet. "You and Mum just want to get rid of me. That's it. I'm in the way, like an old shoe."

"That's not true," Mum said, reaching toward him.

Not knowing exactly what possessed him, he bolted out of the room and down the hallway toward the bedroom where they had left his bag. He didn't even kiss or hug Mum. He wanted to more than anything, but he was also mad at her for leaving him here.

* * *

Totally *knackered*, Abi walked to the car and left her precious son at his new school. As the lush New Zealand countryside zipped by, she gazed out the car window and wondered why things had to be the way they were. It took every ounce of her remaining strength to stop herself from ordering Takahe to turn around and go back for Moa. As Takahe had said before they left the inn, Abi had no business going along, but she could not send him off with someone else – not even Takahe. Eventually, he would only have her and Colin.

She had to think about something else, something like her mother coming. As much as she looked forward to seeing Mama, it also terrified her – and it brought her one step closer to the end. She needed to talk to someone who understood. Takahe sat inches away, but Abi lacked the strength to verbalize what weighed on her heart.

Abi laid her head back on the seat, closed her eyes, and released herself to the refuge of sleep. When the park materialized before her, she heaved a huge sigh of relief and immediately began looking for Garrett. He had never failed to be there or else show up shortly after she arrived. Abi walked around, enjoying the mobility, the sunny day, the gentle breeze, the exhilaration of feeling well, free, and whole – not sick.

When she found Garrett, he was sitting at the base of a tree, drawing on a pad. She stood behind him for several seconds, watching as his hand moved rapidly over the paper.

"I wondered where you were," she said.

Garrett glanced up at her. "Sit down. Be my next victim." He patted the grass in front of him.

"So you've taken up drawing, huh?" She lowered herself to the ground, sitting cross-legged.

"Yes, actually, I started doing this right after our last visit. This is the second sketchbook I've filled." He thumbed through the pages. "Every drawing is of Morgan. Actually, a few in another book were of my nephews. I did those the same day we last met. The rest are of my son – who you never told me about," he chided with a hint of disapproval.

Abi held out her hand, and Garrett handed over the tablet. She examined it, struck by how familiar the drawings looked, how much they reminded her of the sad little boy she had left behind at St. Anthony. She was dreaming, so wasn't it logical anything he drew would look like a child Garrett would never know. "You're a natural," she said, knowing full well that her words meant nothing; they were vapor in a foggy, make-believe, dream world.

He took the drawing pad back from her and began again on a fresh sheet of paper. This time he sketched, glancing back and forth from the paper to Abi. "You look sad. What's wrong?"

"I just left Moa at a private boy's school. He didn't want to stay, but I had to for his sake." Heaviness filled her chest while her throat tightened around her words.

Apparently, undisturbed by the quiver in Abi's voice, Garrett continued drawing. "What do you mean 'for his sake'?"

"We don't have schools in our area because we are so rural." She wiped away a tear.

"So you live out in the country," he prodded.

"Yes, at a bed and breakfast. It's a beautiful part of N– . . . ." She stopped herself short of saying New Zealand. She could not tell him, not even in her dreams. "We have a thermal springs close by, so the tourists come to enjoy that, but there aren't enough locals to constitute a school. So I've home schooled him up until now."

"Why don't you continue doing that?" Garrett asked while he drew an amazing likeness of her.

"Doing that . . . ?" she repeated, so stunned by the drawing that she had lost track of what they were discussing.

"Home schooling, why don't you keep home schooling him?"

"I can't." She took in a long, deep breath. "I simply can't." With that admission, Abi knew she had finally made up her mind about whether or not to contact Garrett about Moa. She could tell him all about his son in her dreams, but she would not tell him in real life. Not even in her dreams would she tell him why she had to leave him in a boarding school or where they lived, not even the closest continent. It was the only way of guaranteeing Vince would not end up with Moa.

"So describe my son," Garrett continued his prodding as he flipped the page and began another sketch of Abi.

"Well, you know what he looks like." She gestured to the pad. "Of course, his picture says so much more to me since I know him." She paused to think. "He likes to read, although not as much as I would like him to. Every night we read *As a Man Thinketh*. He has memorized it since we've read it so often. He says what's on his mind, and he is usually very adventurous. He loves to hunt, and with the game being so plentiful here, he has every opportunity. I suppose ten is too young for him to go out on his own. I used to go with him, but I don't any more. Sometimes Colin does if he is home, which he usually isn't."

"Colin?" Garrett asked casually between strokes.

"He lives here on and off, mostly off. He helped me leave the States when Vince came looking for me in Austin. I thought I told you about that." She could tell by his mischievous grin that he was trying to get more details from her, like he used to. Reassured that it was only a dream, she added, "We live with Takahe. She owns the inn where we live."

"Takahe," Garrett said slowly. "What an unusual name."

"She's a local with a huge belief in witchcraft and the like. Takahe is the name of a bird that was once thought to be extinct. In the last fifty years, it's actually resurfaced."

"Interesting." Garrett added to his drawing of Abi.

"Her B and B is called Birdsong Inn. She was the one that started calling Morgan, Moa, which is also the name of a bird but it is extinct. They were huge, bigger than an ostrich. That's kind of funny since Moa is little for his age."

"Small, like me," Garrett said with a pleased grin.

"Yes, like you." Even though it was only a dream, it pleased her to think Garrett would be happy to know Moa looked so much like him. "Since the inn is called Birdsong, Takahe thought it was wonderful that you called me Bird. She still calls me that, not often, but sometimes it slips out. I think she's afraid it hurts me to hear that name – because I missed you so much."

"Really?" he asked. "I missed you, too."

"But, you've gone on with your life. You're married, you have a counseling practice, and you've written a book."

"That doesn't mean I haven't missed you, that you didn't make a huge impact on my life, that I don't still long to find you." His green eyes echoed the sincerity of his words.

She smiled at the idea that he had yearned to see her even a fraction as much as she had longed to see him, to return to what they had once known together. "You were my life. In so many ways you still are. When I look at Moa, I see you, and I thank God for all you gave me."

"And what might that be?" he asked playfully.

"You gave me myself. You loved me without expectation or conditions. In my heart, I knew that you loved me and you always would. And I will always love you." She had said all of this before in another lifetime and this was only a dream, only a dream. She had to keep reminding herself of that.

Garrett put his pad on the grass. He studied her face. "I want so badly to touch you, but if I do, you'll disappear again."

Abi wanted to touch him too, but what he said was true. She reached out to him. "I'll try to stay here. No guarantees."

With eyes locked, their fingertips met. The current of energy that surged before flowed again, but this time they remained seated, facing one another.

Interlacing the fingers of both of her hands with both of his, she whispered, "We're still here."

Impulsively she rubbed her nose against his. "That's a Maori greeting."

"Maori?" Garrett said, his clear-green eyes questioning her. "What country do you live in?"

She had said too much. Abruptly, Abi left her dream world behind and returned to the car, the scenery rushing by, and the pain, the ever-present pain.

* * *

Frantically, working against the clock, Delthea scribbled notes in the fifth of ten charts she needed to update over her lunch hour. Being gone last Friday had put her behind more than usual. Here it was Wednesday, and she was still trying to catch up. She should never have gone – for many reasons.

The phone rang, and she jerked it up in mid ring. "Yes."

"Wow, that was quick. I've got Rhett Butler on the other line, and he wants to know if you are available. What do you say, Scarlet?" Judy asked with a chuckle.

"I'll take it, and don't ever call me that again," Delthea said, terrified at what Rhett might have already said to her.

Delthea pressed the button for the second line, "This is Dr. Richards."

"Hey, Delthea. You are one hard maverick to track down. I've spent fifty-two dollars in long distance charges just trying to find a phone number for you." He said this lightly.

He wouldn't sound so jovial if she told him to take a flying leap. In fact, now that he had tracked her down, he had everything he needed to make her life totally miserable.

"I'm so sorry. I'll be happy to reimburse you. I had to leave to catch my plane, and I didn't even have a chance to drop by your room and say good-bye." Maybe if she acted like nothing happened, he wouldn't remember since they had both been drunk.

"Hell, you could have at least given me a nudge when you got up." This time he sounded a little more pissed.

Panicked at the realization that Judy could be listening in on the line with her handy dandy little pull back lever, Delthea said, "Got up, you mean from the table?"

"No, I mean out of bed. Were you that soused that you don't even remember coming to my room?" he asked indignantly. "I've got your ring here to prove it."

"My ring?" she repeated, ready to forfeit it in order to get rid of him.

"Your Grandmother's ring. Oliver, the guy who was supposed to have given that speech, said it was yours. That's the only way I got your number. He thought you would want it back."

Dear Lord, now Oliver was part of the fiasco. "Did you tell Oliver how you came by it?" Delthea asked weakly.

"I didn't give him a detailed account of what went on, but I imagine he can put two and two together, don't you?"

"Yes, I'm sure." What she really wanted to know, but she had no way of asking was did he realize she was married to a semi-famous author, and was he looking to blackmail her? "What did Oliver tell you about me?"

"He said you are a workaholic, and he was glad you finally let your hair down for a change."

Delthea breathed a huge sigh of relief. "Well, he's right. I am a workaholic. In fact, I've got a mountain of work in front of me right now. Let me give you a post office box you can mail the ring to."

"Hold your horses. I'm not sticking something like that in the mail. It's irreplaceable. I'll bring it to you."

"That's awfully nice of you, but I'm going to be out of town for the next three weeks and then with the holidays, I'm not sure what will be happening." Delthea wondered if her lies sounded as fake to him as they did to her. "Besides that's a long way for you to drive."

"Well, I guess, I'll just have to hold onto it until after the first of the year."

"Are you sure you wouldn't rather mail it?" Delthea realized by his adamant tone that she couldn't dissuade him, but she felt obligated to try. "I'll be happy to reimburse you for your expenses. I need to pay you for the phone calls anyway."

"Nope, it's already settled. I'm coming to see you after the first. I'll be down that way to take my state board exams in Austin about mid-January, so we'll just call it a date."

"State board?" Delthea asked, not sure what he meant.

"For my nursing license. Remember? I told you I was finishing school in December. You said you have a sister that's a nurse. Maybe she can party with us."

"Perhaps." Elaine would be a good match for Rhett. They both had that devil-may-care attitude.

"Well, I guess I better let you get back to all that work."

"Yes, and I hate to run up your phone bill any more. Nice talking to you. Good-bye." Delthea mechanically hung up the phone, feeling sick to her stomach.

*   *   *

In total disbelief, Garrett stared at one of the drawings of Abi in his sketchbook. Berta had bought drawing supplies for him when she went grocery shopping after she saw how much he had drawn in his journal. Somehow the picture that he dreamed of drawing while he was asleep had materialized in the book and was there when he woke up. It was one thing to dream about drawing something; it was quite another to have that drawing appear after sketching it in a dream. He simply could not believe it.

When Delthea arrived home, Garrett slipped the sketchpad into the space between the cushion and the arm of the chair. She hated to see the drawings of a boy, so she would probably go ballistic over sketches of Abi. She had seen her photograph, and she would recognize her. He had done a decent job of it if he did say so himself – even if he had done it in his sleep. How insane was that?

Delthea and Berta went through daily updates on what Garrett had done all day: drawn, read, didn't eat much for breakfast, ate a good lunch, had a long nap, watched a little of the news about the terrorist explosion in Beirut and the U.S. invading Grenada.

The front door opened and shut. Then Delthea walked into the living room. She looked more tired than usual.

After collapsing on the couch, she said, "We need to talk."

"Okay?" He hoped she would explain where she was when he tried to call her in Austin.

"Obviously we've grown apart – what with your book tour and then your illness. I'd like us to reunite, find that common ground we once stood on – together." She wrung her hands while her gaze bounced around the room, looking at anything but him.

She had not mentioned Austin and Garrett was not sure he wanted to go there, so he said nothing. Delthea was talented at dancing around a subject and then coming in for the kill. Her intention could be to confront him about his drawing, or she might be backing into asking him for a divorce.

"Last week while I was in Austin, I realized that we have not been on the same page – so to speak – in a very long time."

The topic of divorce was looking more and more likely, and Garrett could not blame her. He had not been a husband to her in longer than he cared to remember. As insane as it felt to consider the possibility, it would almost be a relief to free her rather than put her through any more of this.

"Anyway, I'd like to talk like we used to." She gave him one of her desperate smiles.

Delthea's behavior reminded Garrett of the time she accidentally deleted three chapters of his book from the computer. Or was Garrett seeing guilt in her because of his own shame for having imaginary rendezvous with Abi?

"Of course," he said. She had not mentioned his declining health, which was the basis of all this.

"Well, what shall we talk about?" Delthea clasped her hands together and rested them on her knees. She usually said that and made this gesture when starting a counseling session.

"Let's talk about how the practice is going." That seemed like a reasonable topic since they once had that in common.

"It's fine." She nodded with the upper half of her body.

They stared at each other.

"There's nothing new – at all?" Garrett asked, beginning to take on her uneasiness.

"No, everything is the same. Mrs. Wood is still neurotic about what the neighbors are doing, and Mr. Holding is still wearing his wife's underwear, and Mrs. Simpson is still toying with the idea of going to Russia when she retires."

The whole idea of therapy struck Garrett as useless, which also struck him as incredibly odd since it had at one time been his whole life. "It all seems sort of pointless, doesn't it?"

"What?" she asked blankly.

"What we do, what you do, psychotherapy," he replied.

Her gaze took in the room as a whole. "I don't know; it makes a living," she said defensively.

"Don't take my comment as criticism. I simply meant it must feel pretty futile to work with someone for years and not really see any progress." Garrett sensed he was painting himself into a corner, but he wasn't sure how to get out of it.

"How would you know? You haven't been there in over two years. Not that the patients have quit asking about you. Silly me, I keep telling them you're coming back." Tears filled her eyes.

Guilt, pure unadulterated guilt tightened around Garrett's heart like a hand squeezing it. "I'm sorry, Delthea, that I haven't been there for you." He reached his arms out to her.

She crossed the room, knelt before Garrett, and embraced him. For a long, tender moment they held each other. Then she stiffened within his arms and pulled away.

"Let me see your drawings." She sounded like a mother who had spotted pornography in her ten-year-old son's bedroom. Her gaze was riveted to the gap between the pillow and the chair.

"Delthea, it's not what – "

"Let me see them." She held out her hand.

"I'm afraid you'll get the wrong idea."

Without another word, she grabbed the sketchpad and examined the two pictures of Abi, the ones that had magically appeared, somehow materializing into reality out of a dream. Her jaw worked and her face took on that stoic expression she used when she was protecting herself. "The wrong idea? How could I get the wrong idea from this? It's fairly obvious who you think about, who you care about, what occupies your mind – all of the time. How idiotic it was of me to think that tearing up her pictures would stop you from obsessing over her." She climbed to her feet, threw the tablet on the floor, walked to the guest bedroom, and slammed the door.

Garrett stared at his sketch of Abi, half expecting it to come to life – it had such a magical quality to it. He regretted Delthea seeing it for her sake, but that didn't stop him from being drawn to it, from remembering how strong, how healthy he felt in his dream. The drawing lying on the floor was tangible evidence of the normalcy he now only felt in his dreams.

*   *   *

Moa sat on his bed, leafing through the books Mr. Perkins had brought to his room, so he could get an idea of what was going on before he showed up for class tomorrow. The head master had also suggested that Ian, his roommate, might want to 'familiarize' Morgan with what they were doing in their classes. When Moa asked Ian where the class was in each subject, Ian had shrugged his shoulders.

At dinnertime, Moa followed Ian out of the room and walked beside him, fully aware that the boy who was supposedly his age stood a head taller. When they reached the dining room, Ian suggested Moa sit at a particular table after he went through the food line. When he insisted Moa go first in the line, Moa thought he had misinterpreted Ian's aloofness. But when he ignored Moa who sat alone while Ian joined a group of boys on the other side of the large room, Moa understood Ian's goal, to make Moa look and feel stupid. As a result, Moa had eaten the tasteless meal by himself, fully aware that every boy in the place was looking at him and sizing him up.

The clock said 10:15, fifteen minutes past the time Mr. Perkins had ordered lights out and the boys were to be 'bedded down and resting for the next day.' Ian sat at a desk that was between their two single beds, struggling over math equations. He had erased and sworn and erased some more. Moa had always found math fun, figuring out the answers to the formulas Mum came up with, but he figured Ian would not appreciate his help, so he threw his books in the pile with the others at the foot of his bed, lay down with his back to Ian, and closed his eyes.

Of course sleep did not come. What showed up instead were images of his mum, painting a picture of his dad, laughing at something Moa had said, outside shooting a gun, sitting beside him as they read *As a Man Thinketh*. That last picture was the one that got him. This was the first time since Mum stayed in the hospital that he had gone to bed without her and him reading that book. He tried to say the words to himself, but his mind flooded with thoughts of her dying, and he started to cry. Unable to stop himself, he sobbed like a stupid baby.

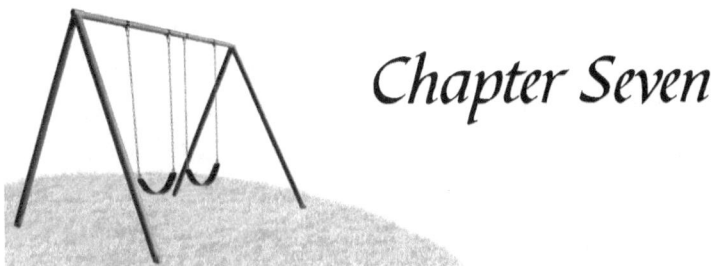

Chapter Seven

*I*t had been a week and a half since Mum and Takahe dumped Moa at this crappy school. In those ten long days, he had continued to sit by himself in the dining room. He had walked alone to classes. He had made it a point to speak to the other boys in the hallway, who nodded and gave him timid smiles, but he had not attempted to join any of the various groups that hung around between periods and after classes were dismissed for the day.

The other boys seemed nice enough, but no one made an offer of friendship. Moa had never really had a friend, and he did not have a clue how to make one. Not knowing what else to do, he operated much as he would have at home, doing his lessons and keeping to himself. Here at St. Anthony, though, he could not go out and shoot, he did not have anyone to talk to like Mum or Takahe, and he did have to follow the school's stupid rules.

One day last week on the way into the library, Moa noted a plaque above the door that had Witherspoon, Ian's last name, engraved on it. While he read it, a boy Moa recognized from his English class walked past and said in a low voice, "Lucky you, rooming with, Prince Ian."

After that, Moa noted how the other boys treated Ian in class, in the dining room, and on the soccer field. No one seemed particularly close to him, yet everyone gravitated toward him and deferred to his wishes. Ian had not spoken to Moa since he directed him to sit alone in the dining room. While Ian struggled with his course work every night, Moa debated offering help and then thought better of it.

The first time Moa went outside to play soccer, a fat kid who struggled to keep up told Moa that he had drawn the short straw by ending up with Ian. That day while Moa stood on the sidelines, he struggled to understand what was going on. Moa wasn't surprised when Ian, the tallest kid out there, took possession of the ball, but he was shocked that no one sincerely tried to take the ball from him – not even the opposing team. Having never played on a team, but having done a lot of one-on-one with Colin and kicking the ball around on his own, Moa decided that someone needed to bring Ian down a notch or two.

Today, as they all grabbed for jerseys to determine which team they would play on, Moa watched Ian who pulled a blue one out of the pile. Moa snatched a red one, slipped it on, and immediately volunteered when the coach asked for a lead on the red team. Without asking, he handed the ball to Ian. His plan felt somewhat suicidal, but the best that could happen is that Moa got kicked out of school for breaking a sacred unspoken rule – don't cross Ian.

When Ian started leisurely kicking the ball toward his team's goal, Moa charged toward him at an angle, kicked the ball, and immediately began steering the ball toward the opposite end of the field. Stunned-faced, the boys from both teams watched as Moa raced toward the goal and shot it into the net. Moa jumped in the air and cheered for himself while the rest of the boys stared at Ian who stood at mid-field with his hands on his hips. The coach blew his whistle, handed the ball off to Ian, and Moa charged him as he had before. This time Ian was ready for him, which Moa had anticipated, so he made a forty-five degree turn when he reached Ian and stole the ball from the other side. Moa's team members cheered when he, again, easily directed the ball past the goalie.

The coach handed the ball off to Ian a third time, winked at Moa, and said, "Looks like we've got a real game today."

Ian glared at Moa. Moa ran backwards while Ian built up speed as he approached his goal. At the last possible moment, Moa made a lateral approach, kicking the ball toward the sideline. A fellow red-shirt streaked down the field, intercepting the ball right before it went out of bounds. Moa ran side-straddle while he guarded his teammate. Out of the corner of his eye, he saw Ian approaching, but the tall blue jersey was not running toward the boy with the ball. He ran squarely into Moa, knocking him to the ground.

Initially winded, Moa struggled to catch his breath.

"Is baby going to cry again?" Ian taunted from a few feet away. He turned and smiled at the blue-shirted boys around him.

Moa looked to the coach who should have called a foul, but he seemed preoccupied with retrieving the ball. Ten days of putting up with Ian made Moa do something he had never done before. He scrambled to his feet, crouched, and ran toward Ian, hitting him low and hard. When he made contact, he heard something crack. They landed in a heap with Moa on top, and Ian crying out in pain. Grabbing his leg, he kicked at Moa with the other leg while he rolled away.

Moa scrambled to his feet, peeled off the red shirt, and threw it in the storage box as he stalked off the field. His shoulder hurt where he had hit Ian, and he was in trouble, but it was worth whatever Mr. Perkins decided to do to him. Ian had been asking for it. Moa hated this school, and he hated the way everything operated around certain people, namely Ian.

*   *   *

When Berta finished vacuuming and finally sat down to take a break, Garrett asked, "What are you doing for Thanksgiving?"

"Gonna go see my sister in Salt Lake. What about you?"

"Elaine has invited us over, but Delthea hasn't agreed to go." He wasn't sure how to gracefully maneuver into what was on his mind, so he blurted out, "Does Delthea seem a little testy to you – since she came back from Austin, I mean?"

Berta sipped her diet root beer. "Yeah, I'd say she's a little more pissed off acting than usual."

Garrett smiled at her candor. "I love the way you never mince words." He pulled out his drawing pad, now filled with drawings that had appeared while he slept, sketches that he did not remember drawing, even in his dreams. They were all of Abi – in front of a Victorian style home, sitting in a porch swing, perching on a stool in a glassed in studio with a paintbrush in her hand. He handed the tablet to Berta. "Tell me what you think."

Berta leafed through the pages, a look of amazement growing on her face. "These are good. But how did you do them? You haven't looked at your pictures in a couple of weeks."

"I didn't do those. At least I don't remember doing them." Garrett knew it sounded preposterous. That was one of the reasons why he needed to talk to someone. "Every time I wake up, there's another picture in my tablet. And I'm not drawing them. They just appear."

Berta knitted her brow and looked back and forth from Garrett to the drawings. "They just appear," she repeated.

"Yes," Garrett answered, thinking how absurd this sounded.

"Are you still dreaming about Abi?" Berta asked.

"It's been over a week. The last time I dreamed about her, I was drawing her in my dreams. And then when I woke up, the first two drawings of her were in my tablet, looking just like they did when I dreamed about her. Ever since then, a new drawing appears every day, but I don't have any memory of drawing them, except the first two and that was in my dream."

"Has Delthea seen these?" Berta tapped the sketchpad.

"The first two. She saw them that day. Since then I haven't really talked to her. She spends most of her time in the guest bedroom. In fact, she's been sleeping in there."

"Sounds like she's not too happy with your artistic endeavors." Berta laughed her deep, ex-smoker's chuckle.

Garrett also wanted to make light of it, but there wasn't anything humorous about his situation. "You're right; she's pissed. What concerns me is that my mind is going the way of my general health. I should remember drawing these. It doesn't make sense."

"Why don't you check in with Abi?" Berta rocked forward a couple of times before she finally got enough momentum to stand.

"If you mean talk to her in a dream, I'm not sure I can just go there. There's no rhyme or reason for when that happens." Garrett had wondered why he had not dreamed of her, or if the pictures meant he was dreaming, but he was not remembering it.

"Yours is the most unusual situation I've ever seen." Berta shrugged. "Do whatever feels right for you. Fuck the rest of the world – even Delthea. When it all comes down to it, what have you or any of us got left, except our dreams?"

Berta sauntered into the kitchen and turned on the water. She hummed a musical jingle from a commercial that always came on midway through her soaps. Her words hung in Garrett's thoughts, weighted with finality, truth, and doom.

Garrett examined the pictures, each one a mystery unto itself, each one telling him something he could not understand. They seemed to be calling to him, and he wanted to follow Berta's advice. He did not want Delthea to walk in and see him snoozing with Abi's new pictures in his lap, though, so he struggled to his feet and crept down the hallway toward his bedroom, today just like yesterday, moving slower than he had the day before. He locked the door behind him.

After crawling onto the queen size bed, he sat in the middle, tore the pictures out of his tablet, and arranged them all around him. "Okay, Abi, it's time we got together again."

A wave of fatigue passed over him, and he lay back, immediately drifting into sleep. He saw the park and began scanning for Abi. The trees had lost their leaves and the grass had turned brown. A strong wind howled and gushed around him. Abi stood by the swing set, her hands rubbing up and down her arms while she bounced up and down at the knees. She wore a blue corduroy jacket over her usual sweater and jeans.

"Abi!" He waved and ran toward her.

She waved back at him and held her arms open as if she expected him to run into them and hug her. He half feared she would disappear, but he did it anyway, so pleased that she was making this gesture of openness. Even though it was simply a dream, he needed someone to want him, someone to need his touch as much as he needed to receive it. He wrapped his arms around her, lifted her almost weightless body off of the ground, and spun around with her in his arms. She laughed, her high-pitched voice pure music next to his ears. When he finally set her down, she continued to laugh.

"Oh, God, I needed that." She grabbed his hand. "Let's find someplace to sit where we can get out of the weather."

Without discussing it, they walked toward her black Volkswagen parked on the street. He opened the driver's door and waited while she got in. After shutting it, he walked around and got in on the passenger side. She had already pulled an army blanket out of the back seat and was arranging it across her body while leaving the other half for him.

"I had forgotten how cold it gets here. Where I live, we're in the middle of summer." She laughed, her cheeks flushed from the wind and freezing temperature.

Summer, Garrett thought, at the same time recalling what had prompted her to leave the last time – his question about where she lived, what country. It must be below the equator to be warm there while it is cold in Texas.

"What are you thinking about?" she demanded happily.

"It's been a while since we got together." He didn't want to say or do anything to make her evaporate again.

"I've been very depressed about leaving Morgan at school. I know he's not happy, but I'm trying to do what's right for him. You understand, don't you? He needs an education."

"I can also see his side of this." Garrett thought about all the time he was away from Loc when his son lived in Houston and Garrett stayed on in Oaces to finish his course work. That was the semester he had met Abi. "I'm sure he misses you, especially if he's never been away from you."

"He hasn't." She drew in and released a long, ragged breath. Looking out through the windshield at the trees whipping in the wind, Abi said, "There are some days that I have to take medicine to sleep, like this past week. On those days I can't find my way here."

"Medicine? Are you sick? What's wrong, Abi?" A wave of panic washed over him. He was sick, but he never imagined she might be as well. It was just a dream. But the pictures, they were real.

"I'm not sure how much longer I'll be able to come see you." She looked at him, her chocolate brown eyes filling with tears.

"What is it? Tell me what's going on." He wanted to reach out and grab her, but he feared she would vanish with his touch.

"I'm not sure. Let's just hold on to this precious moment in time." As if she lacked the strength to hold up her head, she rested it on the steering wheel and smiled at him.

Just as Berta suggested, Garrett suspected that she held the key to who or how her pictures had appeared in his sketchbook. "I have a mystery I need you to help me solve."

"What is it?" she asked, raising her eyebrows.

"Since the last time I saw you, ten more pictures of you have magically appeared in my sketchbook."

"Besides the two you drew?" she asked.

"Yes." He was amazed that she did not seem as perplexed as he felt. This dream felt so real that he had to keep reminding himself that it was only his imagination.

"Did you bring them with you?" she asked.

"No, they're on my bed at home." He studied her head resting against the hard, gray plastic of the steering wheel. There was something very odd about her today. She was not solid. He imagined that he could reach out and move his hand through her, like she was a cloud or a holograph.

"Let's go there," she suggested.

"Back to my house?" he asked, amazed she would suggest such a thing.

"Yes, why not? If we can come here, why not go there?"

"Sure. But next time I want to see where you live."

"Of course." She reached over and covered his hands with hers, and then she closed her eyes.

Garrett followed her lead, and when he opened his eyes, he sat on his bed with Abi sitting next to him. The pictures lay on the bed as he had left them. She examined each one, picking them up, and then laying them back down exactly where they were.

At last she turned to him. "I didn't draw these. I think they are pictures from my memories, images of me doing things I love." She picked up the tablet that lay on the edge of the bed and began examining the picture that had newly formed there, a picture of her with Morgan. They were sitting next to each other while holding a book. "This is my favorite memory."

She handed the tablet to Garrett. "Mama's coming to see us next week. I doubt I'll be able to visit you during that time." She disappeared; just like that, she vanished.

Garrett looked around the room. He couldn't remember waking up, but he had. He looked down at the new picture, and he remembered what Abi had said about it being her favorite memory. It made less sense than it had before he had this last dream, but it also seemed crystal clear – in an insane sort of way. He was getting Abi's memories. Somehow she was transmitting them onto his sketchpad. The idea was absolutely insane.

*   *   *

Takahe pushed the door open and said in a whisper, "Little Bird, I heard you stirring and thought you might take some soup and fresh bread." She carried a tray laden with dishes of food that filled the room with an aroma that should have made Abi hungry instead of nauseous. Setting the tray on the nightstand, Takahe said, "Do you think you can eat something?"

Abi shook her head, too weak to speak. She had recently awakened from dreaming about Garrett for the first time in a week. In her dream, she had met him in the park, but then they went to his house where they looked at drawings of her memories that were spread out on his bed. He said they had mysteriously materialized in his sketchbook. Takahe might have some insight as to what the dream meant, but Abi lacked the strength to describe it to her.

"We got a call from Moa's school today," Takahe said with forced cheerfulness. "Moa had a bit of a tiff with his roommate. Mr. Perkins thinks it will all work out."

"A tiff?" Abi managed to utter.

"Apparently, they had a disagreement on the soccer field." Takahe picked up the spoon and poised it over the soup. "Let's see if we can't get some food inside you."

Abi wanted to shake her head, but it wouldn't move. She needed to ask questions about what was going on with Moa.

"We need to build your strength up before your mother gets here. She called yesterday to tell us when her plane will arrive. Colin can pick her up." When Abi didn't respond to her offer of food, Takahe straightened the sheets, re-tucking them in at the foot of the bed. "She said she was bringing a tin of cranberry sauce to make it more like an American Thanksgiving. I warned her not to, but she insisted, so I told her she would get in trouble if she did not declare it in customs."

Abi smiled, knowing her mother would not understand this hard and fast New Zealand law. She did need to do all she could to prepare for her mother's visit. After moistening her lips with her tongue, she said, "Eat."

"That's the spirit," Takahe said, moving to her post beside the bed and preparing to spoon the soup into Abi's mouth.

It tasted good, but it did not want to go down. Abi swallowed several times, before her throat allowed the small portion of liquid to pass. She accepted a bite of bread that Takahe tore from the wedge on the blue-rimmed plate.

While Abi chewed and chewed on it, she thought about the afternoon she arrived at the inn. Takahe had been making bread. That night Colin, Takahe, and Abi had eaten it from the plates that they still used.

*   *   *

The phone rang again as Delthea walked to her office door. She started to let the answering service get it, but on impulse, she wheeled around and grabbed it before the fourth ring. "This is Dr. Richards. May I help you?"

"Hello, is . . . ahhh, is Garrett Clay there?" The woman's voice had a distinctly Texas accent, but slightly different, more nasal than the ones Delthea was used to in Houston.

"No, he's not. May I help you?" In the past few months, fewer and fewer calls came in for Garrett. In fact, Delthea couldn't remember the last one they had received.

"I'm an old friend of Garrett's – from the Panhandle area," the woman explained.

"The Panhandle?" Delthea repeated, thinking of one person. But this voice sounded older than Abi would. Of course, she could easily disguise her voice.

She laughed a little, and then she said, "I'm Betty Barker. Garrett used to come in my shop and get his hair cut. He wanted information about my daughter, Abi. Of course, I didn't know that at the time." She paused as though giving Delthea a chance to speak, but after a few seconds of silence, she added, "I found Garrett's, or rather, Dr. Clay's book at a garage sale, and I recognized him from the picture on the back flap where they tell a little bit about the author. That's how I knew to call information in Houston to get this phone number. The book says he has a psychology practice."

"Currently, he's on sabbatical, not available. He's writing his next book." Delthea cursed herself for picking up the damned phone. If she had simply let it ring, she would not need to decide what to say to Abi's mother or how to deal with this situation.

"I'm going to see Abi and her little boy, and I thought Garrett might want to send some sort of message to them."

"I have no idea how to reach him to ask. Dr. Clay goes to remote locations, so he has plenty of quiet in which to write."

"Would it be possible for me to leave a phone number . . . just in case he checked in from his remote *location*." The sarcasm in her words screamed of her ability to see through Delthea's lies.

At least she wasn't asking for blackmail money – not yet, at least. "Oh course. I'd be happy to take a phone number. Let me get a piece of paper."

While she wrote down the number that Betty rattled off to her, Delthea asked herself why she was writing it down. Relaying a message to Garrett or giving him another means of contacting Abi was the last thing she wanted to do. He obviously had already taken care of that himself – sick or not. She tore the paper from the pad and poked it in the folder containing Morgan Barker's birth certificate. It had no apparent use at the moment, but there might be a time when she needed it – for what she did not know. Still, as crazy as her life was these days, who could say?

After a final plea to be sure and let Garrett know she had called, Betty Barker hung up.

Delthea sat heavily in the desk chair. The phone conversation played again in her mind, Abi's mom calling, wanting to know if she could talk to Garrett, wanting to relay a message to Abi. She stopped when she got to the part about finding Garrett's book at a garage sale. The idea of that made her want to cry. Imagining his book lying in the midst of trashy romance novels and selling for a quarter was more than she could take.

Delthea dropped her forehead on her folded arms that rested on her desk. She didn't need this on top of everything else. It had been four weeks since she slept with Rhett, and she had not started her period. What else could go wrong?

*   *   *

Instead of sitting at his desk and laboring over his studies, Ian now sat on his bed with his left leg in a cast. Moa sat on his own bed, working through the math homework for tomorrow. He did not want to get behind since neither he nor Ian would be going to class. They still had not spoken, but they ultimately would have to before either one of them could leave their room, except to go to the toilet. Mr. Perkins was even having their meals brought in until they got their differences sorted out. Moa wasn't about to apologize, and, apparently, Ian wasn't either.

Moa hoped Old Perky, as the boys called him behind his back, hadn't any ideas about keeping Moa from going home next week when his grandmother arrived. He was curious enough to meet her, but most of all he had to see Mum. It had been two and a half weeks, seventeen days since he had seen her.

He thought about how weak Mum had been the day she and Takahe drove him to this place. Soon she would be dead. How was he going to live without her? The way things were going here at school was not a good indication of how well he could do on his own.

Tears welled in his eyes, but he willed them away. He wasn't about to give Ian the satisfaction of seeing or hearing him show any emotion. He could still hear Ian's words right before Moa got totally fed up and knocked him off his feet: "Is baby going to cry again?"

Chapter Eight

"The mountain has come to Mohammed," Mr. Perkins said, looking extremely pleased with himself.

Moa didn't have a clue what he was talking about.

Mr. Perkins took a long hard look at Ian's bulletin board full of ribbons and stickers and then at Moa's plain side of the room. "I've been placed in a quite precarious situation. As you know, your task is to come to some sort of agreement before either one of you resumes classes. But you haven't, and I have already given my word that Morgan may go home to meet his grandmother who is arriving this afternoon from the States."

It would be just like this old fart to think of some way of going back on his word and somehow making it sound legit.

Clearing his throat, Mr. Perkins went on, "I've decided the only thing I can do is to send both of you to Morgan's home."

"That's not fair," Ian protested, the first words out of his mouth in a week. "My father will have something to say about that. You can't just ship me off to some hooligan's home. You are responsible for my welfare."

"Witherspoon, I realize that. As for your father, it was his idea to send you home with Morgan. And since Miss Takahe has graciously agreed, that is what we shall do."

Moa would never have imagined this turn of events. He was going home as promised, but now he had this problem going with him, sort of what Mum would call an albatross around his neck.

* * *

"I remember how you used to love to draw, even when you were just a little thing." Mama studied one of Abi's old paintings that leaned against the wall of the studio. Colin had delivered her from the airport only a few hours ago.

It was already Thursday, Thanksgiving Day in the States, but nobody here knew the difference. They would celebrate tomorrow since Moa wasn't arriving home until later today. Takahe said he was bringing a friend. Abi was glad he had settled in and already felt comfortable inviting someone to his home. She also experienced an insane wave of jealousy. This friend and others in Moa's life would eventually replace her.

Leaning against the door frame because she didn't have the strength to stand, Abi tried to remember the last time she had been out here in the studio. She recalled the many long afternoons she sat in a pool of sunshine with Moa at her side. While she painted, he read or wrote an essay for social studies or science. "Art has been my therapy." She tried to smile at her mother, but the pain pills were getting in the way. They along with her will and Takahe's encouragement were allowing her to keep going, although not nearly as well as she would like.

"I'm so glad you called, Baby. You can't imagine how many times I've prayed for that phone to ring and pick it up to hear your voice on the line." She gave Abi a longing look, the same one that spread across her aged face when she walked into Abi's bedroom and saw her daughter's condition, the one that said she couldn't believe her only child was dying.

"Moa convinced me to. Otherwise, I guess I wouldn't have ever gotten around to it," Abi admitted. "He's worried about what is going to happen to him."

Mother nodded. "You know I'll take him, don't you?"

It was the answer Abi had expected and could not accept. "That won't work. He can't go back to the States – not ever."

"Sweetheart, it might take a while, but Morgan and I would get used to each other." Mama propped an elbow on the drawing table. "We don't know each other yet, but with time . . . ."

"It's not you I'm worried about." Abi slumped onto her stool. She had been out of bed more today than she had in the last month. "Like I told you on the phone, Vince is the reason we left and the reason Moa will never go back."

"I understand. Vince comes by periodically to check on me. Not as often now as he did right after you left." She put her head in her hands. "I'm sorry I told him about you and the baby. It's just that I wanted to see you so badly. It never occurred to me that he wasn't the father. I told myself you were just going through that postpartum thing, the baby blues."

"Even if he had been Morgan's father, I wouldn't have gone back to him. He beat me. You saw the bruises and my black eyes." Abi could not understand how her mother could remain so passive.

"I thought it was just normal fighting. You know the kind that everyone has." Mama wiped at her eyes with her sleeve.

"It was the same kind you and Daddy had, but that's not normal," Abi said, the old anger building. "I didn't realize women don't have to put up with that shit until I met Garrett. He's the one who taught me what real love is."

"But he was married," Mother countered, like that somehow negated what he and Abi had shared. "When I think of the times he came in my beauty shop, asking to get his long hair cut. He never said a word about knowing you, but he sure as hell asked a lot of questions about you."

Abi didn't have the strength or desire to spend this precious time arguing. "Morgan is staying here. Takahe will be his legal guardian, and you can come as often as you like, but you can't tell Vince where Moa lives."

"All right, Baby. It's not what I want, but I said I wouldn't tell him, and I won't." She examined the unfinished sketch on the table. "What about Garrett? Why don't you tell him? I bet he would take the boy. I tried to reach him before I left Texas, but I couldn't get through."

"You what?" Abi asked, totally dumbfounded.

"I called his office and the lady who answered the phone said he was 'unavailable,' working on his next book." Mama picked at a piece of lint on her slacks. "I found him in the most peculiar way. I was at a garage sale a while back, and I picked up a book with a catchy title, *I Am*. After I leafed through it, I saw the author's picture on the back inside jacket flap, and I knew he looked familiar, but I couldn't place him. I figured I had seen him on television or something."

Abi remembered Garrett telling her in a dream that he had written a book by that title. The medication kept her from thinking clearly, but she knew this wasn't possible – her mother saying something about Garrett that he had told her in a dream.

"Actually, it wasn't me who figured it out. I bought it for a quarter, and when I took it to the shop, Charlene started looking at it, and she recognized him the first time she picked it up."

Mama watched Abi before she spoke again. "I brought the book with me. It has his office phone number written in it – just in case you want to use it."

Abi slowly stood up and shuffled toward the door – her knees, threatening to buckle. If she didn't start now, she might not have enough energy to get back to bed. "There are problems with calling Garrett. Number one, he's not here, and I'm not about to risk sending Moa to him. But more important than that, Garrett doesn't know Morgan exists."

Mama held Abi's arm, supporting her. "You haven't had any contact with him?"

"No, I haven't, and I don't intend to." Dreams didn't count, regardless of how real they felt.

"Garrett called nearly a year ago, but I didn't tell him anything. And then he sent this detective guy around looking for you. The detective even talked to Vince – which of course got Vince all riled up." Mama looked at Abi and must have seen the horror on her face. "I shouldn't have said that. No need to worry you any more than you already are." Mother shut the door on the studio.

With Mama supporting Abi, they walked across the grass and entered Abi's room through a patio door that Colin had installed to make it easy for Abi to access her studio. Then Mama helped her into bed. While Abi settled herself, Mama watched her every move.

"I'm so glad you're here, Mama. Thanks for bringing the cranberry sauce. I'm surprised customs didn't take it away from you," Abi said, exhausted yet needing to keep her mother engaged.

"I could not imagine Thanksgiving without it. Besides, it was something I could bring you from home." She stood back, eyeing Abi with that look that said she wished she could do something to help.

"Actually, I'm pretty proud of you for not declaring it since you've never really defied authority," Abi observed.

"What do you mean?" Mama asked, fiddling with a curl that had escaped the cluster on top of her head, a new 'do' Charlene had constructed just for Betty's trip.

"I was thinking about Dad and the way he pushed you around." They had never talked about Harold Barker's reign of terror, yet they both had been undeniably affected by it.

"After Harold got sick, he said he sure regretted the fact that you two never got along." Mama hugged herself as if trying to contain something or maybe offering herself comfort.

Abi recalled the time her father found his hammer in the rain then switched her legs until they bled. He turned his wrath on Mama when she reminded him he was the culprit. "I don't miss him," Abi admitted. "I'm sorry if you do."

It pained Abi to admit it, but Vince was a hell of a lot like her father. Why had she married him? Why had she tolerated the beatings and mental anguish? She'd still be with him if not for Garrett, and she would not have Moa. Why did Vince still haunt her? Because he would take Moa if he could. He was that kind of a bastard. He took what he wanted, however he could get it.

"You look sleepy, Babe." Mama kissed her forehead. "I'll leave you for a while." She slipped out of the room.

Abi was glad she had called her mother. She wanted to see her. But Abi didn't like the idea of Vince having a connection to Garrett through her mother. That news made Abi more determined than ever not to tell Garrett about Morgan.

*   *   *

Thanksgiving morning Garrett studied the ceiling above his bed and thought about the turkey in the refrigerator. Yesterday Berta carried it in saying, "They're practically giving them away." She didn't speculate as to who would cook it or if it might be there when she got back Monday. Delthea had refused Elaine's repeated offers to spend the holiday there.

For the first time in close to a year, Garrett eagerly crawled out of bed. The mysterious disease had not left him. He still lacked strength and energy, but he had decided. They would celebrate. For a change, he would be happy.

On the way down the hallway, he peeked inside the bedroom Delthea began using after their confrontation over his sketchpad. Her sleeping face, pinched into a permanent frown, lay on the satin pillowslip. An empty wineglass sat on the nightstand. In the last month, she spent most of her time at the office, and when she was home, they hardly spoke. Not wanting to wake her, he pulled the door shut. He wanted to talk to her about his dreams where he visited Abi, although they had not reoccurred since Abi came back to his bedroom with him to look at the sketches. He wanted to discuss what had happened in Austin, but she didn't seem receptive. The wall between them remained intact.

Yesterday, before Berta left for the grocery store, she and Garrett counted his remaining sketchpads. She bought them out of the grocery money Delthea left on the kitchen table. They agreed five would suffice, but Berta said she'd get a few more for good measure. When she returned with watercolor paints and paper as well, Garrett experienced an excitement that did not make sense. He had never had the desire to paint – or draw, but creating these images now filled most of his waking hours.

His subject matter had expanded beyond the young boy to include variations of the pictures that continued to mysteriously materialize while he slept, like the Victorian style house surrounded by lush vegetation. At first he drew the outside. Then he traveled within the numerous rooms, sketching the many people who talked, laughed, and ate at a cluster of tables. The boy lived there along with two other people, a man in his sixties whose eyes danced with mischief and an older woman with heavily tanned skin. All of this felt bizarre to say the least, but his life for the last year had been one unexplainable development after another.

Garrett checked the refrigerator and found it well stocked with other holiday foods besides the turkey. A row of useful looking items like cooking bags sat on the counter. What temperature should he set the oven? And how long should it cook? He wished he could talk to Berta. They spent most of their time in the kitchen. She cooked or crocheted while he drew. Last night, she flew to her daughter's house. He didn't even know how to reach her.

Feeling lost, Garrett called Elaine. She answered, obviously still asleep, and told him to read the instructions inside the cooking bags box. They discussed a menu, who would cook what, and agreed to eat at her house mid-afternoon.

Nearly overpowered by the turkey's weight and size, Garrett wrestled the twenty-two-pound bird into a bag within a roasting pan and stuck the whole thing in the oven. An exploration of the cabinets and freezer produced what he needed to make three beans salad, an apple pie, and dressing. While he worked, a tune Garrett did not recognize floated through his head. He hummed it, not noticing Delthea until he looked up and saw her sitting at the table.

"What are you doing?" she asked, shock written on her tired, drawn face.

"Cooking. I've already checked with Elaine on what she needs." He knew Delthea would find something wrong with his actions. They had not agreed on anything in quite some time.

"I can't believe you're doing all this." She smiled as though perplexed and gestured at the flour-coated cabinets.

"Cool, huh?" he asked, checking the apple pie for doneness.

She got up and walked over to him, her eyes riveted on his. "Where did you get all of your energy?"

He wanted to tell her how much he loved her, how much he missed what they once shared, but he feared her rejection. Instead, he said, "I'm not sure. Actually, I'm still in a lot of pain, but I can't let this day go by like all the rest have. You know what I mean? We need to go over to Elaine's and see the boys, be grateful for what we do have."

"You're absolutely right." She slipped her arms around his waist and hugged him.

Garrett held her for what seemed like the first time in years. God, how he missed the smell of her hair, feeling her heart beat next to his, knowing that she cared about him as much as he cared about her. He was miles away from being well, but he felt happy for the first time in a long, long time.

*   *   *

In spite of Garrett's insistence that he could do it, Delthea drove to Elaine's place. She didn't want him to overexert. The cooking and getting dressed on his own completely shocked her. Delthea wanted to believe a shift in perspective could change the situation as Garrett had always preached, but his slow, unsteady gait attested to the fact that his health had not changed, only his attitude.

After they parked, she rushed to his car door and grabbed his arm to assist him up the stairs. He gave her a quick peck on the cheek and opened the back door.

"We really should have put this in the trunk." He rubbed a towel on the juice from the pie that had spilled on the seat.

They had debated that issue when they loaded everything. It took every lame excuse she could think of to keep him from opening the trunk and seeing Abi's stuff. Rather than deal with it, Delthea had ignored the three boxes. She couldn't let them go on sitting there.

Delthea grabbed the salad and followed Garrett up the stairs. At Elaine's door, she gave Kent the keys and asked him to get the turkey. David immediately cornered Garrett and begged him to draw him again. Garrett agreed to, smiling broadly. He looked so much younger today.

Not even the prospect of him drawing bothered Delthea. She wanted to kiss Garrett and tell him how pleased she was by his progress. Something stopped her, though. That something was the guilt that grew in her heart – and in her uterus.

Over lunch, Garrett asked the boys about school. Delthea recalled David's outburst when she had pursued the same topic at a previous encounter.

"Actually, he's gotten himself into a bind." Elaine scooped out a spoonful of mashed potatoes. "He cut a deal with his school counselor, and now he has to fulfill his end of it."

"What's that?" Garrett struggled to cut up his meat.

It took all of Delthea's willpower to resist taking the knife and fork out of his hands and doing it for him.

When David did not answer, Elaine said, "Tell them, David."

All heads turned toward David. He said nothing.

"Tell them now or leave the table." Elaine took a bite out of a radish and eyed her youngest son.

"I got in trouble for smoking in the restroom," David said, his chin an inch from his plate, his eyes cast downward.

"And . . . ." Elaine prompted.

He took an enormous breath. "And stealing and lying."

Garrett put his silverware down. "Sounds like you've been busy."

Delthea suppressed a smile. It was so Garrett. Comments like that popped out of his mouth when he counseled. They lightened the moment and gave the client the freedom to say more in a supportive environment. She loved hearing it.

"Yeah, well that's not all of it." Elaine took a long sip of wine. "He told the principal about his famous uncle, the shrink, and said that you would counsel with him, so he wouldn't have to go to an alternative school."

It was Garrett's turn to draw in a deep breath. "I don't know if I'm up to that or not." He looked at Delthea. "What do you think?"

"I think it's a good idea. David can come to our apartment. It will give you something to do while keeping your hand in the business." And away from that goddamn pencil and sketchpad.

Garrett agreed and they went on to easier topics like who would win the football game and what the boys wanted for Christmas. After the meal, Elaine assigned the boys to clean up the kitchen while Garrett supervised. She motioned for Delthea to follow her outside.

On the way down the steps, Elaine lit a cigarette. "What's new?" she asked, opening the door to all those topics they couldn't discuss around the kids and Garrett.

"I guess everything is about the same," Delthea reported, wanting desperately to unload her heavy heart.

Elaine looked at her and nodded. "Garrett's lost more weight, but he's acting like he feels pretty good. You, however, look like crap."

"What do you mean?" Delthea asked, immediately defensive.

"Your eyes are hollow. Your hands are shaking." She spoke with the authority of a good nurse, one who picked up more data from what she saw than what someone said.

"You're right. I'm not sleeping well."

They walked down the street to an empty park and sat on a bench. Everyone else in Houston was either eating turkey or watching the Aggies play football.

Elaine crushed her cigarette butt in the dirt. "Have you thought of what you're going to do?"

Delthea realized what her sister meant, but she lacked the courage to formulate an answer much less say it aloud. Clearly, if Garrett continued his current course, he would die.

"You're going to have to, you know?" Elaine added.

Although sometimes a flake, her sister really was strong, unlike Delthea who pretended to be capable by helping other people solve their so-called problems.

"I know," Delthea finally acknowledged. "But there's a lot of stuff in the way right now."

Elaine silently waited for Delthea to continue.

"When I was in Austin, I had an affair," Delthea blurted out, shocked at her admission, yet glad she said it.

"Holy shit! Way to go, Deli." Elaine slapped her on the shoulder. "I knew you must be getting pretty horny, but I never figured you for that type."

"I'm not. I went to talk to this guy, so I could get away from Abi's stuff, that trunk load of crap I showed you the last time you were over. We drank too much, and it happened. That's it. No passion, no forethought, just a lot of regrets." Delthea picked at the raised grain of the wooden bench.

"I never suspected you were a player. It's a side of you I've never imagined," Elaine said, altogether too delighted.

"Here's another shocking tidbit; I haven't started my period." Delthea cringed, ready for Elaine's predictable reaction. She had debated telling her, but the need for a listening ear, or at least, reviewing medical options had won out.

"How late are you?" Elaine asked, sounding like a real nurse and not her flighty sister.

"Two weeks," Delthea admitted, not wanting to say it was really more like three. "But my breasts are full and tender. Thank God I haven't started throwing up."

"Aren't your breasts usually like that before you start?"

"Yes, but I've never been scared I was pregnant before."

"See there, it's nerves," Elaine decreed. "Considering what you're dealing with, being a little late is normal."

"Besides all of that, I lost my wedding ring in his hotel room," Delthea wailed, glad to purge, but more depressed than ever. Telling Elaine made her feel even more stupid and guilty.

"Grandmother's ring! You lost Grandmother's ring? Do you know how much grief Mother is going to give you about that one?" Elaine quipped, again delighting in Delthea's misery.

"I know. I know. Rhett called and wanted to bring it back to me, but I put him off. I can't deal with him right now." Delthea now regretted telling Elaine anything. "Don't you dare breathe a word of this to Mother. I've got enough on my mind without worrying about what she thinks."

"Did Garrett notice that your ring is gone?" Elaine asked, lighting another cigarette.

"Immediately. I haven't told him about Rhett, although I'm sure he suspects something. Garrett knows me too well, plus he tried to call my hotel room several times during the night Rhett and I were together."

Elaine nodded her smug little 'you're in deep shit' smile. "Rhett is it?" Dubbing her Scarlet, Elaine quizzed Delthea at length about the man who had 'charmed her pants off' while steering around the issue of a possible pregnancy. When Delthea mentioned Rhett's new career as a nurse, her sister's interest turned to disapproval. While they walked to the apartment, Elaine asked if he was gay, which she said most men were if they went into nursing. According to Elaine, any guy who showed up at a cattleman's conference, but in his other life was studying nursing, had to be some kind of closet freak with multiple personalities and a little schizophrenia mixed in?

Delthea ignored her. She had enough problems without adding Rhett's psychological health to her worries.

*   *   *

By the time the football game ended, Garrett was exhausted. David and his team had lost, but it really didn't matter. Doing something besides sitting in his apartment and drawing had been wonderful. Elaine and Delthea had returned from their walk and sequestered themselves in the bedroom. Delthea needed someone to talk to. Her stressed expression had grown more taunt in the last few weeks. Partly, his drawing irritated her, but he conjectured it also had something to do with her lost ring. Hopefully, Elaine's candid attitude would give Delthea the courage to talk it out.

Tired and ready to go home, Garrett struggled to his feet. The illness left him weak and sitting for long periods of time made it worse. "Kent, do you still have our car keys?"

"Sure do." He pulled them out of his pocket and dangled them in midair.

Recalling how he had loved to handle those chunks of steel when he was a teenager, Garrett said, "Would you and David help me load our leftovers?"

The boys argued about who had to take the big roasting pan, and David lost since Kent had brought it up in the first place. Garrett grabbed the bean salad, and they trooped down the stairs.

"Let's put it in the trunk," Garrett said, recalling Delthea's illogical idea about putting the food in the sloping back seat so it wouldn't slide forward while they drove.

Just as Kent started to unlock the trunk, Delthea shrieked, "Don't do that!"

Garrett couldn't understand her objection to using the car trunk.

"What do you want us to do with this stuff?" Kent held up the pie, directing his question at Garrett and ignoring Delthea.

"Put it in the back seat," Garrett said, unwilling to cross Delthea.

She marched down the steps and thrust out her hand to Kent who ignored her, slammed the car door, and handed Garrett the keys. Obligatory hugs were exchanged all around before Delthea casually slipped the keys out of Garrett's hand.

They were halfway home when Garrett asked, "What was that all about?"

"What?" she asked, her gaze riveted on the street beyond the windshield.

All at once the real question occurred to him. "What's in the trunk? Why are you so fanatical about me not seeing it?"

"It's a Christmas present." Delthea shot a quick glance at Garrett. "I wanted to surprise you." Her clenched fist pivoted back and forth on the steering wheel.

Garrett knew she was lying, but if she wanted to pretend it had something to do with Christmas, he'd humor her. Considering how tired and weak he felt, he didn't have the strength to argue. Nor, did he honestly expect to live that long.

Chapter Nine

The Monday morning after Thanksgiving, Abi lay in bed, exhausted from more activity than she had attempted in months. Her entire body ached. Each breath required effort. Over the last few days, she and Mama had talked with an unspoken need to cram the last ten years into a few short days. Pain pills and sheer determination had enabled her to keep going. She was running out of the latter.

Moa lay next to Abi, never far from her side since he had arrived home again. They, too, had talked until she was worn out. Obviously, he did not like school, but he was making a gallant try at doing what he had to do considering the circumstances. She suspected his concern about her was getting in the way of him being fully present for his classes or making friends. He seemed to understand this would be their last time together.

Someone knocked lightly at the door. Then Mama walked in, smiling timidly. "Hi, Sweetie." She held up a paper sack. "I have that book I told you about."

Abi knew what she meant, and she wasn't sure Moa should see it. She ran her fingers through Moa's mass of ringlets. "Is Ian up to a short hike?" Abi asked, needing to temporarily distract Moa, yet concerned that, to her knowledge, the two boys had not spoken to each other. This made her wonder why Moa had asked Ian to visit – in light of her condition.

Moa sighed deeply. "I get it. You want me to get lost." He got up on all fours, and turning to face her, pressed his nose to hers twice, his green eyes too serious. "'The world is your kaleidoscope.'"

" 'And the varying combinations of colors . . . .' " she answered, cutting the quote short and hugging him. She did not have the strength to finish it. He would have to understand.

"You are my special mum," he whispered, his breath warm against her chest.

"You are my special boy," she answered like always.

Moa slowly climbed off the bed and turned before he stepped outside, blowing her a kiss and then gently closing the door.

Concerned about what he was going through, but powerless to change anything, Abi tried not to think about it.

"What's that all about, that thing you two say every time he leaves the room?" Mother asked.

"It's our ritual. The nose bit is a New Zealand custom." She could tell her much more, but she lacked the strength.

"What you and Moa say sounds like something out of a book," Mama said, sitting in the chair next to the bed.

Abi nodded. "It's from that thin one on the top shelf."

Mother retrieved *As a Man Thinketh* and opened the front cover where something seemed to catch her attention. "I didn't realize Morgan was Garrett's middle name."

Imagining what her mother was looking at, Abi said, "Morgan's middle name is Clay."

"So he's named after his father." Mama returned the book to the shelf.

"I gave him my last name since Garrett and I were not married, but I named Garrett as his father on his birth certificate."

"Is that legal?" Mama asked, always concerned with what was acceptable.

Abi shrugged. "They didn't tell me I couldn't."

Mama pulled a book out of the sack and handed it to Abi. "Here's Garrett's book, the one I told you about."

"Thanks." Abi studied the front cover and the title, *I Am* and *My Thoughts*, in a smaller font printed in royal blue against a yellow background. What a perfect title for the philosophy Garrett had preached from the inception of their relationship. She pictured him sitting next to her in the library at the University of the Panhandle, or UP as the locals called it. His long hair was a tangle of ringlets that bounced as he enthusiastically explained how our thoughts determine our words and our words dictate our actions and our actions create our world. He believed emphatically in what he called the only conceivable explanation for how we got to where we were.

Abi glanced around her room, the world she had created, according to Garrett. She thought of the pain that never left her. When it finally ended, not when she escaped it by dreaming, then she would be dead, a whole different world. She could not imagine what that would be like, although she did not fear it as she once had.

"Are you too tired to look at it?" Mama held her hand out as if to take the book.

"Show me his picture," Abi said, wishing desperately to stay awake, to take advantage of this time with her mother.

Leaving the book in Abi's hands, Mama flipped it over and opened the back cover. "See, here he is. Like I said, Charlene recognized him first. But once she did, I did too, especially when I finally put it together with his name. I got this from information." She pointed to a handwritten line of numbers beneath the picture of Garrett, who wore a suit and tie, had short hair and no beard, not at all the character in her dreams.

Abi's focus settled on his clear, piercing eyes. She glanced down at the phone number, all she needed to make contact with Garrett. Her mother had even paved the way by calling. Mama had not reached him, but Abi knew Garrett well enough to imagine that he had gotten word that someone who knew Abi was trying to contact him. He might even be trying to find her this very minute. But he was married. He had moved on. Even in her dream he said he was married. Maybe it said something about all that in the bio.

She pointed to the text above his picture. "Read to me."

Her heavy eyes drifted shut as Mama read about Garrett having a psychology practice in Houston, which he shared with another psychologist,

Delthea Richards. That was the name he called his wife in her dream. Correlating her dreams to reality sent a chill down her spine. Mama said a private detective had come snooping. He had gotten Vince agitated. Why would Garrett look for her if he were married? It didn't make sense.

He had also mentioned his book – long before Mama showed up with it. How had she known about it before her mother told her? Had he talked of writing it years ago? If she had read about it in the news, she would remember, not subconsciously filing it away in the recesses of her brain. She needed to talk to him.

"You look sleepy, Babe." Mother kissed her forehead. "I'll leave you for a while."

"Wait." Abi struggled to open her eyes. "Did that say Garrett was married?"

Mama checked the book again. "No, it just talks about his practice he shares with another psychologist, Delthea Richards."

Abi had not dreamed of Garrett since her mother's arrival. She and Mama were either talking or Abi slept too deeply to remember where her mind wandered while her body rested.

*   *   *

Sitting in his chair, his sketchpad by his side, Garrett pushed the chair back to a full recline and closed his eyes, if possible more exhausted than ever.

It pleased him to immediately find himself at the park, the dream setting he had wished for but had not experienced in over a week. He looked around for Abi, sure he would find her since he had gotten this far. Typical of West Texas, the weather had changed since his last visit, turning not quite warm but clearly pleasant. Following her previous pattern, he walked to a tree that he had come to think of as theirs and found Abi sitting beneath it.

She looked up at him, shaded her eyes against the sun with her hand, and smiled. "There you are." She patted the grass in front of her. "Sit down. Let's talk."

He lowered himself to the hard ground and sat cross-legged. Every time he dreamed like this, he marveled at the joy of being free of the disease that imprisoned him. She grabbed his hands with each of hers. He saw her slender fingers grip his, but he could barely feel her. Even though he felt perfectly normal in this unconscious state, he wondered if his inability to feel her indicated he was, health-wise, losing ground. Shifting his pelvis, he compared the solidness of what was beneath him to the lack of physical connection between Abi and him. It all meant something, but he didn't know what.

"It's been a while," he whispered, focusing on the inviting depth of her dark, hypnotic eyes.

"I know. Mama's been here, and I've been too exhausted to remember where I go in my sleep." She had a glow about her that contrasted with the last time they met like this.

He appraised her smiling face. "Appears that Mama's visit must have been exactly what the doctor ordered."

For a second, her eyes tightened into that quizzical look she got when she seemed to wonder how he knew what she was thinking, which made him even more curious about what was going on. Then as if dismissing her thoughts, she grinned again and said, "Guess what Mama brought me?"

He thought about all the things she hated about the Panhandle. "Oh, let's see. A sandstorm."

"No," she answered, obviously trying not to smile.

"How about a tumbleweed?"

"No," she answered again, this time laughing.

Garrett pondered what she cherished. "Your gun."

"I brought that with me," she said, stern faced again.

He remembered seeing the gun lying on top of the boxes that filled her back seat the last time she came to his apartment. "I don't know. What did she bring you?"

"Your book, the one you told me about the first time we met here, *I Am My Thoughts*. Isn't that cool?" Still holding his hands with hers, she pumped his hands up and down.

He still could barely feel her touch, although he clearly felt his arms moving. "Abi, this is weird. You're touching me, and I'm not feeling it."

She glanced down at their hands and quickly released her grip. "I may not have much time left, so I need to ask some questions about things that don't make sense."

A chill ran up his spine. "What do you mean when you say you may not have much time left?"

She ducked her head for an instant as if regrouping. "Nothing, I'm just anxious to find out some things."

"Like what?" He reminded himself this was all imaginary.

"What's your wife's name?"

"Delthea," he answered.

"Delthea," she repeated. "That's what I thought you said. Does she work with you?"

"Yes, she is also a psychologist. She's kept our practice going while I've been ill. Why are you asking all this?" The urgency of her tone and the look of consternation on her face made him wonder what was going on.

"Give me just a few more answers. Did you send someone looking for me, a private detective?"

"Yes, Bud Anderson. He talked to your mother and to Vince, but neither one of them knew where you were."

"Oh, God. This is insane," she said, shaking her head.

"I've had this overwhelming need to find you. It started over a year ago, about the same time I started feeling sick. The only time I escape my illness is when I meet you here, but I can't get here by myself. I've tried. Every once in a while, I close my eyes, and I'm back here, and I feel great – like I'm thirty again, like I felt when we were together."

She studied him, examining his face, his body, and his crossed legs, as though she was seeing him for the first time. "I've got to think of something to ask that I could not have imagined, some way to prove it," she muttered to herself.

"Prove what?" Garrett asked.

She snapped her fingers. "I've got it. What's your office phone number?"

He had to think. Berta occasionally called to "get permission," but he rarely did since he knew Delthea was too busy to talk. Suddenly it floated to the surface of his mind, and he rattled off the numbers, starting with the area code. On the road, he had always had to dial the complete number.

She repeated the number back to him, repeating it several times as though she was memorizing it. Her eyes lit up like she had thought of another idea. "Give me your house phone, too."

"Are you planning to call?" he asked, horrified at how Delthea would react if she answered the phone and heard Abi's voice or if she even found out Abi had called. He had to remind himself he was only dreaming. None of this was real.

"No, I well, I don't know. I might. I'm too confused." Again she grabbed his hands.

He could not feel her grip. Fear shot through him. He was dying. He was slipping away.

She stared into his eyes, demanding his attention. "Give me your house phone."

He reached up to caress her face, but his hand moved through the space occupied by her head. She seemed to have as much density as a cloud. "I'm losing you."

"Quick, Garrett, give me your house phone," she repeated with the calmness and intensity of an emergency room doctor.

He thought for a few seconds, his mind blank. "I can't remember."

"Think, think," she insisted.

All at once the number spewed from his mouth.

Lips moving as she repeated the numbers, Abi locked her eyes with his. "I don't have much time. I have to go, and I may not be back again. Her hands reached for his cheeks, and he felt her fingers as light as a feather, and then she faded.

Knowing what always came next, Garrett blinked and woke up back in his chair, back in Houston, and back in pain.

*   *   *

It had been a hell of a day. While driving home, Delthea recalled her session with Mrs. Wood, Mrs. Kirby, and all the other clients who droned on about one asinine issue after another. They wouldn't recognize a real problem if it fell off a Neiman Marcus display and hit them on the head.

Since she and Garrett arrived back at the condo Thursday night until she left for work this morning, Garrett had spent every waking moment, which weren't that many, drawing in that goddamned sketchbook. She spent the long weekend fretting over whether she was pregnant and crying when she confirmed it first thing this morning with a pregnancy test. Nobody, absolutely nobody got pregnant the first time they had sex after nine months of abstinence, nobody except Delthea Richards.

At home Delthea found Garrett lying in his fully reclined chair, sketchbook in hand, his eyes at half-mast, everything the same. Berta stood at the stove, her back to Delthea.

"Is this all he's done all day?" Delthea demanded. She paid Berta well to occupy Garrett.

"Yes," Berta retorted, not bothering to turn around.

Delthea dropped her briefcase in the foyer and charged into the kitchen. "You're the one that keeps egging this on, buying sketchpads behind my back."

Berta spun around, holding a wooden spoon and looking like she wouldn't mind walloping Delthea with it.

"All of that keeps him thinking about her," Delthea added, abruptly clear that Berta's day had also been bad, and she needed to do a little back peddling. "Garrett has got to get over this – this Abi thing. We need to work together."

After taking off the apron she always wore, Berta calmly hung it in the pantry. "I wouldn't stop him from drawing if I could. It's the one thing that keeps him going."

"What do you mean?" Delthea followed her into the living room.

Berta gazed at Garrett. Her heavily lined face softened. Still looking at her patient, she whispered, "He's dying."

"No, he is not," Delthea argued emphatically. "A person doesn't die without a reason." She thought of all of the grueling tests Garrett had endured. Then she remembered Berta's experience with terminally ill patients. She had seen people die. She knew the signs and symptoms.

Berta shifted her steady gaze to Delthea. "Do what you can to make him comfortable." She walked to the foyer, grabbed her bag, and opened the door. "My time here is done. I won't be back." She firmly shut the door behind her.

Dumbstruck, Delthea muttered, "Oh no, God, no." She ran to the door, opened it, and saw Berta stepping into the elevator. "You can't quit on me," she called to her, but Berta ignored her and pushed the button to close the doors.

With the ease of moving through quicksand, Delthea walked into the living room and collapsed onto the couch. She watched Garrett who lay in his recliner, his eyes half open, his sketchbook resting on his chest. He smiled at her and raised his hand in a weak greeting. As usual, he seemed content, ready for what came next, whether it was death or more of what they had endured for the better part of a year. How would he react if he knew about the boxes that now sat in their storage closet downstairs, the ones she had Milton move over the weekend? Better yet, what would he say if he knew he had a son? How about the fact that she was pregnant by a virtual stranger?

Propping her elbows on her knees, she held her face in her hands. If she told him all these things, would it agitate him enough to bring him back to life? Or was Berta right? Was Garrett going to die no matter what she did?

In that moment, Delthea wondered if God was trying to tell her something. Maybe all this had happened at the same time for a reason. And if God was in charge of all this, then maybe God could get her out of it. If she just wasn't pregnant. Of course, that wouldn't have happened if she hadn't slept with Rhett. And that wouldn't have happened if she hadn't found Abi's stuff, which she wouldn't have been led to except for Bud Anderson and that stupid birth certificate. Every aspect of her misery seemed so significant that it was impossible to focus on any one part of it. Then Berta's decree about Garrett dying came crashing back into her head, and she knew which issue meant anything at all. Without Garrett, nothing else mattered.

Even though she doubted her ability to exercise much clout in this arena, Delthea began concocting a deal with God. She had tried everything else, why not this? If Garrett lived, if he got well by Christmas, Delthea would tell him everything. The word 'everything' hung in her head as though God wanted a checklist of what that included. She would tell Garrett about his son, about Rhett, and about her pregnancy. *And.* God expected more. Nothing else popped into her thoughts, so she assumed the deal had been deemed acceptable.

Her gaze drifted back to Garrett. Again, he smiled at her, looking so sweet, so weak, so vulnerable. At noon while she ate the burger Judy had brought back to her, she thought about having an abortion. What if she did and then Garrett died? She would lose everything, absolutely everything – even what she was sure she did not want – a child by another man.

The phone rang, startling Garrett who lay nearby. Delthea was glad to see Garrett reach for it, although she ultimately would have to take it. Either Judy failed to give her a message, or Elaine, who usually slept during this time of the day, was calling to check on Garrett.

"Hello," Garrett said into the mouthpiece. In response to what the caller was saying, he sat up, causing the recliner to transform back into a chair.

"I don't understand. You're Abi's friend?"

At the mention of Abi's name, Delthea found hidden energy, raced across the room, and reached for the phone in Garrett's hand. Whoever was talking about Abi had already said too much, but she still might be able to stop irreparable damage. "Let me get that. It's probably someone who's trying to – harass you."

He waved her away. Then he stuck a finger in his unoccupied ear while he asked, "You say she has a message?"

"The dreams are true," Garrett said as though repeating the message, a look of bewilderment on his face as he reached to hang up the phone.

Was this God's way of signing the deal? Or was God providing a means of finding Abi – like a friend with a message.

*   *   *

Mum had suggested it, but Colin was the one who saw to it that Moa took Ian when he went out to shoot or not go at all. At first, his roommate seemed dumbfounded by the idea. Ian used his broken leg as an excuse, although it had not kept him from going up and down stairs and on the trails surrounding the inn.

When Moa said he would carry all of the gear, Ian snapped, "Me go out with you pointing a loaded gun at my back? Never."

"Fine, then carry it yourself, and I'll lead the way," Moa replied, desperate to go out and shoot his gun, even if he would have to share his only real means of escape with the biggest jerk in the world.

In the end, Colin had intervened, insisted he go along, and ended up carrying all the ammunition, while Moa carried two rifles and Colin carried one. Colin was well ahead, having ordered Moa to stay behind with his guest. Ian kept getting farther in the rear, grumbling every step of the way. Moa had given up on actually shooting anything on this trip. Instead, he looked forward to returning to the inn, eating some supper, and trying to forget about his stupid roommate.

A faint yelling sound interrupted Moa's thoughts. He looked behind him and could not see Ian. Retracing his steps, Moa hurried back along the path. If Ian was hurt or had gotten into trouble, Moa would catch all the blame.

When Moa didn't find Ian, he began calling Ian's name. His roommate finally responded by yelling back at him and Moa eventually found him sitting on a boulder overlooking the valley and lake, Moa's favorite spot in the whole world, a place he would not have willingly shared with someone he could not stand.

"What's wrong? Why did you stop?" Moa asked, glad to find Ian, but also pissed off that Ian didn't seem to notice him.

Then Moa saw what he had never imagined seeing; Ian was crying. Tears were running down his face, and he was trying desperately not to let Moa see them.

"Are you hurt?" Moa asked.

Ian shook his head, pinched the bridge of his nose, and dropped his head, taking a long breath. Moa sat nearby and waited, not knowing what to do or say.

After what seemed like an eternity, Ian spoke while he looked out at the lake. "When I shouted for you, it was because I was scared. No, more like terrified."

Moa could not believe Ian was saying this to him.

"I was afraid you'd leave me here." Ian swiped at his tears. He sounded like a little kid, not the tough guy Moa had learned to hate.

"I wouldn't do that," Moa said, although the idea didn't sound half bad in hindsight.

Ian sniffed and glanced fearfully at Moa, "It reminded me of what happened last year. I felt like I was going through it all over again." His shoulders began to shake. "My mum died. She had breast cancer." He started blubbering, not holding back at all, the kind of crying that came from his gut.

Moa understood exactly what Ian was saying. A sense of loss, a feeling that nothing would ever be right again, a huge weight that would never go away hung around his neck. All of it, every bit of it had to do with his mother dying. She was leaving him and when she was gone, he would wake up in a strange forest with no compass and no one to show him his way home.

Unsure as to how Ian would react, but clear he had to, Moa put his guns down and sat next to him, wrapping an arm around the bigger boy's shoulders. Ian cried harder, although Moa didn't think it was humanly possible.

Then he did something Moa had never expected. Ian turned to face Moa, wrapped his arms around Moa's torso. That got Moa started, and they both cried, two big bawl-babies, neither one caring what the other one thought.

When they returned to the inn, the sun had slipped behind the mountain and night was settling in. Takahe greeted them as they walked in the door, but she never said anything about the time or the fact that Colin had returned without them. She didn't even seem to think it odd that they were now talking – not about what happened on the trail, or about either one of their mothers, but just saying guy stuff, being mates.

Chapter Ten

*A*lthough Abi heard birds singing outside her bedroom window, she remained in the shadows of sleep, lost in second guessing herself about allowing Takahe to call Garrett's home phone number. After waking up and finding that the office number Garrett gave her matched the one Mama had written in the book, she wrote his home number beside it before she forgot it. When Takahe came in to check on her and noticed Garrett's book lying on the bed, Abi explained about the phone numbers. It had been Takahe's idea to call, and Abi, needing to verify it, gave her the go ahead. When he actually answered, Takahe silently asked what she would say. That's when Abi told her to say the dreams were real. It felt like the only way to bridge the chasm between the unreal dream world and Takahe talking to him.

How could she dream phone numbers and names that actually existed? It simply wasn't possible. Takahe said Garrett sounded weak, but she might have wakened him, although it was only early evening there. Since it sounded so much like her illness and started at the same time, perhaps she was somehow responsible? Maybe the connection they experienced ten years ago had never gone away.

She needed to consider what all of this meant. She needed to talk to Garrett one more time, but she had no idea how to explain that she was dying, and he could as well. She thought of her last two encounters with Garrett and her lack of solidity. Garrett's body had substance, but hers had not. At that moment, she knew with clarity that he would not die. In fact, her passing might even release him.

Abi struggled to sit upright. With so little time left, she needed to spend every moment with Moa. Heavy footsteps clomped into the room, vibrating the bed.

"Mum?" Moa said, his voice alive with anticipation.

Abi forced her eyes open and in the room lit by early morning light saw her son bouncing slightly. Whatever he wanted to tell her was more than his body could contain. He had done this since he was a toddler. She reached for him, but her arm caught in the sheet. "Moa," she croaked.

He held a glass of water to her lips. Abi tried to sip it, but more of it ran down her chin than stayed in her mouth. She was losing control of her body – of her life – of everything.

He dabbed at the spill with a washcloth, probably mimicking what he had seen Takahe do so often. "It's not really my birthday, but Takahe said we could celebrate early since Ian and I have to go back to school later today."

The fog in her brain wouldn't clear enough for her to find the words to say how much she loved him and how impossible it was that her baby was so grown up and so mature, handling a situation that no one should be asked to face.

"Next week, I'll be ten years old," he announced proudly.

Tears overrode her feeble attempt to smile. She had done nothing to prepare for this milestone in his life, nothing but lie in her bed and inch ever closer to death. Determined to at least touch him, she untangled her hand from the sheet. Her skeleton-like fingers caressed his rosy cheek.

Moa's rough hands clasped hers and his green eyes danced. "Takahe's made a cake, and Colin bought me a gift. By the shape of the box, I think it's a new rifle. Ian's turning out to be a really good shot. Colin went out with us early this morning."

Abi was glad whatever stood between Ian and her son had been resolved. More than that, she thanked God for Colin and Takahe. She had taken Abi and Moa in when they had nowhere else to go. She had acted as friend, confidant, mother, and sister. Colin was the male version of those same roles. In recent weeks, Colin had hung around the inn.

Takahe must have told him the end was near. Something in her wise old brain knew.

That same something now spoke to Abi. It was her only clear thought. She had to make sure everything was taken care of. "Speak to Colin," she whispered.

"I'll go get him." Moa leaned over Abi, not forcing a hug on her, but available if she felt up to it. Takahe must have taught him that, too.

A fresh wave of guilt gripped her heart, and she pulled him to her. "Happy early birthday," she muttered into his hair. He was eager to celebrate his special day with her, knowing they would not be together when it actually happened. She had to hold onto what little time remained. She had to hold onto him.

When he wiggled, Abi hugged him tighter. "Don't leave me right now. Let's just lie here together and talk."

Moa settled next to her like he had so often. They were as close as two humans could be and still occupy separate bodies.

"I won't live much longer," she said, not sure how to prepare him for the inevitable.

"What do you think death is like?" he asked. A tone of quiet wonder permeated his words.

Daily, she pondered that question. "Not bad, but a little scary since I don't remember what it was like before I was born. I'm not sure what heaven looks like either. Streets of gold?" she said, thinking maybe they had read something to that effect.

Moa shook his head, rejecting the idea.

"I really can't picture it," Abi admitted.

"I think it's beautiful," Moa volunteered, his gaze directed to a point in near space. "Like it is here at Jacob's Springs. There are trees and mountains to climb and plenty to eat. And nobody ever gets sick." His words choked at the end.

"That's right. We'll all be healthy there," Abi agreed.

"When I go to heaven, will you be waiting for me?" They had always been together, except for the last few weeks. How terrible it must be to face the rest of his life without her.

"Of course, but I'm not really leaving. My spirit will always be here taking care of you." She wanted to believe what she was saying, to somehow make good on her word.

"What do you mean '*spirit*'?" he asked skeptically.

"That's the part of you that never dies. It has always been and always will be." Abi knew she was right. She just didn't know how it all played out. "It's your soul."

Moa nodded, unusually quiet and still.

After a light knock, Colin stuck his head into the room. "I just got back from seeing your mum off at the airport."

"How did it go?" Abi asked, thinking of how her mom had cried when they said goodbye.

Moa scrambled off the bed and hugged Colin as if he had not seen him in years. He needed someone to cling to, someone who would not desert him. But Moa couldn't count on Colin, either. His surrogate uncle always returned, yet he never stayed long.

Their sailor friend crossed his arms over Moa's back and rocked from side to side. He looked longingly at Abi, no doubt seeing death lurking in the shadows. "How are you?"

"I've been better." Fresh tears clouded her vision. She had known all along that saying goodbye would be the hardest part. "I need to talk to you about some things, wills and all of that." They had discussed all this at length, but at this point, it was all she could do to insure Moa's future.

He nodded and patted Moa gently. "Takahe needs some help." He was talking to Moa, but his eyes never left Abi's face.

*   *   *

"I know I was out all last week," Delthea replied to her frustrated secretary. "Just cancel all of my appointments for this week and tell them I'll try really hard to be there next week or have someone there in my place. Talk to you later."

Late afternoon shadows added to the gloom of Garrett's bedroom. Delthea had barely left her husband's side since the day Berta quit. Elaine dropped by daily to monitor Garrett's deteriorating vital signs and to offer a few words of comfort. When Garrett refused to go to the hospital, Delthea convinced his primary doctor to make home visits. Initially, the white-haired man said they needed to run more tests, but Garrett declined, saying he wanted to die.

Delthea wrung out the washcloth in a bowl beside the bed and carefully folded it before returning it to Garrett's forehead. He brushed it aside and mumbled something incoherent.

"Are you getting chilled again?" she asked, not sure if she should cover him with blankets in hopes of avoiding another seizure-like spell of tremors. His body temperature oscillated between freezing and burning up.

The doorbell rang. Delthea ran to get it, puzzled that Milton had not phoned ahead.

She opened the door and found Berta standing in the hallway, wearing the white uniform and sweater she always wore and carrying a bag that spilled over with a rainbow-colored crocheted afghan. "You said you needed some help."

"Yes, I do. Thank you for coming." The evening Berta quit, Delthea had phoned her and gotten an answering machine. She didn't leave a message, but the next three days she did, each time groveling a little more. The last call had been four days ago. What had changed? Why was she here now?

"I talked with Elaine. Well, actually, she came over and convinced me I needed to come here as much as you needed me." Berta sounded sheepish, like she had done something wrong. "See, I started drinking again."

"Oh, Berta, I'm sorry. Was it what I said the last time we talked? I didn't mean it. I was under stress. It's just that all this has been so overwhelming." She gestured toward the bedroom that drew her back like a huge, unyielding magnet.

"Naw, it wasn't you. Something happened that I've avoided since I first got into this business. I got attached to my patient. Usually I can convince myself that it's okay for them to die, but Garrett was different. I couldn't let him go," Berta said, her voice strained. She looked away from Delthea and swallowed, obviously fighting tears.

Delthea wrapped her arm around Berta's shoulders and guided her into the living room. "Perhaps your need to experience that kind of patient is what drew you to us." It sounded like psychological mumbo-jumbo, but talking like that allowed Delthea to escape the situation. If only for a few seconds, she needed to forget her world was unraveling.

"Well, I'm here – for whatever reason." Berta set her bag in its usual corner.

"I'm so glad. I really, really need you. Elaine has been by every day, and I convinced Garrett's doctor to come see him, but nobody knows him like you do." Plus, Berta gave her an inkling of security.

"I'm gonna be honest with you." Berta locked gazes with Delthea. "Garrett's dying. I've worked with too many terminally ill not to recognize the latter stages. That's what scared me out of here a week ago and drove me back to the bottle. With my other patients I could accept it because there was a reason, but with him there's no explanation."

Delthea's temporary tranquility vanished. Berta had echoed her own feelings. It wasn't right or fair or possible. How could Garrett die without a reason?

"Let me take a look at him." Berta walked into the bedroom, gently took his pulse, and briefly peeked beneath one of his eyelids.

That roused him, and he uttered something unintelligible.

Berta pulled up the covers and stroked his dirty, matted hair. "You getting any fluids down him?" she asked, never taking her eyes off of her patient.

"Some, not a lot," Delthea answered, feeling inadequate.

"Ice chips might chill him since his skin feels cool. Maybe he'd take a cup of hot tea." Berta left the room with an air that said her worst fears were founded, and she was glad she came back.

When Berta returned, Garrett agreed to drink the hot tea and yielded to their efforts to sit him upright. While Delthea held the cup to his lips, he sipped and gradually woke up. His roving eyes drifted to Berta. "I'm glad you're here," he said with great effort.

Berta sat on the bed and patted his leg. "I had to come see my favorite guy. No telling what you'd get into without me here to keep you in line."

Garrett gave her a half-grin and nodded as if to say he had managed to get into more trouble than he could handle. Focusing on Delthea, he said with great difficulty, "Need talk to lawyer. Make sure my will is up to date."

"Of course." Actually, it was an effort in futility since nothing had changed since they set up their wills the same year they opened their practice, nothing except finding out Garrett had a son. Delthea was the only one that knew that, though. If and when Morgan Clay Barker surfaced, Delthea would make sure he was taken care of, whether Garrett was alive to see to it or not. She thought of Abi's friend calling and how Garrett had refused to explain what he meant about the dream being true. For all Delthea knew, the caller could have been a wrong number and Garrett had been hallucinating. None of it mattered now.

She called Phillip Berryman, a lawyer they had used extensively, and convinced him to come to their home. He arrived after lunch. By then Delthea had found their wills in the filling cabinet and had Garrett's ready for him to check.

Garrett insisted on talking to Berryman in private. Berryman stayed in Garrett's bedroom for more than an hour, calling Berta in once to serve as a witness. Once the bald-headed lawyer had left, Garrett made another request. "Need to call Mom and Dad."

Their obligation to call both of their parents had nagged at Delthea since Garrett first developed this insane illness. She put it off, believing he would recuperate. Now she must respond to his wishes. As for her own mother, Delthea would let Elaine tell her and suffer the initial wrath for not relating Garrett's situation sooner. Delthea had enough to handle without dealing with that situation as well.

Anticipating the need to interpret, Delthea dialed the phone she had plugged in at Garrett's bedside while she held the cordless phone in her lap. When Nadine Clay answered, Delthea told her Garrett wanted to speak with her and his father Bill.

"First, he avoids calling for nine months, and then he has you acting like his secretary, getting us on the line before he takes his precious time to grace us with a word or two. I'm not sure we're available," she retorted, as always ready to fight.

Delthea stroked Garrett's pale cheek. Since her first encounter with Nadine Clay, she had understood what attracted her husband to psychology. He, like most shrinks, had personal reasons for learning how to help others cope with their past.

"Nadine, please ask Bill to pick up the other phone. Garrett has been ill. In fact, we're afraid he's . . . ." The words caught in her throat. She could not say it.

"And this is the first we've heard of it? What's wrong with him? That just shows how little Garrett cares. I'm his mother. I should have known about this."

Garrett lifted his hand toward the phone. He knew his mother well enough to guess what she was saying.

Between clinched teeth, Delthea said, "Please, just ask Bill to pick up a phone while I put Garrett on." She held the cordless to Garrett's ear and continued to listen.

After some talking in the background, Bill said into the phone, "Son, what's wrong? Mother said you're sick."

"Dying," Garrett whispered. "Don't have much time."

"What? Where are you? Tell us which hospital, and we'll be there as soon as we can." It was more than Bill typically said in a thirty-minute conversation.

"At home," Garrett managed.

His response launched Nadine into a tirade that spanned the gamut from her disappointment that Garrett had joined the army without their approval to her assessment that he tended to exaggerate 'normal aches and pains.' He always had. Delthea wanted to intervene, but she couldn't begin to explain what had transpired over the past year. Nor, could she justify keeping Bill and Nadine uninformed. The only point that seemed clear was that she and Garrett had been in complete denial.

Finally, Bill interjected, "What seems to be the problem?"

"Doctors can't de-ter-mine." Garrett looked to Delthea and nodded. He had done that when they worked together. It was his way of asking her to take over.

"We've had extensive tests run." Delthea gave an account of the many doctors, both in Houston and elsewhere, which they had consulted without getting a conclusive diagnosis. She ended with, "We should have called before now, but since we had no idea what was wrong, we thought he'd get well."

Before either parent spoke, Garrett added, "Want to say I love both of you." He looked up at Delthea, faintly smiled, and closed his eyes, silently asking her to hang up.

Delthea pushed the off button on the cordless phone. While she moved the other receiver to the cradle, Nadine's shrill voice continued. At that moment, she had more pressing matters to deal with than Garrett's mother.

*   *   *

While Delthea went through the motions of rolling their phone calls to the front desk, something he had never learned how to do, Garrett returned to his mental list of issues he must address before he died. For too long, Delthea had needed from Garrett what he once did well – conversation. Regretfully, he had been too consumed with his illness to deal with what lay between them. He could not change the past, but he would not go to his grave, knowing that Delthea carried an unnecessary burden.

"Talk," he whispered, wishing he had the energy to give her the attentiveness that she needed.

"About what?" Delthea, who sat by his side, had that wide-eyed, just-got-caught look on her face. Doubtlessly, she recognized they had unresolved issues, but, like their clients, it was easier to plead ignorance than to address them.

In an effort to economize on effort and time, Garrett said the one word that might open up the wall between them, "Austin."

Her eyes closed, and she dropped her chin.

Garrett inched his hand toward Delthea's. Noticing this, she tried to lace her fingers between his. He resisted, managing to grasp his goal, the ring finger of her left hand. He had never liked the gaudy relic that once adorned it, but he acquiesced to Delthea's compunction to please her mother. Given time and the energy to do so, he would replace it with a simple gold band, one that represented his everlasting love for her. Sadly, that would not happen.

"Where did it go?" he croaked, unable to say more.

"I-I d-don't know," she stammered. "You know me. I drank a couple of margaritas and after that I can't remember." She knew. The guilty expression on her face spoke volumes.

Already exhausted from his meeting with Phillip and phoning his parents, Garrett chose his words carefully. "I love you. What happened in Austin doesn't matter."

Delthea started to object, but he looked into her eyes and gripped her hand with what little strength he had left. "I haven't been here for you – in a long time. I wish I could have done it differently. Please forgive."

She nodded and pressed her lips together the way she did when she was trying not to cry.

"There's one more thing." He hated to mention Abi in any way, but the message she had given her friend was too poignant to ignore. Besides all that, eventually, Delthea would know about the codicil he had added to his will. "I'm not sure it's true, but I have a feeling – a hunch that I have a child . . . by Abi. He would be ten years old now."

"How did . . . ?" She started to say more but the air escaped her mouth like a balloon slowly deflating. Her face registered puzzlement more than shock, not at all how he had expected her to react.

He thought of his last dream, Abi's insistence that he give her his phone number, and then the friend's call with someone, perhaps Abi, speaking faintly in the background. It had been a surreal experience, much like the dreams themselves, but all of it was convincing enough to make him wonder if everything Abi said in his dreams was somehow true. "If I do have a son, his name is Morgan, and I've set up a trust fund for him."

"M-m-morgan?" Delthea repeated. "You have a son named Morgan?" Her face twisted, and her eyes filled with tears.

"I'm not sure. Bud . . . ." He started to make up a lie, but it took too much effort, and he could not begin to explain about the dreams, those brief encounters with Abi that felt more real than the present moment.

"Bud Anderson told you that you have a son?" she quizzed.

"The pain . . . ." He focused on pulling in a long, painful breath. "I want to die."

At this Delthea burst into sobs and held Garrett, laying her head next to his on the pillow. When her crying had faded to a series of short hiccups, she said, "You can't leave me."

Berta touched his shoulder. "Are you ready for a pain pill? It's been a while since you had one."

Garrett nodded, glad for anything that might minimize the giant claw that seized his entire body. He stuck out his tongue. Berta dropped a pill on the back of it. Then he sipped water through a straw, like he had countless other times.

Right before he drifted into unconsciousness, he realized Delthea had lain down next to him, her face beside his. She fell asleep, exhausted from taking care of him around the clock. He examined the lines of worry that remained between her eyes. In the past year, she had also suffered. Given the chance, he would change what had happened for her sake alone. He loved Delthea more than words could say. And he felt bad about leaving her to deal with life on her own.

* * *

Moa sat next to Ian at his roommate's desk. They were working together on math, which was Moa's strength. Ian, on the other hand, knew how to bullshit his way through an essay, which they had plenty to write after being out of class nearly two weeks. Together they had knocked out nearly every item on Mr. Perkins' list.

The calendar hanging above Ian's desk kept catching his eye, especially today's square, December the eighth. He was ten years old. Neither Takahe nor his mother had called, which in a way was a good thing. It meant she was still alive – he hoped. On the other hand, he knew she was going to die. It was simply a matter of time, and she sure wasn't enjoying being alive. It might be selfish, but he hated for her to go simply because he did not know what to do without her, how to keep on living.

"Ian," he said to his roommate who was bent over the desk.

Ian looked up at him, not saying anything, just asking what he wanted with his eyes.

"When your mum died, how did you feel? I mean, were you kind of lost for a while?" Moa felt dopey asking him stupid stuff, and he sure didn't want to make Ian cry again, but he thought if anyone could tell him what to expect, Ian could.

"It feels like shit," Ian said, putting his pencil down. "Everybody tiptoed around me for weeks." He smiled. "In fact, you were the first person who crossed me. I can't tell you how pissed that made me. But at the same time, I was really glad. Finally, somebody was treating me normal, not like some little baby who might break if they said the wrong thing."

Moa nodded. His roommate was a whole lot smarter than he had thought, but that still didn't help him deal with what he knew was coming. "I just don't know what I'm gonna do when it finally happens. You know what I mean?" He felt the tears burning at the back of his eyelids, and he chewed his bottom lip, determined not to let them get started again.

"Hey, you know what, mate?" He tousled Moa's hair. "That first night when you were crying, I was sitting here thinking, I hope that stupid *drongo* doesn't get me started." He gave Moa one of those looks that said more than words could spell out in a whole book. "See, I never had cried until that day out in the forest. Even at my mum's funeral, I never shed a tear. Everybody, including my dad, kept telling me how brave I was. Bugger. I was petrified, scared shitless."

A light knock on the door preceded Mr. Perkins opening it and poking his bald head inside the room. "Morgan, your mother is on the phone. She wishes to give you a birthday greeting."

Moa walked down the hallway with Mr. Perkins, thinking how Mr. Perkins had said Mum wanted to talk to him. She was still alive. That was all he wanted for his birthday. It had been her birthday when she went to hospital and found out about the cancer. He would never forget that day.

"A penny for your thoughts, Master Barker," Mr. Perkins said in that prissy way of his.

"I was just thinking about the day my mum was diagnosed with cancer. It was her birthday."

"And today is yours?" He checked Moa's face like he was unsure about what he needed to say. "Your mother is quite weak. I expect she wants to tell you goodbye." His eyes got all shiny before he pulled out a kerchief and wiped them.

Moa didn't need the warning, but he appreciated Mr. Perkins being considerate enough to offer it. When they got to his office, Moa saw the handle of an old black phone lying on the desk. He picked it up and said, "Hello?"

"There you are," Takahe said, just like he had walked into the kitchen after going for a hunt.

"How's Mum?" he asked.

It took her too long to say, "Not good."

"She's not already dead is she?" he asked, his heart pounding in his ears.

"No, and she wants to speak to you. What she says may not make a lot of sense, but there's something she wants you to know. It's very important." She spoke to his mum, telling her he was on the line and ready to listen.

"Moa," Mum said, his name a soft whisper.

"Hey, Mum." He didn't know what else to say; besides, he was still trying to figure out what Takahe was talking about.

"Your dad, I saw him in my dreams." She breathed heavily into the phone and Takahe said something about phone numbers, but Mum said, "No," more clearly than she had spoken in a while. After another exchange in which they disagreed again, but Moa couldn't understand exactly what they were saying, Mum came back on the line. "Happy birthday, Moa. I love you."

"I love you too, Mum."

"Good night, Moa," Takahe said, just like she had been saying for as long as he could remember.

While Mr. Perkins walked him back to his room, Moa wondered what Takahe meant about phone numbers, and why she argued with his dying mother. He had never known of them to disagree or for Takahe to challenge his mother on anything that had to do with him. This seemed like a really weird time for them to start.

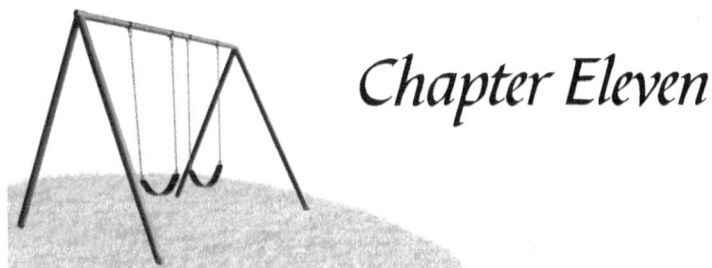

Chapter Eleven

*A*bi drifted in and out of a restless sleep. It had been a while since Takahe phoned the school, so Abi could tell Moa how to reach Garrett. At the last minute, she panicked when she thought about Vince somehow getting wind of Morgan's whereabouts and claiming him as his own. It would be better for Moa to never meet his dad than to grow up with Vince as a father. Besides, she had no assurance that Garrett would live. Since his illness coincided and replicated hers, he might also die, although Abi's conviction that her death would release him had grown.

Takahe had called Mama once she finished her conversation with Moa. Mama confirmed that she had gotten home just fine, that Charlene was glad to have her back, and that the two of them had gone out for Mexican food the previous night. With Takahe conveying the messages back and forth, Abi said she had not had a decent tortilla since she left the States. When Betty said she would mail her one, Abi told her not to mark it consumable, or they wouldn't let it in the country. With that final remark, she told her mother she loved her and asked Takahe to hang up the phone.

She knew it was time to go, to leave this body and go on to something else, but she also knew she needed to visit Garrett one more time. Not knowing what she would say or how honest she would be had kept her from initiating the meeting. As he had indicated the last time, she was the one who seemed to dictate their rendezvous. Knowing she could not put it off any longer, she closed her eyes and imagined the park.

Abi found Garrett sitting on one of the swings, his head bent and shadowed by his floppy hat. She settled into the nearby swing and watched him for a second. "So am I getting the silent treatment because you're mad at me?"

He glanced up at her. "No, I just now realized I was here."

She backed up as far as the rubber seat would permit and then she swung, pumping her legs and going a little higher with each back and forth motion. Garrett watched her movements, his face stony.

"This is it, you know. This is the end," she yelled, not sure what she meant exactly or why she was saying this. Then she thought of the name he had always called her, Bird. He had not used that name recently. They were no longer lovers. And she was not long for this body. None of this mattered, nor did it make her sad. It simply was. What she wouldn't give to be able to fly away and not do the rest of this dying bit. While her swing slowed, Garrett watched her.

"Why didn't you talk instead of your friend?" he asked.

"It's complicated, much too complicated." She debated telling him where she lived and how to find Morgan, but she thought of Vince and why she had avoided telling Moa. Her son would be fine. Takahe and Colin loved him. He was settling in at school. He and Ian were getting along.

"Where's my son?" he asked, clearly angry that she had kept him from Garrett.

"At school. He's settled. He has friends. He doesn't want to be disrupted and jerked halfway around the world. Leave him alone." She had to convince Garrett to back off and essentially disregard everything she had inadvertently told him.

"Does he know about me? Does he know that I would give anything to have him with me?" Garrett asked, his green eyes following her as she glided slowly back and forth.

"He knows your name. He has seen countless pictures I've painted of you. And he knows that I never told you about him," she admitted.

"Except you did – here." He looked around at the leafless trees and the brown, dead grass.

"This doesn't count. This isn't real. It's only a dream." Slowly coming to a stop, Abi realized she would not return to Birdsong Inn.

Abi stood and surveyed the park that had brought them back together. It seemed highly unlikely that she would ever see it again. She stretched out her hand to him. He did the same, but their fingers did not hook or intertwine; they fused. He also stood up. Again, there were no directions, no instructions; she simply knew what to do next. Without forethought or hesitation, she walked forward and stepped into him.

*   *   *

The early gray of morning lit their bedroom. In the half-shadows, Delthea roused and checked Garrett's pulse. He was still alive, yet he had shifted from labored breathing to a breath that was barely detectable. After examining his gaunt face, a new wave of panic washed over her, tightening her heart with a painful realization. Perhaps he lacked the energy to breathe deeply.

In desperation, Delthea once more searched her brain for a solution, a means of escaping this horrific situation. The answer lay somewhere beyond this world. Only a supernatural force could help. She thought of her earlier futile deal with God. Some unexplainable entity had brought this reign of horror upon them in the first place. She had never really believed bargaining with the gods would work, but she had done it none the less, resorting to voodoo and superstition, anything to keep Garrett alive. Her weakening mental grasp clung to the fraying threads that maintained Garrett's fragile life.

Dear God, she thought, *please make Garrett well. I know I've made deals with you in the past, but maybe you didn't get how truly sincere I was.*

Nothing happened. No light from heaven, no angel's songs, not even a rustle of wings.

"Dear God, make Garrett well," she whispered. Terrified that nothing would appease this angry God, Delthea considered her earlier tactic of making an offering. It had to be good, but how could she top what she had already proposed? Perhaps finding Morgan was the ultimate sacrifice.

She thought of Garrett's obsessive drawing and the recent phone call from Abi's friend. That could have been God's way of asking Delthea if she would uphold her end of the bargain.

That was it. Much as she hated the idea of reconnecting Abi and Garrett, it was the only worthy gift she could think of, the only sacrifice that would prove her complete, uncompromising love for Garrett. The whole thing was bizarre, completely insane, the ravings of a woman gone mad after months of battling an invisible foe. How could she hand Garrett over to Abi?

Garrett drew in a long, deep breath. He sounded almost normal. Was this a glimpse of what God might do for her?

Before she had time to give it further thought, Delthea closed her eyes and vowed, "If you let Garrett live, I'll find Abi and Morgan, and I'll deliver them to Garrett. I promise."

Delthea took a deep breath and laid her head on the bed beside Garrett's shoulder, more at peace than she had felt in months. Her end of the bargain sounded impossible, but so was God saving Garrett. If He could do that, she would find Abi and Morgan and somehow deal with the repercussions.

Not sure how she could ever live without him, Delthea ran her fingers through Garrett's long, oily hair. Four days ago when she had suggested he let her bathe him, he refused, too racked with pain and weak to care if he was clean.

His eyes opened, and he lovingly gazed at her as he had the first time they slept together. "Good morning, Glory," he said clearly, catapulting her into the past. That silly phrase was something he had said often in their early days together.

Delthea stared at him, unable to speak.

A look of astonishment that reflected her own feelings spread across Garrett's face. He flexed his arms and hands as though trying them out for the first time. "I feel great," he said with amazement.

"You do?" she asked, completely stupefied.

Garrett sat up and filled his chest with a long, deep breath. "I do. I feel wonderful." He leapt out of bed and ran to the mirror where he examined his face and hair. "Delthea, this is incredible. I feel perfectly normal."

"M-m-maybe it's just a burst of energy. You should lie down and rest, so you won't overdo." She scrambled to her feet. "You remember what happened at Thanksgiving. For a short time you felt better, then the bottom fell out and you felt worse than ever."

"This is not like that." He began yanking off his striped pajamas, his clothes of choice for the last few months. "I've got to take a shower."

Too shocked to try to stop him, Delthea watched open-mouthed. Had her bargain with God actually worked? Was Garrett miraculously cured?

The phone rang. Delthea grabbed it.

Milton cleared his throat, an annoying habit that let her know who it was before he said a word. "Boy, have I got a pile of messages for you. Let's see. Must be ten of them, mostly from Dr. Clay's mother. Just to sum it up, she's pissed that Garrett called and said he was 'gravely ill', her words, not mine, and then she couldn't get through to him last night. I told Leroy to just take messages like you said," he whined, defending both of them.

"That's exactly what I wanted you to do. I'll call her back. Thank you."

Delthea started to hang up when Milton added, "I don't think you'll get her. The last message says she's booked the first flight out of Miami, and she'll be in Houston by eight o'clock." He paused and Delthea could imagine him looking at his watch with his usual goofy expression. "That would be about thirty-five minutes ago."

Delthea hung up the phone and glanced at the clock radio on the nightstand. Dear God, what was she going to do? God? Was all of this His doings? She still might be dreaming, and if she weren't, how long would Garrett feel well? What would keep Garrett from relapsing?

The doorbell rang. Berta no doubt. Delthea had tried to give her a key, but she refused it, saying she didn't want to be responsible for it.

Delthea opened the door and immediately announced to the woman who wore a traditional white uniform every day, "Garrett's had a remarkable recovery."

Shock washed over Berta's wrinkled face.

"He's in the shower, but I'll show you when he gets out." Delthea grabbed her arm and pulled her into the foyer.

The phone rang again, and Delthea switched it on.

"How's he doing?" Elaine asked, but before Delthea could answer, she added, "I've been trying to call all night, but the jerk at the front desk wouldn't put me through. I figured you'd call me if something happened."

"Garrett's better. I'm scared to say it out loud, but he appears to be well."

"Holy shit. That's impossible," Elaine shrieked.

"Come over and see for yourself," Delthea said.

Delthea hung up the phone and returned to Berta who stood in the middle of the living room, her face slack, her mouth gaping. "I want you to see him, so you can tell me I'm not dreaming." She listened to the sound of water running and Garrett singing "Bridge over Troubled Waters" at full volume. Garrett was taking a shower by himself. She could not believe it.

"He just woke up well?" Berta said, the first words out of her mouth that morning.

"Yes, it's incredible." Delthea couldn't wait to show Berta his incredible recovery.

"Delthea, would you hand me a towel?" Garrett called as he had countless times before. He never remembered to get a towel before he started a shower, and he hated to step on cold tile with warm, wet feet. Those once annoying details now added to her elation.

She couldn't believe it. It was unbelievable. He was back.

*   *   *

Amazed beyond belief, Garrett looked down at his skinny body while he waited for Delthea to bring a towel. He had not experienced this exhilarating sense of aliveness in the past year – except when he visited Abi in the park. In fact, he had never appreciated how truly wonderful it felt to be alive, to feel healthy while not dreaming. His arms were

weak, and he felt light-headed, probably from hunger, but he was well –
incredibly, indisputably well. He thought of his last encounter with Abi
and how it had ended with her melting into him. In the past, when he
left the dream, he returned to nagging pain, but he could not remember
anything that happened after they became one. While the whole idea
seemed bizarre, it also felt right. More than that, he had finally lost his
need to find Abi. He finally knew that she was okay wherever she was.
They were both free. He was sure of that.

Delthea hurried in and handed Garrett a towel. She gazed at him,
obviously equally amazed by his abrupt recovery. "Berta's here. She
wants to see you. She can't believe you're well." After another astonished
appraisal of his body, she added, "Do you need help?"

"Thanks, but really, I don't. Isn't this incredible?"

She gawked at him while he quickly dried and wrapped the towel
around his waist.

Not bothering to put on the jogging suit Delthea had laid on the
bed, he raced into the living room, grabbed Berta's hand and yelled,
"Look at me. Can you believe it?" He held her limp arm in the air. "Is
this incredible?"

Berta slowly wagged her head from side to side. "I've never seen
anything like it."

Once more the phone rang. Delthea answered it, and after listening
for a brief time, announced, "Your mother and dad are on their way up.
Better get dressed."

The doorbell rang. Garrett ran to get it, eager to show someone
else, anyone, the miracle that had taken place. He flung open the door
and revealed his parents. They wore suits and expressions, both equally
appropriate for his funeral.

"Mom, Dad, come on in," he greeted enthusiastically.

Rather than move, his mother glared and his dad stared at him. "You
don't look sick," his mother accused, always the spokesperson when they
were together.

His first instinct was to go on the defensive, the only way he knew to deal with his mother. But his heart told him to be patient, that they loved him and were terrified they had waited too long to make amends. "I was, but I'm not now. You won't believe that happened. I can't believe it myself." They didn't look pleased, but they had not gone through what he had endured. "I've been sick for a year."

"Why weren't we informed of this earlier?" Not giving Garrett a chance to answer, she marched past him and into the living room. Dad followed like a well-trained dog. Mother eyed Delthea and Berta as if they were part of the conspiracy to deceive her. "When we spoke yesterday evening, I was too shocked to ask questions. Then last night, I found you were screening your calls, like you didn't want to be disturbed while you're dying." She eyed Garrett, starting with his wet hair and quickly moving to his bare feet before adding, "But obviously, you're not."

"Let me explain," Garrett began.

"You don't have to," she said decisively. "It's quite clear our whirlwind trip was totally unnecessary." Mother returned her glare to Berta.

Garrett put his hand on his mother's back. "Berta, this is my mom and dad, Bill and Nadine Clay. Berta has helped us during my illness."

Dad stepped forward, shook Berta's hand, and uttered, "Pleased to meet you."

Mother turned her assessing gaze back to Garrett and appraised him once more, stopping at the towel wrapped around his waist. "Don't you think you should at least get dressed?"

"How about some coffee?" Delthea asked the room at large. She still wore her clothes from yesterday, and her hair stuck up on one side.

Garrett excused himself and ran into the bedroom. He wasn't about to put on a jogging suit, though, not after wearing them and pajamas for the past nine months. Clouds hung thick in the morning sky, so Garrett opted for a sweater that would hopefully hide his skinny body. What did it matter? He was well! He could walk and talk and even run if he wanted to. God, he felt good.

While Garrett was slipping on a pair of jeans that had once fit snugly and now felt five sizes too big, Delthea ran into the room, shutting the door behind her. She grabbed Garrett's shoulders and looked him up and down. "I still can't believe it. This is just too incredible."

"I know, isn't it?" He pecked her on the nose. "Did you appease the angry mob?"

"Your mother is the only one that's upset. I guess she's disappointed about abruptly flying across country only to find that you aren't gasping for your last breath as promised."

Garrett laughed. He felt too good not to. The way his mother was acting could not affect his overflowing happiness. "That was yesterday's show." Garrett buttoned his jeans and searched his closet for a belt to keep them from falling off.

Delthea stared at him, again her face reflecting the complete awe that filled his own heart. His recovery was a miracle, too wonderful to comprehend.

Glancing at the clock on the nightstand, Garrett said, "It's late enough for lunch. Let's take everybody to Ninfa's." Mexican cuisine, usually his last choice, now sounded wonderful.

"Ninfa's?" Delthea echoed, her face scrunched with bewilderment. "You hate Mexican food."

"Not anymore. It's a new me." He combed his long, wet hair straight back and threw the brush to Delthea. "Get ready, and let's go."

Elaine arrived soon after Garrett walked back into the living room. "Damn, Garrett, you are alive," she declared as she pulled at his sweater sleeve. "This is incredible."

Her remark seemed to mellow his mother. She said in a diplomatic tone, "I still don't understand why we weren't notified earlier. After all, we are your parents."

Garrett had never felt close to his parents, not as a nine-year-old latchkey kid, a teenager who tried drugs hoping that might get him some parental attention, or an eighteen-year-old who joined the army and volunteered for Vietnam. Something had changed. He saw through his mother's tough exterior, and he loved her. He understood his father's silence, and he appreciated the patience and love that had enabled him to live with Nadine, a difficult woman to say the least.

Hugging his mother, he whispered in her ear, "I'm sorry I scared you. Forgive me. You're right; I should have called. Delthea wanted to, but I hated to worry you." Delthea had never mentioned it, but a little PR work never hurt, especially when it came to Mother.

Leaving his mother open-mouthed, Garrett gave his father a hug. "We need to spend more time together, go fishing and golfing." His dad did both obsessively, probably to find a little peace.

"Yeah, sure," Dad said, seemingly as mystified by Garrett's proposal as anything else that had happened that morning.

Delthea waltzed into the room, dressed in a red dress with a fitted waist and long sleeves. Her long blonde hair flowed like water over her shoulders. She looked gorgeous. While struggling to survive, he had lost sight of that and all the incredible things about Delthea that drew him to her.

It took some finagling to first convince everyone to go out for Mexican food and then to sort out who would go in which car. What difference did it make? He had all the time in the world – to enjoy his beautiful, caring wife, to finally get to know his parents, and to show Berta and Elaine how much he appreciated their support throughout this terrible ordeal. All the time in the world. He could not believe it. He was well, and he felt great. He was a walking, talking miracle.

*   *   *

Two days after his mother died, Moa sat on the front row of the dining room chairs he had helped drag into the living room for people to sit in for the funeral. Takahe and Colin occupied a seat on either side of him.

When Takahe helped him call Grandma Betty after he got back home, she cried and said she wished she could be there with him. That made Moa cry too, as if he hadn't already done a bunch of that. When Perky told him the news, he had even gotten Ian started again. They had sworn at each other afterwards, hugged, and Ian helped him pack a bag. He said he would go to the funeral with Moa if he wanted him. It was a tempting offer, but Ian couldn't afford to get further behind on schoolwork. Moa didn't necessarily want Ian or Grandma Barker, but he did want someone or something to make him feel better.

One of his mother's favorite songs played on the record player, "Bridge over Troubled Waters" by Simon and Garfunkel. Who ever heard of using that at a funeral? But then again who would want to have their service in their own living room and with only a few neighbors and friends? His mum. In his dreams, Moa thought he felt her touch his nose and say their special words, but that was only a dream, a wish to hold onto something he would never get to do again. He missed his mum so much it felt like somebody was squeezing his heart.

He thought about that time she had said she would always be with him. Moa wanted to believe she had known what she was talking about, but she was dead. He could see her lying in that stupid coffin. Last night after he and Colin got home from the school, he had sneaked back into the living room and felt her cold face and fingers. Seeing her like that had given him the willies. That lifeless corpse wasn't her. Even when she felt the worst, she still gave him a smile and whispered his name. He had barely slept for thinking about that dead body that wasn't her.

Moa swallowed and tried to stop them, but tears rolled down his cheeks anyway. Takahe handed him a tissue and Colin wrapped his huge arm around Moa's shoulders. Tears were running down their faces too. At least he had them – until he left for boarding school. And then he had Ian.

Takahe nudged him and handed him the piece of paper with the passage he was supposed to read. He knew the words by heart. He didn't need some dumb paper to tell him what to say. He didn't want to do anything that would make his mother's death more real than it already was. He hated this whole thing. Why couldn't he run out into the woods and stay there until he died and joined his mum?

The tears came faster and harder. He tried to stop them, but sobs moved in behind them. "No," he whispered. "I can't do it." She had to understand. Saying good-bye was too hard.

Again, he wondered if his mother's spirit might actually be with him as she had said it would. He wanted to believe it was. Taking a long, hic-cuppy breath, he stood up, and focused on the paper in his hands. The words blurred with his tears. He didn't need them because his mum's voice began saying them in his head, and he knew them anyway.

Along with her, he said, "'Tempest-tossed souls, wherever ye may be, under whatever conditions ye may live, know this – in the ocean of life the isles of Blessedness are smiling, and the sunny shore of your ideal awaits your coming. Keep your hand firmly upon the helm of thought. In the dark of your soul reclines the commanding Master: He does but sleep: wake Him. Self-control is strength: Right Thought is mastery: Calmness is power. Say unto your heart, "Peace be Still!"'"

* * *

Death was not at all like what Abi thought it would be, but then again, she hadn't really decided what it was like yet. After she merged with Garrett, she lost her body, which must have been when she officially died. Since then she found herself showing up at various places, all of them having to do with people who had known her well like Mama, Moa, Takahe, Colin, and even Vince. He was the only one that made her stop and wonder why she was there.

He sat in front of a television, a beer in one hand and two empty cans sat on the floor. No one else lived in the same house she had once shared with him. So far, she had figured out that being dead gave her the ability to know what people were feeling, how they were coping with her death. With each person she had felt a strong connection, a deep caring, love. Somewhere deep in Vince's being, she intuitively knew he also possessed that, but it had gotten covered up with a lot of other negative feelings. Gone were the rage, the jealousy, and the hatred. Now all she felt from him was an empty hollowness, a deep painful sadness. She never imagined she could actually feel compassion toward a man who had abused her physically and emotionally, but she genuinely felt sorry for him.

She looked around the house that had been her home for a dozen years. It had once been a prison. Now, only the warden remained – and he had lost his power. Power. All at once Abi knew what had prompted her to visit Vince. Even after she left him, he had ruled her life, even to the point of deterring her from uniting Moa and Garrett. It had been a huge mistake, an irreparable blunder.

She had never accepted the possibility that she would end up in hell, but looking at Vince and seeing the misery he had created for himself here on Earth made her realize she had fashioned her own punishment. Would she spend the rest of eternity wishing she had told Garrett how to contact Moa, or given Takahe permission to share the phone numbers with Morgan, or, at the very least, acquiesced to Takahe's suggestion that she say something to Moa about how to find his father?

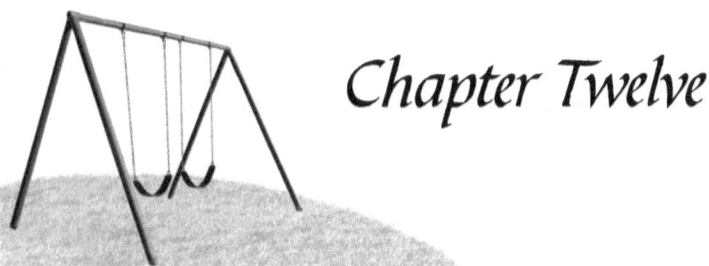

Chapter Twelve

While Delthea returned to work and Berta remained at his side during the day, Garrett painted. Mesmerized by images that birthed themselves, he watched his hand move independent of his conscious thoughts, much the same as when he began drawing during his illness. Along with landscapes that did not look like anywhere he had ever been, he produced detailed images of the curly-haired boy that must be his subliminal version of Morgan, his mythical son. He had not had another Abi-dream after the one in which she merged with him before he miraculously woke up well. He had not felt the need to.

Garrett could not quit thinking about the short phone conversation he had with the foreign sounding woman, whose accent reminded him of the way Abi had spoken in his dreams. Over the phone, she had relayed his one-time-lover's message that the dreams were true. He didn't quite know what to think about all that, the dreams and the phone conversation. Some part of it had seemed plausible enough to prompt him to set up a trust fund for his questionable son. Reason told him he had been hallucinating as Delthea suggested when he talked to her about it. At the time, he had been taking a lot of pain pills. What would be the chances of dreaming about someone he had not seen in ten years, telling her his phone number, and then receiving a phone call from her? It had to be his imagination, along with whatever possessed him to compulsively paint these pictures.

Fully aware of how much he had already abused his relationship with Delthea, Garrett concealed his artwork from her as much as he could.

After his amazing recovery, he and Delthea began sleeping together, which left the other bedroom for Garrett to use as a studio and hiding place. That room was overflowing, though, so he needed to move the numerous canvases to the storage closet downstairs.

Although they shared the same bed, sex had not returned with the reunion. He could not remember their last intimate encounter, and he feared his self-doubts would result in impotency and sabotage any romantic overtures. Delthea seemed content to once again lie side-by-side. Underlying his other reservations was the inescapable awareness that she might have slept with another man since she made love to Garrett. He couldn't be certain, but he usually read Delthea well enough to believe it might be true. If it was, he blamed himself.

Realizing he needed a break from the easel before him, Garrett initiated a game of gin with Berta. They had started doing this in the week since his recovery – after her soaps were over and when he needed to do something besides paint – so Delthea would not come in and surmise that was all he had done all day, which it was.

"Today's my last day," Berta said, discarding a king.

It had been a week since his remarkable recovery. Any minute now Garrett expected Delthea to hurry in the door, throw her briefcase on the couch, kiss him on the cheek, and thank Berta again for "hanging in there while we saw this thing through."

Garrett studied his cards. "Oh, yeah? How are you going to convince Delthea of that?"

"I'm not. We're adults. We can do as we please." She gave Garrett an appraising look. "Or, at least, I can. Besides, I got a new grandbaby ready to make his début."

He drew something worthless off the deck, and discarded his queen. "That's who you were making the afghan for." He hated the idea of losing her. She had been his companion for three months.

"Yeah, and I just won another nickel off of you." Berta picked up his queen and announced, "Gin." With a grin, she slipped his cards out of his hand, tallied his points, and marked their scores.

She stood and stuck out her hand, palm up.

Garrett pulled a quarter from his loosely fitting jeans. "This is for all the times I cheated."

Smiling, Berta pushed his hand aside. "Keep it. How do you think I ever manage to win?" She grabbed her coat and bag. "Take care; you're my only living patient. I wouldn't want anything to happen to you."

"Nor to you, Berta. We would have been lost without you." Garrett walked Berta to the door and then hugged her long and hard.

On the way to the elevator, she pulled tissue from her pocket and blew her nose. He knew how she felt. They needed to get on with their lives, but like Delthea, it was hard to move beyond what had grown comfortable – the two of them here at the condo and Delthea at work every day.

Garrett walked to his closet and flipped through his suits, every one of them three sizes too big. Then he studied himself in the mirror. His hair was longer then it had been since cutting it short right before he started his internship. And his beard was reminiscent of those days as well – not nearly as long, but certainly more like his college days than how he typically wore it now. Looks mattered little compared to what he would actually do once he returned to the office. It had been two years since he practiced psychology. First, editing the book occupied him, then promoting it, and finally the illness. What if he attempted a counseling session and drew a blank? What if someone asked him about his new book, the one Delthea had cautioned him to at least outline enough to discuss? Hell, why didn't he go ahead and write the damn thing? It would be easier than pretending to be a therapist again.

Checking his watch, Garrett wondered why Delthea was late. He picked up the phone to call and suggest she meet him at the Galleria. Then he replaced it, sure she would say something about it being too early for him to get out on his own, and that he could deal with the crowds better after Christmas.

Berta had escaped, and he could too. After scrawling a quick note, Garrett grabbed his leather bomber jacket, the one Delthea repeatedly put in the giveaway pile because it would never fit him again and now did. Garrett dug his car keys out of her lingerie drawer where Delthea had hidden them when she thought he was sleeping. He had to vamoose before he lost his nerve.

The Galleria was decked out in Christmas decorations from the ceiling of the three-story building to the massive Christmas tree on the ground floor. Garrett walked from one store front to another before he found himself drawn inside a toy store where he browsed randomly up and down the aisles, first thinking of Loc and then of Morgan, the mythical son that Abi had told him about in his dreams. A saleswoman stopped him and asked if she could help.

"What would a ten-year-old boy be interested in?" he asked.

"A lot of them like He-man action characters." She plucked a blister card from the wall that contained a muscle-bound doll and handed it to Garrett. "They come with a book," the older woman said, pointing to a tiny paper booklet tucked in behind the grotesque character.

If he had a son, surely he wasn't interested in stupid looking dolls like this. Garrett carefully re-hung the toy and thanked the lady for her help. What did Morgan look like? The paintings? No, they were only his imagination, just like the dreams and Abi's friend calling.

*   *   *

Totally *knackered*, Moa walked while Ian, using his crutches, hobbled beside him. A soccer practice had just ended, and Moa was cooling off while Ian pointed out how he could improve his game. Not about to say it, Moa thought how being a bystander had made his friend an expert. It didn't matter what Ian talked about as long as he kept the conversation going. Moa didn't want his mind to wander because he immediately thought of his mum and how much he missed her.

Finally, running out of anything else to discuss, Moa brought up something that had been bothering him. "Ian, how well do you know your dad?"

"My dad?" Ian repeated, looking at him like he was crazy. "What do you mean? I know him like anybody knows their dad."

Moa stared straight ahead. "Well, I don't. I didn't even know I had a dad for a long time."

"What ya think? You were the immaculate conception?" Ian paused in his hobbling long enough to poke Moa in the shoulder.

"No, I thought he was dead. At least, that's what I grew up thinking. Mum and I used to do this stupid game where we made up stories about a boy and his mum, and the way we told it, I always knew the boy was me. Before she died, Mum told me my dad wasn't dead, but he doesn't even know I exist."

Moa snuck a peek at Ian whose face said to keep talking. "While I was home for her funeral, I found this book in Mum's room. A bloke who has the same name as my dad wrote it. And his picture on the back inside cover looks like the pictures Mum painted of my dad – at least his eyes do, not his long hair and beard like in the paintings."

"All those paintings at your house were of your dad?" Ian asked.

"Yeah. In the book he has short hair and he looks a lot older." Moa bent down and picked up a stick. "I guess, Mum remembered him the way he was when she knew him."

"So, what are you going to do?" Ian asked.

"I don't know that there's anything I can do. Mum didn't want me to go back to the States." Moa bent the stick until it snapped into two pieces.

"The States?" Ian asked, like that meant something to him.

"He's a psychologist in Houston, Texas, or that's what it says in the book. I've been reading it. It's pretty goofy. You know, adult stuff about your thoughts and all that."

Ian nodded like he understood about how strange adults can be. "My dad travels all over the world. He does stuff with oil, and he ends up in Houston a lot. You ever been there?"

"I've never been away from New Zealand. I can't. I heard Mum tell my grandmother that we couldn't leave since we came here without passports. Colin smuggled us in aboard the freighter trip he worked on. Nobody even knows we're here."

Ian scrunched up his forehead. "Of course people know you're here. Your mum registered you for school, didn't she?"

"She has my birth certificate, but that's all." Moa threw one side of the stick as hard as he could.

"I think that's all you would need to get a passport," Ian said, sounding like he knew what he was talking about.

"Why would I want a passport?" Moa asked.

"To go to Houston, of course, you ninny." Using his crutches for additional strength, Ian shoved Moa hard enough to knock him off balance.

Moa righted himself, ignoring Ian's goofiness. "But my dad doesn't know I exist. And Mum said I couldn't ever go there."

"How she going to stop you? My mum told me not to do plenty of stuff before she died."

"Is that when you started going to this school, when your mother got sick?" Moa asked, amazed that Ian could talk about her without acting like a *sook* like Moa always did.

"Naw, I've been here for eight years. My father went here and my grandfather and his father. It's tradition." He didn't sound happy or sad. That was just it, the way it was.

Moa hated the idea of spending the next eight years at this school. Ian made it bearable, but it still was not home.

"You know, I bet my dad's secretary could get you a passport. She could even find information on how to contact your dad. She's great at doing stuff like that. I think she has a crush on my dad, so she does anything I ask her to."

"She doesn't have to. There are two phone numbers written in the book. One says home and the other one says office. That makes me wonder if my mom has called my dad and maybe he even knows about me." Moa was glad he had someone to talk to about all this.

"Great, we'll call him. I've got a credit card I use to call my dad."

"What if Mum hasn't talked to him? That might be too much for an old guy, to all the sudden find out he has a son." Moa got what mum called the *heebie-jeebies* just thinking about talking to his dad, especially since his mother had told him not to.

*   *   *

Abi rested beneath her tree, the same place where she had often spoken with Garrett. Since her death, she had sometimes retreated to this refuge. Of course, Garrett couldn't meet her here now. She could watch him, and she often did. Often, that had to do with time, which didn't have any relevance for her now. She moved forward and backward in time with the same ease that she moved back and forth between Garrett and Moa. She hadn't managed to get her mind around it yet, but it actually felt like she was with both of them at the same time.

"Sort of interesting, isn't it?" a man's voice said.

He was next to her. Although neither of them had a body, she knew he was there and she knew where she was. It was an interesting aspect of her current condition that she had yet to understand. Abi had no idea how or when the man had joined her. She had not spoken with anyone since she left her body. While she did not feel lonely, the prospect of having someone to talk to intrigued her.

"What did you say about something being interesting?" Abi asked.

"The phone number dilemma, isn't it interesting?" he asked. His gentle voice suggested a smile, although she had no idea what he looked like since she could not see him.

"Yes, it is," she agreed, curious how he seemed to read her thoughts as well as Moa's.

"Like you are able to know what your loved ones are thinking, I know what you are thinking," he said, clearly reading her mind.

"Who are you?" she asked.

"It doesn't matter. Just consider me a guide, someone who would like to help you make the transition from your human body to a heavenly being," he explained gently.

"You mean, I'm not completely dead?" she asked.

"Oh, yes, you are most certainly dead in the human sense of the word. It takes a while to acclimate to this new existence. Souls adapt in various ways and with the help of many or only a few others. I suspect, you'll be one of those independent souls, maybe even opting to stay with the living a little longer since you have some concerns for your son and his father."

All this talk about options, staying with the living, and being independent confused Abi.

"I know, it's more than you can comprehend, but eventually you'll understand completely."

Again she could not make sense of what he was saying. Somehow he read her thoughts. Why couldn't she read his?

"You can, my dear," he said, answering her unspoken question. "It will come." He laughed. "I nearly said 'with time' and as you've already discovered, we don't use that illusion here."

Yes, that was one of the few things she had figured out.

* * *

From outside Delthea's office window, the Houston skyline turned from amber to coral mixed with streaks of purple. Christmas lights had begun to twinkle on lamp poles and trees. Everyone was getting into the spirit of the season. She had finished writing her patient notes. A single envelope lay in the center of her clean desk – the call log from the front desk of the condos for the previous month. It arrived a week ago, but Delthea could not bring herself to open it. The report contained the answer to the question Garrett had asked Delthea: Did Abi's friend really call? Garrett had answered the phone, but because he had been taking a strong pain killer, she had convinced him he was confused.

Knowing she had tangible proof of Abi's continued interest in Garrett added to Delthea's guilt. God had done His part in restoring Garrett's health, but she had not upheld her end of the bargain. She had tried while lying next to him in their darkened bedroom, while they ate their evening meal, while they sat next to each other and watched TV, but the words would not come out. Not only had she vowed to admit her unfaithfulness, which would destroy what she had waited and prayed so long to regain, but she had also committed to finding Abi and their son. Plus, Delthea was pregnant by another man, a stranger, a hillbilly who had a huge bargaining chip, her ring.

As much as the thought of it made her stomach churn, she had to find Abi and Morgan. Garrett deserved to know he had a son. As many times as she had repeated this, she could not convince herself. Garrett made a point of closing the door on the bedroom he used as a studio, but unable to sleep for worrying about her unpaid debt, Delthea got up nightly and examined his work. Since his recovery, he had graduated from pencil sketches to vividly colored paintings. It also brought with it an amazing maturity of style. The scenery pictures did not bother her. While they did not look like the local terrain, they could have hatched out of his imagination or the results of a paint-along television lesson. His portraits of Morgan were another matter. They spoke clearly of his growing need to find the boy whose images appeared real enough to speak.

She took a deep breath and sliced the letter opener across the top of the envelope. Her heart ached with the realization that along with God accepting her deal, He also provided a means for fulfilling her end of the bargain. Ceremoniously, she slipped out the folded sheet of paper and opened it. Elaine's name was repeated most often along with the doctor's and lawyer's sprinkled in.

Takahe, appeared halfway down the page next to a phone number one digit shorter than the rest followed with a star. Delthea shifted her gaze to the bottom of the page where a notation indicated that the receptionist had failed to write down the entire phone number. A wave of relief washed over Delthea as she studied Abi's phone number. God had given her a reprieve. How could He expect her to call her with only a partial phone number? Besides, she wasn't even sure this odd name belonged to Abi's friend. Of course, who else could it be? The date and time fit.

On the way out of the building, Delthea whistled a hollow tune. She wanted to feel good about her stay of execution, but she could not. A temporary suspension only added to her misery. Before she opened the letter, she almost believed she could contact Abi. Now, she knew she couldn't – with or without a phone number. She loved Garrett too much to hand him over to another woman. Still, her unpaid debt gnawed at her like something chewing on her insides.

*   *   *

Before they left the house, Delthea asked why Garrett did not get a haircut while he was out last night. If he was determined to come back to work, surely he should look the part. But there was something within him that resisted. He was a changed man. Over the last year, he had become someone he did not know or recognize.

On the way to work, Garrett dutifully took notes as Delthea gave a running commentary on things he should remember about their patients. Mrs. Wood and all the rest would insist upon filling him in themselves. Telling in graphic details about their latest disturbing encounter or emotional setback motivated these patients to come back week after week. Many of them had been their patients since Delthea and Garrett started their practice five years ago.

"Mrs. Hemphill's dog died last week, so if you see her, say something sympathetic. Of course, you'll read their charts before you see anyone, won't you?" The look on her face said she was not sure what he would do. He was, after all, coming to work in spite of her insistence that it was too early.

"Of course." He sketched her profile in the border of the yellow legal pad. The early morning sun bouncing off of her blonde hair gave her a halo effect. "I probably won't see a patient for the first week or so. Like you said, I need to get back in the groove." Most of all, he needed human contact with someone outside those condo walls.

Her jaw set and her eyes darting from side to side, Delthea jockeyed through the congested traffic with the skill of a racecar driver. Garrett recalled feeling the same aggressive tendencies most of his life. When he drove the day of his remarkable recovery and yesterday on the way to the mall, he found himself moving slower than the speed limit and looking for opportunities to let other drivers into the flow of traffic. His illness had changed more than his shirt size.

When they walked into the office, Judy's stood up open-mouthed. "Dr. Clay, is that you?"

"Yes, long-haired and bearded, and you look more lovely than ever." He hugged Judy and made a mental note to order her favorite flowers, pink roses. She and Delthea routinely conflicted, so Judy was probably overdue for a little recognition.

Delthea grabbed his arm, guiding him past the door and down the hall. "That wasn't particularly professional. Do you plan on getting physical with all of our patients?"

"No, I just thought – well, I mean, Judy is more than an employee, she's – "

"– incompetent," finished Delthea, unlocking Garrett's office.

She stepped across the hall to her office and immediately returned with an armload of thick files, which she deposited on his empty desk. "You might want to spend the week re-familiarizing yourself."

As Garrett dropped into his chair and began sorting, Delthea left. Most of the names looked familiar. Leafing through the recent notes, he saw that their problems remained consistent as well. It was a travesty to keep these patients coming back year after year. They would be better served if he encouraged them to get a hobby or join a club or a bridge group or do volunteer work at the hospital. Any of those would be more fulfilling than rehashing the past without resolution.

What would Delthea think, though, if he followed his conscience on this matter? She referred to these long-term patients as their lifeblood, the mainstays of the practice. Didn't that make him and Delthea leeches, sucking their patients for their insurance money or, worse yet, their cash?

Unable to stomach the truth, Garrett shoved the folders to the front of his desk and retreated to the yellow legal pad. Delthea had handed it to him when he reached for his sketchbook on the way out of the apartment that morning. She was right; he had no reason to draw at the office, except that when his hand moved in swift, sure movements over the paper, his heart beat steady and his mind relaxed.

Several drawings later, Garrett remembered to call in an order for pink roses, and then he sauntered down the hall. On his way out of the restroom, he met Delthea coming at him, Mr. Gregory trailing her. The highly educated, middle-aged man began therapy several years ago with a severe inferiority complex, sure that everyone at his work perceived him as inadequate. His cowering expression had not changed.

Mr. Gregory saw Garrett, and his eyes lit up. "Dr. Clay, good to see you, although you do look different. Will you be sitting in on my session?"

Garrett hesitated, reluctant to interfere, but also eager to respond favorably to his former patient's momentary improvement. Delthea gave Garrett a steely gaze.

"Actually, I'm – I'm . . . ." Garrett hedged, not sure what to say.

"Dr. Clay is busy on his next book," Delthea interjected as she ushered their patient down the hall toward her office.

"You're due a short break then," Mr. Gregory called back, as if addressing an old fishing buddy. Apparently, Delthea had made more progress than Garrett had initially thought.

"For only a minute," Garrett relented, unable to resist the temptation to observe exactly how much Mr. Gregory had changed.

Feeling the need for some kind of prop, he retrieved his legal pad from his office. When Garrett walked into Delthea's office, she sat facing Mr. Gregory. The chair Garrett had always occupied was gone, so he rolled the desk chair to his customary place.

Delthea asked Mr. Gregory about his week, to focus on one thing that had gone well since they last met, and finally what he wanted to work on today. It was an old dance with comfortable familiar steps. Fully aware that Delthea would resent his involvement, Garrett resolved to nod and say nothing.

While Mr. Gregory told about making a well-received presentation at work, Garrett began sketching his portrait, impressed with Mr. Gregory's marked improvement from the man he had last seen. It seemed a shame not to give him a final vote of confidence and release him. On the other hand, he dared not challenge Delthea on this issue since she had worked so hard to maintain their practice.

"Mr. Gregory just asked you a question," Delthea said sternly.

"I'm sorry. I was thinking about how much progress you've made, Mr. Gregory, and I didn't hear what you said." Garrett examined his former patient's face.

"You seemed distracted, like you didn't care what I was saying," Mr. Gregory whined, reverting to old behaviors.

"On the contrary, I was blown away by the new you," Garrett countered, not sure how to deal with Delthea and Mr. Gregory at the same time.

"I can tell you weren't making notes. From here it looks as if you're drawing something, like you're bored," he accused.

Delthea gave Garrett a skeptical look.

"During our first sessions, you wrestled with how others saw you, isn't that right?" Garrett asked, inspired, but not sure if he should follow his instincts.

Mr. Gregory nodded.

"Look how you've changed." Garrett handed him the pad.

Mr. Gregory examined the drawing, his face reflecting the confident image on the paper. A toothy grin beamed at Garrett when he looked up. "This is amazing. May I keep this? I'll put it in my planner to remind me of how much confidence I have gained." His glow had returned.

The session continued with Garrett steadily building up Mr. Gregory's ego as Delthea faded into the background. Garrett knew it was not right, and he was creating a rift between him and Delthea, but he felt powerless to do otherwise.

Chapter Thirteen

*A*bi and her newfound friend sat under her tree. Neither one of them had a body, yet she somehow knew he was male. The physical limitations of earth had left her, but she was keenly aware that she had not fully reached heaven, what or wherever that was.

"Our clarity from this perspective is amazing," Abi's companion said. "Like this family."

A scene unfolded before them of a man and woman in their late thirties surrounded by five children of varying ages from three or four to mid-teens. They sat around a table, each one focused on their sparsely filled plates and eating in silence. Empty serving dishes sat in the middle of the table.

"I don't understand. What's happening?" Abi asked, confused by his comment about clarity.

"Listen to their thoughts," he said.

Abi focused on the smallest child who was imagining herself outside playing house under a big tree in the backyard.

"You're getting it," he said. "Now try someone else."

She shifted to the oldest child, a boy. Angry images churned in his head of fist fighting with the man who sat next to him. The young man mentally cursed him and shouted his desire to leave the farm, start his own life, and be free of his father's expectation that he stay there and continue in his footsteps.

"Now check out what his father is thinking," he coached.

The older male was adding up a series of numbers having to do with the cost of seed, what they owed the bank, the car note, the taxes, and the payment on their equipment. He thought of his son next to him and thanked God for giving him a healthy boy to keep the farm going. With time, the boy would understand the opportunity he had in inheriting the land and a means of providing for his own family.

"We see clearly both of their perspectives," her companion said. "But neither of them can understand the other's. I was that young boy. I grew up resenting my father and the burden I perceived he had saddled me with, rather than appreciating the gift he had to offer."

Abi wondered if her new friend was more than a random stranger who had elected to help her.

"I am, but you won't recognize me until you're ready," he said, vague as usual.

She sensed a warm glow from him, which she interpreted as the equivalent of a spiritual smile.

"There you got it. That's exactly what I sent you," he affirmed, again reading her mind. "Have you experienced anything similar to what we have seen with this family in your own life? Think back to someone whom you now see differently."

Abi reflected on the people she had observed since leaving her body, Moa, Garrett, Takahe, Mama, Colin, and Vince. She recalled the scene of Vince sitting in front of the television. "Yes, there is one who really stands out, my ex-husband. I now realize how lonely and pathetic he is, not the intimidating brute that I once lived with."

"What else do you understand about him now that you did not realize before?"

With her developing ability to tune in to people's emotions, Abi listened carefully to Vince's thoughts. Initially, she got nothing except a hollow feeling. Then she picked up a sensation that she knew well – fear, of being alone, of not being worthy of another person's love, of dying without anything to show for this life. "We were so much alike," Abi admitted, stunned by the revelation.

"Most humans are alike in that respect. Fear is what disables everyone. It's not just you and Vince. Take a look at Delthea."

She focused on the woman who had married the man Abi spent the last decade loving from afar. Delthea sat at a massive desk in an expensively decorated office. Visions of her Austin lover, an unborn child, Abi's old things, and a lost ring clouded her vision. "She's already lost sight of how thankful she was that Garrett lived."

"See how fear has kept her from the very thing she bargained with God to get?" he asked.

"But God didn't make Garrett well, did He?" Abi asked, still not sure what had happened when she left her body and merged it with Garrett's.

"No, *God* doesn't make anything happen," he said, emphasizing the word God. "Humans decide. You have free will. Cutting deals with someone in heaven who is supposedly playing chess with people's lives is futile. It's what a human thinks that decides everything about their life, or rather how they perceive it. It's all about thoughts and attitude."

"Are you telling me it was what I thought that created the whole scenario that is now continuing on earth without me?"

"You're still very much there," he responded.

"How?" she asked, again confused.

"You are in your loved ones thoughts," he explained.

"But that's not me being there," she argued.

"The essence of you are in their subconscious thoughts. Newly born souls are totally aware of their divine connection. Then little by little as they grow into consciousness and lose touch with that."

Abi thought of Morgan and the totally consuming love she felt for him even before he was born.

"Exactly. The subconscious is actually where the soul resides. It is who you are, whether you inhabit a body or whether you are sharing other souls' current bodies. When you and Garrett met at the park, those were your semi-subconscious thoughts, halfway between conscious and subconscious. You are still and will always interact with those you are connected with on a soul level. Because you are not ready to shift to a subconscious state, you are still tuning in to their conscious thoughts, which are mostly clouded by fear, not the truth of who they are. What humans do in their daily lives is nearly always far removed from their soul selves."

"Wait a minute. Are you saying that I had dream experiences with a lot of people, not just Garrett?" Abi asked.

"You are still communicating with others on a subconscious level. Most souls are not as connected as you and Garrett. When you are ready, you will move fully into a subconscious state of being, but you will never lose your connection to Garrett. Once you enter completely into your subconscious thoughts, you will have the option of remaining in the spirit world or returning to the physical plane in another body."

Excited by the prospect of choices, Abi asked, "Have you lived more than one life?"

"Yes, many, and most of them with you in some form or fashion, but that is beside the point. Let's get back to your conscious merging with your sub-conscious."

"Are you at that subconscious level now?" Abi asked.

"Yes, but that doesn't keep me from communicating with you. It's part of what we do at this level of existence; we answer the questions of the new arrivals and guide them along the path." He gave her one of his spiritual smiles, and she picked up on an aspect of his personality that had attracted her initially but she hadn't deliberately thought about; he had a genuine, loving nature. He was, in fact, the epitome of love.

"That's the essence of who I am," he explained. "I see the same in you. That's what our souls are, an expression of love without the trappings of the human ego."

Abi did not understand how all of this fit together, not the mind reading that seemed so easy for him, or the part about being in a subconscious state of being. None of it made sense.

"When you are ready, it will make perfect sense," he said, his presence leaving her.

Glad to be alone again, Abi pondered what they had discussed, specifically about still being alive in her loved ones' subconscious. That idea appealed to her, but she had no idea how to get there.

*   *   *

"This is the book I was telling you about." Moa laid his father's book on the desk where Ian was studying. Opening it to the back cover, he added. "And this is my dad – I think." Ever since they talked about it yesterday, Moa had been considering Ian's offer to call his dad.

Ian studied the picture. "He looks pretty normal to me."

"Of course, he is," Moa said. "Why wouldn't he be?"

"Psychologists can be really weird. My dad sent me to one after my mom died. He was strange," Ian explained.

"Mum was daft about this guy." Talking about Mum made Moa miss her.

"Yeah, I figured that from all the paintings. Except he looks really different in this picture." Ian pointed to the older, more dignified version of Moa's dad.

Moa preferred the portraits Mum had painted that hung all over the inn. The painted version looked like he wanted to laugh and talk and he might even want to go out hunting. This *tightarse* looking bloke wouldn't want to do anything fun. "I hate to spend your money on calling my dad," Moa said, knowing it must cost a lot. Plus, the idea of talking to a man he might dislike, gave him the willies.

"It's my dad's money; and he won't know since his secretary will pay the bill," Ian explained.

"When should we call?" Moa's stomach was doing flip-flops.

"Well, the time difference will get in our way. You've got two numbers here, one for his office and one for his home."

Although the handwriting was faint and shaky, Moa recognized it as his mother's. She must have done it when she was really sick, probably toward the end. Again, he wondered if she had talked to his dad. Maybe that was why she was so intent on Moa not calling him. The last time she called, Takahe had tried to get her to say something, but she wouldn't. After the funeral, Takahe encouraged him to look through Mum's things and take what he wanted. She had to know he would find this book.

"It's tricky to get my dad at his office number," Ian explained, like they were working through a math problem, except this time he understood better than Moa. "If he's at his office, and I get Lisa, no problem, but most of the time, he's at somebody else's office, and I've got to convince them that I really need to talk to him. Then you've got the time difference problem."

Amazed by Ian's worldliness, Moa waited for him to finish working through the problem aloud.

"At your dad's house, we'll have to deal with other people who might pick up, like a girlfriend, or he may be married."

"Mum said he was, and they have a son. That's why she left when she found out she was pregnant with me." Remembering that conversation made his chest feel like a brick rested on it.

Ian grimaced. "That will make it difficult, but I still think that is our best bet. We're only allowed to use the phones in the early evenings, except on weekends, and there is a six-hour difference in the time. They are six hours ahead of us. Actually we are eighteen hours ahead of them, because the time changes to a new day here before it does there, but it feels like they are six hours ahead of us since it's twelve o'clock noon there and only six in the morning here."

Moa was glad Ian had all that sorted out in his head, which was pretty amazing since he generally wasn't good with numbers.

"Let's call Saturday morning before we get on the bus to go to the game," Ian decided.

They had a soccer match, Moa's first game with another school. With his leg still in a cast, Ian would sit on the sidelines and cheer. Funny, but the cast or why he wore it didn't seem to bother Ian. It sure hadn't kept him and Ian from becoming the best of mates. Even though Moa was not sure about the whole idea of calling his dad, he was glad to have Ian as a roommate. It felt weird to remember now how much he had once hated him.

*   *   *

As quietly as possible, Garrett slipped out of bed. He wanted to move the paintings down to the storage closet before Delthea woke up. Since it was Saturday, they had not set an alarm. Like most nights, she had gotten up around two or three and been out of bed for several hours. He did not know if she read or wrote, but she obviously needed the time to process what was going on for her.

Garrett pulled on a pair of jeans, glad to wear his grunges again instead of the suit office life dictated. Back at work less than a week, and he was already dreading the idea of returning Monday morning. It wasn't the patients, although he often found himself thinking that very few of them really needed him or Delthea. The problem was actually his wife. He loved her, but he could not please her. If he sat in on a session, she expected him to say and do what they had always done. It no longer worked for him. He could not continue taking people's money and giving them practically nothing but friendship in return. When these people originally sought a psychologist, they needed help, but now they needed to get a life.

Fully intending to move the finished canvases, Garrett entered the second bedroom. He walked past the easel where a half finished picture of the curly-haired young boy sat. An almost physical force pulled at him, telling him to sit down and work for just a little while. Hopefully, Delthea would catch up on her sleep. Thinking he would only be there for a minute or two, Garrett settled himself in the chair and picked up his paintbrush. That peaceful, relaxed feeling returned. It was so highly addictive that hours passed unnoticed while Garrett labored over the eyes, bringing them alive with the perfect spec of color, shading the cheeks with just the right combination of pigments to get skin tone, adding highlights to the lively halo of hair. How did he know all of these techniques or that they even needed doing? Why was he so obsessed with spending his time this way?

When the phone rang, Garrett checked the clock. It was past eleven-thirty. It rang a second time as he reached for it. He and Delthea said hello at the same time. Elaine answered and she and Delthea immediately began talking. Garrett put the receiver back in the cradle and decided to take advantage of what likely would be a long conversation.

He randomly selected ten paintings and stacked them. Berta had bought the canvases for him, all of them the same size and stretched over a thin piece of cardboard so they stacked easily. While he handled the commercially prepared canvases, he mused over the possibility of building his own frames and stretching canvas over them. This might give them more bounce, which could possibly allow him to more effectively make the images come alive. This idea, like so much of what he worked through while creating a painting, seemed to come from an unknown source.

The down elevator was already occupied by a neighbor who lived one floor up. The man wore his graying hair in a ponytail that hung down his back, and he dressed in jeans and a denim shirt. He wore massive turquoise rings and bracelets. Somewhere in the recesses of his long-term memory rested the man's name, but Garrett could not remember it.

"How are you?" Garrett asked, feeling obligated to speak.

Ignoring the question, the neighbor said, "What do you have there?" He took the top canvas, one of the boy, out of the stack in Garrett's arms and scrutinized it with knowing eyes.

"It's just a hobby really," Garrett explained, uncomfortable with others viewing his work.

"This is actually quite good. Who have you studied with?" Mr. Ponytail asked, turning his scrutiny to the other canvases.

"Studied with?" Garrett repeated.

"This is not amateur work," the man remarked.

"Oh, yes, it is." Garrett wanted to take the painting back from him, but his hands were full.

The man lifted the next painting from Garrett's stack, another one of the boy. The elevator doors opened at the bottom floor as the man stared at it, apparently captivated.

"This is my stop." Garrett moved forward, hoping to discourage the man.

"There's something about your painting, man." Still holding the paintings, he followed Garrett out of the elevator and outside to the closets on the backside of the main floor.

The storage units were an option that Delthea had insisted they take advantage of even though Garrett had argued that they should get rid of stuff they no longer had room for in their condo. He doubted the storage unit contained much, and whatever was there needed to go in the trash. At number thirty-three, he set the paintings down next to the door. The nameless neighbor was still by his side.

"Look, I'm sorry, I don't remember your name, but I really don't think these paintings are worth your time."

"Harrison," the man said, adding the painting he carried to Garrett's stack and sticking out his hand. "I run an art gallery here in town, The Pentacle. Maybe you've heard of it. I'm generally not so taken with unknown artists, but this stuff is good. Have you done any shows?"

"No, I just started painting a few weeks ago." Garrett dug in his pocket for his phantom keys.

"No way, two weeks! That's unreal." Harrison began lining up the paintings along the wall.

"Look, I've forgotten my keys upstairs. Would you mind staying with these while I go get them?" He hated to leave a stranger with his work, but he sort of knew Harrison, and he could move more paintings while he got his keys.

After Harrison agreed, Garrett ran to the elevator. In the condo, he overheard Delthea still talking to Elaine. He rummaged through the kitchen drawers, looking unsuccessfully for the key. Sure that they had a duplicate at the front desk, he retrieved nine more paintings, the rest of them, from his studio and returned to the storage closet where Harrison was studying the original batch he brought down. Harrison eagerly grabbed the latest paintings, and Garrett walked to the front desk in the lobby.

Milton sat behind the counter, his eyes blood shot, his shirt wrinkled and buttoned crooked. He brightened when he saw Garrett. "Hey, Dr. Clay," he said, his words thick and slow.

"Hey, Milton. I'm trying to put some stuff in my storage unit, and I can't find my key. Do you have a backup?"

"I'm your man," he said brightly as he opened a drawer. "Let's see number thirty-four, right?"

"No, I think it's thirty-three," Garrett corrected.

"Really, I could swear I put that stuff for Dr. Richards in thirty-four." The phone rang and Milton absently reached for it. After slurring out the name of the condo building, Milton listened, and then replied, "I can try it again. Let's see that's five-thirty."

Still wondering what Milton meant about moving stuff for Delthea, Garrett was further intrigued when Milton said the number for his condo, five-thirty. On a clipboard, Milton wrote the name, Ian Witherspoon. The name was now written three times. The times were noted next to it, 11:45, 11:50, and now he wrote 11:55. Who was Ian Witherspoon and why was he calling his home? Maybe it was whoever Delthea would deny she met in Austin. Chill bumps prickled up Garrett's spine.

* * *

Delthea had barely had a chance to pee after getting off the phone with Elaine when the phone rang again. She hurried to it, thinking Elaine needed to reschedule the date they had set up for the next day. It was just like her to forget something like the fact that she had agreed to take an extra shift.

After Delthea answered, a jostling noise followed. It was probably a random sales call or a wrong number. "Is someone there?" No doubt Milton had switched the phones to ring without going through the front desk switchboard. She had seen him do that when he stepped out for a smoke.

"Hello," said a timid young boy's voice. "Could I speak with Garrett Morgan Clay?" He had a foreign sounding accent, not quite English, but very close.

A young boy asking for Garrett by his complete name could only be his son. But where had the accent come from, and why was he calling instead of Abi? Delthea had absolutely no idea how to respond. Her mind was blank. She could deny he lived there, but Milton may have rung them through, which meant he had verified their name and who they were calling.

"Is he there?" the boy wanted to know.

"No, he's not. He's gone on a business trip," Delthea blurted out, needing to get rid of him. But if he didn't reach Garrett by phone, he and Abi might show up in person.

The boy conferred with someone in the background, no doubt his mother. She was certainly the clever bitch, putting Morgan on instead of asking for Garrett herself. No doubt she knew about Delthea and did not want to deal with her directly.

"Has he gone on a book tour?" the boy asked.

"Yes, that's exactly where he is. He won't be back for three weeks." By then Delthea could have their phone number changed. She should have done it right after Abi's friend called, but at the time, she had thought Garrett was dying. That's when she made a deal, which might have everything to do with this phone call. Was this God's way of making her fulfill her side of the bargain?

"I'll call back then," the boy said sadly.

Delthea hung up and stepped away from the phone.

"Who was that?" Garrett stood in the bedroom doorway. How long had he been there? What, if any, of the conversation had he heard? Delthea could not remember the last thing she said to the boy.

"Are you all right?" he asked, moving toward her.

"I'm fine. I just have to pee." Delthea raced to the bathroom and sat on the commode behind a closed door and shook.

After a light tapping on the door, Garrett said, "Who is Ian Witherspoon?"

"Who?" Delthea asked at a total loss.

"Ian Witherspoon," he repeated.

"I have no idea."

"He's the person you were talking to," Garrett shot back.

She had to think fast. New client? No, Garrett would never buy that. She wouldn't give out their home number. How the hell did he know who had just called? She would find out later. "Oh, Ian. You're not supposed to know about him. It's a Christmas surprise." The lies came easier and easier.

"Sorry, I didn't mean to spoil your fun." His voice got farther away. "I'm putting some stuff in the closet downstairs. Do you have anything that needs to go down there?"

No! She could not let him find Abi's things. She had to stop him, but how? Dear God, how?

*   *   *

Intrigued by the complexity of the scenario, Abi watched Garrett ride the elevator to the ground floor, totally baffled by his wife's illogical actions. He wanted to believe Delthea was planning a surprise for him, but her irrational behavior of late did not coincide with what she had said. Her negative reaction to him moving his paintings further confused him. At first she hated the paintings, but now that he was moving them out of the condo, she was begging him to leave them be.

At the same time, Delthea conjured possible explanations concerning Abi's things while she quickly dressed. As she rode the elevator down, she felt a wave of relief that the truth was finally going to come out. As hard as it was to deal with how badly it would hurt Garrett, at least, she could quit living a lie.

After Garrett introduced her to Harrison, she surveyed the storage closet, which now held Garrett's paintings and the few items she had placed there herself. Milton had screwed up – again. Thank God. But what had he done with Abi's boxes?

"She's still stuck, isn't she?" Abi's companion said, close by once more.

"Her dilemma reminds me of myself. I was sure I shouldn't tell Garrett about Moa. Now I see that they need each other desperately. When I was there, I couldn't see it."

"Of course not. Here you have several advantages. For one thing, you have a clear view of all the players, so to speak. Secondly, you don't have the human involvement, the distortion that comes from living in a body and seeing from only one point of view. Thirdly, and probably most significant, you've moved beyond the fear. That's what kept you married to Vince, but once you got beyond that, it also kept you away from Garrett or from anyone who wanted to love you."

"Are you talking about Colin?" Abi had viewed Colin's thoughts where she verified that he loved her dearly and would have gladly given up the sea if she had been willing to marry him.

"But you were too scared, weren't you?" her companion asked.

For a loving being, her guide could also be very annoying.

"The truth does hurt," he said and once again left.

"No, wait, don't go."

"Yes?" he answered.

"Is this the price I have to pay? Do I have to realize all of my mistakes before I go to the next level, to my subconscious like you mentioned before?"

"There is no price to pay. That sounds too much like what humans call hell. When you are ready, you'll move on, not before." His spirit faded again.

"Good riddance," she muttered, annoyed at the ambiguity of this place that wasn't really a place.

Chapter Fourteen

*A*ll around her, people entered the coffee shop, sat down, were served, and left while Delthea waited for Elaine, who was later than usual. She would breeze in an hour from now, not even bothering to explain why she couldn't get here on time. When they set up this meeting yesterday, Elaine hesitated to commit since David or Kent might come up with something to do since they were off for Christmas break. Delthea wanted to leave, but she needed what Elaine had promised to give her.

"Hey, Dilly Deli, what's cooking?" Elaine slid into the booth opposite Delthea. Her hair had been cut short and permed into tight corkscrew curls all over her head. She poked at it with her fingers. "What do you think?"

"It looks . . . youthful," Delthea said. And it looked ridiculous on someone Elaine's age and size.

"No more fuss – just wash it, shake it out, and go." Elaine demonstrated by shaking her head.

The waitress arrived with a menu and a glass of water for Elaine, who ordered the breakfast special, coffee, and grapefruit juice.

"You don't even know what the breakfast special is," Delthea scolded, as she watched the thin waitress saunter away.

"So I'll be surprised. It'll be the highlight of my day." Elaine took out a cigarette and tapped it on the table. "Don't let me forget to call Monday and schedule a time for David to see Garrett. The school is giving me a hard time about David not fulfilling his end of the bargain on that discipline thing. When they go back from Christmas break, I've got to have something going or David is off to juvee."

"I'll tell Judy to call you about it." Thinking what an unfit parent Elaine was, Delthea pulled her planner from her bag and noted David's need for an appointment. She thought about why she and Elaine were meeting and what kind of parent that made her. "Did you bring that name and number?"

Elaine cleared her throat. "Yeah, I got it." She lit her cigarette. "Are you sure that's what you want to do?"

It had been a hard enough decision to make without her sister second-guessing it. "I can't have this baby. Garrett would know it's not his. We haven't had sex in over a year."

"But is an abortion going to solve the problem? You tell me if not telling your husband what happened in Austin is going to magically make it go away." Elaine blew a plume of smoke above their heads. "Obviously, it hasn't if you haven't resumed sex since Garrett recuperated."

Delthea chose to ignore Elaine's comments by changing the subject. "You won't believe who called after you and I got off the phone yesterday morning."

After screwing her mouth sideways, Elaine guessed, "Abi's mom called again."

Her response impressed Delthea. She never knew when her sister was really listening. "No, worse. Her son. I'm sure Abi was coaching him, but they were smart enough to give him an alias, Ian Witherspoon. Doesn't that sound like some hunky guy in a cheap romance novel?"

Elaine stared at her, uncharacteristically silent.

"I'm having my phone number changed, so they can't call again." Elaine didn't respond, so Delthea lifted crumbs from the table, using the tip of her index finger and dropping them on her plate.

The waitress returned with two platters that overflowed with eggs, ham, and blueberry waffles. It looked much more appetizing than the dry toast Delthea had eaten an hour ago.

"What if they get the new one the same way they got the last one?" Elaine cut up her waffles and drowned them in syrup.

"I'll cross that bridge when I get to it." Delthea eyed Elaine's breakfast, wondering if she would eat all of it. "I have other issues to worry about – like what happened to Abi's things. I asked Milton to put them in my storage closet, but when Garrett took his paintings down there, they weren't there."

"Sounds like God is giving you a reprieve on your deal you told me about yesterday. You get an abortion, a new telephone number, forget about Abi's stuff, and things can go back to normal. Right?"

If only it were that simple. Delthea stole a quick look at Elaine's somber expression.

"You know you can't do that, Deli. I don't have any room to talk when it comes to successful marriages, but I can tell you living a lie is not going to get you back to where you want to be." She bit into a huge piece of ham.

Delthea knew that. She had mentally gone through all of this a thousand times. Nothing was right. She felt guilty for everything she had done. Besides all that, Garrett wasn't happy at work. He obviously had no interest in what she had worked so hard to maintain. He would rather paint than do anything else. And he was good, even that goofy looking gallery owner said he would like to do a show for him. Eventually, Abi would make contact with Garrett. She had tried three times, first through her mother, then her friend, and yesterday her son.

"What are you thinking?" Elaine asked around another mouthful of ham and eggs.

"That you're right, but I have no idea how to deal with all this. I've buried myself so deep in lies that I have no idea where to start being honest with Garrett."

"Start at the beginning. Tell him about getting the birth certificate and deciding to go to Austin to check it out. Tell him you found Abi's stuff, and it upset you so much that you left the room and ended up spending the night with some guy you barely know, that you lost your ring in his room, but you picked up a souvenir of the evening. Tell him about Abi's mom calling, that someone really did call and say that his dreams were true, and that his son called yesterday looking for him. Let him know that Milton put Abi's stuff in God knows whose storage unit. And that you're thinking about having an abortion, but you thought you would check with him before you proceeded."

"Oh, sure, why not? It would be suicide to tell him all that. Elaine, he'd leave me – with good reason. He'd go looking for his son and for Abi." Tears threatened, but she wasn't about to break down now, not after all she had been through.

"It's your decision. With the way things have shaken out, you could probably get away without telling Garrett anything that's happened. You could probably even convince him to start a family if you ever resume having sex. That is what you wanted, isn't it, to have kids and do the mother routine?"

"Yes, that's exactly what I want." Delthea understood what Elaine was saying. She understood it altogether too well.

"What would you tell one of your patients if they were in your position?" Elaine shoveled a fork loaded with waffles into her mouth.

"I'd tell them that dishonesty was not a sound foundation for a marriage. I'd tell them that communication was the only real solution to any relationship issue." How many times had she preached those ideas to couples in the middle of conflict?

Elaine downed her grapefruit juice. "When are you going to tell him?"

"I don't know," Delthea muttered.

"Set a time and a place. Make a commitment to yourself, or it simply will not happen, and years from now, you'll still be kicking yourself." Elaine shoved the half-full plate to the center of the table. "I see two or three suicide attempts every week. Most of them are about guilt over something they wish they had said or done differently. Last week, I had a sixty-nine-year-old who emptied her medicine cabinet into her stomach because she regretted not telling her son that she loved him."

Delthea waited for the rest of the story.

Elaine sniffed. "The bastard died thirty years ago. They had argued the night before he left to go overseas with the army. She had forbidden him to join because she was scared he would die. And he did, and she never forgave herself. Is that fucked up, or what?"

More ravenous than she had ever felt, Delthea picked up Elaine's fork and began eating her leftovers. She had to abort the baby, but that didn't stop her body from wanting to eat.

"It's not going to be easy no matter which way you go, but you gotta try to look down the road and see where you eventually want to be," Elaine advised. "You could probably avoid telling Garrett any of this, but it's not really him you have to live with. It's you."

Elaine slid out of the booth, picked up her purse, and walked out. As Delthea polished off the ham, eggs, and waffles, she realized what Elaine had given her rather than the abortion doctor's name and phone number. She had confronted Delthea with what she could not accept – the truth, which made her harebrained, irresponsible sister right and Delthea wrong. There was no justice in that, none at all.

*   *   *

Seated in the back corner of Ninfa's, Garrett watched Delthea study her menu. She had reluctantly agreed to this place when she said at lunch today that they needed to have an in depth talk in a neutral spot. He wasn't sure what she wanted to discuss, but he still had an insatiable hunger for Mexican food, so this seemed as good as any. The waiter came by, so Garrett ordered two margaritas, figuring Delthea would sip hers. As soon as the waiter returned, set them on napkins, and walked away, Delthea drank half of hers and asked Garrett to order her a second one when he got a chance. She rarely drank more than one drink and even that she often left half finished.

Starting on the second drink, Delthea asked, "What do you want for Christmas?"

Garrett thought of her response when he asked about Ian Witherspoon. "The surprise you have planned sounds intriguing. You don't need to overdo." He had no idea what to get for her.

"Surprise?" she asked blankly.

"It has to do with Ian Witherspoon," he prompted.

"Oh, that," she said dismissively. While she finished the drink, she chatted about their quirky patients and what she wanted to buy Elaine and the boys for Christmas; remarkably, the two disjointed topics merged well under the influence of liquor.

While she talked, Garrett thought about her odd behavior Saturday when he was moving his paintings to the storage closet and how she had spent most of Sunday after she met Elaine for breakfast sequestered in the bedroom. He had suggested they take a walk, but she had opted to sit alone in the darkened room. In bed that night, she lay with her back to him, and when he put his hand on her shoulder, she had stiffened and said she really needed to sleep.

Delthea flagged the waiter over and ordered a third drink. She had not eaten any chips, and they hadn't even ordered food.

Garrett laid his hand over hers. "What's wrong? You're drinking too much too fast."

She chewed her bottom lip, not a good sign. "I've thought long and hard how to tell you this, whether to do it in a public spot or in the privacy of our home." She looked across the room and stared, blinking ever so slowly. It was her way of composing herself when she thought she might start crying.

It suddenly occurred to Garrett what troubled her. She wanted a divorce. It made sense. After putting up with his writing and book tours and then a lengthy illness, he now was unsupportive at work, a practice he had insisted they start in the first place.

She had never been able to resist his I-need-you grin, so he squeezed her hand, trying to get her to look at him. "You're the most precious thing in the world to me."

"Don't make this harder than it already is." Her drink arrived, and she gulped half of it.

"I haven't been there for you, but I can change. We can start a family. You've always wanted that. I've been selfish. Our lives have been focused on me, and that's not right. I'll do whatever it takes to keep the practice going, so you can be the stay-at-home mom you have always wanted to be."

She glanced up at him and immediately dissolved into suppressed sobs, her white cloth napkin pressed to her face.

"Look, don't say something tonight that you may regret tomorrow," he reasoned, her mounting sobs adding to his growing sense of urgency. What could he tell her to make her see that he loved her more than life itself?

The cloth napkin remained in front of her face as Delthea began to speak. "Garrett, I have to tell you this tonight, while I'm drunk, and I have the courage to say it. If I don't, I won't be able to live with myself. In forty years, I could be emptying my medicine cabinet into my stomach."

"What?" he demanded and pulled the cloth out of her hands.

"Never mind. I've just got to say it." She took a deep breath. "Do you remember the day I tore up Abi's pictures?"

He nodded. That seemed like a lifetime ago.

She grabbed the napkin back from him and dabbed at her eyes. "I did that because Bud Anderson gave me something that really upset me."

Bud Anderson? "Is this about Abi."

Delthea reached into her purse and pulled out an envelope. She handed it to Garrett. "This is what Bud gave me."

He looked at the outside of the blank envelope, and then he glanced up at Delthea. Ever since he had gotten well and the dreams stopped, he had not thought about Abi, although he did think about the mythical son she had described in his dreams and continued to show up in his art work.

"Look at it," Delthea ordered, taking another swig of her drink.

He pulled out a piece of paper. Three smaller slips fell on his lap and one of them on the floor. Delthea watched him pick it up. The one on the floor had a phone number and a name, Mr. Truman. He glanced up at Delthea who offered no explanation, so he picked up the other slips in his lap. One had 'Abi's mom' written above a phone number with an eight-zero-six prefix, a Panhandle number. The last note had an Austin address and Abi's name written above it.

Delthea took another drink from her margarita. Garrett unfolded the full size piece of paper. At first it didn't make sense. It was a form of some kind. Then he saw his own name and Abi's name and the name of the son Abi had told him about, Morgan Clay Barker. "Bud Anderson gave you this?"

She nodded, her face twisted with anguish.

"She told me in a dream that I had a son, but I thought he wasn't real because it was a dream. I even thought someone called and told me the dreams were real, but you said . . ."

Delthea's head was bowed. Her long blonde hair hung down hiding her face. "I lied to you. Someone did call. You talked to them. You do have a son."

Garrett cupped her head in his hands and forced her to look at him. "We have to find him."

"That's what I told God I would do . . . if he would make you well. And He did, and here I am fulfilling my part of the deal." Her red, swollen eyes brimmed with tears.

"Is this where they live?" Garrett held up the Austin address.

"No, I went there in October when I did that speaking engagement for Oliver. Mr. Truman was her landlord." She pointed to the paper he had picked up from the floor. "He gave me three boxes of her stuff, clothes, sketch pads . . . journals."

"Where are they?" Garrett couldn't believe what he was hearing. He felt like he was in another dream, one that made much less sense than the one he had shared with Abi.

"I don't know." Delthea propped her elbow on the table and supported her forehead with her hand. "I asked Milton to put them in our storage unit, but when you moved your paintings this weekend, they weren't there like I thought they would be."

"Did you ask Milton about that?" It wasn't like Delthea to let something like that go unchecked.

"No, no, I didn't." She lined up the silverware.

"Maybe we should go home and ask him." He grabbed her hand and pushed his seat back.

"There's something else I have to tell you." Without looking him in the eye, she told him about taking Abi's stuff back to her hotel room because she did not want it to fall into the wrong hands, reading her journal, and fleeing to the room of a cowboy who had taken her out to eat and dancing. "I don't remember making love, but . . ." She glanced up through her blonde bangs. ". . . I'm pregnant."

If someone had hit him in the head with a baseball bat, he would not have felt as stunned. He had thought she might have been with someone, but he never imagined this.

Even though he was numb and in shock, he understood why she had been so upset. He was too, but he didn't know which part of it to try to think about. "So you're telling me I have a son, and you're having another man's child."

Delthea nodded, her head bowed again.

Nothing had changed. But why hadn't it? It was one thing to rationalize that her having an affair with someone else was his fault. It was quite another to hear the words come out of her mouth. Remarkably, he still loved her as much as he ever had – maybe more so. His illness had changed him in ways he could not explain or comprehend.

Again, Garrett lifted Delthea's chin. "Do I still have a wife?"

"If you want me," she whispered.

"I love you, Delthea. You're the one who helped me put my life back together, not just once but twice. Nothing is ever going to stop me from loving you." He put his hand on her back, leaned forward, and kissed her salty-tasting lips. "But no more margaritas. They're not good for our baby."

"Our baby? Oh, Garrett, you called it our baby." Totally and undeniably drunk, she brought his face to hers, touching foreheads and noses.

He carefully wiped the tears from her face. No wonder she had been so upset. Realizing she had carried that burden alone while he was ill made him even more in love with her. A part of him wrestled with jealousy and betrayal, but another stronger side rejoiced at having his wife back and learning that he truly did have a son, a ten-year-old son. The dreams had been real.

* * *

"That's very nice," said Abi's sole heavenly acquaintance.

"Yes, it is," Abi agreed, glad to have someone with whom to discuss Delthea and Garrett. "Garrett seems all right with this situation, Delthea's affair and her pregnancy. His reaction is not a typical human response."

"There are several factors going on here, one of which both you and Garrett are totally oblivious – you are part of him now. Subconsciously, you've always been linked," he explained.

"Well, all the more reason for *us* to be a little upset. If I am part of what's going on here, wouldn't I be jealous of Delthea, the woman who loves my ex-lover?"

"You are now part of Garrett, and you are looking out for the best interest of yourself, Garrett, and also your son. She is your potential replacement, a mother to your son."

Her guide had a point. Meanwhile, Garrett was in the midst of searching his memories for other clues in his dreams. He reasoned that if the fact that he had a son were true, then other things Abi had said would help Garrett find him. When or if Garrett found Moa, Delthea would still be part of the picture. They had weathered much and would likely remain together.

"Garrett has seemingly dismissed what other men would hold against their wives forever, but he will revisit this in the future. After all, he is still human," her companion said.

"Vince nearly killed me when he suspected I had been unfaithful to him," Abi recalled.

"I remember that," he said.

"You were there? You knew me then?" She searched her memories for who this man could have been in her life.

"Oh, I was there, and an integral factor in shaping your life, but I didn't really know how closely our lives had been interwoven until I found myself in your current position."

Again, Abi explored her memories for who he could have been to her, a teacher, or a friend, which seemed highly unlikely since she never had any male friends – except Garrett.

"Not even close," he assured her. "Let's get back to Garrett and Delthea and your part in their future."

"What does that mean, my part in their future?"

"Your dying has allowed everyone to stop interacting with you on a conscious level. Except, Delthea, of course. She will battle with you until she realizes that you are no longer a threat to her. Right now you are engaged with all of them, even Delthea, on a subconscious level, a level beyond where you are now and beyond what most people can contact in human form."

"What does that have to do with *our* future?" Abi asked. "Am I going to end up with them?"

"If you want to," he said gently.

"But how? I mean, in what form, as an angel, or what?" she demanded, confused and frustrated by his ambiguity.

"You'll have to see how it unfolds."

A wave of panic told her she would spend the rest of eternity stuck in uncertainty.

"As I've said before, you'll go on when you're ready. What you're seeing now gives you insight into where you may want to go upon leaving this level."

"You mean I have a choice?"

"Of course, everything is a choice. Choosing your life as Abi was a choice, one you and Garrett made together before either of you was born."

"We decided that together?" She could not get her mind around such an idea. But why not? They had the same birthday. And they had instantly felt connected upon meeting.

"And when you were ill, he was too – for no apparent reason. You are soulfully connected."

"Could I join him?" She asked, still struggling with the limits or lack of limits in this situation.

"You always have been – as well as many other souls. You're just not aware of that yet since you are clinging to your humanness. In human form, it is nearly impossible to understand that your soul, who you really are, is not restricted to one body – even when you are inhabiting a body."

She was trying to take this in when he said, "Ask yourself what you fear. That will help you see what you still need to release."

"What I fear? My concern is for Moa. I want him to find Garrett, but I don't want him to go back to Texas. Vince isn't the threat he once was, but all Moa knows is Takahe and Colin. I don't want him to lose them for the sake of finding his father."

As if by mentioning him, another scene appeared. Moa and Ian were in their dorm room where Moa was packing his bag while Ian sat on his bed and watched him.

"Come to my house when you get back from seeing your dad?" Moa offered, as he wadded up a shirt and crammed it in the duffel bag.

He and Ian had been discussing their plans for the holiday break. Ian was flying to see his father for a few days, but most of his days off would be spent here at the school with Mr. Perkins. Moa thought it sounded like the dullest holiday imaginable. As for himself, he looked forward to going home, but he also knew that everything there would remind him of Mum.

"I'll talk to Perky about driving me over to your place." Ian wanted more than anything to spend the time he wasn't with his dad at Moa's home, but he wasn't sure how welcome he would be. During the holidays they might have a lot of guests, not that his dad wouldn't pay for him to stay there. For once in his life, he wanted someone to like him for who he was, not his dad's money. Ian figured money was the reason Perky let him spend the holidays there while everyone else was gone.

"The really sad part about this scenario is that Mr. Perkins relishes the idea of having someone to spend his holiday with. He has spent many years by himself," said Abi's guide.

Another scene appeared before them in which Mr. Perkins sat alone, staring blankly into space with an open book in his lap.

Abi wondered what purpose seeing all these scenes served.

"These scenes do have something in common," her guide explained. "They are all wrestling with fear. It is the factor that keeps you tied to

Moa. It is as disabling here as it was on earth. Imagine how much better Delthea feels now that she has faced her fear and told Garrett about Morgan and her pregnancy. Garrett's reaction was nothing like she imagined."

His presence began to fade. "What are you afraid to face?"

Abi thought about it. She was scared she wouldn't ever find the key to getting beyond her current condition. She feared never interacting with those she loved. She feared fear itself and the insidious hold it had on her life – even after she had died.

*   *   *

When Garrett got his inebriated wife home, he helped her undress, in the middle of which she needed to throw up. While she babbled about how grateful and wonderful Garrett was, he thought about his son. As soon as he had Delthea tucked in bed, he sat in the living room and went back through his journals from the end of his illness. Within them he searched for notations concerning the details Abi had given him in his dreams, clues to his son's whereabouts.

Finding nothing in his writing, Garrett returned to his sketchbooks, especially the ones that contained images of Abi drawn during the time when he dreamed about her. If he could only take himself back to that time, maybe he could remember exactly what she had said. He started a list along the edge of the paper as he recalled her mentioning a bed and breakfast in a rural setting that attracted visitors because of the thermal baths. She had friends there, Colin and Takahe. That name, Takahe had some significance. It had something to do with what they called Morgan, which was Moa. A bird. That was it. She had said Takahe knew that Garrett had called her Bird. And Moa and Takahe were also names of birds. Takahe, Songbird Inn, it now fit together as it had not when he was dreaming.

She had touched her nose against his as a greeting, which seemed like an Eskimo custom, but she had an accent, not English exactly, but like it. He thought of the phone conversation that Delthea had only that night admitted actually happened. The lady he spoke to also had an accent, the same as Abi's, but more pronounced. He intended to call Milton in the morning and find out where he put Abi's things. Garrett also decided to call Mr. Truman and Abi's mother. If he didn't have a clear idea of how to find her after chasing all of those leads, Garrett would call Bud Anderson and give him all of the information, along with whatever money it took to get him back on Abi's trail.

Garrett wondered how much his intended actions would disturb the bliss that his acceptance of Delthea's infidelity and pregnancy had induced. When she returned to a sober state would things still be *wonderful,* the word she had used over and over again on their way home. How would she feel about him finding his son? He had to. That was all there was to it. One son had slipped away to death's angry grasp. He would not lose another.

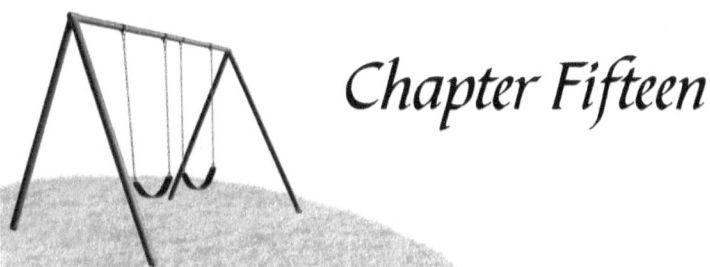

Chapter Fifteen

*H*er head pounded. It had ever since the alarm began screaming at her this morning. At first Delthea could not remember what happened last night. Then she caught a fleeting memory of Garrett tucking her into bed and telling her that, yes, everything was wonderful. When she staggered toward the kitchen sure that coffee would help, she saw Garrett asleep in his chair with sketchbooks and journals lying on his lap and on the floor, each one open to a picture of Abi. She was back.

Now Delthea sat at her desk at work, willing her headache to go away while she worried about what affects the alcohol might have had on her unborn child. When she began drinking last night, she told herself she needed the courage it gave her. Otherwise, she would never have been able to admit what she did in Austin. That was another time she had gotten drunk.

She couldn't change what she had done, but, at least, she could start taking better care of herself. She picked up the phone and made an appointment to see her gynecologist. Then she called Elaine, waking her from a sound sleep to tell her about how Garrett had reacted to her truthfulness. She carefully steered clear of relating how she had mustered the courage to tell him.

"Cool, I'll send you my bill," Elaine said, sleep slurring her words. "While I've got you, let's make an appointment for David with Garrett, or is he already off in pursuit of his son?"

"No, he's here." Delthea recalled that neither she nor Garrett had spoken in the car as she drove to the office that morning. He seemed preoccupied with notes he was making on a legal pad. Her head hurt so badly that she welcomed the silence. As soon as they walked in the office, Garrett went to his office and began making telephone calls, most likely to the numbers she had given him along with the birth certificate.

Elaine made rustlings noises in the background. "I think David's taken my cigarettes again. We got to get on this intervention thing."

Rather than preach to her about being a model for her children, Delthea set up an appointment for David to talk with Garrett the next day after school. She had to work on her own behavior before she started passing out advice about parenting.

She had barely hung up the phone when it rang again, Oliver calling to say he had heard Garrett was seeing clients again and was he up for taking a couple of domestic violence cases, a specialty Garrett had always eagerly accepted. She wrote down their phone numbers, thanked Oliver for thinking of them, and hung up, wondering if he remembered the cowboy who had called inquiring about how to reach her. What had Rhett told him to get her phone number? No matter. Garrett knew the truth, and he still loved her. While it would take Garrett some time to adapt to the idea of having a baby, he had made a commitment to do whatever it took to keep their business and their marriage intact.

The fog of alcohol would not allow her to remember clearly, but in hindsight, she recalled he said that immediately before she dropped the bomb about her affair and pregnancy. Still, he had taken her home, put her to bed, and driven to work with her. Without Elaine's disarming honesty, she might have aborted her baby and tried to hide the truth from Garrett. She had much for which to be thankful – even if guilt continued to nag at her for getting pregnant in the first place, and her head hurt like hell.

To make sure they got them in before the holiday weekend that was coming up, Delthea called the two couples, set up appointments, and wrote a note, alerting Garrett about David's as well as the two domestic violence appointments – all of it happening the following day.

* * *

Garrett sat at his desk, sketching Abi as he sifted through the foggy memories of his dreams.

After a quick knock, Delthea opened his office door. She shot him a happy grin, and literally waltzed toward his desk, a piece of paper flittering as her arms glided up and down. "You know how eager you've been to get started on seeing patients again. Well here are three appointments for tomorrow. David is last, so you can finish up with an easy one." As she laid the paper on his desk amidst the sketches of Abi, she visibly stiffened, her brows arched, and her smile faded.

Garrett had an urge to minimize what was clearly evident, but what could he say?

"What are you doing?" she asked stiffly.

"Trying to remember what Abi told me in my dreams. She said some things about where she lived, but she never gave me a specific town or even a continent. I need to look at the call log from last month. If Takahe is listed as the lady who called, then that verifies what I'm able to recall."

"He's ten years old. She may have remarried by now. If she wanted you to know where he was, she would have told you by now," Delthea reasoned in her most soothing therapist voice.

"I think she didn't tell me because I told her I was sick. She may have expected me to die, just like you and I thought I was going to die."

"But you didn't. You're alive, and you have a child to look forward to. I know he's not your biological son, but he's mine, and yours by extension. I can't tell you how happy it made me to know that you were willing to forgive me for my indiscretions."

He saw disappointment and fear in her eyes. "There's no forgiveness to it. Delthea, I love you, but that doesn't make me not want to find my son. I have to."

Needing to assure her of his allegiance, he considered telling her the phone calls had been futile. Even Abi's mother had denied knowing where she was. And Milton, moron that he was, did not have a clue about Abi's boxes. His ex-lover had always been a threat to Delthea, not just when he was sick, but from the very beginning, even before Loc and Trang died. Better to not say anything else about it.

The following day at lunch, Garrett and Delthea discussed the two cases he would see that afternoon. All morning he had attempted to read the files Oliver sent over via a courier, and all morning he had repeatedly retreated to his sketchpad as a knot grew in his stomach. He wanted to believe his ambivalence had to do with his preoccupation around finding Morgan, but the closer they got to the appointment times, the more he knew it had to do with the cases themselves.

Scowling and glancing in his direction while he sketched, Delthea peered at the folders before her. "It says here the police have come twice in response to the neighbor's calls. In fact, the judge has mandated these counseling sessions, or else the state will intervene by taking the kids out of the home."

"How old are the kids?" Garrett asked, doing his best to act the way Delthea expected him to.

"Ten, eight, and six. God, they're just little stair steps." Delthea pulled his drawing pad to her side of the desk. "You really need to eat something before you go in there."

His stomach churned even harder. Now the kids' welfare was part of the picture, which made his anxiety grow exponentially. When he read 'spousal abuse' on that piece of paper that Delthea put on his desk, he immediately felt a sense of apprehension. It didn't make sense. Back when he saw eight patients a day, a lifetime ago, he felt good about what transpired with his domestic violence cases. Was it simply so long ago, or was there more that fueled a growing wave of panic within him?

"The couples' names are Wayne and Valerie. They've been married fifteen years." Delthea bit on a carrot and read around chewing. "Right now the family is intact – everyone living under one roof."

He tried to process what she was saying, but all he heard was the pounding in his head. When she paused to take a breath, he interjected, "So why did Oliver send them to us?"

"It's not 'us' he's interested in. Oliver specifically asked that you take these cases." She pointed the carrot at him. "He thought you could help them."

Garrett turned his attention to his untouched salad. "We don't have any abuse cases right now."

Delthea glanced at her watch. "Last year I referred them to Paul Jackson since you two did so many of those together when we worked with Oliver."

"I'm not sure we should start with anyone else right now. Paul can take them," Garrett argued.

"You said you wanted to get involved again, and this is your specialty," Delthea countered.

"We shouldn't overdo, though, since I'm so out of practice and now that you're pregnant. Let's call Paul's office to see if he can take them." He hated to disappoint her, but it felt preferable to facing the demons that were clawing at his psyche.

"They're on their way if not already here." She gave him a stern look.

"You should've consulted me before accepting these," he argued, feeling a fresh wave of panic.

"You said you were eager to get back to work. Monday night at the restaurant, less than two days ago, you said you would do whatever it took to keep this practice going. Have you changed your mind?" She put the lid back on her bowl, covered his untouched food, and stuck both of them in the refrigerator hidden behind a filing cabinet.

Garrett's hand shook as he reached for his water glass. "I can't do this."

"Of course, you can, sweetheart." She put a reassuring hand on his shoulder. "You'll do fine."

When they walked into the waiting room, a small woman with mousy brown hair sat stiffly on the couch beside a huge dark-haired man. They were the new clients, Valerie and Wayne Olney. For some reason, the enormity of the man and the small woman sitting beside him felt miserably familiar. Garrett's dread gave way to an even stronger wave of terror that continued to build.

Muttering, "I'm sorry," to Delthea, Garrett hurried down the hall toward the restroom as he suppressed the bile in his stomach fighting its way upward.

*   *   *

Abi understood Garrett's anxiety because it matched her own when she looked at Wayne and thought of Vince. This was the first time since her death that she saw how much of her Garrett had inherited in her passing. Obviously, he had taken on her drawing and painting, but now she saw he had gotten the less than desirable traits as well, her specific fears. She thought about what the guide had said about her connection to Garrett. If she had the power to do so, she would give Garrett the strength to deal with what felt like an impossible situation.

She watched Delthea open Garrett's office door and stick her head inside. He sat at the desk, his head in his hands, his mind racing with paralyzing anxiety.

"Come on, Garrett. They're waiting," she said.

Mustering all the strength he had, he rose to his feet and slowly followed her.

When they entered the room, Mrs. Olney returned Delthea's smile with a timid grin while Mr. Olney bowed his head and played with a paper cup. Abi read Valerie's fear, Delthea's concern for her husband, Garrett's building anxiety – everyone's thoughts, except Wayne's. All she got from him was his sullen attitude, but she didn't get that from his thoughts. It showed in the scowl on his face.

"Dr. Clay, this is Mr. and Mrs. Olney," Delthea said. "He is an operator at an oil refinery, and she is a domestic engineer."

Wayne snorted and muttered, "That's a fancy way of saying she don't work."

Valerie glanced at Wayne and wrapped a tissue around her index finger on her left hand as her eyes darted around the rest of the room. "You can call us Valerie and Wayne," she muttered.

Garrett nodded and sat down heavily, at a loss for what to say or do.

Sure that Garrett would return to normal once they got started, Delthea took a seat and opened their chart. "To save time, let me go over the notes I received from Dr. Matthews. I'd like for both of you to add important details or correct errors as I go through it."

Valerie continued winding her tissue. Wayne slumped lower in his seat.

"Are you agreeable to that?" she asked cautiously and raised a questioning eyebrow toward Garrett who stared at Wayne as his mind raced with both anxiety and abhorrence.

His size reminded Abi of Vince who would never have gone to a shrink, whether or not it meant hopefully saving his marriage. Granted, this guy was here under court orders. When she tried again to tune into his feelings, all she got was Garrett's growing urgency to maintain self-control.

Abi thought about the price Valerie would pay for this counseling session. When they got home, Wayne would drink a few beers, and then he would start lashing out. Wanting to protect the children, she would take the brunt of his anger. She dreamed of leaving him, but she had no way to support herself and her children. Still she wasn't doing them any favors by staying. This was something else Abi understood. Getting pregnant with Garrett's child had given her the courage to leave Vince.

Wayne propped his foot on his knee and drawled, "I don't know why we have to go through this fucking shit again."

Wayne's comment compounded Garrett's tide of emotion. He wanted to waylay this bully.

"Dr. Clay, perhaps you could address Wayne's concern," Delthea said diplomatically, glancing from Wayne to Garrett.

The most civil words Garrett could form were, "Because you hurt your wife."

Abi applauded his boldness, but worried that Wayne might react as Vince would have.

"What the hell?" Wayne turned an accusing glance at terror stricken Valerie. "Did you put that in that goddamn report?"

A long, chilling silence hung in the room. Delthea was confused by Garrett's unorthodox approach. She wondered if this was typical or reflective of his obvious anxiety. Garrett continued spiraling downward, both physically and emotionally. All he wanted to do was escape what felt like a confrontation with his worst enemy.

Wayne pointed to the chart in Delthea's lap. "Is that what your fucking folder says?"

"No, ahh . . . No, it doesn't," Delthea stammered. At a loss for what to do next, she prayed that Garrett's strategy worked. Abi did, too.

"I only agreed to this to keep her happy. I didn't know I'd be attacked with some trumped up charge." He turned to Valerie as if ready to attack her.

By then Garrett had established a silent communication with Valerie. His eyes squinted slightly as he held her gaze. She relaxed, drawing strength from him.

Seeing this, Wayne turned on Garrett. "What's going on between you two?"

After taking a deep breath, Garrett asked Valerie, "Does he hurt you?" She nodded quickly.

"The hell I do!" Wayne shouted.

"What does he do?" Garrett asked, totally ignoring Wayne's outburst. Still locked in Garrett's gaze, she stammered, "He . . . he . . . ahh."

"Valerie Sue, you better not start with those lies again," Wayne hissed through clenched teeth.

She glanced at him and said just above a whisper, "He gets drunk sometimes, and he doesn't know what he's doing."

"And now you're making excuses for him. You do that a lot, don't you?" Garrett replied, his voice calm and supportive.

She nodded her head with quick, jerky motions. "I know I do things he don't like, but when he's drunk, there's just no pleasing him." She quickly peeked at Wayne, fearful that he might hit her now.

Red-faced Wayne shouted, "You're putting words in her mouth, mister. She's just saying what she thinks you want to hear. Believe me, I've heard it myself for years. She'll lie 'til the day she dies."

Garrett shifted his focus to Wayne and continued in his slow even cadence, "You're already thinking about how you're going to take her home, down a couple of beers, and then you're gonna fix her little wagon, aren't you?"

Although Abi couldn't read Wayne's thoughts, Garrett seemed able to, or perhaps he was picking up what Abi was getting from Valarie. If her companion was right, they may all be connected subconsciously – each getting what they need from the other, no matter how bad it looks on the surface.

"That seems to be the case," said her guide who had materialized without Abi knowing it.

Wayne jumped to his feet. "What I do in the privacy of my own home is no concern of yours, you little bastard."

Garrett slowly rose, keeping his eyes fixed on Wayne. "Once you chug a few beers, you'll be strong enough to do what you always do when she gets out of line."

Wayne stepped toward Garrett.

Terrified by what might happen next, Delthea stood up. "This has gone far enough."

Garrett continued, "She'll say something. It doesn't have to be much. Just anything will do, 'cause you can get mad enough to beat the crap out of her for practically no reason at all, can't you?"

Wayne charged forward, and Garrett stepped up to meet him. Nearly a foot taller than Garrett, Wayne glared down at him while his fist flinched spasmodically at his side.

Speaking slowly as if to control a growing rage inside himself, Wayne said, "I'm going to be real nice to you, doc. We're leaving now, and I won't even press charges." He took a slow ragged breath and shouted in Garrett's face, "Just stay the fuck out of my life."

"Valerie's not going anywhere," Garrett declared.

Wayne rolled his eyes. "I don't have to take this shit, not from you or her or anybody. Come on, Val, let's go." He grabbed her arm.

Valerie hunched her shoulders and drew her hands to her stomach. Her limp brown hair swayed slightly from side to side.

He bent his mouth to her ear. "I said come on!"

After jerking her free hand to her ear, she said timidly, "No, Wayne. Not this time."

Wayne gawked at her with disbelief, and then he threw her arm down. Veering far off course, Wayne swaggered past Garrett, hitting him with his broad shoulder.

Garrett quickly regained his balance, yet the shove seemed to awaken him from a daze. He glanced from Delthea to Valerie as if trying to make sense of what he was seeing.

At the door, Wayne surveyed the room. "This is a fucking kangaroo court." He left, slamming the door behind him.

"You did well with that," the guide said.

"What do you mean, I did well?" Abi asked.

"You were cuing Garrett with subconscious messages," her guide explained.

"But I wasn't thinking everything he said," she protested.

"Yes, you were – subconsciously. You had concluded that right before you realized I had joined you. You're linked with all of your loved ones on a subconscious level," the guide explained.

"Will Valarie be okay?" Abi asked.

"We can only speculate. As you know, the great human gift is free will, so it all depends on her choices. Your lesson in all this is to see that you do have the ability to empower your loved ones, especially those you feel most connected to."

Abi thought about who that included. Only two people came to mind, the two people she wanted desperately to bring together, the two people she had resisted finding each other when she was on earth. Again Abi wondered if her guide was someone she had known who had died before her. Could he fit in the category of a loved one? He felt oddly familiar, but no identity came to mind.

*   *   *

The next day, Delthea sat at her office desk. She heard the lobby door open, so she glanced at her watch. Judy wouldn't arrive for another thirty minutes. It had to be Garrett. After they got home last night, he locked himself in his studio and had not come out when she departed this morning. She left a note on the kitchen table, telling him she had rescheduled the second abuse case for this morning. It was her way of giving him permission to not show up – not that she wanted to see them by herself. Still, that would be preferable to what had transpired yesterday.

After lightly tapping on the door, Garrett walked in wearing one of the suits Delthea bought for his book tour. Although he had regained a few pounds, it was still three sizes too big.

"I apologize for hiding out last night." He closed his blood-shot eyes. "I needed some time."

At two when Delthea got up to use the bathroom, the light was still on in his studio, and she heard movement from within. When she tried to open the door, she found it was locked. He didn't respond when she called to him, so she returned to bed, hurt and mad.

"Actually right now I'm more worried about Valerie Olney." Her gaze shifted to an open folder.

He cocked his head to the side, causing her to question whether he knew who she meant.

"I sent her to a shelter yesterday. This morning the director of the center said she was with her sister, but I'm scared she's gone home – because of her children, which I certainly understand."

Garrett walked with halting steps toward her desk. "What can I do?"

"You know what I'm scared of, don't you?" she asked.

He nodded and focused on the chart.

"I'm afraid, I'll only make it worse if I try to talk to Mr. Olney." He lifted his gaze to meet Delthea's. "I can't explain what happened yesterday. I've rehashed that session a thousand times, but I can't figure out what possessed me. It feels like someone else took over my mind."

"What I don't understand is why you attacked him?" She stood up. "There was probably no hope for their marriage, but now I'm worried about the kids."

"Let's call Oliver and ask him to make contact with Mr. Olney," Garrett suggested weakly.

She walked to the window, noting the endless traffic on the 610 Loop. "I think *we* should do something. *We're* the ones that fucked it up," she said, nastily emphasized the use of '*we.*'

Garrett didn't respond.

With her back still to him, she said, "Why don't you call the center? Tell them who you are and why you're concerned. See if they have the phone number for her sister."

He quietly got the chart from her desk and walked toward the door.

Delthea spun around and said, "Garrett."

He stopped, but didn't turn to face her.

"What were you doing last night?" she asked, knowing she shouldn't, but unable to stop herself.

Still facing away from her, he said, "Painting – and thinking."

"Dare I ask what was on your mind?" She knew, but she didn't know if he would admit it.

"We can talk about it tonight," he answered, moving toward the hall.

"Let me know what the center says," she called after him.

She returned to her desk. Her head swam with feasible scenarios of why he had shut her out. Abi's image reappeared every time she mentally shoved it away.

Ten minutes later, Garrett returned, carrying a slip of paper. "Here's her sister's number."

Sure that Garrett was emotionally unprepared to do so, Delthea took the number and dialed it. When a woman answered, she said, "This is Dr. Richards. I'm one of the psychologists who worked with Valerie Olney yesterday. The shelter gave me your number. I called to see how she's doing."

"Just a minute. I'll get her," the woman responded.

Muffled voices, followed by sounds of the phone being handed to someone else preceded Valerie's voice saying, "Thanks for calling. When I can, I'm going to pay you back that money you gave me yesterday."

Relieved to hear Valerie's voice, Delthea blurted, "Don't worry about the money. I'm just glad you haven't gone back to Wayne." It was probably unethical to say this, but she could not stop herself.

"After Dr. Clay gave me all that courage yesterday, I decided I had to do what was right for me and for my kids. My sis helped me go get them last night. Wayne didn't like it, but we did it anyway."

Delthea cringed at the idea that Garrett had somehow achieved hero status out of yesterday's debacle. "That's wonderful. We want to make sure that you get the follow-up counseling you need."

"I can't afford that. I don't have a job, and I gave the money you gave me to my sis since she's keeping me and my kids here at her place."

"Don't worry about the fee," Delthea replied. "Our main concern is that you get the support you need right now. Dr. Clay and I feel you could benefit from individual counseling."

"I don't have a car to get over there, and I hate to ask my sister for anything else."

"We can talk on the phone a few minutes every day – until you have a plan in place?" Delthea suggested. "That way we can deal with things as they come up."

"I guess that might work," she said hesitantly.

They talked for fifteen minutes about what it had taken to get her kids safely out of the house and what she planned to do in the immediate future. Garrett stood by Delthea's desk, silently waiting.

When she hung up, Delthea looked at his haggard expression.

Garrett splayed his fingers on the desk as if he needed to steady himself. "How did she sound?"

"I think she's all right." After shuffling through some patient charts, she met his gaze. "Why don't you get ready for your session with David, and I'll handle the other case by myself?"

"Good idea. I think you're much more capable," he said, as his shoulders visibly relaxed.

"Oh, incidentally. She said to tell you thanks for giving her the courage to do what she's been wanting to do for a long time." It galled Delthea to admit he had come out looking like he knew what he was doing, but she had promised Valerie she would relay the message.

*   *   *

Preoccupied with a comic book, David sat slouched on the couch in Garrett's office. Garrett thought how close in age he was to Morgan. He wondered what his son, Moa, as Abi had called him liked to read.

David lowered the brightly colored pages that featured a lady with huge breasts accented by a plunging neckline. "What?"

"I was just wondering what you're reading?"

"Spiderman," David answered, tossing the magazine on the coffee table between them. "What do you want to talk about?" he asked, obviously eager to get the ordeal finished.

"What do guys your age like to do?" Garrett asked.

David raised his shoulders up and down. "I don't know." His face brightened as if he had thought of something. "Do you want me to think of things to do besides smoking?"

"Not necessarily. It's been a long time since I was your age. I wondered what you like to do. You know, stuff like that." Actually conversing with David would do more good than scolding or reasoning with David, which was what the school and Elaine expected.

"What I like to do," David repeated. "Well, see that's the problem. Me and Kent get home from school and there's nothing to do except watch stupid cartoons, so we start messing around."

"What does that mean?" Garrett asked.

"We go through my mom's drawers, looking for quarters, so we can go buy stuff at the grocery store. Usually we don't find much, but we nearly always find cigarettes, so we smoke them. I do. Kent doesn't. He says it's stupid. But I take them to school and the other guys think I'm cool because I have cigarettes. If I like somebody, I give them a smoke, but if I don't like them, I make them pay."

Nodding, Garrett asked, "So it's kind of a reward system you've got for guys being nice to you."

David sniffed and twisted his face to the side. "The last guy I charged ratted on me, and . . . ."

Garrett waited.

"The principal said I was going to get kicked out if I ever brought smokes to school again." He picked at a hole in the knee of his jeans.

"What would happen then?"

"My mom told me she would send me to live with my dad, and she said he would probably send me to military school since he wouldn't put up with crap like that." His voice grew strained as he spoke.

"Military school. How would you like that?" He pictured Elaine making rash threats about the elusive man who had fathered David and then disappeared.

"I wouldn't," David shot back. "But if I don't have nothing to offer or no reason for the guys to listen to me, I'll just be what I've always been, a lump, a nothing."

"Is that how you see yourself, a lump with nothing to offer except cigarettes?" Garrett asked, his heart breaking for the sad little boy.

"Pretty much." He sighed. "I wish I could do something cool like draw."

"You think that would help?" Garrett asked.

"Yeah, I do," David answered defiantly.

Garrett got up, grabbed his sketchbook and pencil from the desk, and sat next to David on the couch. "Drawing takes practice, and you have to learn to look at things differently." He wasn't sure where that concept had come from, but he decided to see where it took him.

David grabbed the pencil and pad, apparently eager to try.

Garrett pointed to the other side of the coffee table. "See that armchair. Let your eye follow the outline of it. At the same time, move your pencil on the paper, echoing what your eyes are seeing."

He scrunched his face up at Garrett.

"Tell you what, I'm going to sit over there in that chair and talk you through drawing me without looking at your paper." It felt risky, but Garrett decided to go with his instincts.

After moving back to his original seat, Garrett imagined he was David and methodically talked his nephew through the process of drawing him. Periodically, David glanced down at his paper. Otherwise, their eyes stayed locked. When he had finished drawing himself through David's perspective, Garrett told his nephew to look at what he had done.

"Whoa, this is cool," David said, obviously impressed. He turned the pad, so Garrett could see.

"You got it," Garrett whispered. Chill bumps swept over him. The style looked similar to his original drawings – the ones he had done of Abi at the park – in his dream and later in his bedroom. "Take that pad home with you. I want you to practice drawing."

Once he had David out the door, he returned to his desk and a phone number he had found in a pocket after rummaging through his brief case, drawers, and every folder in his office. He dialed the number, prepared to leave a message if he needed to.

Bud Anderson answered on the third ring. "Hello."

*   *   *

Delthea rearranged the Chinese take out on her plate. What Garrett had been thinking while hold up in his studio last night niggled at her. She was pretty sure what, or rather who was on his mind, but she hated to ask. Still, she was, as usual, the elephant in the room.

Garrett took a long drink from his water glass. "How did the session go with Oliver's other referral?" It was the closest he had come to addressing the Valerie and Wayne disaster.

Not wanting to admit her own floundering attempt at counseling them, she said, "It was fine. We talked about communication strategies, and options they may want to take. She's already in a shelter, so I wasn't afraid I would run into a situation like you . . . well, like what happened yesterday."

"About that," Garrett said as he laid his napkin on the table and pushed his chair back. "Delthea, I'm not sure I'm up to seeing patients again. I thought I could, but when I think about yesterday afternoon, I just . . . well, I don't think I can do it."

"I pushed you into that. You weren't ready. With a little more time, you'll get back in the groove," she said, not actually feeling what her words suggested.

"The idea of counseling that type of patient again terrifies me. I couldn't sleep last night for thinking about what irreparable damage I may have caused." He ran his hands through his hair. "I know I told you I would do whatever it takes to keep the practice going, but I'm not sure I can. That's what I was thinking last night."

"We don't have to take any more spousal abuse cases. You did fine with Mr. Gregory. Of course, you convinced him he was fine without us, but he left happy," she argued.

"That's just it. I'm a genius if they don't really need me, but if I get in a situation where it might literally be life or death, I'm incapable." Garrett drank the rest of his wine.

"Christmas is Sunday, and Judy has blocked out the following week. Let's reevaluate after we come back. By then, you'll have a new lease on this," Delthea said with more optimism than she felt.

"You know what I want for Christmas?" Garrett asked as if that was part of their conversation.

Delthea knew, but she could not say it aloud.

"To find my son," he said, studying her face like he suspected that she knew how to do that.

When she did not respond, he walked toward his studio/bedroom. "I'm going to paint."

*   *   *

It had only been two weeks since his mother's death, but it felt like a lifetime. Just knowing she was not there had made coming back to the inn that much harder.

Early afternoon when Moa was sure Takahe was busy with dinner preparation in the kitchen, he slipped into Mum's room. It still smelled of her, an odor he could not put a name to. It was simply her, a combination of turpentine, a soapy scent, and an indefinable ingredient that he associated with her paintings, especially ones of him. It had to be love, but that didn't have a smell.

Moa sat cross-legged by her bookcase and pulled out the book they had always read together, *As a Man Thinketh*. He didn't need to open it to know what it said, but it made him feel good to leaf through the familiar pages, sort of like holding his mother's hand. The idea of doing that made his eyes fill with tears. Lately, it didn't take much to do that.

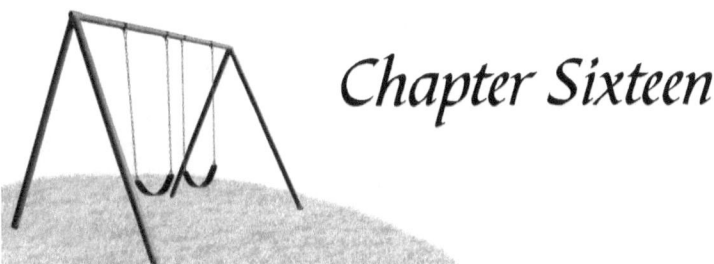

Chapter Sixteen

*C*hristmas morning, Delthea rolled over in bed, opened her eyes, and saw Garrett smiling at her. He stroked the hair out of her eyes.

"Merry Christmas," he said, with that mischievous grin that told her he was up to something.

"Merry Christmas," she repeated, looking back at him. After a minute or so of staring, she demanded, "What?"

"Nothing," he answered, but obviously there was something, something he planned to do, had done, something he could not wait for her to figure out.

Because lately she always needed to go to the bathroom, especially when she woke up, Delthea decided to play his game later. She slipped out of bed and walked to the bathroom. While she sat on the toilet, emptying her full bladder, she pulled off some toilet tissue. A simple gold band was on the ring finger of her left hand. "Garrett," she shrieked. "When did you do this?"

He cackled with delight. She could imagine him tucked into a ball and laughing with his whole body. He was still chuckling when she returned to bed and snuggled up next to him.

"When did you do this?" she asked, admiring the simple gold band that looked and felt so perfect on her left hand.

"Last night after you went to sleep," he said, obviously pleased with himself.

"Thank you. It's perfect, just perfect." She touched her lips to his.

"You're welcome. That's the ring I've always wanted you to have, simple, strong, and without any ins and outs, just like my love for you." He wrapped his arms around her.

This was the man she had fallen in love with, and the man she would always love. This was the perfect moment to give him his Christmas present, but she did not have one. She had racked her brain for what she might buy that she could say Ian Witherspoon had helped her secure, but absolutely nothing came to mind, so she had decided to default to a semi-truth.

Snuggling up next to him, she ran her fingers along the center of his hairy chest. "I don't have a present for you. I honestly could not think of anything you would like – except having me." She gazed into his smiling face and gave him her most coquettish grin.

He pulled her to him and murmured, "You are all I have ever wanted."

They lay there together, but neither one of them made the first move toward intimacy. Delthea was not sure if she was disappointed or relieved. It had been too long and there was still too much she had not told him – like who the hell was Ian Witherspoon, which she did not know.

Later that morning, Garrett sat at the piano plunking out a crude version of "Bridge over Troubled Waters." Delthea had not heard that tune in years and wondered why and how Garrett knew even a very limited version of it.

She sat next to him on the bench and wrapped her arm around his thin waist. "Thanks for my ring. Now I'm legal again."

"That's right." He pecked her on the cheek then returned to the piano, obviously lost in thought.

"You about ready for Christmas dinner? Elaine and the boys will be over soon."

"Sure." He played a few notes. "When you talked to Betty Barker, exactly what did she tell you? I mean, why did she call in the first place?"

Delthea was confused why Betty Barker had not told Garrett where Abi was. When she called before Thanksgiving, she was eager to relay messages from Garrett to Abi. "I don't know. Maybe she got nostalgic with the holidays coming up. It could've been a shot in the dark at finding her lost child."

With her last, poorly chosen phrase ringing in Delthea's ears, Garrett turned to her and searched deep within her soul with his penetrating green eyes. "When I talked to her, she said she didn't know anything about Abi, but when I asked her about Morgan, she started to tell me something, and then she stopped herself. She knows more than she's saying. It doesn't make sense."

"Most things in life don't." If she told him that Betty had said she was going to see Abi, he would wear Betty down until she finally told him Abi's whereabouts, which was according to her deal with God something Delthea should find out and share with Garrett.

The doorbell rang followed by pounding on the door, muffled voices, and laughter. Thankful for the interruption, Delthea opened the door to Elaine and her rowdy boys. Since she didn't have a tree or any other Christmas decorations, she told them to put their presents on the piano along with the ones she had bought for them. Still taking his jacket off, David cornered Garrett. Kent turned on the television while Delthea and Elaine retreated to the kitchen. They heated up the prepared meal she had bought at the grocery store last night on the way home from work. Then they set it on the table and called everyone to eat.

Once they had filled their plates, Garrett stood up. Delthea wondered what would come out of Garrett's mouth. He had a way of surprising her – in not always a good way.

"I'd like to propose a toast," he said.

The group looked up at him expectantly.

"You may have noticed that Delthea is wearing a new piece of jewelry." He gave her a wry smile. "As she confided to me just before you guys got here, she is now a legal woman. And she is giving me the ultimate gift." He locked his gaze with his wife's. "This summer, we'll be parents."

"Hot damn, Garrett. You still got it in ya'," Elaine said as she clinked her wine glass with his.

The boys laughed and made a big production of clinking their glasses of milk with Delthea's. Hearing Garrett assume equal responsibility for her child made his toast nearly as wonderful as finding the ring on her finger. Whatever she had endured over the last year was now bearable – except she had not actually fulfilled her end of the bargain with God.

Still standing, Garrett cleared his throat. "Another addition to our family, actually not an addition, but someone I've just verified the existence of is my son Morgan. He's ten years old. I'm just not sure where he is, but I'll find him."

Kent and David looked quizzically at each other.

Elaine glanced at Delthea. "So how's that going?"

Delthea shrugged her shoulders.

Garrett sat down and apparently overhearing Elaine's question said, "I've called her former landlord and Abi's mom, but neither of them seems to know a thing."

Elaine gave him a confused look. "Really? I would have thought Abi's mom could – "

"You know what?" Delthea interrupted. "We need Christmas music." She jumped up from her chair and prayed that Elaine would take her hint to shut her big mouth.

While Delthea busied herself with the record player, the sound of forks and knives resumed a steady rhythm of clicks.

After she had reseated herself and began slicing her ham, Garrett said to the table at large, "I think he lives in a foreign country because in my dream Abi had a strange accent."

Delthea wondered what the boys must think of their uncle. She had lived through a year of such bizarre talk, but they probably thought he was totally losing it.

"Somebody talked to you in a dream?" David asked, obviously fascinated. "Was it someone you knew a long time ago?"

Garrett looked purposely at Delthea. "Yes, the mother of the son I'm looking for." Elaine's unfinished comment and her blatant interruption had not escaped him. He knew she talked to Elaine, and he was determined to get whatever information Elaine had, with or without Delthea's cooperation.

The doorbell rang.

Garrett shot a questioning glance at Delthea who shrugged her shoulders and said, "It's not Berta. She's still gone."

Garrett answered the door. Harrison, the art dealer who lived three flights up, refused to come in and apologized for interrupting, but he really needed to talk to Garrett and thought maybe Christmas Day was as good as any to catch him at home. They stepped out in the hall for at least half an hour. By the time Garrett returned to the table, the boys had settled themselves in front of the television, ready to watch the football game.

Garrett laid a business card beside his plate. "Harrison wants to do a showing of my paintings. Seems his next artist didn't officially cancel or even answer his calls when Harrison tried to reach him. He says we're temperamental like that."

"You're not an artist; you're a psychologist." Delthea began clearing the table. Harrison had nerve, showing up on Christmas Day and suggesting Garrett further sidetrack his profession by commercially pursuing this obsessive hobby of his.

When she returned to the dining room, Garrett was explaining to Elaine that Harrison had promised him a large advance on the show and that all he had to do was turn over the paintings in the storage unit. He wouldn't need to paint anything else. Plus, he was interested in Garrett's drawings.

"Your drawings," Delthea blurted out. "My God, those are just sketches of someone you don't know." She immediately regretted her words on two counts. First, it brought them right back to Morgan, the phantom idol of the day, and it would be just like someone as brazen as Harrison to use that concept as a marketing piece. Delthea imagined the byline beneath a picture of Garrett at his easel: Psychologist turned artist paints pictures of lost child whom he desperately seeks.

*   *   *

Exhausted from emotionally battling Delthea, Garrett took his uneaten plate of food to the living room to sit with his nephews. For his son's sake, he needed to get back in the groove of being a guy by doing guy stuff like watching football, or whatever they played wherever he lived. He remembered Abi telling him that Morgan liked to hunt. She had said they had plenty of game where they lived, and he was as good a shot as she had ever been, which spoke highly of his ability. Hunting was not something Garrett had ever cared about, although, he now curiously relished the idea.

David crawled onto the arm of his chair, and they picked up where they left off perusing his drawing pad when Delthea called them to the table for dessert. He had been practicing since his first lesson with Garrett, and he was good. "David, you have a gift. You need to stick with it."

The phone rang.

When Delthea muttered something about people having the decency to leave other people alone at least one day out of the year, Garrett answered it, so Delthea wouldn't feel compelled to.

"Dr. C, I got a Christmas present for you," Milton said.

"You didn't need to do that," Garrett answered, wondering what hot item Milton might have 'picked up' for him.

"I found those boxes you were looking for. You know the other day when you wanted your key, and I said number thirty-four and you said number thirty-three. Well, that's where I put them. For some strange reason, I woke up this morning thinking about you asking about those boxes. It just suddenly popped in my head." Nothing worked very fast in Milton's head, but, at least, it had finally registered. Garrett should have thought of that himself.

"I'll be down in five minutes."

Garrett raced to the elevator without explaining to anyone where he was going. He helped Milton move the boxes to his storage unit right next door, the whole time thanking Milton again and again for letting him know that he had found them. Garrett told him it wasn't a problem that he had guests right now, although he knew Delthea would disagree.

When Milton finally left, Garrett began riffling through Abi's things, knowing he should come back later, but unable to force himself to leave.

He looked inside each box and decided the one labeled personal had the most potential. As he sat cross-legged on the concrete floor and began going through her sketch pad/journals, Garrett had a sense of Abi looking over his shoulder. He was fascinated by the drawings of himself, holding up his infant son and nuzzling him under the chin, cradling him in his arms, and perching him on his shoulder. In each, Garrett appeared happy, exactly the way he would have been had he actually been there.

After he put the spirals in chronological order, he began reading the journal entries, determined to scrutinize each one for a clue to where Abi went after she left Austin. He was halfway through the first one when David appeared at the doorway.

"Delthea is really pissed. My mom said you might like to know that," he reported.

He appreciated Elaine's concern, but Delthea's irritability was nothing new. "Oh, really?"

David sauntered over to a box, opened it, and began sorting through tiny sleepers and nightshirts. He then played with a rattle and a crib mobile. Torn between wanting to protect the remnants of his son's baby days and glad David had found a way to occupy himself, Garrett continued to read.

*   *   *

The day after Christmas, Moa woke up early, excited that Mr. Perkins was bringing Ian in a few hours. Moa had slept in his mother's bed where he had fallen asleep the night before. Takahe had not moved him as he expected she would. She was a lot more relaxed now about stuff she used to get in a dither over. He didn't know if it was the fact that Mum was dead or that Takahe missed him now that he was in school, maybe some of both.

Takahe was already in the kitchen cooking breakfast for the guests. Mr. Perkins and Ian would arrive before lunch, probably using the school van since Moa doubted he owned a vehicle, or if he did it was probably an old rust bucket. He would accept Takahe's predictable lunch invitation since he didn't have anyone to cook for him at school. Yesterday when Ian called, he said that Mr. Perkins was hesitant to let Ian stay with Moa for the rest of the school holiday. Moa figured Mr. Perkins would be glad to have some time by himself given all the dodgy stuff that took place when school was in session.

Moa crawled out of bed and began making it. Takahe was particular that he did that immediately and correctly, which meant it had to be perfectly straight, no wrinkles showing through, and the bedspread had to be even all the way around. What a pain. He slipped his mum's favorite book in his backpack along with his dad's vest and the dog tag he had found in her jewelry box, the one that once hung on a chain around his mum's neck. He wanted to take these things back to school, and he didn't want to have to sneak them out of the room right before he left.

He padded to the kitchen in bare feet and offered to help Takahe. Once Ian got here, he wanted to spend every minute with him. Maybe Takahe would consider extra help a deposit on free time later.

She told him to set the tables. After that, she sent him outside with a pair of scissors and instructions to cut enough flowers for several bouquets. A few of their guests were Americans who were fascinated by the fact that it was summer in New Zealand while it was snowing at home. As Moa trudged about in his *gummies* as it had rained the night before, he snipped roses and daisies and wondered what kind of weather Houston had right now. Ian said it was nearly always hot there even though it was their wintertime. He said it was close to the coast and had a lot of humidity, the traffic was terrible and there was all kinds of crime. Moa puzzled over why anyone would want to live there instead of someplace wonderful like Jacob's Springs.

When Moa laid the flowers on the big wooden table in the middle of the kitchen, Takahe thanked him and said to go play until after the guests had finished breakfast when he would be expected to help clear the tables.

On the way out the back door, he grabbed a sausage and a hunk of Takahe's homemade bread, the best in *Aotearoa*, according to Takahe herself.

It was way too early, but he decided to sit on the front porch and watched for Ian and Mr. Perkins to come over the rise on the only road that led into or away from Jacob's Springs. Close to noon a new convertible parked in front of the inn. Mr. Perkins wore a sporty cap, which he tossed into his seat. He then helped Ian get out of the car since his left leg was still in a cast.

"When you getting rid of that thing?" Moa asked as he snuck up behind them.

"Oh my, there you are," Mr. Perkins said, still as *tightarsed* as ever. "The holiday seems to be treating you well." He shook Moa's hand as he looked at the inn. "What a wonderful home."

"Yup, it's nice," Moa answered.

"You'll have to give me a tour," Mr. Perkins said.

Ian hopped while he maneuvered the crutches under his arms. "You're ugly as ever," he snarled at Moa with a lopsided grin.

Moa wanted to come back with something, but he was too happy to see him to think of anything, so he rested a hand on Ian's shoulder to help steady him while he got situated.

Takahe opened the front screen door and stepped out onto the porch. "*Kia Ora, Tena koutou,*" she called, a Maori greeting that she gave every guest that came to the inn. "So good to see both of you," she continued. "I would have come to the school to get Ian, but we are full with guests."

"Perhaps you don't have room for Ian then," Mr. Perkins answered.

Moa gave Takahe his most pathetic look. "We'll sleep in the studio."

"We'll hang them somewhere. It's not a problem. Come on in. Lunch will be served in a bit." She held the door for Ian, but Mr. Perkins, always a goon about manners, insisted that Takahe go in ahead of him.

Takahe asked Moa to give Mr. Perkins a tour of the inn and grounds while she finished setting lunch. Before he had time to ask, she told him she would need him to help clear the lunch dishes, but after that he was free to go tramping in the woods.

Mr. Perkins asked lots of questions as Moa pointed out everything. He commented on Mum's paintings, which hung on nearly every wall. In the studio, he studied the paintings Mum had not finished and said what a shame it was that she had been taken so young. He made it sound like someone had snatched her off the stool while she was busy working. Moa supposed he meant well, but when anybody said anything about his mum, it made his chest ache.

Takahe called them to lunch and told Moa to sit with Ian and Mr. Perkins just like he was a guest. She got the help started, and then she sat with them, too. While they ate *chook* or chicken as Mum called it, spuds, *veges*, and yeast bread followed by hokey pokey ice-cream for dessert, Mr. Perkins asked one question after another about the inn, Takahe's Maori heritage, and the community of Jacob's Springs. He said he was thinking of retiring and had been looking for a place like this. Moa wondered what it would be like to have Mr. Perkins as a neighbor, but there really weren't any houses available to buy or rent. People came here for the springs, otherwise locals who had been here forever owned the land. Takahe and Mr. Perkins each said they had never married. Mr. Perkins said St. Anthony's boys had always been his children. Takahe said she considered herself a mum to Mum and a nana to Moa. That prompted Ian to snort and kick Moa under the table.

As the guests left their tables, Moa scurried about clearing them. When he had finished, including the one where Takahe and Mr. Perkins continued giving each other an ear bashing, Moa and Ian hurried outside. They couldn't go far since it had been raining, and Ian still had that stupid cast, but they mainly wanted to get off by themselves. On top of the knoll, they sat on a large, flat rock.

Ian reached inside his jacket, and from an inside pocket, he pulled out a legal size envelope. He handed it to Moa. "Here's your *Chrissy pressie.*" He gave Moa a smirky grin.

"Bugger, mate. I didn't get you nothing." Even if Moa had not been strapped for cash, he doubted he could think of a thing to buy that Ian didn't already own.

"You're putting up with me 'til school starts, and besides all that, you've given me more than money can buy. I got to sit on the bench the whole season, didn't I?" He gave Moa a friendly punch in the arm. "This one's my shout. Seeing you use that will be my gift."

Curious to know what Ian meant, Moa opened the envelope and slipped out a passport and a ticket of some kind. Inside the passport, he found a picture of himself.

"How did you get this?" Moa asked, totally dumbfounded.

"It's amazing what money can buy," Ian said, looking pleased with himself. "Check out what else you've got there." He pointed to the other piece of paper in Moa's hand.

Moa couldn't think of what to say, so he stared at it.

"It's an open-ended ticket to Houston to go see your dad. You can use it anytime you want."

"I've never even been on a plane," Moa admitted.

"I was thinking, we could say we felt sorry for Perky and wanted to visit him. My dad's chauffeur could drop you off at the airport on the way back to school. I could tell Perkins that you got sick and couldn't come. By the time, he figures out what is going on, you'll be there."

"But how will I know where to go, and all that?" Moa asked.

"We'll plan it out before you do it," Ian said confidently.

Moa wasn't so sure about all this.

*   *   *

David returned to the group and announced, "Garrett said he would be right up, but I doubt it. He's had his nose stuck in those tablets since I went down there an hour ago."

Elaine gave Delthea that I-told-you-so look. Saying she needed to go home and get dressed since she was getting triple time for working the evening shift on Christmas Day, Elaine herded the boys out the door, carrying their unopened Christmas presents from Delthea and Garrett.

Delthea sat in the empty condo and looked at what money had bought them, a lot of nothing. Elaine's presents still sat on the piano. She was happy to be pregnant, even if it wasn't Garrett's baby, and she was glad Garrett had so easily accepted her condition. Few men were that understanding. Still, she sensed that her days with Garrett were limited. Within those numerous pages that David had alluded to Garrett reading, he would find some clue. It didn't have to be huge, simply something that halfway jived with the dreams, the telephone calls, and the insanity that had taken over their lives.

She called her mother and wished her a happy Christmas, telling her that she and Garrett had spent their day with Elaine and the boys. Yes, they left, so Elaine could go to work. David seemed to be doing better. Garrett was teaching him to draw. She hadn't told Mother about her husband's latest hobby? Well, she would have to send her some photocopies of his drawings, better yet the originals. God knew they had plenty of sketch pads lying about, in the living room, the kitchen, beside his side of the bed. Oh yes, Mother, life was going well, very well.

"I have a surprise for you. You're going to be a grandmother," Delthea said, not sure how her mother would react.

"Elaine's pregnant again?" Mother asked indignantly.

"No, Mother, I am." Elaine wasn't married. That wasn't a requirement for Elaine. Come to think of it, it wasn't a requirement for her either – or at least not being married to the biological father.

"You?" her mother said indignantly. "I thought you and Garrett couldn't have children."

"We can, and we are," Delthea said, hearing the chill in her own words.

"Congratulations. When's it due?" Mother still didn't sound as though she believed Delthea.

"The middle of July. By then Garrett should be ready to handle the practice by himself." She wished that were true, or that she could even fantasize in that direction.

"So you're going to stay home to raise it?" Mother asked with a hint of skepticism.

"Why bring a baby into the world if I don't intend to be its mother?" Why indeed. Even though she had not conceived this child by choice, Delthea would be the best mother any child ever had.

"Well, I stayed home with you and Elaine, but that's not what young mothers do any more," Mother said self-righteously. Her mother cleared her throat. "It wouldn't hurt for you to call a little more often. Up until a couple of months ago, I could count on you to call every Saturday morning."

Delthea promised to phone more often and hung up.

She watched television, ate leftovers, and read in bed, hoping Garrett would come home, but she fell asleep with his side of the bed still empty.

The next thing she knew, Garrett was slipping into bed behind her, his cold hands on her belly and his icy feet against hers. He snuggled his bearded chin against the side of her face, his lips next to her ear. "New Zealand," he whispered.

"What?" she answered, already knowing.

"On the last page of the last journal, she made a notation about leaving the next day with a guy named Colin who lives in New Zealand. She mentioned him in my dream. That's where she went."

"New Zealand is too big to go and just start looking?" she muttered.

"I have a few clues. For one thing, the inn is close to some thermal springs. I talked to Bud Anderson about helping me, but he wants an arm and a leg up front, so I decided to go myself."

Glad the room was dark, but still needing to say this to his face, Delthea rolled over. "Since you brought up money, let's talk about that. You haven't worked in two years. Your book sales have fallen off. And now that I'm pregnant and hopefully going to stay home to raise this child, I really don't think we have the money for you to gallivant all over the world looking for a child who may or may not want to see you. Abi could be married to someone else who's adopted him." Or, at least, she hoped as much.

"No, she hasn't remarried," Garrett replied.

"How do you know that?" Delthea persisted. She knew how he would respond, but she wanted him to say it, so she could point out the absurdity of his answer.

"She told me in my dreams."

"In your dreams," Delthea repeated slowly.

"Yes, in my dreams where she told me she worked in a restaurant and that a man named Colin helped her escape because Vince was looking for her – exactly like I read in her journal."

Delthea had no rebuttal. She couldn't argue with these incredible details. They were simply too outlandish to be coincidental. Desperate, she returned to her original argument, "You still haven't told me how you're going to afford this."

"I'm going to sell my paintings. Harrison offered me a two thousand dollar advance. If he sells everything and gets more than that, he'll give me more. I won't spend a penny beyond what I get out of the paintings. Harrison contacting me about wanting to show my work and Milton finding the lost boxes has been a double Christmas miracle."

While Garrett fantasized aloud about leaving as soon as he could arrange it, Delthea saw her own dreams for the future evaporate. Once he left for New Zealand, she would never see him again.

* * *

"She's right, you know. It is amazing that all these things are coming together right now. And she doesn't even know about Morgan and Ian's plan for Moa to go to Houston," Abi said to her guide who had also watched the events of the day unfold.

"Seems that way, doesn't it?" he agreed. "Do you remember writing that entry in your journal, the one about leaving Austin with Colin who was from New Zealand?"

"Yes, I remember writing it. At the time, I thought if Garrett ever found my things, and if he read that, maybe he would find me, but I certainly never thought it would take this long or so much would have happened."

"Interesting that you left that door open," he answered.

"Yes, very interesting. Did I do that knowing the events of this day would eventually happen? Do humans know all this?"

"On a subconscious level they know the possibility is there. Right now you are operating on both levels, getting closer and closer to moving into a fully subconscious level."

"Will I stay there?"

"As I told you before, where you are right now is a continuum of what you experienced on earth. You may chose to stay in this interim level of existence or go on to a purely subconscious state or return to a human body."

"I don't know what I want."

"Don't concern yourself. It will come together, just as this day has come together for Garrett and Morgan. That passage in the Bible about everything having a time and a season is very true."

This was her guide's first reference to religion. Abi wondered if he had been one of the ministers of her childhood.

"Hardly," he said, answering her thoughts.

"You said you were someone I knew. I need to know who that is." She didn't understand why her guide's identity remained a secret.

"Sometimes the role a person places in the lives of others gets in the way of individuals seeing their soul, or who they truly are, especially on earth," he answered and was gone.

Chapter Seventeen

*D*elthea was in session with her last patient of the day, Mrs. Wood, who blabbered nonstop with only an occasional, "Yes, I understand," or "How did that make you feel?" to keep her going.

Meanwhile, Garrett was likely executing one more detail toward getting ready to leave tomorrow. The more she thought about it, the madder she got that he had banked their future on that one tiny clue, a ten-year-old chance reference to a man she also mentioned in a dream. A dream! How could a woman she had yet to meet have complete control over Delthea's life? Abi had, since Delthea fell in love with Garrett, which was the day she met him.

When the clock had finally reached an acceptable time, Delthea cleared her throat and shifted in her chair. This was Mrs. Wood's cue to wrap up her tirade on the evil of neighbors allowing their pets to poop in other people's yards.

"I think it's disgusting to find dog shit on my lawn. Don't you?" Mrs. Wood wanted to know.

"I do." Delthea stood up. "Next week we'll talk about what you can do to minimize that."

Mrs. Wood muttered to herself as she struggled to her feet. She was still muttering as she left the office. At the front desk, she asked Judy, "Do you think dog poop is nasty?"

Judy shot a questioning look at Delthea who nodded with exaggeration. "I do," answered Judy as she opened her appointment book and prepared to schedule her next appointment.

On the way back to her desk, Delthea glanced into Garrett's office. He had stacks of folders on every flat surface, including a huge pile at his feet where he sat in a chair next to a filing cabinet.

She leaned on the door jam. "What are you doing?"

He glanced up at her, and then quickly returned to the open file drawer. "Going through all our patient files to see if there is anyone you're seeing who couldn't live without you."

"What are you suggesting, that what I do here has no meaning, that my work is not valid?" With every word, her pitch got higher and her volume increased.

Garrett faced her again. "That's not at all what I'm saying. I would like very much for you to go with me, and I am trying to convince you that you can."

Garrett knew exactly why she could not drop everything and go with him, she had admitted it many times in the last two weeks, but she vowed to keep Abi out of this argument. "We really can't afford that. Besides I do happen to be pregnant."

"All the more reason for you to go. You need to rest."

"I hardly think traipsing around a foreign country looking for your ex-lover is a vacation," she countered, inadvertently bringing up Abi once more.

"I'm not looking for Abi. I'm looking for my son." He spoke with that same forced patience he had used over the last two weeks in response to her constant objections to his ridiculous plan.

"Really?" she shot back. "And what are you going to do with Abi once you find him? Ask her to step out of the picture while you get to know Morgan? Or better yet, maybe she'll offer you her blessings to bring the child back to Houston with you?"

"I don't know what I'm going to say to Abi. I'll have to cross that bridge when I get to it." He returned to his file.

"Whatever point you are trying to make by emptying your files is lost on me. I am not going with you, and as I have told you countless times, I do not want you to go. I think it is a crazy idea. It is a waste of time and money. Plus, I need you here."

"Delthea, we have been through this over and over again. I will come back when the money runs out, and I will not spend more than Harrison gets from the show." Still focused on his task, he dropped a handful of folders on the pile. "He called this afternoon and said it was going really well. He wants me to send over some more drawings, so he can get them framed. My picture in the paper with the caption about me looking for my son has sparked a lot of interest."

"I bet it has," she muttered as she spun on her heels and strode to her office.

* * *

As the chauffeur pulled away, Takahe stood in the driveway and waved. When he couldn't see her anymore, Moa poked his head out the window of the limousine and waved back at her until she disappeared in a cloud of dust kicked up by the car. He wanted to tell her he would be fine, and not to worry, and that he would be back, but he didn't say any of those things for fear of giving away the secret he and Ian had spent the last two weeks planning. When they rounded the bend and the inn was out of sight, Moa sat down on the seat next to Ian. The window he had been hanging out of began rising as if by magic.

They had timed it so that they should get to the airport with plenty of time for Ian to help Moa find his gate, get checked in, and get ready to board the plane. Then Ian would leave for school in the limo. Fredrick, the driver, seemed to know Ian and whatever Ian said to do was just fine with him.

On the way, they went over the plan for the hundredth time.

"Remember, act like you do this all the time. Confidence is the deciding factor, just bluff your way through," Ian said.

"Easy for you to say since you have done it before. When I get to customs, they'll know I've never gone anywhere. They can tell by looking at my passport."

"True, but you have two advantages. First, you're a kid, and everyone assumes you are scared, so they'll be eager to take care of you."

"Which is true in my case. I've got the willies big time."

"Once you get on the plane, use that. Make the stewardess dote on you. By the time you get to California, you should have her wrapped around your little finger. Tell her you're going to see your sick dad, that he may die, or that he is too sick to come get you." Ian looked like he was enjoying all this. Moa would love to send him in his place.

"So what's the other point?" Moa asked.

"You've got dual citizenship. You're as much a Yank as a Kiwi. Even though you don't have an adult with you, you belong in the States. You're a citizen there. They can hardly keep you out. Besides once we get you on that first plane, you're practically there."

"How do you figure that?" Moa's stomach was getting more and more upset.

"What are they going to do with you? Kick you off the next plane with no one to take you? You've got a plane ticket and just as much right as anyone else to fly."

"You've done this before yourself, right? You've flown to Houston by yourself?" Moa asked, suddenly losing confidence in the whole scheme.

"Well, not exactly. I've always had an adult, but with that letter of instruction that my dad's secretary wrote, I don't think you'll have any trouble." This was the first time Ian had admitted this minor detail.

"I'm doing something you've never done?" Moa asked, his terror turning to anger.

"You've always been better than me, mate." Ian tapped his cast. "I've got the scars to prove it."

"That's what this is; your chance to get back at me for breaking your leg," Moa accused, half joking, half not.

Ian laughed. "Good on you. You figured me out." He punched Moa in the arm. "I want you to see your dad. And the next time I come to Houston, I want to come see you, and see what it's like to live with a famous psychologist and author."

"Right," Moa answered, still not sure what part of Ian's statement he believed. "*Bugger.* This is *daft.* What if I get lost, or what if I can't find my dad once I get there."

"You'll be all right. In Los Angeles, you'll have to change planes once you get through customs. That's the hardest part, because you usually have to go to a different terminal."

All of this was written down in case he forgot, but it still helped to hear Ian go over it one more time. They rehearsed with Fredrick what he would say to the person at the ticket counter. Fredrick parked the car and carried Moa's duffel as they walked inside the huge building with Ian pointing the way with his crutches. They checked the board with all the flights listed and figured out which gate to go to for his flight. Once they had decided to carry out this *daft* scheme, Ian had used his dad's calling card and called the airport to make Moa's reservation. Without Ian, Moa would be totally lost. Without Ian, Moa would never have tackled such a scary plan.

The lady at the gate said it was highly unusual for children Moa's age to take international trips alone. Fredrick stepped forward at Ian's cue, said he was authorized by Moa's father to put him on the flight, and showed her his driver's license. Ian chimed in that he was Moa's older brother and that their father would be waiting for Moa in Los Angeles. She frowned and glanced at the line that had formed behind them and said Moa should sit over in the pre-boarding section. She pointed to a set of doors.

"I'll take him over there," Ian said, sounding an awfully lot like a real older brother.

When they were out of earshot, Moa muttered to Ian, "Older brother, my *arse.* I'm the oldest."

"Yeah, but I'm taller, you little runt."

Ian and Fredrick stayed with Moa until the plane arrived. When a man came to get Moa, Ian hopped up on his good leg and gave Moa a bear hug. "Tell Dad *gidday.*"

Moa hugged him back, all of a sudden daft with worry that all of this was a very bad idea. He started to tell Ian that he couldn't do it, but Ian shoved him toward the plane. As Moa walked beside the man, he looked back and saw Ian and Fredrick moving through the crowd away from him. He wondered if he would ever see his friend again.

The stewardess stuck Moa's duffel bag in an overhead locker. Then she seated him in the seat below it, which was at the front of the plane next to a window. Before they took off, she was already offering him something to drink and a flannel to wash his hands and face. He asked for a fizzy drink and eagerly waited for the plane to start moving.

It took a while for everyone to get on. A tall man wearing a cowboy hat sat in the seat next to his. When the plane did finally take off, Moa felt himself pinned against the seat like someone was holding him down. He understood why Ian enjoyed flying. It was fun.

They had barely gotten into the air when the stewardess came around again, offering food and more drinks. Moa chose the fish and chips from the three choices she gave him. She handed him a package of cookies and crackers wrapped in cellophane and said they were to tide him over until the real food arrived. He decided to stow them away in case he needed them once he got to the States. The man in the next seat, who was eating prongs on a bed of ice, watched Moa poke the food in his backpack. Smiling, the man asked the stewardess for the snacks she had given Moa, which he handed over to Moa when she brought them to him.

"*Ta*," Moa said, and then added, "Thanks," because he was sure the man was a Yank, and he might not know what he meant.

The *greasies* tasted all right, but not nearly as good as Takahe cooked. The man in the next seat had lobster. Halfway through their meal, he commented that he wished he had gotten what Moa chose. Moa offered him what he had left since he couldn't begin to eat it all. The man laughed and ate a few bites. Moa could tell he was trying to be friendly. He talked loud, laughed loud, and sounded like he might be a Texan. Moa wondered if he lived in Houston.

They watched a movie called *Flashdance*. In the middle of it, Moa fell asleep. He knew the stewardess was adjusting his seat to lay flat and covering him with a blanket, but he could not wake up enough to thank her.

* * *

Garrett's plane arrived in Los Angeles at noon, but the flight to Auckland did not leave until 3:00, 5:00 o'clock Houston time. For the first hour, he sat in the waiting area with an open book in his lap. He didn't read a word. Instead, he kept replaying the fight he and Delthea had before he left Houston. She had gotten so mad she refused to take him to the airport. He understood how she felt. Abi had always been a threat to her, but this was not about Abi. It was about finding his son. She didn't seem to get that.

He opened his briefcase and went over the notes he made about New Zealand. His research had shown there was a great deal of thermal activity in the North Island, so it made sense to start there. He had found several bed and breakfast inns that had access to thermal baths. Even though none of them were named Songbird Inn, he hoped one of them could direct him to the right place.

For what felt like the one-millionth time, he went over the clues that he had remembered from his dreams. He could list them in his sleep, but that had not gotten him any closer to finding a specific place to look for his son. When he pulled Morgan's birth certificate out of the envelope, Betty Barker's name and phone number fell out. He picked it up and examined it. She would be at work right now. Still, he wanted desperately to talk to her once more. He had called several times since Christmas, but she had not given him an ounce of information. Every time he had spoken with her, she seemed a little less adamant about not revealing Abi's whereabouts.

Garrett saw a pay phone across the way and decided to make one more plea. She would not be home yet, but he could leave a message, so that she knew he would be calling back and hopefully she would relent and give him what he wanted. Delthea often said he was good at wearing people down. He left the message and returned to his seat.

After arguing with Delthea until late in the night and then fussing with the viscous doubts that kept running through his head, Garrett had slept little. He scrunched down in his seat low enough to rest his head against it. What seemed like only seconds later, he was awakened by the announcement that his plane was preparing to board.

A wave of panic flooded over him as he hurried back to the bank of pay phones. As luck would have it, all of them were occupied. Several planes must have arrived and all of the business men needed to call their stock brokers or wives or mistresses. He shifted from one foot to the other, watching the line of people destined for his plane filing into a corridor.

Finally a phone opened up, and he grabbed it, dialed the number by memory and waited for it to ring. While it was ringing, a man wearing a Stetson walked by with a boy who looked amazing like his drawings of Morgan. His head was covered with loopy curls, and he was small in stature, as Abi had described him. The most compelling detail, though, was what he was wearing – a leather vest with long fringe. In college Garrett had worn a vest identical to that one. Abi had taken it with her. The boy wore a backpack and carried a duffel bag. He was looking up at the tall man who walked next to him.

"Hello," Betty answered.

Garrett had a strong urge to catch up with the boy and ask him his name. "Hello, Garrett, is that you," Betty said, bringing him back to the reason why he had a phone in his hand.

"Yes, this is Garrett. I'm in the airport on my way to New Zealand. I thought maybe you had remembered something that might help me find Morgan." He stretched to see if he could still see the boy and the man.

They were standing in front of the flight schedule board and apparently discussing which gate they needed to go to next.

"I've been thinking about that. In fact, Charlene and I discussed it today. She said she thought you would call again."

She hesitated, so Garrett prompted her with, "Yes, and did you think of anything you could tell me. I hate to rush you, but my plane is boarding right now."

"Oh dear. I told her I wouldn't, so the only way I can live with my conscience is to give you a clue. She lives in a town that is a biblical name. It's so small that you'll be able to find the inn when you find the town."

She had just blurted out more than Garrett could process in the one minute he had left before he had to get on the plane. "A biblical name?" he repeated, not sure what she meant.

"Yes, the town is a spring, but the first part of it is a name from the Bible. Charlene said you should be able to figure it out from there. That's all I can say." She hung up.

Garrett saw the boy and the man walk away from each other. The boy called something to the man that Garrett could not begin to hear for all the commotion going on around him.

"Last call for Pan Am's flight leaving for Auckland," a voice said over the loud speaker.

The boy was simply a product of his overwhelming need to find his son. He would think about Betty's clue later. Right now, he had to get on that plane.

*   *   *

"Okay, tell me why Garrett didn't run after Morgan. He saw him. He recognized the vest," Abi said to the nothingness that surrounded her; she figured her guide was close by. He seemed to show up when she needed him.

"Sort of defies logic, doesn't it?" her guide agreed. "Instead of going after what is right in front of him, he stays with his plan which will take him around the world, looking for what he has just seen."

"What are the chances that Garrett and Morgan would end up in the same airport at the same time on the very same mission – to find each other? Garrett's refusal to respond to his instincts goes against what I really thought he would do."

"He obviously has a strong need to go to New Zealand, in spite of what his logical mind and you were telling him to do."

Abi knew exactly what her guide was talking about. She had sent one message after another into his brain, alerting him to the fact that Moa was there.

"Don't forget Morgan. You were also sending him messages about looking for his dad. Why do you think they ignored all that? Better yet, does it concern you?"

When she had first left her body, she was consumed with her need to bring Garrett and Morgan together. "They will eventually find each other." She now knew that without reservation.

"Of course, they will," her guide agreed. "Because they both have a clear intention to do so."

"Is all of life like that, predictable, preordained to a certain destiny?" It felt too much like God had created humans to fill various roles in a never ending play called *Life*.

"Not exactly a predetermined script, more like a lesson. Everyone has freewill. They are given the opportunity to learn the lessons; it's up to the individual whether they take advantage of that or not."

She didn't understand.

"We each go into a human body to learn a lesson. Some people do it efficiently and move on to the next lifetime and new lessons and some people live several lives before they learn the lesson."

"What was my lesson?"

"To love without fear."

"Did I get it?"

"Did you?"

"I loved Garrett."

"Without fear?"

"No. I loved Morgan."

"Without fear?"

"No." If she still had tears to cry, she would shed them.

"Abigale, please understand that few of us, including me, get it right the first time or even many times after that. I spent my last lifetime trying to learn to love, but I failed miserably. Part of why I am here with you now, is to assess the damage so to speak, to perhaps do it better next time."

She felt such warmth, such love in his words.

"You think I am your guide, but it is actually quite the opposite. I come to you because I was unable to love you when I had the chance. You made much more progress than I did, and certainly more than most."

"Tell me who you are."

"You can't guess that I am the man who instilled fear within you at a very early age, the one who gave you the greatest opportunity to overcome the road blocks to love?"

All at once she knew. She understood why she had married an abusive man, why she could not risk loving Garrett except from afar, why she could never give herself to Colin, why she eventually even had to leave Morgan. Her guide was her father. As an infant, she had interpreted her father's actions and reactions as a clear message that she did not deserve a man's love. It was a lesson that she had never been able to unlearn.

Chapter Eighteen

"*P*ardon me for doubting you, but you are simply not the same man who raised me." Abi remembered her father losing his temper over the least offense, not helpful and loving like this person had been.

"You've hit the nail on the head. When you knew me as your father, I was very much a human, living a very separate life from my soul existence."

"Not only that, but you were a jerk. You treated Mama and me like shit. Why did you act like that if you are really such a nice person?"

He laughed, and she almost laughed with him – almost. It was not funny. Her lifetime had been a series of difficult relationships with men, even with Garrett, whom she had truly loved, but could never allow herself to have.

"As a human, I made choices just like you did. I often deviated from my soul-self. This gift of freewill nearly always separates humans from their divinity. Everyone interprets the world based on how they perceive it. I saw my life as most humans do – with a child's first impression."

"So how we live our lives is dictated by our distorted perception of childhood?"

"Exactly. You spent a lifetime living your life based on incidents that you could not consciously recall. Let's look at one now."

Before them appeared a scene of a six-month-old baby lying in a frigid, dark room and crying inconsolably. Her wet diaper had soaked her gown and sheets. Abruptly a large man stormed into the room. A leather belt dangled from his hand, dancing like the toys her mother often used while trying to console her.

"You want to cry! I'll give you something to cry about." He began lashing at the child with the leather strap. The sides of the crib kept his weapon from making full contact, but enough of his attempts found their mark to add a searing pain to what the child was already feeling. She cried even louder. At that, the man reached inside the crib, grabbed her arm, and lifted her. The shock and pain was so immediate and strong that she could not catch her breath.

"My God, what are you doing?" her mother shrieked.

Abi felt herself being flung onto her parent's bed, a surface she had often laid on while her mother changed her diaper. While pain began radiating out of her arm socket into the rest of her body, she smelled the scent of baby powder mixed with her mother and father's familiar odor. A swishing sound followed by a loud whack preceded a sharp pain. Again and again the belt stung her legs with loud slaps. Her pain was so intense that she could not catch her breath enough to cry out. A wrenching knot of pain had formed in her gut. She twisted and turned, clear she needed something to relieve her anguish, but oblivious as to how to get relief.

"Is it any wonder that you would develop a basic mistrust of men?"

Her father's words abruptly brought her out of the paralyzing memories and back to him. "That baby was me, and you were the man."

"Yes, sadly, that's true. I was operating out of a need to be in charge and get what I wanted no matter what it cost others, even my baby girl."

Abi understood how much seeing this must hurt him.

"It is painful, but also insightful – for me at least. Is it any wonder that you chose to leave the Panhandle rather than face the pain of pursuing a relationship with a man – even someone you thought you loved?"

Again, what he was saying made perfect sense. Her marriage to Vince had only reinforced what she already believed about men.

"When you married him, he felt very comfortable, a good substitute for me. As we said at the beginning of this conversation, life is about choices. And what each of us chooses makes a difference in what others do. For instance, you could have chosen to stay in Oaces and let Garrett work through his issues of having two families. As it was, you left, making it easy on him. Of course, he has had his own agenda of lessons to learn, some of them he has mastered and some he has not. Losing his first family was certainly a challenge. Patience and fidelity were overriding themes. Delthea has been a challenge for him on both counts."

"I can see where she would test his tolerance, but why is she an obstacle in the fidelity department? Isn't that her stuff since she was unfaithful to him?"

"He is receiving what he gave. Now bear in mind, I am not passing judgment on either one of them. Everything that happens and the decisions we make that create those events are all part of creating an opportunity to learn. Garrett was unfaithful to his first wife, and now he is living the other side of that experience. Right now he is preoccupied with finding Moa, but eventually Delthea's unfaithfulness will haunt him. Also, there is a child to consider, a child who he will connect with at varying degrees, depending on which soul enters her body."

Her father's last statement struck Abi as odd. "What do you mean by that? Why do you say 'her' and 'varying degrees'?"

"A girl's body is forming. That was decided at conception, but the soul that will occupy that form is still up for grabs."

Abi wondered if he was baiting her. Surely he knew she would be interested in returning to human form as that soul. It would be the best of all worlds along with the obvious challenges. She would be with Morgan and Garrett . . . and Delthea would be her mother. She could think of more pleasant people to raise her.

"The position definitely has points to be considered," he concurred.

"How does this work? Do I have to get in line, fill out an application, talk to the big cheese or go through an interview?"

"No, none of that. The position is yours if you want it. You and Garrett and Morgan have spent several lifetimes together. Delthea has been with you before as well."

"What?" Abi asked, shocked by the idea.

"She's one of your soul family, but you've never been so closely associated. It promises to be both a rewarding and challenging assignment should you choose to take it."

"What happens if I don't?"

"Someone else will take it, or the position will be recalled."

"You mean she will lose the baby?"

"Don't concern yourself. Surely you realize by now that death is not the tragic ending that humans make it out to be."

"In fact, death is an illusion, isn't it?" She had not fully understood that until she reflected on her own state. She was not lifeless. Her earthly body was gone, but that didn't stop her from existing. She had always been and would always be – in some form or fashion.

"Yes, you're really getting it. Another choice would be to remain in the subconscious state to which you are evolving until Garrett or Morgan comes to this stage. You would be to them what I have been to you. It is a gratifying stage on which to linger. There is no hurry in deciding."

Abi decided she would wait until Garrett and Morgan had found each other before she decided. Much could happen before then. She also needed to observe Delthea extensively before she made a choice that she would literally be forced to spend a lifetime enduring.

*   *   *

The nice man, Bill Turner, whom Moa had met on the first plane, lived in Houston, had four boys of his own and said that Moa made him think of them and how much he missed them and looked forward to seeing them again. In Los Angeles, Bill stepped in when the customs agents wanted to know why a ten-year-old boy was traveling alone from one continent to another. Like a fairy godfather, Bill said he was escorting Moa to see his dad, the famous author and psychologist, Garrett Morgan Clay.

On the second plane, Bill got his seat assignment changed, so they were next to each other again. Like the other flight, the seats in the front of the plane where they sat were large and spaced apart. The ones in the back of the plane, beyond a curtain that the stewardesses kept shut, were smaller and closer together. Ian had told him he was going first class, which at the time had meant nothing to him.

Every time a stewardess brought him another *fizzy* drink, Moa said, "*Ta*," which made Bill smile. Bill had asked him about what he called the soda pop and how he thanked the stewardess. That got them onto all the *kiwi* terms that were different from the way they talked in the States like *big smoke* for a large town or city and *Pakeha* for a non-Maori person, which was what Moa was, unlike Takahe who was officially his guardian. Moa explained that his and Takahe's names were bird's name and that at one time they were both considered extinct, except his really was and hers wasn't. Moa had told him about his dad and shown him the book his dad wrote. He then pulled out his father's dog tag from beneath his shirt.

Moa told Bill about Mum and how she had died on his birthday, the eighth of December. They had talked and talked and Bill never seemed to get tired of him. He said he liked Moa's accent, and Moa told him he liked Bill's because his mum spoke somewhat like that, especially if she was mad or excited. When Bill said he was looking forward to meeting Moa's dad when they got to Houston, Moa admitted that he did not have anyone meeting him there. The plan was to look up his dad's office in the phone book, then get a cab to take him over there. At that, Bill said he doubted the flight crew would let him go without someone waiting at the gate.

That made perfect sense, but Moa could not change things now.

"How about I tell them, I'm taking you to your dad's place?" Bill offered. He said he had lived in Houston nearly all his life, and it would not be a problem. When they got to Houston, he got off the plane with Bill just like he had always known him. Bill helped him look up his dad's office in the unbelievably thick telephone book at the pay phones.

Right now he was in Bill's car headed for his dad's office. If Takahe or Mum could see him, they might be worried about him getting in the car with a stranger, but he had decided he had to trust that someone would help him, and Bill seemed to be the best and only person for the job. While he drove, Bill said that his dad's office was on the west side of town close to the Galleria. Moa had never seen so much traffic. The cars were bigger than they were in New Zealand, and the steering wheels were on the left instead of the right, and they even drove on the wrong side of the road.

When Moa commented on that, Bill said, "You Kiwis drive on the wrong side. We drive on the right side." He laughed like it was a big joke, but Moa just looked at him.

"Get it? We drive on the right side." He held up his right hand and waved it.

Moa couldn't think clearly enough to respond. A heavy fog was moving into his brain. Even though he had napped on the plane, he still hadn't really slept in the last couple of days. The night before he left New Zealand, he lay awake worrying about what might happen.

"Uh-oh, I think somebody has jet lag." Bill glanced at the sea of cars that surrounded them. "We're getting on the other side of this *big smoke*. See if you can hang on a little longer, Sport."

When Moa woke up, Bill's car was pulling to a stop.

"Okay, Sleepy-head, time to find your famous dad," Bill said, opening his car door.

They walked into an office building and found the correct office number, but the door was locked. Bill knocked and then checked his watch. "It's after five. I bet they've shut down for the day. Don't you have your dad's home phone number or address?"

Moa's heart sank. With all of their planning, how had he forgotten to bring that one piece of information. "I had his home phone number, but I forgot to bring it with me."

A deep line formed between Bill's eyes. "I'm not sure what to do. I could take you to the police station and let them see if they can find some information on your dad, but I hate to abandon you."

"That's all right. I'll just wait here until morning." Moa did not like the idea of getting the police involved since they might decide to ship him home, and he didn't want to be a pain to Bill.

Bill glanced down the empty hallway. "I don't think that's a good idea."

The office door they had knocked on opened barely a crack. A narrow slice of a blonde-haired lady looked at Bill. "May I help you?"

"This young man is looking for his dad, Garrett Clay," Bill explained.

Her eyes shifted down to Moa and widened as she took in a sharp breath. Then in a creepy robot voice, she said, "Dr. Clay is not here."

"Will he be back today?" Bill glanced down at Moa.

"No, uh, let me think. This is highly un – Maybe we should – No that wouldn't – Oh, God, I haven't even asked the child's name?" she said, sounding all flustered.

"He's named after his dad, Morgan Clay. He's even got Dr. Clay's dog tag." Bill sounded sort of angry now, like he was mad that the lady didn't believe him. Maybe he had jet lag, too.

She opened the door wide enough to step into the hallway. Kneeling down, she carefully examined the dog tag that hung from a chain around Moa's neck. She looked as old as his mum, but she was healthy and very pretty, but not at all happy. When her eyes met his, she seemed to see something that bothered her because she abruptly stood up.

"I didn't introduce myself. I'm Dr. Richards. Garrett and I have a practice together." She stuck out her hand to Bill.

"Bill Turner," he said all business like. "Morgan and I met on the plane from New Zealand. He was traveling by his lonesome, and we just sort of buddied up to keep each other company." He was back to his nice guy way of acting.

"That's awfully gallant of you to take care of Morgan like that. I had no idea he was coming here, so you have to excuse my lack of hospitality. Morgan, I guess, we'll just have to find you a place to stay until your dad gets back." She used his name like she knew he existed, but Mum had said his dad didn't know about him. Moa and Ian had practiced over and over again what Moa would say to his dad when they finally met, especially the part about introducing himself and making it clear who he was and how they were related.

"Where is my dad?" Moa asked.

"He just left this morning on a business trip. Bill, thanks again for looking after Morgan. We owe you a debt of gratitude." She shook his hand again.

Bill reached in his back pocket and pulled out a wallet. From it, he got a card and squatted down to hand it to Moa. "If you need anything while you're here, you give me a call. It's been super getting to know you."

Moa hugged Bill as tight as he could. "Ta, mate."

Bill's whole body shook with laughter while he hugged Moa back. "You're the best."

As Bill walked away, Moa stopped himself from calling after him. Bill paused before he rounded the corner and waved. Moa waved back. He wanted to go home with him rather than stay with the lady standing next to him with her hand on his shoulder. Still, finding her had gotten him closer to finding his dad.

Moa wondered if this lady was the same person who answered the phone when he and Ian called his dad's house. She sounded pretty much the same, except all Yanks sounded alike. She didn't say she was his dad's wife, and besides, she was named Richards, not Clay, but Barker, his mum's last name was also different than Clay, so they could all be related. She might be his stepmother. *Bugger.*

*   *   *

"Holy crap, what am I going to do? I mean, Jesus Christ, what am I going to do?" Delthea exclaimed into the phone's mouthpiece. The fact that she was asking Elaine for advice spoke volumes about her current level of desperation.

"Where's the kid now?" Elaine asked.

"In the guest bedroom asleep. He kept nodding off in the car which was just as well since I didn't know what to say."

"About what?"

"About Garrett and where he is," Delthea shot back. She knew what was coming next before Elaine even started speaking.

"You didn't tell him where his dad is?" Elaine asked indignantly.

"No, I didn't tell him. Maybe I'm not supposed to. Maybe this is God's way of letting me off the hook." Delthea paced up and down the length of the living room. She knew she wasn't making any sense, but she could not and would not accept the idea that she had to be the one to bring Garrett and his son together.

"Cut the crap about what God does or doesn't want you to do. That is bullshit. You never believed in God until you finagled this stupid deal on Garrett's death bed, and now you're going back and forth daily on whether or not you have to hold up your end of that absurd bargain."

"I don't even know how to contact Garrett right now," she lied, knowing full well that Garrett had left that information on the fridge.

"What does that have to do with anything?" Elaine demanded.

"How can I tell Garrett his son is here if I don't even know how to reach him?" Elaine was supposed to say something to make her feel better, not make her feel worse.

"Absolutely," Elaine taunted with sarcasm. "There would certainly be no point in telling a ten-year-old kid where his dad was if you couldn't reach him, especially if that kid came from half-way around the world to find him." Elaine had this insidious way of making what she considered obvious sound like the only way to look at something.

"Well, no, but I'm not sure I have to. Maybe I should just tell him to go back to his mom and give up on the idea of finding Garrett. You know his mom put him up to this. How else would he have gotten here? She's probably waiting for Garrett to surface."

"Yeah, like she's going to throw a bag over Garrett's head and kidnap him." Elaine laughed that smug little laugh of hers. "What did he say about Abi?"

"Nothing. I haven't broached the subject. I haven't even told him that I'm married to his dad."

"Delthea!"

"How would you feel if your husband's bastard child ended up on your doorstep? And let me remind you there's more to this picture than that. I am pregnant – not with Garrett's child, but by a man I barely know. Garrett has every reason in the world to ask me to send his child to him, so he can stay there with Abi and his son."

"You're right. It is complicated, and I've got to get ready for work. I'll bring David over tomorrow for his session, and we'll talk about all of it then." Elaine hung up.

"Fine," Delthea told the hollow sound radiating from the phone. What had she expected Elaine to do, except state the obvious? She needed to tell Morgan the truth, but in doing that she would surely be sealing the death of her marriage. She and Garrett had fought before he left. In a moment of anger, she had said things she now regretted, hateful things like knowing that he had never stopped loving Abi, and that she knew his purpose in going was to find Abi as much as, if not more, than the son he had never known, and worst of all, that he would never love her child because it was not his. That had brought tears to his eyes and to hers as well. She had to quit thinking about all this, but how?

*   *   *

During the eighteen-hour trip from L.A. to Auckland, Garrett sat in the middle seat with two couples on either side. Before they were fully airborne, the women who sat at his right and left miraculously discovered that they knew someone who knew someone who knew the other one. When Garrett suggested he would trade places with either one of them, they both said they would stay seated next to their husbands. That didn't keep them from talking all the way across the Pacific Ocean.

While they chatted about how small the world was, Garrett thought about Betty Barker's clue – Abi lived in a town with a Biblical name. He had studied the map and the only city that had any kind of Biblical connection was Christchurch, which he knew couldn't be it since it was not a small community as Abi and Betty had both indicated. Another point that steered him away from it was its location on the South Island. Abi had said the bed and breakfast was located close to a thermal bath. From the guide books, Garrett had learned that Auckland in the North Island, the city where his plane landed, was built on volcanic cones. There were various thermal sites in the North Island, so Garrett surmised that Morgan had to be there.

After Garrett got through customs, he hailed a cab and gave the driver the address for *Mary's Inn* where he had a reservation. His cab pulled up in front of a plain house in what looked to be a modest neighborhood. Garrett paid the cab driver with New Zealand money he had gotten from his bank in the States. The lady, who opened the door, introduced herself as Mary. She showed him to a bedroom in the back of the house.

"The toilet is across the hall here. You can drop your gear in there or here in your room." She pointed to a door beyond which Garrett saw a sink and a bathtub.

"If you'd like to eat the evening meal with us, it's at seven and there's an extra charge."

"Thanks, but I need to get some sleep," Garrett said, totally exhausted.

"Yup, takes some time to get your clock turned around. You'll be awake in the middle of the night," she predicted. "There's a flannel and a towel next to the basin. Let me know if you need anything else. Me husband's a *brickie*, works hard and likes to give it a rest at the end of the day. He'll be home soon, and we're likely to go out for a few *handles*. He ain't a *pisshead*, just likes to yack with his mates. May come home happy as *Larry*, so never you mind."

"Right," Garrett answered, mysteriously understanding that her bricklayer husband was not an alcoholic, but he did like to visit friends and have a few beers. "If I don't come to breakfast, would you mind waking me?"

"Not a problem," she assured him as she walked away. "At *sparrow fart*, I'll be checking your pulse." She laughed and rounded the corner.

Garrett washed his face and returned to his room where he undressed and slipped beneath the sheet. His mind whirled with thoughts of calling Delthea and letting her know he had gotten here safely, not that she would want to hear that since she was adamantly against him making this trip. The night before he left Houston, he and Delthea had the worst argument of their marriage, which left him weighing his need to find his son versus keeping his marriage intact. His purpose for the trip was not to find Abi, but he could not convince Delthea of that.

For the first time, he doubted his decision. Maybe she was right. How did he propose to find one person in a country the size of Texas? No one wanted him to, not Abi or her mother or his wife. And what about his son, the person he had come to find? How would he feel about Garrett showing up? Abi had said Morgan didn't know Garrett existed. In his dream, she told him that, and so far everything she said had been proven true. Was he still dreaming? Was all of this simply a nightmare, a fantasy he had created? If so, he wanted to wake up.

*   *   *

Moa awoke, needing to go to the loo in the worst way. At first he wasn't sure where he was, much less how to find the toilet. When he crawled out of bed, he realized he was still dressed in his jeans, shirt, and his dad's vest. He opened a door and found a toilet across the hall. After he took a piss, he walked down the hallway, past a closed door, which he figured was Dr. Richard's bedroom. At the end of the hall, a huge black piano sat in one corner of a large room. He didn't dare play it since it would wake Dr. Richards.

Beyond the piano room, he found a small kitchen. He turned on the light and opened the refrigerator door. Unlike Takahe's well-stocked fridge, there was practically nothing in this one. He settled on a slice of cheese and a small shriveled up apple. In a cabinet, he discovered a box of crackers and some peanut butter.

A note was stuck to the fridge with daisy magnets. It said *Mary's Inn* and a phone number was written below it. Moa wondered if it was where his dad was staying. He studied a metal box sitting on a cart. It had a door that swung open when he lifted a latch on the front. On top of it lay a spiral that looked like his mum's sketchbook. He laid it on the table to look at while he ate. Mum would be mad at him for snooping in other people's stuff, but he needed to find his dad. Besides, she shouldn't have died. He wouldn't be here doing this if she had stayed alive.

Several of the pages had been torn out. He could tell because little bits of paper remained inside the metal coil. Moa leafed through it.

The pages were blank. A small newspaper article was stuck between the pages in the back. He pulled it out. It showed the side of a bearded man who sat in front of an easel painting a picture of a boy that looked like something Mum would have painted of him, but the picture wasn't clear enough to make out the details of the painting. Moa read aloud, "Garrett Clay, psychologist/author/artist has pledged to find his ten-year-old son Morgan, who he has never seen. He knows of the boy's existence based on a birth certificate and artifacts that were recovered from an apartment in Austin where the child once lived with his mother. A showing of Dr. Clay's art work is now on display at the Pentacle Gallery on Montrose."

"Wow," he whispered to himself. If Ian were here, he would tell him to keep the article.

The newspaper said his dad was looking for him. He wondered if that's where he was, but wouldn't Dr. Richards know that? She hadn't said a word about it. None of this matched what she told Bill or Moa after Bill left. Moa looked at the phone number for the inn. It wasn't familiar, but it could be a kiwi number with extra numbers for the country code. He and Ian had discussed the fact that Yank numbers had seven numbers and Kiwi phone numbers only had six.

He didn't have the whole picture yet, but he knew this much: his dad was looking for him, and Dr. Richards was not interested in getting Moa and his dad together. He had to watch what he said to her and how much he let her know about what he knew.

Not exactly sure when he might need it, Moa dug in the drawers until he found a pen. He took the note about the inn off the fridge and copied the name and number onto the back of the newspaper article. Careful to put everything back where he found it, Moa turned off the light and quietly returned to the room where he had slept. He hid the newspaper clipping in his backpack and lay down again, *knackered* but no longer hungry, just worried.

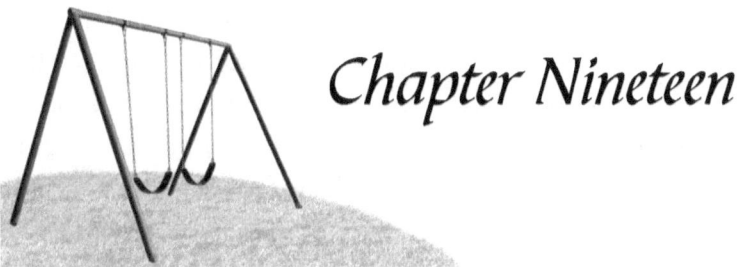

Chapter Nineteen

"The last time we talked, you mentioned the possibility of me choosing to return to earth as Delthea's baby. That feels like it would be a wonderful existence, living with Garrett and Moa. Even though they are not together yet, I expect they will find one another," Abi told her father/guide.

"It's highly likely. But will Delthea sabotage that?" he asked.

"Moa is with her, which means all of them will eventually end up together," she responded.

"Not necessarily. Moa triggers all of Delthea's insecurities. She is not sure Garrett has enough love for her and her child as well as his biological child, especially since her child is not his."

"Yes, that's true, but she can hardly put Moa back on the street at this point," Abi pointed out.

"People do all sorts of things, especially when they are afraid. At the time, it seems normal. When they get to your current state, they often wonder why they did it. I did," he confessed.

"Give me examples of souls who wondered why they did what they did on earth," she requested.

"Hitler and Stalin are extreme examples of people who totally deviated from their inner guide and dismissed any regard for the souls they encountered."

"Why would someone assume a human form and act that way?" she asked.

"Who we are in human form is almost never a true depiction of our soul-self, or who we really are. Self-actualized people like Gandhi, Mother Theresa, Jesus, and Buddha are rare, and even they were more human than most people want to believe," he admitted. "Those ideal individuals have been working at living their true identity for many lifetimes. Hitler and Stalin are examples of the extreme opposite while most of us are somewhere in between."

"Were Hitler and Stalin on their first lifetimes? Is that why they made such horrific choices?" she asked, fascinated by reincarnation, a concept she had heard of but never gave much credence.

"They could have been, but I expect not," he said thoughtfully. "Every soul has always been. When a soul chooses to assume human form varies from one to another. Plus, chronological order and progression are human concepts. Remember we are not shackled with those concepts here. Since Hitler and Stalin's lives had such universal shock, I suspect they selected those assignments for that reason – to experience that vast impact."

"What they did was terrible. Why would anyone want to live such a life?"

"By human standards of death and suffering, they were certainly despicable individuals, but look at what the world learned from these people, from the settings they created."

"People are still waging war and killing one another. We haven't learned much," she countered.

"That's true, and a time may come when they once more totally destroy human existence on earth. At which time, life will once more begin to evolve out of the ocean."

"Are you saying this has happened before, that life as we know it has evolved more than once?"

"Think about it."

Abi opened her mind to the possibility of knowing the answer to her own question. She received an image of the world covered with a cloud of smoke followed by a series of pictures of life evolving from the sea, on the land, and in the air. All of this flashed through her mind like a high-speed movie.

Do you realize how far you've come since you left your body? It was a phrase she had heard him say a number of times, but this time it was different. She wasn't hearing his words; she was thinking his thoughts. They were communicating without conversation.

That's right. You've crossed a chasm so as not to speak.

She understood completely, and it felt wonderful.

You are in a new space. I'll leave you here to enjoy it.

He was gone, and Abi was fine with that since she understood that there really was no place or time. She had finally left her human form. Until now, a part of her had clung to it. Now she was completely free of the limitations that had kept her human. She had returned to her soul state, and it felt truly heavenly, better than she could have imagined as a human.

*   *   *

Delthea finished making notes on her last session. Morgan was up front, sitting in Judy's chair since she was out sick, which was just as well. If Judy had been at work, she would probably say something on the phone in front of Morgan about Garrett being in New Zealand. Lying awake practically the whole night, Delthea had thought about what she should do with this child, how she could get rid of him before Garrett returned. Since he was supposedly looking for his son, his investigations should lead him back home when he didn't find him in New Zealand.

On the way to work, Delthea had asked Morgan how he slept. Rather than answer her question, he told her to call him Moa since that was what everyone called him. He said only his mum used the name Morgan and that was when she got mad at him. When Delthea asked if his mother got mad at him often, he stared out the window for a minute before he answered that he got madder at her than she got at him. Delthea saw right through his ploy of trying to weasel his way into their lives, coming here under the guise of being unhappy at home and looking for a sympathetic parent who would love him.

Children were experts at manipulation. David was a perfect example of the child snowing the parent. Elaine just needed to take charge of those boys. She noted the time and decided she should go up front and wait for David and Elaine. His appointment was due to start in ten minutes.

She opened her office door and heard Elaine's voice – of all days for her to be early. Delthea could not believe it. By the time she opened the door to the waiting room, Elaine was saying, "Moa is Garrett's son, the one he told us about at – "

Moa? Elaine wouldn't know that unless they had been talking for a while? "David, I didn't know you were already here," Delthea interrupted, hoping she had discovered them before Elaine had said too much. "I'm glad to see you've met Garrett's son. You two are similar ages."

"Moa was telling us about the kind man who brought him to the office." Elaine was asking in her roundabout way what was going on, how much Delthea had told him.

"Yes, Bill. He's an awfully nice fellow." She had already decided she would ask Elaine to join David for his session, so Elaine wouldn't have an opportunity to talk to Morgan alone. "Well, we better get started. Elaine, we need you to join us."

"I don't want her back there," David protested.

Delthea had been ready for Elaine to resist, but not David. She decided to use the same strong arm approach with him that she had planned to use on his mother. "I'm sure you don't want to go to a probationary school, do you David?"

"Garrett talked to me without Mom," he argued.

"I'm not Garrett, am I?" Delthea asked, growing increasingly uncomfortable with the situation.

Elaine cocked her head toward Morgan. "Can you believe how much he looks like Garrett?" As usual she was oblivious to her own children. Plus, she was asking in true Elaine fashion if Morgan knew who Delthea was and where his dad had gone.

"Yes, he does." She turned on her heels and opened the door to the hallway. "If you two will join me, we'll get – "

"You still haven't told him?" Elaine fixed her eyes on Delthea's and smirked. "How long can you keep that going?"

"As long as I need to." Delthea had not decided what to do about Morgan, and she refused to give in to Elaine's blackmail tactics. "Elaine, why don't you and David – "

The door to the outside opened, and a man wearing boots, tight jeans, and a plaid shirt walked into the room. Everyone turned and looked at him. Delthea had hoped to never see this man again, but here he was, big as life and grinning like a Cheshire cat.

"There you are, just the lady I was looking for," he said in that unmistakably West Texas drawl.

If Delthea could have died at that very moment, she would have elected to do so. Since that was not an option, she moved toward him with her hand extended. "So good to see you."

"Hell, what's this? Aren't we on a hugging basis by now?" His arms wrapped around her in a strong embrace, and he held her for several seconds.

She had to get out of this. Somehow, someway she had to get out of this situation. Breaking free, she turned to the group. "Rhett, I want you to meet my sister, Elaine. She's an ER nurse. I think I mentioned her to you."

Elaine's gaze moved slowly over his tall, muscular frame. "When Delthea said you were training to be a nurse, I never pictured someone quite so – handsome."

"I hate to be rude, but I've got a session with Elaine's son David." Delthea was still struggling with what to do with Rhett, how to gracefully ask him to leave.

"Well, hey, Deli. What are you going to do with Mr. Butler here while you talk to David and me?" Elaine was still sizing up Rhett, obviously pleased with what she saw.

"Delthea didn't say my last name was Butler," Rhett challenged.

"No, she didn't, but what else could it be." Elaine smiled and batted her eyes playfully.

He smiled back at her. "What else?"

"From what I heard, Austin was a great encounter," Elaine drawled.

Elaine was acting like a bitch in heat, and Rhett was responding like a dog ready to service her. Delthea had an idea. Whether or not it was necessarily good, she didn't have time to decide. "Actually, Austin was nice." She read Rhett's face, which was preoccupied with looking at Elaine. "But good things don't necessarily last." She held up her left hand. "I got married a couple of weeks ago."

This bit of news seemed to wake him up from the spell Elaine had cast upon him. "Well, how about you? Here I go bringing you back your grandmother's ring, and you've done got your own."

"That's right." Elaine pointed to Morgan. "In fact, this is her husband's son Morgan." Her extended finger shifted to David. "And this is my son, David."

Delthea clamped her hand on David's shoulder, ready to steer him away, but more than that needing something to hold onto, something to keep her upright. She had to get rid of Rhett and Elaine, not that sending them off together wouldn't complicate things, but she had to do something. "There's a coffee shop downstairs. Why don't you two get to know one another?"

"Are you sure?" Elaine asked. "I thought I needed to go in with David?"

"No, it's fine. He and I can meet on our own this time."

"Well, here let me give you this." Rhett dug in the pocket of his skin-tight jeans and pulled out Grandmother's ring.

"Actually, I'm the one that should have gotten that." Elaine took his arm. "Let's see if that thing doesn't fit me."

Rhett looked to Delthea who smiled and nodded her agreement to Elaine's suggestion. Not that she was blessing their union, but she wanted them to get the hell out of there. They walked out, and Delthea watched David watch them go. She wondered what was running through his mind. Then she turned to the other boy in the room and noted Morgan was silently taking in all of this.

"Morgan, do you need anything before I talk with David?"

He shook his head no, but he kept looking at her, apparently processing the fact that Garrett was her husband and Delthea was his stepmother.

"We'll be through in about an hour." She steered David to her office and shut the door.

They both plopped in a chair, and he waited expectantly.

"What do you think about what just happened?" she asked, genuinely curious, but also at a loss for anything else to say.

He shrugged his shoulders as he often did in response to a question. This time she understood his answer completely.

"Well, what do you think about your mom leaving with Rhett?" Surely, this had made some impact on the child.

"Who's Mr. Butler?" he asked, his forehead knitted.

"Oh, that was a reference to an old movie, *Gone with the Wind*. Rhett Butler was the main character. Scarlet O'Hara was in love with him from the minute she laid eyes on him." Delthea considered how similarly Elaine had acted in the waiting room.

Again he shrugged his shoulders in response, but this time he rocked his head from side to side, the way Elaine often did. "I guess if she likes him, and if they end up getting married, we might get to move away from Houston. Looks like he's a real cowboy."

In that brief encounter, David had read his possible future. Delthea had no idea how accurate he might be. Knowing Elaine, anything was possible. She had jumped into two failed marriages and had gone through numerous short term relationships between and since them. "Would you like that?"

"Sure. I hate this place."

Once more Delthea's concern for David grew. He had voiced similar sentiments on numerous occasions. He was not a happy child. She noticed the sketchbook in his lap. "What's that?"

He showed her his drawings and talked about each one, obviously in love with drawing, and actually quite good at it. Garrett's newest passion had rubbed off on David.

While she took time to look at the sketchbook, Delthea thought about Elaine and Rhett. Letting Morgan know she and Garrett were a couple was the payment Elaine had demanded for taking Rhett off her hands, but it wasn't like Delthea was getting rid of him. It was all still in the family, very incestuous with far too much latitude for Rhett to find out about the baby. Of course, Elaine wouldn't keep Rhett around long. She never did. Hopefully, if this immediate infatuation did develop into a romance, she wouldn't feel compelled to tell him about his parental rights to Delthea's child.

*   *   *

Amazing. That is simply amazing, Abi thought.

Isn't it? All things work together for good, her guide answered.

But we don't know that this will necessarily have a happy ending, she countered.

Not by worldly standards, but every encounter, every person is part of the experience that makes being human a learning arena. The potential is there for everyone to get what he or she wants. It's up to the players involved to make the right choices.

And what about Rhett? Is this really best for him?

Oh yes, this is exactly what Rhett wants. As we have discussed before, all souls communicate on a subconscious level. Rhett's soul has been communicating with Delthea's soul since before they met in Austin. They were drawn together with full intention to do what happened there.

What about Elaine and the boys? How do they fit into all this?

That same divinely guided energy brought Rhett here at this specific moment to find Elaine and to potentially be the man she has been seeking and the father her boys have needed. Every player in this encounter has free will and is not required to respond to their soul's direction. From the looks of things, though, I would say, they are very tuned in to their soul's guidance – even Delthea who responded to her soul's suggestion to send Rhett and Elaine to the coffee shop.

How long have you been tuned in to the people who directly and indirectly affected me?

Ever since I got to where I am now.

So you were sort of my guardian angel?

Not sort of, I am. Your soul, Garrett's soul, and my soul collectively decided to get you and Garrett together in a state that was neither conscious nor subconscious, so we gave you the idea of dreaming about Garrett.

That was a good idea.

Thank you. It was divinely inspired, as is all creation.

Abi understood that. She didn't need any sort of explanation. God was creation. Everything made sense. It was the beauty of her present state. She understood what being on earth had been all about. It was nothing like what she had thought when she was there. Currently, she was experiencing heaven, and it felt wonderful.

*   *   *

These Yanks were crazy, totally daft. Morgan flipped the pages of the comic book David had given him before Delthea came out, the Rhett bloke arrived, and everybody left again. He had thought Delthea might be married to his dad, but he still didn't understand why she had tried to keep that a secret. Where was his dad? Delthea knew, but she wasn't going to tell him. Elaine would; he just needed a chance to talk to her. Morgan studied the strange characters in the comic book. The girls all had big chests and the men were all muscle bound. He didn't see much that was funny about it. Every time he looked at the wall clock, it had barely moved since the last time he checked it.

When nearly an hour had passed, the phone rang. He looked at it wondering if he should pick it up. That was the job of the person who usually sat here, so maybe he was supposed to. It rang again. During the day, it had rung several times, but Delthea always answered after the second ring. It rang again. When it rang a fourth time, he reached over and, still not sure he should do this or not, he lifted the receiver. As he was about to speak, two people said, "Hello," at the same time. One of them was Delthea and the other was a man. Moa remained silent.

"Garrett, is that you?" Delthea asked.

"Yes, yes, it's me. Can you hear me okay?" he answered.

"Yes, you're coming in loud and clear. What time is it there?" she asked.

"Late morning, around 11:00, I think. I arrived here yesterday afternoon, and I got some sleep, but my internal clock is still haywire. What's going on there? How are you doing?"

"I'm fine. The baby's fine. David and I are finishing up a session. He was showing me his drawings. They are really wonderful. You've done a terrific job of teaching him to draw."

"Great. I appreciate you working with him. He's a super kid." It sounded like a car was driving by in the background.

"Where are you? I hear a lot of traffic noise," Delthea yelled into the phone.

"At a pay phone. The door's broken, so I can't shut it, but it was the closest one I could find to the bed and breakfast where I'm staying." Another car drove by, making a lot of noise. "I'm thinking about leasing a car, but I'm not sure since they drive on the left hand side of the road."

His dad talked about the bed and breakfast where he was staying and the amazing fact that he understood a lot of what the owner was saying even though it should be foreign to him. Delthea said she was sorry they had argued before he left and that she didn't mean any of what she had said. His dad said he knew she didn't.

"Delthea, I had the strangest thing happen to me in Los Angeles. I was on the phone calling Betty Barker, trying to get some information out of her about how to find Moa and a kid walked by with a guy wearing a cowboy hat."

Like the newspaper said, his father was looking for him, and he knew how to reach his grandmother. They both wanted to find each other.

"What's so unusual about that?" she asked. "I'm sure men wear Stetsons in other parts of the world besides Texas."

"The boy looked like Moa, in the face I mean. He had curly hair, and this was the really odd part, he was wearing a vest that looked identical to the vest I used to wear in college. It was something Abi took with her."

He and his dad had been in the same airport at the same time! And his dad had seen him. It had to be impossible for that to happen, but it had. Moa remembered walking through that airport and thinking that he was actually in the States and that he needed to start looking for his father. If he had only looked around more, he might have seen him.

"Wow, Garrett. That's really unusual." Delthea sounded sick, like she might *chunder*.

Moa wished he could see her face.

"I guess I'd better let you go. It's terribly expensive to call, but I wanted to let you know that I got here, and I'm all right. I'll call you back in a day or so, after I've had a chance to look around and get the lay of the land."

"Keep me posted," she answered, still sounding a bit ill.

Bugger. Moa wanted to shout that he was here, and that his dad needed to come home right away, but he thought better of it. Delthea wouldn't be at all happy with him, and for right now, she was the person he had to get along with. Besides, it was enough to know that his dad knew about him and that he was looking for him.

They said their good-byes and Moa held the phone over the cradle, so he could hang it up as soon as he heard them do the same. He had just dropped it into place when David came out of the room they had gone into. By the time Delthea walked into the waiting room, Moa had his head bent over the comic book like he was busy reading it.

"Did Elaine come back?" she asked.

Moa looked up at her and shook his head.

"Well, now what are we supposed to do?" She looked at David. Then she turned to Moa. "How do you two feel about pizza?"

"Yeah, that sounds good to me." David nodded and gestured to Moa in a way that clearly meant he needed to agree.

"Sure." Moa didn't know whether he liked pizza or not. Takahe never cooked it, and they had never had it at school. Maybe David could tell Moa what was going on.

*   *   *

With Mary's help, Garrett found the city bus. On it, he toured Auckland, getting a feel for the area. Even though he knew it was summer here, that had not fully sunk in. The weather was similar to Houston's winter with moderate to cool temperatures. He watched the traffic traveling on the opposite sides of the street from what he was used to, and without reason, it occurred to him that he could drive a car here if he decided to.

He opted for the tourist-guided trip up to the top of a flattop mountain formed from a volcano. There he walked around with others and marveled at the lush green expanse. He felt like he was on top of the world, and for some strange reason totally at home, actually like he had returned home. It was the oddest feeling.

*   *   *

Delthea, Moa, and David parked her car in the valet parking at the condo close to ten in the evening. The boys were full of pizza, and she hoped spent from playing video games. She had used the pay phone at the pizza place to call Elaine's home, but no one answered. Typical hairbrained Elaine. What was she supposed to do with David? Didn't she realize he had school the next day? On the way through the front lobby, she checked with Milton to see if anyone had left a message.

"Nope," he answered, his sleepy eyes settling on Morgan. "Who's the kid?"

"This is my new cousin, Moa," David said proudly.

"New, huh? He looks like he's been around for a while."

Before Milton could start prying into their business, Delthea headed for the elevators, dragging David with her and trusting Morgan would follow. She needed to get these two in bed and then sit down and figure out what she was going to do. The noise and trying to make sure the boys were not talking to one another about what was going on had taken every bit of her attention. And lest she forget, she was still pregnant. That, along with a lack of sleep, explained why she felt totally exhausted.

She had just handed David a pillow and a blanket and told him to sleep on the couch when the phone rang. Thank God. It had to be Elaine. She had better have a good explanation for her behavior. Delthea stuck the receiver to her ear.

"This is the answering service. I have a message from a woman who calls herself Ta-ka-he." She said the name like she was not sure how to pronounce it.

Delthea sank into Garrett's chair. This was it. Abi had sent Morgan here as a set up. Next they would be asking for money. Somehow they knew Garrett was gone, had probably even baited him into going to New Zealand, or maybe he was part of it. It would be far too coincidental for him to see Morgan in the Los Angeles airport. They were fucking with her mind.

"Are you there, Dr. Richards?" the service asked with an impatience that said she had asked more than once.

"Yes, yes, I'm here. What's the message?"

"Actually, all I got was a phone number, but it's out of the country. I think she said it was from New Zealand." She rattled off a series of numbers, including a country code.

Delthea studied the phone number. It was the same as the one that had appeared on her phone log, the one that was incomplete. "But this doesn't have enough numbers."

"I repeated it back to her, and she said that was it."

After thanking the service, she made sure the boys were in bed before she went to her room and returned the call. As the phone rang, she berated herself for not changing the phone number as she had originally intended to.

"*Kia Ora*," a woman's voice said, "*Tena koutou tamariki ma.*"

"What's that?" Delthea asked, stupefied by the greeting.

"It's a Maori way of saying hello. You must be a *Pakeha*. Who's calling?" she asked, her tone turning serious.

"My name is Delthea Richards. I got a message from someone at this number named Takahe, and I'm returning the call."

"I am Takahe. I am looking for Morgan Barker. His friend Ian says he went to Houston to find his father." She sounded concerned, but not frantic as Delthea would have been in a similar situation.

"Well, where's his mother? Shouldn't she be the one making this phone call?" Delthea saw right through them.

"Abi? He didn't tell you?" she asked.

"No, all he has said about his mother is that he gets madder at her than she gets at him – whatever that means."

"So he's there with his father?"

"Yes, Morgan's here, but his father is not." They knew all this. Why was this old lady playing stupid? "I don't expect Garrett back for several weeks."

A long silence followed. Delthea was used to that in her work. She would force this woman to make the next move. Two could play this cat and mouse game.

"He is not eager to meet his son?" she finally asked.

"Garrett has a life. He has a wife and a child on the way. He doesn't need or want some mistake from the past to deal with. In fact, he would rather not see Morgan." The words were not fully out of her mouth before a wave of guilt washed over her.

"This is how he feels?" she asked quietly.

"Yes, that's how he feels," Delthea replied, telling herself she couldn't back down now.

"Moa must come home then. It will be several weeks before I can come. Perhaps Colin can make the trip there. It will take me several days to contact him and see if he will be able to leave his ship." She spoke as though she was thinking out loud.

"Perhaps, I could bring him home." The words had slipped out before Delthea could stop them.

"That would be very generous. I will pay your expenses."

"No, it's fine, its the least we can do." She got the address, a little place called Jacob's Springs. The woman said it was in the South Island and gave her directions. Delthea told her she would call back with details of their flight and arrival time.

Delthea went to bed that night, composing a letter she would leave at the front desk for Milton to read to Garrett should he call while they were gone. She knew she was doing the right thing, protecting Garrett from the past, but that nagging voice of guilt kept gnawing away at her.

Chapter Twenty

*D*elthea had told Moa and David to go to bed when the phone rang, but Moa was able to hear enough to know that the caller was talking about a phone number that didn't seem to be long enough. Ian had pointed out to him that the phone numbers in the States were longer, so he guessed they were talking about a kiwi number. He wondered if the muffled sounds he heard through the wall between their bedrooms were Delthea talking to his dad. Moa lay awake long after he heard the noise stop.

From the conversation in his dad's office earlier that day, he knew for sure that Delthea was married to his dad. While they were playing video games, David said a few things, like telling him that his dad was in New Zealand looking for Moa and that Delthea was strange. From his dad's phone call to Delthea and the number on the refrigerator, Moa already suspected where his dad was, and anybody could figure out the other. She was more than a bit daft. Both Elaine and Delthea were odd, but each in their own way. Moa had never seen a woman meet a man and then disappear with him like David's mum had. It must be something they did here in the States.

He had a phone number, so he could call his dad and tell him he was here. Or he could tell him how to find the inn. The only problem with that was getting back home. He had Bill's card, so he might call him. If he got really desperate, he could call Ian's dad, who he didn't know at all. What about calling Ian? It was midnight in Texas. He thought about it a moment and decided it was six o'clock in New Zealand.

Because he didn't want Delthea to hear him talking, Moa took the cordless phone and his backpack to the closet. Remembering what Ian had told him about how to call, he first pressed in the numbers from Ian's calling card and then the school's number, not sure who would answer since school was not in session.

Mr. Perkins answered, sounding all business like.

Not expecting him, Moa spat out the first thing that popped into his head, "This is Ian's brother. May I speak to him?"

Immediately, Mr. Perkins shouted into the phone, "Morgan Barker, where are you? Do you know how worried all of us are, especially your grandmother?"

He had to be talking about Takahe since Moa figured his grandmother here in the States didn't have a clue what was going on, but Mr. Perkins' angry tone warned Moa not to ask who he meant. "No, sir, I didn't know that."

"Where are you?" he demanded again, not his usual happy self.

"I went to the States to find my dad."

"Well, did you find him?" He sounded a little calmer.

"No, sir, I think he's in New Zealand looking for me."

"Well, now that is an odd twist of events, isn't it? Sounds like you need to come home."

"Yes, sir, you're right, but I don't know when that will be. I have a phone number for where my dad's staying. Could you give it to Takahe?" Moa wasn't sure this was a good idea. He should call her himself, but that would mean listening to her holler at him. She would be doing that soon enough.

Moa rummaged through his pack and found the picture from the newspaper that said his dad was looking for him. He read the number he had copied from the note on the refrigerator. Again, Mr. Perkins asked where he was, and Moa told him about finding his dad's wife and staying with her. That seemed to make him feel better.

After Moa hung up from talking to Perky, he dumped his pack on the floor of the closet and looked at the book his father had written and the book Moa and his mum had always read together. He put on the vest and the dog tag. A sad feeling moved into his heart. All of a sudden, he wanted to be home where he knew what was going on and where people knew and liked him.

*   *   *

After spending the day wandering from place to place and finding no real leads, Garrett walked along a street of businesses. A sign in one of the windows said they rented and leased cars. He had watched the motorists all day and tried to picture himself driving on what felt like the wrong side of the road. Still, something nudged him to go inside. Looking through the window, Garrett saw a woman close to his age who sat at a desk. She glanced up and waved at him. If nothing else, she might offer a suggestion on how to find Songbird Inn, so he opened the door and stepped inside. Again, an odd feeling told him this was the right thing to do.

As Garrett approached the desk, he read a nameplate on her desk. "You must be Heidi." He stuck out his hand.

She stood up, reached across her desk, and took his hand. "I must be. And who do I have the pleasure of meeting."

"Garrett Clay. I'm from the States."

"Yes, I can tell by your accent. Dallas?"

He laughed, thinking of the popular television show. More than one person had made the same assumption. "No, but you have the right state, though, Houston."

"Yes, I thought I heard a bit of Texas. How may I help you?" She gestured to a chair.

Garrett felt his lips moving, and he knew everything that came spilling out of his mouth, but it felt like someone else was telling the story of what had brought him to New Zealand, his dilemma about finding the inn, which he mistakenly called Birdsong Inn and then corrected it to Songbird Inn. He related the clue Betty Barker had given him and finished with his desperate need to find his son.

Still smiling as she had throughout his monologue, Heidi said, "The best I can do is offer you a car to rent and suggest a few bed and breakfasts where you can ask about the one you want to find. I've not heard of the one you mentioned, but I would think someone might have a directory of all the Kiwi inns. As for a town with a Biblical name, I'm not that well versed on the Bible. And as for the matter of thermal activity, all of New Zealand was formed from volcanoes, so you may find what you are looking for on the South Island."

Her response left him dazed. Delthea had been right. This wasn't going to be easy.

She shuffled some papers. "We just need to fill out some forms in order to get you into a car."

He filled in the blanks, opted for all the insurance they offered, gave her his credit card number, and left with a set of keys to a tiny red European looking car that was parked in a nearby lot. Even though Garrett had never driven on the left hand side of the road, he felt totally at ease. Again, it seemed like someone else was operating his body, telling him which lane to pull into and how to negotiate a turn. As he drove back to the bed and breakfast, he thought about Heidi's suggestion to look on the South Island and decided he would venture in that direction, stopping at the inns she had suggested along the way. She had given him a map and instructions on how to find them. It felt good to have a plan. Tomorrow night, he would call Delthea and let her know where he was.

*   *   *

Interesting how easily you now work through Garrett.

Yes, I literally feel I'm operating his body.

You are. You have always been and still are very much a part of him.

It feels good to be home. I mean back in New Zealand.

I'm sure it does.

What seems really strange is that I have no concern for Moa. Not that I don't care, but I'm simply not worried about him. I know he will be okay whatever happens.

Yes, worry is a human activity.

Everything will turn out perfect.

No matter what happens.

That's the nicest part about being here. I understand that perfectly. I wish I could have known that as a human.

Then you wouldn't be human. That's what kept us going as humans, all the worry and struggles that we put into everything.

You're right. Realizing that has also made me think about whether or not I want to return to earth. I'm already there as Garrett, although I'm not really in charge of his body.

Yes, you have influence, and from this perspective you can make some strong suggestions, not that you won't continue to influence him should you decide to return to earth. You two have always been closely linked. Should you return, it will give you another opportunity to experience love while inhabiting a human body – not always an easy earthly assignment.

Since you were my father, what do you think I should do?

Throughout eternity, you and I have had a variety of relationships. In most of them, you showed me more than I ever taught you, which is ironically what fathers supposedly do for their children. The most important lesson I ever got from you was the one I will offer back – follow your heart.

You know that's what I'm going to do anyway, right?

Of course, what else can you do? That's all we have to follow – only humans usually get distracted by what seems to be important, like resentments or things like time and money.

Yes, that's key. They get busy with what seems more important or old unresolved issues.

*   *   *

When the alarm clock woke her, Delthea ran to the bathroom. As usual she needed to pee. This baby must be sitting right on top of her bladder. Thank God she had not had to contend with morning sickness. As she sat on the commode, she asked herself why she had said she would bring Morgan home. She didn't have the time, and she sure couldn't justify spending three thousand dollars on airfare to New Zealand. She had to, though. When Garrett gave up looking for him, he would be home in a couple of weeks. Her efforts to keep all this from Garrett were probably futile. David knew, and he would tell Garrett. Still she felt compelled to try – as compulsive as any patient she had ever encountered.

She checked her watch and thought about the two boys she had to get ready as well as herself. When she opened Morgan's door, she found the room empty. Right before she left to look for him in the bathroom, she noted the light radiating from beneath the closet door. Inside she found Morgan sound asleep, wearing the vest he had worn when he arrived, the one Garrett had said he had seen in the Los Angeles airport. What were the chances of them being at the same place at the same time?

As she bent to wake him, she noted a newspaper clipping, the damned picture Harrison had submitted to the newspapers. What was Morgan doing with this? Something made her flip it over where she saw a line of numbers, the phone number Garrett had stuck on the refrigerator. Then she spied the cordless phone and the calling card. This kid had been calling someone, although it couldn't have been Garrett since he was no longer at the original bed and breakfast.

"Morgan, wake up." Delthea shook him, wishing she could erase the fact that he existed, or at the very least ship him back to New Zealand and somehow eradicate him from her life.

"Mum, I'm sorry. I had to," he muttered, his eyes still closed, his arms reaching for something.

"Morgan, wake up," she barked. He'd have plenty of time to talk to 'Mum' once she got him back to where he belonged.

His eyes popped open, and he focused on her. "What?"

"We need to get ready to go." She could drill him with questions about whom he had called and what was going on, but he wouldn't tell her. The little bastard and his mother were in cahoots.

If he had talked to Abi and somehow gotten her in touch with Garrett, so be it. All Delthea could do was fulfill her commitments. She would drop David at school and trust that Elaine could take over from there – if she wasn't too busy playing ride the range with Rhett.

It took some heavy duty pushing, but she managed to feed the boys, deliver David to his school, and get to the office before her first appointment. When she walked into the waiting room with Morgan by her side, Judy raised questioning eyebrows.

Delthea tossed a to-do list on Judy's desk. "I've got a session in five minutes. This is my friend's nephew. He'll stay in my office, so you don't have to worry about him. Like my notes indicate, I'll be out after today, so cancel the rest of this week and don't schedule anything until the middle of next week." No telling what might go wrong while she was in New Zealand.

She started toward her office and turned back abruptly, plowing into Morgan who was walking in her wake. "Sorry, Morgan. Are you feeling okay, Judy – I mean since you've been out sick?"

Judy coughed, probably to validate her absence. "I'm still congested, but better."

"Great, great. Good to have you back." She grabbed Morgan's arm and pulled him toward her office. He would just have to sit in on her sessions. There was nothing else she could do. God, if she could just get the stupid reservations and get this kid back where he belonged. She knew in her heart of hearts this was not going to work, but she didn't know what else to do.

Between her first two sessions, Judy buzzed her and said that Elaine was calling. Delthea pushed the blinking light.

"Oh, my God, Deli, I'm in love," Elaine gushed.

"Okay now, wait a minute. Elaine, you know what's going on here, right? This is the man – " She looked at Morgan sitting across the room and listening to every word she was saying. "Look, Elaine, you need to make sure you're not getting in over your head."

"Deli, don't burst my bubble. This guy is perfect. He is the answer to my dreams. We were meant for one another. He is my soul mate." Elaine sounded like a teenager.

"Elaine, you have two sons, David and Kent. They need you right now."

"I am thinking about them. He wants sons. He is thrilled to death that we have a custom made family." Someone said something, and Elaine giggled. "Oh, Rhett, you're so cute."

"I hate to rain on your parade, but I'm leaving town, and you're going to have to deal with Rhett on your own." She turned away from Morgan and lowered her voice. "My advice to you is to cool your jets. At this point, you're operating on hormones. In six months, he won't look nearly so good when you roll over and find him in bed next to you."

"Yes, Mother." Elaine laughed before she hung up.

Her sister deserved whatever heartache she got.

*   *   *

All day long, Moa sat on the carpet behind Delthea's desk. She told him to be as quiet as he could while she talked to her clients. Because she said she had to for ethical reasons, she told them he was there, and asked if it was okay if he sat and colored or drew while they talked. They all said it was okay, but he could tell they thought it was weird; he did too. Part of the time, he slept. He still couldn't get his days and nights straight. At one point, he woke up and heard the end of Delthea's phone conversation. She was scheduling something.

When they got back to the condo, Delthea told him to pack his bag because she was taking him back to New Zealand. Moa couldn't believe his luck. Maybe she had talked to his dad last night, and he had convinced her to bring him home. She was still acting pretty weird, though, not like a mum or that she cared even a little bit about him.

While he was sorting through his bag, the phone rang. Delthea answered it in the kitchen, and he could tell right away that she was talking to his dad. He snuck into the living room and listened from there, so Delthea couldn't see him.

"Well, everything's going fine here. How are you doing? Have you managed to find the inn or Morgan?" she asked happily while not saying a word about Moa being in Houston.

She listened for a while, and then she said, "Oh, so you've gone to yet another B and B." Her heels clicked as she moved around the kitchen. It smelled like she was cooking broccoli. Yuck. "And this new place doesn't have Songbird Inn in their directory either. Now that's odd. You would think it would show up. Maybe your dreams weren't that accurate after all."

Songbird. That was the problem. He wasn't looking for the right place. And Delthea wasn't about to help him. He listened until it sounded like she was getting ready to hang up, which told him he better head back to his bedroom.

That night, long after the condo had gotten totally quiet, Moa lay awake. He worried about how to tell his dad where to go. Once they left Houston, he would have no way of contacting his dad. His stomach growled, so he decided to check the kitchen for something to eat. On the way, he saw that Delthea had put her suitcase next to the front door. On top of it lay her purse and an envelope. On the outside of the envelope she had written, "Read this to Garrett Clay if he calls."

Moa picked up the envelope. It wasn't sealed. The flap was tucked inside. He slipped it open and read, "Garrett, I had to do an unexpected talk for Oliver, and I didn't know how to reach you since you were moving from place to place. I am anxious to see you when you get home. Love, Delthea."

No longer hungry, Moa grabbed the sketch pad from the kitchen and returned to his bedroom. He wasn't sure what he would do, but this felt like a chance to turn everything around.

*   *   *

Delthea hurried through the condo lobby with Moa at her side. She saw Milton perched on his stool behind the reception desk, talking on the phone, no doubt to another deadbeat while he was supposed to be working. She detoured his direction, laying the letter on the reception desk.

Milton looked up at her, the phone still seemingly attached to his face.

"Garrett may call in the next few days. Read this to him if he does."

Milton looked at Morgan and his backpack and her suitcase. "You want me to tell him where you're going?"

"Just read him the letter. That's all you have to do. All you have to do," she repeated slowly. Dear God, trying to communicate with him was like trying to talk to the village idiot.

Milton nodded.

Delthea did not have time to worry about him. She grabbed Morgan's hand and pulled him toward the door. While she lay awake unable to sleep, she had decided to call a cab and leave her car in the garage. Morgan said nothing as they rode to the airport, waited for the plane, and boarded.

When they were settled in the plane on one of the back rows, he looked around as if acclimating himself. "On the way over, I rode in the front. There's more room there, and the stewardesses were coming around to bring food before we even got off the ground."

"Apparently, you were flying first class. That's very expensive." Delthea wondered where he had gotten the money, or rather where Abi had gotten that kind of cash.

"My friend Ian gave me the ticket for my *Chrissy pressie*."

"What?" Delthea asked, baffled by his odd terminology.

"That's what us Kiwis call Christmas presents. My mum talked what she called Texan and Takahe used Maori words, so between the two of them I had a lot of choices."

"I see," she responded, wondering what it must have been like to have a mother from the States and grown up in a country that was totally foreign to her. "Did your mom tell you what it was like growing up here?"

"She told me it was hard because her dad was a son of a bitch," he said with total innocence.

"Morgan, surely she didn't use that kind of language with you." Dear God, what kind of mother would say such a thing?

He looked to the side as if he could read a script in his mind. "No, she probably didn't say it quite that way. It was more like . . . Well, she had her own way of saying things." The plane started rolling forward. He sat back, his eyes wide. "This is the part I love."

Delthea loved his youthful exuberance.

When the stewardess came around to take drink orders, he asked her to repeat the list of choices, and then he chose the first thing she had mentioned.

The young stewardess glanced at Delthea and said, "Cute kid. You must be proud of him."

Until that moment, Delthea had not imagined that the rest of the world would assume Morgan was her child. Of course, she could easily have one that age. She was nearing her fortieth birthday. Having a ten-year-old was much more believable then being pregnant for the first time.

Delthea looked at Morgan who was engrossed in figuring out the device for watching movies. Over the last few days, she had noted features that looked similar to Garrett's, but she had not had the luxury of simply studying him. He was a little Garrett, a ten-year-old version of the man she loved more with each day that passed. Moa was really easy to like. Why had she been so afraid of him?

"Morgan, tell me about your school," she said, remembering he had mentioned a boarding school, which at the time made her wonder why Abi was shipping him off for an education.

He told her about Ian, Mr. Perkins, and the soccer team that he played on. He went into detail about getting mad at his roommate for treating him badly when he first went to the boarding school and how Ian had finally told him that his mother had died of breast cancer. At that point Morgan got quiet, his face as set as stone.

"Have you ever known someone that died?" Delthea asked, struck by his sudden shift in mood.

"Do you think people have a life after they die, like their body goes on to something else?"

"I suppose that's possible. What do you think?" Someone he had known had died. Delthea had worked with too many children that had that look of shock mixed with awe, like they could see beyond this world – perhaps because of their goodness, or their lack of bad choices. Thinking of bad choices, Delthea wondered how her current deception with Garrett might come back to haunt her.

*   *   *

After settling into one of the bed and breakfasts that Heidi had suggested, Garrett found a phone booth next to a tavern that was only a short walk away. He gave the operator his calling card number and the number for the condo. His efforts to find his son had been useless. Someone at both of the inns he had stopped at along the way as well as the one where he had opted to spend the night had looked in a directory and no one could find Songbird Inn. Every other detail garnered from his dreams of Abi had materialized. Why was this point the exception?

Milton answered the phone with a jovial lilt in his voice.

"This is Garrett Clay. Will you ring my condo?"

"Certainly, but no one's home," he said, his words slurred. "I do have a note, though. I'm just supposed to read it. That's it. Just read it." He sounded like he was parroting someone, no doubt Delthea. Milton and Delthea had waged their own private war since Milton started working there several years ago.

"Let it rip," Garrett suggested, sure that if there had been a note, it had surely disappeared by now. It would be interesting to hear what Milton would adlib.

"Let's see," Milton mumbled. "Where is that thing? Oh, here it is. You ready?" Paper rattled in the background.

Surprised that he had actually found it, Garrett said, "Certainly, proceed." He missed Delthea, her obsession with order, her need to be needed, her beauty, her basic goodness, her desire to be a great wife, not just any old wife, but a great one.

"Okay, here goes. It reads: Dearest Garrett, I am thrilled to tell you that I have found your child Moa. I am taking him back to Birdsong Inn, not Songbird as you had thought, on the South Island in Jacob's Springs. I will meet you there. All my love, Delthea."

"Birdsong," Garrett repeated. That was it. That was the name of the inn. He had jumbled the name. "Did she say she had my son, that she was taking him home?" Garrett could not believe his ears.

"Y-e-p," Milton said, making a three syllable word out of it. "She had a little kid with her. Your nephew, David, he was the cutest damned thing, said this kid Moa was his new cousin, new cousin. Isn't that a gas?"

"Absolutely. Now read that note to me again." He wanted to savor every syllable.

In his absence, a miracle had taken place. Somehow his son had found Delthea, probably while looking for him. Plus, Delthea had taken it upon herself to bring Moa home. This thrilled him more than anything. Garrett had never heard her refer to him as Moa, which could mean that she now accepted him.

The child that Garrett had seen in the Los Angeles airport must have been Moa, but who was the man with the Stetson hat? Delthea's note had not offered an explanation, only that she would meet him at Birdsong Inn. Of course, that sounded more correct than what he had been saying. As a matter of fact, he had used the correct name when he was talking to Heidi at the rental agency. While his ability to drive here was only a small miracle, it represented all the other wonderful, unexplainable things that were happening.

* * *

After Moa and Delthea had claimed their luggage and gone through customs, they got on another plane and flew from Auckland to Christchurch. Once outside the airport, Moa spotted a row of taxis. "Jacob's Springs is a long ways from here, but there isn't any way to get there except by taxi."

Delthea set two huge suitcases on the sidewalk. "Well, I guess that's our only option."

Moa wondered why she had brought so much stuff. If she was trying to trick his dad into believing Moa had never come, she would need to go home and be there when he got back. The daftness of that idea struck

Moa as just plain stupid. Didn't she know that David, or Elaine, or the doorman or the secretary would tell him that they had seen Moa?

As they got closer and closer to the inn, Moa began to notice a red car that turned where they turned and repeatedly ended up on the only road that finally ended at Birdsong Inn. It was too good to be true after going all the way to Houston looking for his dad.

*   *   *

It pleased Abi that all of this had unfolded just as she had predicted it would, but even if it had not, everything would be perfect. It already was. While struggling with the day to day issues of living, humans had simply forgotten to accept this marvelous gift of peace. She prayed that she could remember this when and if she returned to earth.

She watched as the two cars pulled up to the inn at the same time. Morgan piled out of the cab and ran to the red car that had trailed them all the way up the mountain. He grabbed the handle and pulled open the door. His dad eagerly climbed out of the car and wrapped his arms around Moa.

With one arm locked around his son, and Moa clinging to him, Garrett walked to the cab and helped Delthea, who could not believe her eyes, out of the back seat. Still holding Moa, he kissed her. Then he whispered in Delthea's ear, "You have made me the happiest man in the world."

If Abi still had a body, she would smile and cry and laugh with pure joy.

Chapter Twenty-One

*L*ooking back over his shoulder, Moa ran around the side of the inn toward the rubbish bin. He and Ian were competing to see who could get their chores done first. David and Kent were due to arrive this afternoon with their mum and her husband, the bloke she had met in his dad's waiting room in Houston. Moa couldn't believe a full year had passed since Mom, what he now called Delthea, had brought him home.

Ian raced around the corner of the house with another load of rubbish. "Where are they getting all this crap?"

Moa helped him dump it into the bin. "Takahe and Mom want everything perfect before they get here." Moa thought of Ian as his brother since they still shared a bedroom here at the inn and everyone treated Ian like they treated him. Ian complained, but Moa could tell he liked living in a family instead of at the school. "And we gotta do our lessons before I go to the airport with Mom." Moa was ready for Ian to also gripe about doing their schoolwork, but any dope could see he was learning ten times more with Mr. Perkins teaching just them.

At first Moa didn't think he would like Perky living with them at the inn after he retired, but it had worked out okay. Once Moa overheard the adults talking about the fact that Ian's dad was paying Perky's salary to tutor Ian and Moa, and he was also paying Takahe for Perky and Ian's room and board. He was probably also responsible for making it possible for his dad and mom to stay in New Zealand. In only a few months' time, Takahe had gone from living alone and managing the inn with a few local workers to Dad, Delthea, Ian, Moa, and Mr. Perkins living with her and pitching in to help.

Mr. Perkins wasn't suppose to do any of the work, except teaching, but Moa had seen him peeling potatoes on more than one occasion. He seemed to like Takahe. Occasionally, the two of them sat on the back porch after supper, with her knitting and him reading poetry aloud. That made Moa want to *chunder*, but they seemed okay with it.

"I-a-n, M-o-a," Mr. Perkins called from the other side of the house.

"Let's get it over with," Ian suggested and moved toward the sound of Perky's voice.

Moa thought of what day it was – his mum and dad's birthday – March 6. Moa remembered visiting Mum in the hospital when she had an operation. He thought of the cake he helped decorate and eating a slice with Mum before he returned to the inn with Takahe and Colin.

When Perky called again, Ian answered, "We're coming," as he turned around and saw that Moa wasn't following him. "What you thinking about?" Ian asked as he walked back to Moa.

"My mum. It was two years ago today that we found out she was dying," Moa said.

Ian nodded, wrapped his arm around Moa's shoulders, and steered him toward Perky who was hollering again.

Moa missed Mum, but he had grown to love Delthea and was glad to call her Mom. The way it all worked out was incredible. Moa's heart still beat fast when he thought about how right it had felt to finally hug his dad. That he knew of, neither Mom nor Dad had ever talked about going back to Texas. She spent her time with his little sister and helping Takahe while Dad painted pictures that looked a whole lot like Mum's style of painting, although he never did pictures of himself like Mum had painted.

Most of his dad's paintings were shipped to a gallery back in the States. That Harrison bloke called every week or so wanting to know how dad's paintings were coming along. The last time he called, no one else was around to answer the phone, so Moa picked it up, and Harrison said he was thinking of making a trip to New Zealand to visit his favorite artist.

Moa thought that was funny since Dad painted exactly like his mum and no one had taken any interest in her work. Maybe Harrison would if he came and saw her paintings.

Thinking about Harrison made Moa think of his trip to Houston and traveling on his own. He still marveled that he had been clever and brave enough to replace Mom's letter to Dad with his own; otherwise, they might not have magically become a family. Ian was the only one who knew the truth about that, and they had both sworn on their mother's graves to always keep it a secret.

On the way to pick up Elaine and her family at the airport, Moa sat in the middle seat of the eight-passenger van next to his baby sister who was strapped into a car seat. Mom was driving, and she kept looking at her rearview mirror. He saw a deep worry line between her eyes.

Mom had suggested they buy the van for this reason, to pick up passengers at the airport. She had also said they should start advertising in the States and offer stuff like massages. So far Takahe had only given in on the van idea. Lately, his dad left the room smiling when Mom started talking about what she called her latest brainstorm. He seemed happy to let Takahe deal with that.

His sister squealed and stiffened her arms, shaking the rattler she held. She gave Moa one of her toothless smiles. After he made a funny face at her, she did it all again. Mom glanced at them and tried to smile, but she still looked worried.

When they got to the airport, Mom set her parking brake and said, "Morgan, stay with the baby while I run in to help." She jumped out and hurried into a building swarming with people.

Mom was the only one that called him Morgan, and he liked that. Saying he was a great big brother, she nearly always asked him for help when his sister needed something.

In a few minutes, Mom came charging back to the van leading the way with a suitcase in each hand. Elaine, Rhett, David, and Kent followed, each carrying a bag. Mom set down her load and opened the side door of the van. She began unbuckling the straps that held in his sister.

Just as she pulled the baby out of her seat, she motioned for Moa to get out. Mom faced the group, holding his sister with one arm and wrapping the other around Moa, she said, "Well, here are my two beautiful children. Of course, you know Morgan, and this is Abi."

*   *   *

The anticipation of Elaine and her family's visit had just about done in Delthea. Not since she left the States had she gotten caught up in what ifs and regrets about the past. Living in New Zealand had allowed her to wipe the slate clean and start over. She checked the rearview mirror and surveyed the van. Elaine, David, and Kent were in the back seat. Morgan and Abi remained in the middle. Rhett sat in the passenger seat to her left since he and the boys were too big to all sit in the back. She could not bring herself to look Rhett in the eye.

"Hey, Deli," Elaine called from the back. "How did you get used to driving on the left-hand side of the road?"

"It took a few driving lessons – and a few near calamities. Garrett picked it up immediately, which is odd because he usually doesn't know his left from his right."

"So how are y'all liking it here?" Elaine yelled back.

"We love it. I've never seen Garrett happier. He wanted to come with me, but there wasn't room." So far things were going okay, but Delthea wasn't sure what would happen with Rhett. When she located them in the baggage area, she had managed to hug Elaine and the boys while avoiding any contact with him.

"Do you miss home at all?" Rhett asked.

Delthea glanced at him, seeing the kind eyes and easy grin that had once charmed her. Now they were simply features of her sister's husband. "Life here has been busy," she admitted. "What with the kids and helping run the inn, I haven't had a chance to miss what we left behind."

Of course, she had thought about it, and every time the idea of returning to Houston occurred to her, she asked herself what there was to go back to. Nothing. It was funny how Garrett knew that before they each left on their separate journeys and ended up together, which still felt like a miracle.

When they got to the inn, Takahe stepped onto the porch and offered a traditional Maori greeting, "*Kia Ora*." She touched noses with each of their guests, another *Aotearoa*, or New Zealand practice. It sometimes amazed Delthea how quickly she had assimilated into this culture, but nothing like Garrett who almost seemed like a native in no time.

Morgan disappeared with Elaine's boys, no doubt to find Ian. She had overheard Moa and Ian making plans to take their guests hunting. This gun business was one thing Delthea had not gotten used to. She understood that the abundance of game made it a necessary sport, but eleven-year-old boys carting around lethal weapons did not feel right. On occasion, Garrett trekked through the woods with them, and he sometimes hunted alone – again something Delthea saw as odd based on what he said about guns prior to getting sick.

While Delthea led the way, showing them the grounds, Elaine and Rhett followed with their arms around one another and occasionally gave each other moony-eyed looks. Predictably, they found Garrett in his studio, focused on a canvas and dressed in his usual paint-stained shorts and tee-shirt. He jumped up when Delthea opened the door.

"Hey, Garrett, happy birthday," Elaine squealed as she ran and tackled him with a hug. In the excitement of their arrival, Delthea had failed to notice that Elaine had lost weight, at least thirty pounds.

Laughing and still hugging Elaine, Garrett reached out to shake Rhett's hand. "Garrett Clay. You must be Rhett."

"Yeah, that's me." Rhett made a circling gesture with his index finger. "This is quite a place you've got here."

"None of it's mine. We're just Bohemians sponging off the locals." He released Elaine who returned to Rhett's side. Then he slipped his arm around Delthea. "Isn't that right, Sweetie?"

"Absolutely. We're here until they kick us out." In Houston, Delthea had fought Garrett's relaxed approach to life, especially after his miraculous recovery when all he wanted to do was paint. Here she embraced it, fully aware of how much it had improved the quality of their lives.

Delthea suggested that she show Elaine their rooms while the guys got to know one another. It had been too long since she had alone time with her sister. If she had missed anything about Houston, it was Elaine.

Upstairs, Delthea opened the door to their largest room. "Well, here it is."

"Oh, Deli, this is incredible." Elaine walked to the window where the new lacy curtains that Delthea had purchased last week in Christchurch fluttered in the breeze. She sniffed at a bouquet of roses, daisies, and sweet peas. Delthea had arranged them from the ones Morgan and Ian picked that morning. Their fragrance filled the room.

"Who brought up our bags?" Elaine pointed to the two huge suitcases sitting in the middle of the wool rug that partially covered the hardwood floor.

"Friona or possibly Colin. She works here and Colin occasionally lives here. Mostly he's off to sea, but you've caught him on a week's leave."

"Colin? Wasn't he the guy who helped Abi leave Austin," Elaine asked, as usual recalling the minutia of life.

"Yes, he was." Delthea studied Elaine. Something radical had shifted between them. In the past, she would be thinking about how often Elaine had remembered details like who Colin was while forgetting her own kid's father's names. Instead, Delthea was truly glad to see her sister.

"I got to tell you, Deli. When you said you had named that kid of yours Abi, I thought something major was going down." Elaine made a goofy face, which reminded Delthea of how she had always been the clown in every situation.

Delthea picked up a rose petal from the floor and rubbed its velvety surface. "Using that name was actually Morgan's idea, but the more I thought about it, the better it felt. Once we learned about Abi's death, and realized it was essentially what had brought us all together, I knew we needed to honor her memory. She wasn't the enemy anymore."

"Probably never was." Elaine's gaze lightly assessed Delthea. "You know, you've changed as well. Just look at you, wearing an old shirt and shorts." She gestured toward Delthea's clothes.

"Sorry I didn't have time to change. Abi decided she needed to nurse, and it seemed like everybody had a question or request as I was racing out the door."

"No, you look great, a vast improvement from that three-piece-suit crap that you used to wear. But it's not just that. You've changed." After scrutinizing Delthea from head to toe, Elaine snapped her fingers. "You're happy. That's it. I've never seen you like this. It's just incredible. I love it." She spontaneously embraced Delthea with a tight hug.

Delthea held her close and breathed in the sweet smell of Elaine's hair, a scent that reminded her of when they had shared the same bed and stayed up late into the night telling each other ghost stories. The smell of smoke had disappeared. She pulled away enough to look Elaine in the eye. "You've quit smoking."

Elaine laughed. "Don't need them anymore."

Delthea looked her up and down. "I should have mentioned it when I first saw you; you look fabulous. And it's not just your weight. There's something else."

Smiling, Elaine said, "I'm happy, and my boys are happy. What else could I want? What else could any of us want?"

"Yes, that's exactly right." That part had not changed. Elaine was still two steps ahead of her on figuring things out.

* * *

That evening, Garrett held Abi while Delthea finished her meal. Elaine and Rhett sat across the table from them. The boys had already eaten and left. Not entirely comfortable with a new batch of company, Colin had gone to a nearby pub, The Red Bull, to throw darts with the locals. Mr. Perkins had excused himself with Takahe leaving immediately afterwards. Those two were becoming an item.

"What are you so happy about?" Delthea asked Garrett as she brought her wine glass to her lips.

That made him grin even bigger. "You," he answered and kissed her on the cheek.

Delthea stroked his leg and squeezed it lightly. Garrett thought of the conversation they had last night in the wee hours of the morning when he rolled over and realized that Delthea was wide awake, but Abi wasn't in bed with them. Without much prompting on his part, she had wondered aloud how difficult it would be to face the man who had fathered their baby. The same thoughts had crossed his mind and now that person sat opposite him, firing one question after another about New Zealand and their new home. He was a nice guy, treated Elaine well, and was great with the boys.

All that aside, he was Abi's biological father. With the need to find his son, Garrett had never addressed that issue. Now it was staring him in the face.

Rhett drained his wine glass and set it on the table. "I sure appreciate y'all having us here. I never thought when I went looking to find Delthea last year that I'd end up married to her sister and visiting you guys in some foreign country. You just never know." He wrapped his arm around Elaine. "Do you, Babe?"

"No, you don't." She patted his thigh with the ease of someone who had been married many years rather than just one.

"I can't get over how lucky I am to have a ready-made family. Kent and David are truly a Godsend. Here I thought I'd never have kids, and I end up with two of the best boys on the planet." He drew Elaine closer and nuzzled her neck.

Garrett shifted his sleeping daughter to his shoulder. He wondered where Rhett was going with all this talk about thinking he would never have children. Surely to God he wasn't getting ready to claim the child Garrett held in his arms.

Rhett looked at Delthea. "I came to Houston praying you'd see me again, but I figured I didn't stand a snowball's chance in hell since I couldn't give you what you really wanted."

Delthea cleared her throat. "I'm not sure I know what you mean." Her voice quivered.

"You don't remember our conversation, do you?" he asked, grinning with the apparent confidence of someone who has a decided advantage.

"I'm afraid you've got me there." Delthea reached for her wine glass.

"By that time of the evening, I think you had already put away a few drinks, so I guess you don't recall the conversation." Still looking at Delthea, he stroked Elaine's arm. "You said the only thing you had ever really wanted in life was to have a family." He laughed. "You got to understand, by then I was falling for you, but that sort of put a screeching halt on things since I can't have kids."

Delthea shifted in her chair, and Garrett patted Abi's back when she began to squirm. He felt more and more uncomfortable with this whole situation.

"That day I came to your office, I was looking to return your ring and look what I found – the family I thought I'd never have. And my luck kept getting better because Elaine didn't want any more kids." He was still grinning with his arm wrapped around Elaine.

This was not making sense.

Elaine turned to look at her husband. "Rhett, Honey, you should explain what happened to you."

"I guess you don't remember us discussing that either, huh?" he asked Delthea.

She shook her head, her face a picture of bewilderment.

"When I was a kid, I had this freak accident on my bike. I'll never understand why somebody designed boy's bike with that bar at the top." He laughed and held up his free hand with the thumb and index finger slightly parted. "I came this close to having a permanent position in the boys' choir."

"I still don't understand," Delthea admitted.

"Let's just say I had an unintentional vasectomy at eleven." He put his hands on his belt as if ready to unbuckle it. "You want to see my scar?" he asked with the enthusiasm of a kid with stitches or a newly acquired cast.

The group offered a collective and uneasy chuckle.

"But you are using protection, aren't you?" Delthea asked.

Garrett knew she was thinking of Elaine at this point.

"There's no need to. We can play all we like without a worry in the world," Elaine chimed in.

"Maybe the vas has grown back," Garrett suggested, imagining the trouble they were headed for when Elaine ended up pregnant and proving the reality of Abi's parentage.

"Naw, I'm firing blanks." Rhett resettled himself next to Elaine and returned his arm to her shoulders.

"Hey, remember who you're talking to. I made him go down and get a sperm count. He's right. He's got a nifty little pistol there, but the ammunition is harmless." Elaine beamed up at him.

"I have to admit, I came to Houston thinking you might be willing to compromise, but I know now you were simply a means to an end." Again, he kissed Elaine on the cheek. "I've got my boys and the best wife a man could want. I am the happiest man in the world."

Afterwards in their bedroom, Garrett slowly undressed and thought about the after-dinner talk. He looked at Delthea who sat in bed nursing Abi. "What do you think about that story concerning Rhett's sterility? Could that be true?"

Delthea stroked Abi's hair. "I don't know if it's possible or not. I don't remember having sex with Rhett or with you, but I'm sure no one else was involved, and I'm sure it wasn't the Immaculate Conception."

Garrett recalled the months of his illness and how often he barely knew what was happening. He slipped into bed next to his wife and daughter. "You think I really could be her father?" he asked, picking up her foot and rubbing it against his cheek. She looked like Delthea, blonde, straight hair, blue eyes, and even tempered. That part is the new Delthea – the one that had emerged since they had been living here. Of all of them, Delthea seemed the most changed, something that never ceased to amaze and gladden him.

* * *

The next morning, Abi rested in Rhett's arms. He and Elaine were sitting on the front porch, both of them drinking coffee and trying to adjust to the time change. Still connected to her soul's subconscious as she had been at birth, Abi wondered when she would lose that ability to know what others were thinking. Daddy, her guide before she came here, had told her she would, and along with that, forget all she had taken in since she was born, although the impressions and lesson would go on to steer her throughout the rest of her life.

Elaine looked over her shoulder and all around her. "You think they bought that story about you being sterile."

"I don't know. I hope so." Rhett looked Abi in the eyes and thought about the miracle she truly was. What had initially been a wild hair during a trip he made on a whim had given him what he had always wanted, a loving, fun wife and a family.

"You know, Rhett, when you said you thought we should tell them you were shooting blanks, I thought you were crazy. Now I realize it is just one more example of what an incredible guy you are. Not everyone would be that noble." She kissed him.

Rhett held Abi up in the air and gently turned her side to side. "I could not imagine allowing my baby girl to be raised in a situation that was at all questionable. She deserves the best, and it looks like she's getting it." His throat tightened with emotion. "After all, it don't matter who her biological father is. That matters little compared to what her mom and dad think of her and how they treat her while she's growing up."

"I believe Abi is an angel sent to bring all of us together. But I still can't get over Delthea giving her that name. That in itself proves how far my sister has come. When she did that, I knew she was a different person."

Moa opened the screen door and walked onto the porch. Without a word, he walked over to Abi and slipped her out of Rhett's hands. They both struggled with their emotions, Rhett clinging to the limited time he would have with his daughter and Moa jealous of anyone who entertained Abi except Mom or Dad.

"I'm supposed to take my sister for a walk." Without further explanation, Moa hoisted Abi onto his hip and walked down the steps, headed for his usual early morning destination.

When he was out of sight, he brought Abi's head to his lips and kissed her downy hair. He loved his sister with his entire being. Not knowing how or why, she reminded him of Mum. It wasn't important to understand this strange phenomenon; he simply appreciated that he felt it.

After walking for several minutes, he reached the place they had always gone since Mom and Dad started allowing Moa to take Abi for a walk. He sat on the bench Colin constructed and held Abi in his lap. As had become their practice, he turned Abi to face him and stared into her eyes. He wasn't aware of it, but their souls were talking to one another. On a deep subconscious level, they both knew the truth of who they were and how all of this had come into being.

After a few minutes, Abi squirmed to get down. She was learning to walk, and she liked practicing that here in this special place and time that she shared with Moa. Her toes dug into the loose ground as Moa held her hands and walked her toward what brought them to this particular place.

When they were squarely in front of it, he paused, holding his hands still and allowing her to take those last few steps on her own. She staggered forward, grabbing the granite marker. Her fingers traced the words that had been etched into the stone:

Turn your face to the sun and
the shadows fall behind you. -Maori Proverb

Abigale Barker
March 6, 1943 – December 8, 1983

Acknowledgments

Living with Abi

Prior to spending the summer of 2007 in New Zealand, I contacted all the people in my travel club who lived there. I told them about the novel I had written that took place in both New Zealand and Houston, Texas, and I asked if any of them would be interested in reading it for authenticity. A special word of thanks goes to Gail and Doug Bayne as well as Pamela and Hywel Davies for accepting my offer and for meeting with me in person to discuss their Kiwi insights. Jette de Jong, a friend I met during my time there, also read it and gave wonderful feedback from a younger Kiwi's perspective.

My everlasting appreciation goes to my long-time critique partners, Marsha Harris and Debbie Sanders (now deceased), for holding my hand throughout the initial formation of this novel over twenty years ago. Our collective encouragement for each other to "Never Give Up!" reverberates with me still.

Another debt of gratitude goes to Dorthy Edwards Hawkes for also reading it and giving me an honest response. Finally, heartfelt thanks goes to Yvonne Vermillion of *Magic Graphix* for her expertise in graphic setup and cover design. Please, forgive me if I have overlooked someone as this novel has taken its time finding its way into the world.

www.ingramcontent.com/pod-product-compliance
Lightning Source LLC
Chambersburg PA
CBHW031553240626
47153CB00002B/487